TIME REICH

DAVID HEALEY

INTRACOASTAL

TIME REICH: A Novel

By David Healey

Intracoastal Media digital edition revised September 2019. Print edition revised September 2019.

ISBN 978-0-9674162-2-9

Cover art by Juan Padron

BISAC Subject Headings:

FIC014000 FICTION/Historical

FIC032000 FICTION/War & Military

It is not in the stars to hold our destiny but in ourselves.

— WILLIAM SHAKESPEARE

1

Germany, 1945

W ind roared through the German forest, bending the pine trees and driving pellets of ice into the faces of the sentries. The light was fading as a winter's night came on. The storm and the forest gave the dusk a timeless quality so that it could have been the twelfth century or the twentieth. But these men wore the black uniforms of the *Waffen* SS, and they were armed with machine pistols instead of spears and shields.

Their modern weapons did not prevent them from watching the deepening shadows nervously, fingers never straying far from the triggers of their weapons. They shivered as had their ancestors, but they did not complain, standing guard over the structure that had been built beneath the forest floor to hide it from the Allied bombers that now flew overhead daily.

Deep underground, an SS *obersturmbannfuhrer* glanced at the clock on the concrete wall, then tightened the straps that secured him to the seat. *Time.* He had just a few minutes before a scheduled telephone call from Berlin, and he was sure there would be trouble when, instead of the *obersturmbannfuhrer* himself coming to the telephone, his adjutant would calmly explain that an experiment was taking place.

Though he was in a hurry, the Nazi made a point of tightly belting himself inside the steel cage. A safety harness had kept him alive through two crash landings, the most recent just three weeks ago when an Allied fighter had shredded the Junkers flying him back from headquarters. He found it amazing that the skies above Germany were no longer safe. The *Luftwaffe* was spread too thin. He hoped his journey today would go better than that trip had. He might even be in for the ride of his life. He took a deep breath and gave the strap a final tug.

In many ways, the machine surrounding him was not so different from the cockpit of an airplane. One of the earlier prototypes had even been equipped with instruments similar to an airplane or an automobile, but these had been eliminated after swarming shards of glass had blinded three test subjects in a row. A steel cage now enclosed the seat. Looking out from between the struts, he could see electrical coils and thick rubber wires snaking off in all directions. A blue spark of electricity snapped at the base of the cage. The air smelled of ozone, like it did after a fierce lightning storm. He was grounded here inside the machine, but he knew that if he so much as set one foot on the floor while the current was on, he would fry like a moth in a flame.

"All set, *Herr Obersturmbannfuhrer*?"

He nodded at the technician. The man had been reluctant to help, but he did not dare disobey a direct order from an SS officer. The Nazi had found that fear was a great motivator.

"You know what to do," he said.

"I'm not sure of all the settings, *Herr Obersturmbannfuhrer.*"

"I have made all the necessary adjustments. Pretend that this is another drill. You have practiced countless times."

"But never —"

"Pay attention to the controls!" the Nazi shouted.

The technician fell silent, assuming the blank expression of a dutiful German soldier. Taking a red lever in both hands, he pulled it down.

A deep rumble began in the depths of the facility beneath them. The Nazi found that his mouth was very dry. He had watched this machine work many times, but always from a safe distance. Now he was the one strapped inside.

The machine did not always produce good results. He thought of the charred mess left in this very seat the first time they had thrown the switch. Their test pilot had looked like a piece of meat left in the fire too long.

He forced himself to think of something else.

Russia. All that snow. Shivering in the cold at Stalingrad, he had wondered sometimes if he would ever be warm again. A sniper's bullet had almost done for him. One of the best sights he had ever seen was from his bed in the medical evacuation train, watching through a crack in the wall of the box car as they pulled out of the station. After Russia, there was little anymore that he feared.

The machine shuddered.

His next thoughts were of his wife and children. He had not seen them much during the war. It was unlikely that he would ever see them again, but he was comforted by the knowledge that they would survive. He had made arrangements for them to flee Germany when the time came. They would be going to South America.

More sparks snapped. The noise reached a high-pitched shriek. The world beyond the steel cage where he sat was a blur. The *obersturmbannfuhrer* felt himself dissolving. He began to swirl like water going down a drain, his body making long, greasy spirals as it entered a yawning black hole.

"*Nein!*" He could just hear an echo of someone shouting as if from a great distance. "The setting—"

Then the Nazi was gone.

THE BOY WAS AROUND twelve years old, T shirt, and jeans hanging off his skinny frame, shaggy hair like one of the Beatles. That hair style had been popular, what, forty years ago? If there was anything that Hans Schmidt had learned in his long life, it was that given time, everything comes around again. Short hair and long hair, peace and war. That was history for you.

"Pack of Marlboros," the boy said in a squeaky adolescent voice.

"What do you want with cigarettes, boy?" Hans asked, his "w" sounding like a "v." Even past eighty, he could put steel in his voice.

The boy managed to stammer, "They're for my mom."

Hans fixed the boy with a penetrating stare, his face a mask, though deep down the boy's nervousness made him want to smile. "Four seventy-five."

The kid put a handful of change and crumpled bills on the counter. He felt his palms start to sweat. Old Hans was creepy. He didn't wear glasses like most old people and he had intense blue eyes that seemed to look right through you. He had a stare like a lizard. If his friends hadn't been waiting outside, the kid would have turned around and left.

Hans felt something clench inside his chest. His heart had been giving him trouble again lately. He sighed. He was too old to act tough. Hans didn't care if this mop-headed kid smoked or not. He just didn't need any grief about selling cigarettes to minors. The town police had already been on him about that, with that lard-ass Chief Wagner giving him a warning.

He slid a box of Marlboros across the counter. "Next time, tell your mother not to give me all these *gott*-damn quarters."

The kid snatched the cigarettes off the counter and hustled out the door, dodging around a tall man in a black uniform who was just coming in.

Hans felt his heart making a fist again.

This is not possible —

Like someone in a dream, Hans watched the Nazi walk through the doorway of the store he had owned since retiring from the munitions plant. The man was tall with the strong cheekbones and blond hair of a true Aryan. Twin lightning bolts slashed across the collar of his black uniform. He wore a cap with a polished leather brim and the silver death's head badge of the SS. At his throat was the Knight's Cross, the greatest honor a soldier could receive, awarded by the Führer himself.

"You've come," Hans said in a voice that rasped like dead leaves blowing away in the wind.

"What have you done?" the Nazi demanded in the same tone Hans had feared all those years ago. It was a voice used to giving orders. "I had to come looking for you."

At that moment, *Unterscharführer* Hans Schmidt knew the end of days had finally arrived. So many years had passed that he no longer believed what he had lived and breathed and killed for as a young man. Sixty years. *Vor sechzig Jahren.* He wondered if living in America for so long had made him soft. There was a time when the sight of that black uniform coming through his door would have inspired joy. Now Hans looked around, wondering how he could escape, but he was trapped behind the counter. He suddenly felt enormously tired.

He knew why the SS officer was angry. Full of doubt, Hans

had taken the beacon entrusted to his care from its hiding place and buried it in the back yard. He wished now that he'd had the courage to destroy the *gott*-damn thing, but he had wanted to keep the beacon close. It was the same instinct, he supposed, that made murderers on the TV shows he watched late at night bury the body in the back yard, where they could keep an eye on it. He thought he might cheat the future by hiding the beacon in the earth itself.

But the *obersturmbannfuhrer* had not forgotten about him, even after all this time.

Deep within his chest, the old man felt his heart stagger like a drunkard.

No —

The Nazi grabbed the old man by the shirt. "Answer me, *Unterscharfuhrer!*"

Hans Schmidt only opened and closed his mouth silently, like a large white carp. He wanted to tell the colonel that he was too late, that too much time had passed, but no words came out. The old man's last thoughts were of himself as a boy in Munich, going to get his father a newspaper, the first time he had been trusted with an errand. He could still feel how warm the coin felt pressed deep in his palm. And then darkness came on like a rushing tide.

The Nazi stared at him quizzically. "Hans? What is wrong with you?"

But the old man's eyes had all the life of marbles. He let go of Hans' shirt and the withered body slumped to the floor. Dead weight.

Hans' heart had given out before he could explain where the beacon was hidden. The Nazi had come all this way for answers and now only had more questions. Frustrated, he stared down at the crumpled figure of the old man, his flesh pale in the store's harsh lighting. What had the old man said?

Sixty years. That was a long time, and there wasn't another moment to waste.

The Nazi made a quick search behind the store counter but found nothing useful, certainly not what he had come for. He took a pack of cigarettes — American cigarettes, Marlboros — then turned to go, stepping outside into the gathering dusk.

2

Baltimore

Much later, while I was recovering from being shot, I realized that the hunt for the last great Nazi war criminal had started because of a hunch I'd gotten while reading the newspaper. All I had to go on that morning was a name and an address, which I looked up online.

An hour and a half after leaving Baltimore, I took the North Bay exit off the interstate and drove past the store where the robbery had taken place. It was a squat, brick building with plate glass windows filled with lottery advertisements and a hand-lettered sign offering hot dogs for ninety-nine cents. The storefront was wrapped in yellow crime scene tape that flickered in the winter wind.

I pulled over and unfolded a clipping from the *Baltimore Sun.*

ROBBERY SUSPECT WAS WEARING **WWII uniform**

NORTH BAY, Md. — A convenience store owner suffered a fatal heart attack Tuesday during an apparent strong-arm robbery by a man wearing a World War II-era German officer's uniform.

Hans Schmidt, 86, was pronounced dead at the crime scene, according to town police.

Images taken by the store's security camera showed the robber shaking the man, evidently demanding money from the elderly victim.

"It's weird as hell," said Police Chief James Wagner. "We've had everything here from purse snatchings to horse thieves, but no one's ever been robbed by a Nazi."

I DROVE on to the old man's house, parked at the curb and got out. The house was located in a row of modest ranches, in the middle of a blue-collar neighborhood with campers and boat trailers in the driveways. Nobody was around, except for a seventy-something woman next door who was raking leaves.

I climbed the steps to the front door. The outside of the house was neatly kept, with a few shrubs in a mulched flower bed around the foundation. A clay planter filled with silk geraniums added a spray of color to the drab concrete stoop. I pressed the doorbell and waited, shivering. The pale sun offered little heat and the winter air felt especially cold after the warmth of the car.

"Nobody's home," said a voice behind me.

I turned to find that the woman had made her way over from next door, rake in hand. She wore a loose-knit Cardigan sweater the same color as the leaves. "Is this where Hans Schmidt lives?" I asked.

"This is his house," the woman said. "But he died, you know."

"The robbery." When the old woman nodded, I added, "I read about it in the paper."

"I'm Nan from next door," she said, waving in the direction of the yard where I had seen her working. "Can I help you with something?"

"Nan, I'm Bram McCoy." I came down the steps to offer my hand. Her grip was dry and leathery. I hesitated, searching for a way to explain what I was doing there. I wasn't so sure myself. It had been a long time since I had called myself a Nazi hunter — or even a professor — so I told her the closest thing to the truth. "I'm a writer. I came up here to see if I could find out what happened."

"You want to write about Hans?" She sounded surprised.

"Can you tell me about him?"

Nan nodded, as if thinking it over. "I don't want to speak ill of the dead," she finally said. Nan had a frank manner that I liked, looking right at me when she spoke. I knew from experience that meant she had nothing to hide. "But the truth of the matter is that I wouldn't have much to say that was good. Maybe you should find someone else to talk to."

"Was he a bad neighbor?"

"Let's just say he kept to himself. He waved hello, but that was about it."

"Do you know where he was from originally?"

She shrugged. "He lived here in North Bay since the war."

I nodded encouragement. It struck me how people of a certain age simply said "the war" as if there had never been another one since 1945. "How long were you neighbors?"

"He moved in next door about twenty years ago. He lived in town before that, but I don't know where. I'm not sure where he was from *before* he came to town, but I suppose he was Dutch or German. He had that kind of accent, you know?"

"Did he ever have any visitors?" I asked.

"Well, sure. A few. Mostly men he had worked with over at

the munitions plant. He started the store when he retired from there. But there were fewer visitors the last couple of years. All of them getting older, I suppose, or passing on." She looked at me curiously. "You heard that the robber came around here first?"

"No."

"I didn't see him, but someone else did. He was wearing that uniform. The Nazi one. We told the police."

"Do you have any idea what the robber wanted here?"

Nan plucked at the sweater, pulling at a loose strand of yarn. "I have a feeling, with the way that the robber was dressed in a uniform and all, that it was something out of his past. Somebody caught up with Hans in the end."

"Oh?"

"Well, that's what I think," she said hastily. "Maybe I've been watching too much TV. I don't suppose these things happen in the real world."

"I don't suppose you have a key to the house?"

"A key? No, nothing like that. I've never even been inside, as a matter of fact. All these years I lived next door to the man, and I never went in his house and he never went in mine. It's strange how you can be neighbors so long, eat and sleep within spitting distance of somebody and feel like you never really know them."

We both stood there in the wind, thinking about that. I shivered again and wondered if I was getting soft. The cold didn't appear to bother the old woman.

Nan hefted her rake. "I ought to get back to work," she said. "When you get to be my age, you realize every minute counts."

I smiled. "Mind if I look around?"

"Go right ahead."

I went around back, out of the neighbor's sight and screened from the street by the house itself. The back yard was not very private and I paused to fiddle with a gutter downspout as if checking things out. If any other neighbors were watching, I couldn't count on them being as easygoing as Nan. There was a back door — locked, unfortunately — and I hunted under the mat and then under a flower pot for a key, but no such luck.

The small back yard itself was tidy, though mostly barren. A garden shed held a few tools and a wheelbarrow. A screen of shrubs bordered one side of the yard and the rear boundary while the other side was open to Nan's lawn next door. Hans must have been digging recently because the ground had been disturbed in a couple of spots.

I inspected the foundation plantings. Behind a large forsythia bush, its bare branches like a thick, upturned broom, I found what I was looking for — a basement window that wasn't latched. Just large enough to squeeze through. The dense branches of the forsythia would screen me from any observers. Did I really want to commit breaking and entering because of a feeling? But over the years I had developed a kind of sixth sense about these things and right now it was tingling.

I stopped to look around. Nobody in sight. The wind grazing my cheek reminded me of a winter a long time ago. I had been hardly more than boy then, and foolish — playing at hunting Nazis in East Berlin. Back then it had seemed like a game. Only later did I realize what danger I had been in.

I remembered standing before a dilapidated town house in East Berlin when it was still Communist, my notebook and pen in hand. The door at the top of the steps was open just a crack and an old man glared down at me with a lizard-like stare. It was Hermann Ubrecht, who had butchered thousands at Buchenwald. "Are you going to come in or not?" he asked, then turned and went inside, the open door beckoning.

Well, are you?

3

The window swung up with a burst of powdered rust and I brushed the cobwebs away. I wedged my body through the tight space and lowered myself to the floor. It took a moment to allow my eyes to adjust to the darkness. It smelled musty down here, with a hint of machine oil mixed in. There was just enough light from the windows to avoid having to reach for the pull chain that hung from a bare light bulb in a fixture overhead.

The basement had three cinderblock walls and one finished wall covered with drywall. An orderly workbench sat against one of the block walls and above the bench were shelves filled with jars of screws, tubes of glue and caulk, and cans of paint with a dot of color on the label. Hans Schmidt had been an organized man. I grabbed a rag hanging from a nail to wipe away my fingerprints.

I decided to leave the basement for later. The door at the top of the stairs was unlocked. I found myself blinking as I stood on the sun-washed vinyl flooring in the dead man's kitchen.

You could learn a lot from how someone kept his kitchen. Clearly, Hans Schmidt was a man concerned about the smallest details. I studied the spotless floor, the clean counters. The place smelled strongly of cigarettes. The old man must have smoked like a chimney.

I moved on, opening and closing cabinets. A box of cereal, crackers, sack of ground coffee. The refrigerator was just as sparse and neat. Inside were bottles of mustard, horseradish, pickle relish, eggs lined neatly in the molded holder on the door. A few bottles of Becks beer. Frozen dinners in the freezer area, a tray of ice cubes. Not so much as a stray crumb anywhere.

I surveyed the living room next. It was filled with an old man's furniture: oversize recliner made of tan leatherette facing a large TV, a sofa in plaid fabric popularly known as "Early American" and a rectangular coffee table on which resided a single porcelain Hummel figurine of two children poised for a kiss. Positioned next to Hans' recliner was a folding metal table for eating TV dinners. On it was the remote control and a copy of *TV Guide*. The stark, white walls were nearly bare except for an elaborate Bavarian-style wall clock complete with hanging chimes — a timepiece far too ornate for this humble room — and a painting of an Alpine scene in the Thomas Kincaid-style, with the snow on the mountain peaks glowing in luminescent white. Garish though it was, the painting was oddly peaceful. You just wanted to stare at it for a minute and be in that scene. Had it reminded Hans of home?

I could imagine the old man watching television and eating TV dinners from the tray beside his recliner. Passing his time. Passing his days.

The bedroom was more of the same. Double bed, neatly made. Drawers pulled open and closets slightly rummaged. That would have been the doing of the police. Hans would have had everything neat as a pin, judging from what I had seen so far. I did find a stack of well-read *Playboy* magazines under the bed. I picked up the top one and thumbed through it, admiring the glossy photographs. So Hans was a dirty old man. I'd been called that myself not so long ago.

There was a second bedroom, made up into a kind of den or office. Apparently, Hans had no need for a guest bedroom. I tugged at a stuck drawer, my nervous hands fumbling the job. Feeling my snooping time running low, I spent an anxious ten minutes poking through the desk drawers and a filing cabinet. Hans had all his bills methodically organized going back ten years, but unless you wanted to compare his electrical usage from one month to the next, there wasn't much of interest. If Hans had gone to the trouble of keeping his *Playboys* out of sight, I was confident the old man hadn't kept a file folder labeled "Nazi stuff" in plain view. Nothing I found explained why someone wearing a German uniform had shown up at the old man's store to rob him.

Living in Baltimore had taught me there was seldom rhyme or reason for violent crime, but North Bay was a two-hour drive from the city. People here still left their doors unlocked. No, the robbery wasn't random. Someone had singled out Hans Schmidt. Considering that Hans was of an age to have seen SS uniforms first-hand, it was just possible that something from his past had come back to haunt him.

I was running out of time. Next door, Nan would be keeping an eye on the house, wondering what was taking me so long. The last thing I needed was for her to find me poking around and call the police.

I went back through the living room to the basement door. I hadn't left any trace behind and I had used the rag from the basement to wipe down anything I touched.

Back down in the basement, I took a quick look around. Nothing there but that workbench and shelves as neatly organized as a hardware store.

Disappointment tasted sour in my dry mouth. I was taking an awfully big risk to come away with nothing. I also felt somewhat betrayed by the victim, as if he were keeping something from me when all I wanted was to help solve the riddle behind his death. A current of chill air from the window made the coveralls dance eerily on their hooks along the finished wall. Glancing at my watch, I imagined the seconds ticking off like drumbeats.

Time to go.

I dragged a milk crate over to the window and was about to wedge myself back out when a thought occurred to me: why the finished wall? The other three walls were concrete block painted white.

I walked toward the far end of the basement, reached between the dusty coveralls, and thumped at the drywall. It sounded normal enough, but I forced my way deeper into the dead man's work clothes.

They were dark and musty, smelling faintly of old motor oil. Spiders had built sticky nests in the folds. A cracked rubber raincoat was coming apart at the seams. I rapped at the wall again. Judging by the placement of the window I had crawled through, it dawned on me that the basement did seem oddly foreshortened — if this was a full basement, it should have stretched a few feet further under the full length of the house.

Something wasn't right.

I shoved the raincoat and coveralls aside. Behind them was a door that I hadn't noticed before because it was painted the same color as the wall. Also, the door was flush with the drywall so that it became part of the wall around it, without any of the usual trim molding. Your eyes drifted right over it if you weren't looking for a door. I pushed, felt the door give. The darkness inside exhaled a smell of mice and damp.

Carefully, I felt around inside the doorway on the right-hand side. Hans had been thoughtful enough to install a light switch. I found myself standing in the doorway of a well-lighted room. Most of the concrete floor was covered with a worn carpet remnant, with one corner flipped up. The walls of the hidden room were lined with homemade shelves filled with cans of food and jugs of water, flashlights and spare batteries. Hans had been ready for anything from a power outage to a nuclear war.

The air in the room felt undisturbed and I was sure no one had been in here for a long time. Moving slowly, I poked through the cans and jars, but all I found that was even somewhat unusual was a box of mouse poison and a pump action twelve gauge wrapped in an oiled cloth. Disappointed, I put the shotgun back and closed the door. Then I squeezed back out the window.

Nan hadn't come looking for me yet, which was a relief. I shut the window and straightened up, picturing all those rooms with their almost military neatness. Something nagged at me. In my head, I replayed snapshots of what I had just seen. My mind went back to the basement storage room. The flipped-up corner of carpeting on the floor. The magazines under the bed. The Bavarian clock with its hanging weights and carved wood, better suited to a Teutonic castle than a modest tract house. I started to walk away.

The carpet flashed in my mind again. I had wanted to kick it flat. I felt sure Hans wouldn't have left it that way.

I knew then that I had to go back into the house.

I felt like I was in one of those horror movies where you want to shout at the actors *don't go in there*. But I slid into the basement anyway and pawed aside the old clothes until I found the door. The storage room looked even more ordinary the second time around. I flipped back the carpet. Hidden beneath was a wooden trap door set into the concrete floor. An iron ring that folded down flat served as the handle. I reached down and pulled the door up. A ladder led down into darkness. I grabbed a flashlight off the shelf and climbed below.

"Hans Schmidt," I said into the stillness as the flashlight beam played over a swastika. "You Nazi son of a bitch."

That's when I heard the footsteps in the house above.

4

I snapped off the light and held my breath. Muffled voices drifted down and I could hear two people in conversation, although I couldn't make out the words. One set of footsteps was heavy enough to make the floorboards creak, the other was lighter. If they came in the basement I'd be caught like a rat in a hole.

I scrambled back up the ladder and shut the trap door as quietly as possible, then dragged the carpet back over it. I closed the door of the storage room and slipped like a ghost toward the window. The voices and footsteps above me stopped. I climbed out and walked quickly toward my car. Nobody around. I got in and slumped down in the seat, curious about who was in the house. I could see a marked police SUV and another vehicle in the driveway.

A woman came out of the house. She was tall and dark-haired, good looking, wearing a business suit. I guessed that she was a cop. She seemed to be taking in the street and the front of the house, as if trying to picture what had happened there. That's when Nan rounded the corner, talked to the cop a minute, then pointed at my car. I slid lower in the seat. The woman studied my Volvo for a moment like she had x-ray vision and I was afraid she could see me. She looked away and continued talking with the neighbor. After a minute the neighbor wandered off and the cop went back in the house.

I started the car and got the hell out of there.

I SPENT the drive back to Baltimore wondering about Hans Schmidt and his Nazi shrine. Breaking into the house had been risky, though the sight of that hidden room in the flashlight beam had been worth it. That one glimpse told me a great deal, but left me with so many questions. The robbery at the old man's store now seemed even less likely to have been a random act.

I turned my thoughts to the town of North Bay. Located as it was on the upper Chesapeake, I had expected something more scenic. You could cross North Bay off as a tourist destination. It was a backwater town that was long on fast food restaurants and short on charm. There was also an oddly Southern flavor to the place. "We serve grits" a sign in a diner window had noted. I couldn't remember the last time I had seen so many Confederate flags and pickup trucks. Now I had seen swastikas as well. The more I thought about it, the more North Bay seemed like a good place for a Nazi to hide.

Back home, there was a message from my literary agent on the answering machine.

"I'm just calling to check your pulse," he said in his clipped New York accent. "Bram, are you working on anything? People are going to forget about you. It's important to stay relevant."

I deleted the message.

Relevant. I remembered my father the Holocaust survivor, sitting at the kitchen table and working a cardboard matchbook cover under his greasy fingernails. I wondered what he would have thought of that word.

The truth was that I *had* been thinking about writing again. Now that I had time on my hands, I thought maybe I'd get started on some articles, book reviews or essays. I had even thought about another book, but the idea wasn't quite formed. It would have something to do with Nazis, of course. My own white whales. Maybe I would write about the ones who had gotten away. Stories with real-life mystery. But a book was a big project. I needed something in between until I was ready for that. I knew from experience that you had to get in training for a book, just like a runner working his way toward a marathon.

I spent the rest of the afternoon tidying up, adding the newspaper to the stack in the recycling bin, wiping the crumbs off the table. There was no one but me to clutter up the rooms, yet I still managed to find opened books scattered like wing-shot birds on the leather sofa and armchair, an empty coffee mug and snifter sticky with cognac. My running shoes were sitting in the middle of the oriental carpet in the living room and I couldn't for the life of me remember leaving them there. I put the books back on the shelves, rinsed out the mug and glass in the sink, tossed the running gear in a closet. Keeping busy. My mind kept coming back to Hans Schmidt and his hidden room, like a splinter I kept picking at. I could almost hear the whirring of my own imagination above the noise of morning traffic on Light Street several floors below.

I did some of my best thinking when my body was busy doing something else, so I thought about going over to the martial arts school and getting in a workout, but I didn't feel like going out again. Instead, I changed into workout clothes, stretched, and went through a series of front kicks, blocks and punches. My joints creaked and popped until I really warmed up. The secret to martial arts, when you really observed, was not youth with its speed and fierceness. In martial arts, there was something to be said for the cunning that came with age. Time and again, an old fat guy was able to beat a faster young one on points. I wasn't that old fat guy yet, but I found something reassuring in the fact that youth did not trump experience.

It felt good to move and sweat. When I'd had enough, I got a beer from the fridge and plunked down on the sofa. The condo had a good view of the city to the north; to the east I could see the cobalt blue harbor. Before the recession, developers were selling waterfront condos for more than a million dollars. My own place had cost well under half of that, but it still had a great view. At the moment, I found the sight of all those tall buildings and scurrying people reassuring. Whatever had taken place in that little ranch house on the Eastern Shore might as well be a million miles from here.

I was ready for a second bottle of Fort McHenry ale when the door buzzer rang. I don't get many visitors these days, so I had no idea who it could be. I pressed the intercom button and said hello.

"Abraham McCoy, this is Agent Kate Crockett with the federal Office of Special Investigations."

"Yes?" A cold knot formed in my stomach.

"I think I'd better come up."

I buzzed her in because I knew I had no choice. I was very familiar with the Office of Special Investigations. OSI was a branch of the United States Justice Department's Criminal Division whose sole function was to track down Nazi war criminals from World War II, prosecuting them and sometimes deporting them. What I didn't know was whether I should pack my toothbrush and call my lawyer. In my favor was the fact that OSI is made up of prosecutors, investigators and historians. OSI agents do not carry badges and guns. They aren't law enforcement officers with powers to arrest. That didn't mean Agent Crockett couldn't call the police.

The woman at the door was the same one I had seen in North Bay. Up close, Agent Crockett was older than I expected, with the beginnings of crow's feet at the corners of her eyes. Those were the kind of premature wrinkles you got from being outdoors a lot and she looked fit and shapely in her smartly tailored business suit. Tennis would be her sport. Or maybe running. She extended her hand and gave me a quick, firm handshake. We sat in the living room and Agent Crockett didn't waste any time getting to the point.

"What were you doing in North Bay today?" she asked.

"I don't know what you're talking about." My first rule when dealing with anyone in authority was to deny everything.

"I got your license plate number after the neighbor pointed you out," Agent Crockett explained. "I had some friends at the FBI trace it for me."

"What can I do for you, Agent Crockett?"

She paused to tug the edge of her skirt across her knees and I was momentarily distracted by her legs. I noticed she wore good shoes and jewelry. I caught a whiff of perfume. Agent Crockett cleared her throat.

"Look, this isn't going the way I planned," she said. Some of the official tone was gone from her voice. "Maybe I should start over. First, I wanted to tell you that I've read your books. Professor McCoy, I have to say that *Journey of Hope* was very moving. More than anything else it's what steered me into this career."

"I hope you're not here to blame me for that." I didn't bother to correct her about calling me "Professor."

Agent Crockett laughed, then gave me the kind of appraising look I hadn't experienced since a friend talked me into trying speed dating. I felt my face flush. "You're much younger than I expected," she said.

"Let's just say I'm old enough to remember *The Rockford Files* on television, even though it was on after my bedtime."

"I was more about *X Files*," she said. "David Duchovny, you know."

I changed the subject before I carbon dated myself any further. "I'm glad you read my book. I sometimes wonder if anyone has."

"I've read it twice, if that counts for anything," Agent Crockett said. "I keep a copy of *Leaders of the Third Reich* on my desk. It is without doubt the best reference on Nazi war criminals ever published."

"I hardly know what to say."

"Then tell me why you were in North Bay today."

"You're not giving up, are you? Okay, I was curious. I saw the robbery as a news item in the paper and thought I would take a drive and see what I could find out. It just struck me as very strange."

"You think he was a Nazi?"

"That's an interesting question." I was about to step into some very deep water here, and I wasn't sure I wanted to. The silence stretched for several seconds.

"Professor McCoy?"

"He was a Nazi, all right."

"How do you know he was a Nazi?"

"The basement."

"What are you talking about?"

"There's a hidden room down there."

"You went in the house? Oh boy. Don't tell me that. You didn't break in, did you?"

"Does it count as breaking in if somebody left a window unlocked? Anyhow, I found all the proof I need that Hans Schmidt — or whatever his name was — actually belonged to the *Schutzstaffel*."

"He was SS? How can you be so sure? The local police didn't find any room in the basement."

"Maybe they weren't looking. It's there. There's a trap door in the floor."

"What's in the room?"

"A portrait of Hitler. An SS uniform. Some Nazi flags and photographs. It's a shrine to the Third Reich."

"You think someone came for him? They found out who he really was and decided to exact revenge?"

"I don't know."

"Well, it can't be coincidence, having someone in a German uniform show up and scare him to death."

"No, it's probably not coincidence," I agreed.

"We're curious enough that OSI is going to trace the victim's background and find out what he did during the war. There's a good chance that he wasn't just Hans Schmidt, mild-mannered retiree. If someone went after him out of revenge, they might have harassed him first to let him know they were coming. We'll check his phone records to see who was calling him. That could lead to the suspect, or at least offer some clue. One thing for sure, it wasn't a simple robbery."

"Sounds like you have a good handle on this," I said. "It's just a suggestion, but you could have the medical examiner see if there's a blood type tattooed under Schmidt's arm."

"Good thinking," she said. "That would definitely ID him as SS. You know, Professor McCoy, it just so happens that I have some budget for consultants in cases like this. Unusual ones. Would you be interested?"

It slipped out before I could stop myself.

"Very," I said.

5
_____

After Agent Crockett left, I wandered from room to room, already wishing it was tomorrow. I was that excited, like a kid on Christmas Eve. As much as I was glad to be helping OSI, I was also interested in working with Kate Crockett. She was smart and attractive and seemed to have a sense of humor under that tough shell. It felt as if there was some kind of spark between us that could be fanned into something bigger.

For some reason I thought back to my father, to his measured patience. He never understood this Nazi business, this need to dwell upon the past.

My father. Sitting at the kitchen table. He was using the corner of a matchbook cover to pick at the grease under his nails. He hated the thick, gummy grease. He never really got his hands clean so that the grease was a kind of badge to the world that he was a manual laborer, a blue collar worker, this man who had studied engineering in Vienna and Paris and designed some of Berlin's office buildings as Germany emerged as a financial powerhouse in the late 1930s. When he came to the

United States after the war, none of that meant anything; it only mattered that he was German.

By the time I was a teen-ager he had given up hope that he would be anything more than a foreman in a machine shop. By then he was an old man, growing heavy, his graying hair still thick and combed back like Charlton Heston's.

"Were you down at the library?" he asked.

"Yeah."

"Reading about those *gott*-damn Nazis again, I bet."

I didn't say anything.

He frowned down at his nails. "I don't know why you care so much about what happened. You need to think about the future, not the past."

I moved around to the refrigerator, got out the orange juice. The sweetish chemical smell of hand degreaser hung in the air. The kitchen was worn but neat; the same wallpaper with a pattern of blue flowers had been on the walls ever since I could remember. My father had recently replaced the linoleum himself and the floor looked too new, out of place beneath the dated fixtures and kitchenette set with metal legs showing age spots of rust.

I poured the juice into the glass, something with a cartoon character on it that we'd gotten free as a McDonald's giveaway. As I drank, I watched him through the thick glass bottom.

He was still going at his nails, trying to get them clean. He always scrubbed them with a nail brush when he first got home but it didn't remove all the grease. He would sit there for twenty minutes until he had picked away the last of it. He had changed into wool slacks and a clean white dress shirt, even though he wore a blue uniform at work with his name embroidered above the pocket.

It did not help that he had an accent like the bad guys in World War II movies, or that he was Jewish — a fact that he did not hide but did not advertise, either. He never complained about not getting ahead. As he grew older, he seemed content.

"You're never going to get those damn nails clean."

"Don't let your mother hear you curse like that," he said. He looked up and pointed the creased matchbook cover at me. "And let me tell you something. The last thing a man has, after they take everything else away, is his pride. That's why I sit here every night cleaning my damn nails."

Looking back, I know I loved him then. I was sixteen years old and he was my father. My old man. He really *was* old compared to my friends' dads. It was almost like being raised by your grandfather.

I knew about the camps, and how he had survived. It was something I didn't share with my friends, not because I was ashamed but because they wouldn't understand. They were too removed from the war and its pain.

Dad did not seem bitter. I hated the Germans for him. Back then, I wanted to kill them all.

I put the empty orange juice glass in the sink. "Dad, I never understood why the Jews didn't fight back."

"We did fight back. We survived. Hitler's gone. I'm still here." He held up his hands and smiled. "See? Finally clean."

"Good morning, Professor McCoy," the girl said. "The usual?"

"Thank you, Rachel." Baltimore was enough of a small town that the girl in the harborfront coffee shop had gotten to know my name. I knew hers, too, but I was cheating: a plastic name tag was prominently displayed on Rachel's chest. I tried not to stare, since I already had a reputation as a dirty old man where young women were concerned. "Cold," I said, shoving my hands into my coat pockets and stopping just short of adding "as a witch's tit" by way of a Freudian slip.

"You want a sweet roll or something with that, Professor?"

"I always like a little something sweet," I said. "But maybe I'll just stick with the coffee this morning."

Rachel giggled. "You got it, Professor."

It would have been easier to brew a pot of coffee at home, but I liked the harbor in the morning. Gulls wheeled overhead, dodging through the rigging of the tall ship *USS Constellation* that even at this early hour attracted a handful of tourists. The salty winter wind bit and nipped at the people heading to work. I watched them hurrying along with their briefcases, coat collars turned up, and for once I didn't feel a twinge of guilt. I had gone back to work.

I had not been idle in the long months before this morning. I was lean and muscular in a way I hadn't been in nearly twenty years because I had time to run and work out. I read *Gone with the Wind* and *Moby Dick* and half a dozen other classics. I had felt a strange kinship with Ahab, chasing after his white whale. The captain and I knew something about obsession.

At first, after losing my teaching job, I had welcomed the time just to think. Money wasn't much of an issue. I still had some income from my books, enough to keep me going if I didn't waste too much on fancy coffee. I wasn't cheap, but I always had been careful with money. My late parents, who like most of their wartime generation had endured one hardship after another and saved every dime they could, had passed on that much.

Coffee in hand, I stopped and bought a paper, then walked back to the condo and got in my car for the drive to North Bay. Normally, my old Volvo had a stale funk, but this morning the smell of the newspaper was better than any air freshener. I inhaled the acrid scent of the ink that mingled with the aroma of strong black coffee. It was the smell of promise.

AGENT CROCKETT WAS WAITING for me in front of Hans Schmidt's house.

"I was starting to wonder if you were going to show," she said.

"I had to stop for these." I reached into the car for three coffees in a cardboard tray and a box of doughnuts I had bought on the outskirts of town. There didn't seem to be a Starbucks in North Bay.

"Good timing," she said, nodding at the driveway behind me. An SUV with a light bar and "North Bay Police" stenciled on the doors pulled in. The man who got out was big and beefy, wearing a blue nylon windbreaker over his uniform. He was in his late forties or fifties, thinning gray hair, a pale Irish face. His first reaction when he saw us was to frown, but his look softened when he realized I was carrying coffee and doughnuts.

"Agent Crockett," he said, nodding almost gravely at the OSI investigator. He turned to me. "I'm Chief Wagner."

"Bram McCoy," I said, juggling the coffees so I could take hold of the chief's meaty hand. The rest of him looked soft, but he had a strong grip.

"Professor McCoy is here to assist the Department of Justice with this investigation," Agent Crockett explained.

"A professor?" The chief raised his eyebrows.

"Professor McCoy is a leading authority on fugitive Nazi war criminals," Agent Crockett said. "He's written two books on the subject."

The chief took one of the coffees, then reached into the box to fish for a doughnut. He came up with a fat cruller. "Hey, anybody who brings coffee and doughnuts is OK in my book. You get any creamer?"

"It's here somewhere under the napkins."

The chief nodded and spent a moment fixing his coffee,

using the hood of my car for a table. The metal ticked as it cooled. The air temperature wasn't much above freezing, but without any wind it was pleasant enough to stand there in the driveway, sipping from our hot coffees. "Hell of a thing that happened," the chief said. "Old man has a heart attack like that during a robbery."

"Did you know the victim?" I asked.

"I knew him from the store," the chief said as he put the lid back on his coffee. "You wanted a pack of gum or a quick cup of coffee or a gallon of milk, that store was one of the places you stopped. Hans had owned the place for a while."

"He owned the store where the robbery took place?"

The chief smiled. "Hans owned a lot of property in North Bay. You wouldn't know it to look at him. Rental properties, the store, even a car dealership for a while. He wasn't exactly what you'd call a community booster. Hans kept to himself. He acted like it cost him money to smile."

"Chief, we have reason to believe that Hans may have had some kind of Nazi background that he was trying to hide," Agent Crockett said.

"Oh, for crissake," the chief said. I could see that he was getting exasperated with Agent Crockett, but he was making an effort to be polite. He made a face as if the coffee had suddenly turned sour. "Hans Schmidt was not a Nazi. He was an old man who died of a heart attack because someone robbed him. *That* was the crime. You wanted to see the inside of his house again, so here we are."

"I appreciate it, Chief," Agent Crockett said. Then her eyes locked on mine. "Before we go into the house, you should know that Professor McCoy found some Nazi memorabilia here yesterday."

Wagner rounded on me. "You were in the house?"

"One of the neighbors said I could look around," I said, which technically wasn't a lie.

The chief shook his head. "All you got to do is ask, right? We were about to hire a locksmith until we got hold of the old man's keys at the store. Normally, we wouldn't have bothered going in the house since the crime was elsewhere, but the old man didn't have any next of kin. What did you find?"

"I think it's better if I just show you."

"Fair enough." Chief Wagner drained his coffee. "Shall we?"

The chief unlocked the front door. As we stepped inside, I traded a look with Agent Crockett, grateful that she hadn't revealed to the chief that I had broken in. I doubted that the local chief of police would be very understanding. Maybe Agent Crockett wasn't so by-the-book as I'd thought.

Stale cigarette smoke once again assaulted my nostrils. I saw Agent Crockett wrinkle her nose as well.

"Whoever buys this house is going to have one hell of a time getting rid of that smell," the chief said. "That tar gets on everything. You have to scrub it off. I know because I used to be a smoker myself. Haven't touched a cigarette now in ten years."

"Let's check out the basement," Agent Crockett said.

The chief shrugged and started to lead the way, but she slipped in front of him. Agent Crockett and I were on the same side — she was my new employer, as well — but I decided she was pushy all the same.

The basement stairs groaned under Wagner's weight. As I followed him down, I noticed the chief's feet were big and clumsy as cinderblocks on the narrow steps. Agent Crockett ran down them like an elf.

At the bottom, breathing heavily, the chief asked, "Why are we down here?"

"That wall," I said, nodding toward the far end of the basement. Just as I had done yesterday, I found the door and pushed it open.

"Another storage room," the chief said. He picked up a can, put it back down. "Nothing important in here that I can see."

"The rug," I said, and swept it back to reveal the trap door.

"I'll be damned," said the chief. He reached down, hooked his meaty hand through the handle and tugged the door loose like it was weightless.

Agent Crockett had come prepared with a flashlight and she slipped down the ladder ahead of us. She tugged a pull chain to turn on a single bare bulb overhead.

The secret room measured no more than a few square feet, but it was crammed full of Nazi memorabilia. Old Hans had built himself a shrine to the Third Reich. The walls were cinderblock, painted white, and the floor was covered in the same thick carpet as the living room. Directly across from us was a large portrait of Adolf Hitler, his dark eyes glaring out from a gilded frame. That was the most prominent item in the room. The rest of the pictures had been clipped from magazines over the years. Many were yellow with age, but they were neatly framed.

There were photographs of a massive rally at Nuremberg, Hitler speaking behind a podium and making his signature stiff-armed salute, German troops goose-stepping.

"My God," Agent Crockett remarked.

"More like *Mein Gott,*" I said.

The shrine didn't stop at photographs and portraits. One wall displayed a Nazi flag with the swastika on a round white field surrounded by a blood red background. The sight of it made me turn cold. On a shelf the old man had arrayed a collection of Nazi daggers and a couple of Luger pistols, along with a German combat helmet. The *piece de resistance* appeared to be a full SS uniform worn by a mannequin. There was something oddly appropriate in that the mannequin's face was utterly featureless, not unlike the blank stare one usually saw on the faces of soldiers at attention.

"I wouldn't be surprised if that was the bastard's uniform from the war," I said.

Agent Crockett reached up and gingerly took the hat off the mannequin, examined the black *schiff* with its silver skull emblem, and put it back.

"Amazing," she said. "He must have been building this collection for years."

Chief Wagner stood quietly, taking it all in. "I guess it just goes to show you never really know some people," he finally said. "Old Hans. Spends his days selling packs of gum and the whole time he probably can't wait to get home and play with his Nazi toys."

"Now what do you think about the robber wearing a German uniform, Chief?" Crockett asked.

The chief didn't answer, but he moved to take a closer look at one of the handguns. "Do you know anything about guns, Professor?"

"Not really. But I'd say it's German."

"1944 Luger, Model P8," the chief said. He smiled. "I'm into guns. Those Lugers are worth a lot of money."

"Who cares what it's worth," Crockett snapped. "What does it *mean*?"

"Very valuable stuff," I chimed in, siding with the chief on this one. I ignored Agent Crockett's glare. "Do you collect guns, Chief?"

"Shotguns," he said. "I do a little trap shooting."

"How much does a good shotgun bring?" I asked. "A real top-of-the-line trap gun?"

"Several thousand dollars."

"What would you say a German Luger is worth?"

He shrugged shoulders that were rounded and heavy as a sack of grain. "A couple thousand, at least."

"I don't know guns," I admitted. "But that flag there — if it's the real deal — might bring twenty thousand."

The chief gave a low whistle. "That much for some old Nazi shit?"

"People love Nazi paraphernalia," I said. "They'll pay a lot. They know that dad or granddad was in the war and they want a physical piece of it, or they're caught up in some kind of Third Reich fascination and they want a relic of that era."

"You think somebody robbed the victim because they wanted his Nazi collection?" Agent Crockett sounded skeptical. "The only problem with that theory is that he didn't find it."

"Hans had a heart attack," I pointed out. "We may never know what the robber intended."

The chief was moving slowly around the room, pausing to look at the pictures on the walls or to study some item on a shelf. He was careful not to touch anything. "What's this?"

A metallic disk sat on a table in front of the chief. The disk was about eighteen inches across and maybe three inches thick. It was utterly smooth, except for a design in raised relief that showed an eagle gripping a swastika in its talons. The disk might once have been shiny, possibly made out of burnished brass, but time had dulled the finish. Slowly, I reached down and traced the outline of the eagle. The metal felt buttery, like a worn coin, and the disk was warm — or maybe that was my imagination.

"I've never seen anything like it," I said. "Somehow I don't think it's a paperweight."

"Chief, I'd like to take this thing back to D.C. with me and have it analyzed at the FBI lab."

"Be my guest," he said. "Ask the experts. But I'm thinking that the professor here could be right. I doubt this thing is a paperweight, but it does look like it has a decorative purpose. I have some evidence bags in my truck."

"That would be great, Chief. Thank you."

Chief Wagner clumped up the stairs to get an evidence bag, leaving me alone with Agent Crockett in the Nazi mausoleum a strange old man had secreted beneath his house. She reached out to touch the disk, then snatched her hand away. "Ouch!"

"What?"

"I just got a little shock. Must be static electricity." Agent Crockett hugged herself and rubbed her arms as if she was cold. "This place gives me the creeps. Let's go. Chief Wagner can bag up that disk."

She started up the ladder. I lingered for a moment, getting a last look at the SS uniform, the Nazi flag, the outstretched eagle's wings on the gleaming disk. Hitler's imperious gaze keeping watch over it all. Then I followed Agent Crockett up the ladder.

6

The North Bay Police Station was a surprisingly modern facility, given the fact that the rest of the downtown had such a shabby feel. The station was built of brick, with soaring windows and airy architectural beams more suited to an office building than a law enforcement agency.

The interior was neat and sterile, full of echoes from the expanses of glass, steel and tile floors. Many of the cops had shaved heads, and I had a disconcerting image of them shouting "*Ja vol!*" and goose-stepping down the hallways when none of the civilians was around. In most police agencies, the days of kindly Officer Malarkey walking the beat were long gone. Now, the ranks of small-town police were often filled with paramilitary types who subscribed to *Guns & Ammo* magazine.

Chief Wagner led us into his own office, a large space decorated with shooting trophies, including a gold-plated clay pigeon. The "wall of fame" behind his desk featured a large map of North Bay and framed photographs of the chief accepting awards from various public officials. In one photograph, he wielded a shovel alongside the Maryland governor, apparently breaking ground for the police station. He had a sprawling desk that he settled himself behind, taking command, waving his mitt of a hand to indicate we should sit.

"You two might be used to this kind of thing, but I have to say that was some weird shit we found at Hans Schmidt's place," he said, shaking his head and appearing a bit dazed and tired. "With that discovery on top of the strange circumstances of his death, the truth is that I'm going to be under some pressure from the community to figure out what the hell this is all about."

"It's like picking up a rock and finding a big spider under it," I said.

The chief looked at me steadily, then got up from his chair, shut the office door, sat back down heavily.

"Look," he said. "Just so you people know this is *my* rock — and *my* spider. Just so we understand each other. I've got the mayor, the local newspaper, practically the whole goddamn town wondering when we're going to catch this guy who held up the store. In their eyes, he killed that old man. Then we find a Nazi flag and a portrait of Hitler in the victim's house. What the hell am I supposed to do with *that*? I'm inclined to keep it quiet for now."

"Like you said, it's your rock," Agent Crockett said. "If you feel inclined to keep hatred like that hidden because it's the easy thing to do, that's your call. You do what you feel is right, Chief Wagner."

The chief's face reddened. *Ouch.* I felt for him. He had bared his soul and the big shot OSI agent from Washington had stopped just short of saying he was sweeping something ugly under the rug. I looked at the photographs on his walls. Here was a man with an accomplished small-town career that he took pride in. The chief would be inclined to keep local secrets. Maybe it wasn't so strange that an old Nazi would pick a place like this to hide. I glanced at Agent Crockett, but her face was carefully blank. She was making it clear that what the chief decided to reveal about the discovery in Hans Schmidt's basement didn't concern her.

"Of course, the Department of Justice will be glad to extend any assistance you request," she continued. "Now what Professor McCoy and I would like to do is see the surveillance video from the store."

"Fair enough." Chief Wagner opened a notebook computer on his desk and turned it so that we could all see the screen. "One of my men transferred the images from the store camera to a DVD. Believe it or not, we *are* familiar with the twenty-first century in North Bay."

We watched several minutes of customers coming and going through the front door. The surveillance camera had made a frame every few seconds so that the people seemed to march like penguins in the black and white images. The picture was sharp enough to see the faces. A time counter in the bottom corner got to 13:00 hours, around when the robbery took place.

At 13:55 a tall man with fair hair appeared on the tape. He had on a long leather coat that made it hard to tell if he wore a uniform under it. That was definitely a military hat on his head and I was pretty sure he had on jackboots. He paused long enough to hold the door for someone and in that moment he not only tilted his face toward the camera but also turned to offer his profile. Then he was gone from the screen.

"That's it?" Agent Crockett sounded disappointed.

"Hans had a basic surveillance system," Chief Wagner replied. "That's all we've got, but at least it's something."

"Could you play it again?"

The chief shrugged, then had the computer run through the sequence again. The image was grainy, but there was something vaguely familiar about the high cheekbones and the sharp nose. *A harsh face.* Where had I seen it before?

The chief closed the computer, then handed us a still photo made from the tape. "I'll have one of my guys put a copy on DVD for you. Do you want to talk to the kid we found digging the day before yesterday in the old man's back yard?"

"Where is he?"

"Last time I saw him, he was looking miserable in one of our holding cells. The kid's name is Jason Moody. We're holding him on possession of CDS. He's been sitting there for two days because no one's been around to bail him out. You're welcome to ask him what the hell he was doing with that shovel."

"What's his relationship to Hans Schmidt?" Agent Crockett asked.

"The kid lives in the basement of his grandmother's house, which is two houses away from the old man's place."

"Any connection to the robbery at the store?" I asked.

The chief shook his head. "This kid is what we call a frequent flier. He's got an extensive record, but it's all minor shit like shoplifting. Not a bad kid, if he could get off whatever crap he's on."

We followed Chief Wagner out of the office, then passed through a maze of hallways to a barred doorway. Behind it was a short corridor with three cells. I couldn't help but flinch as the door slid shut behind us with a metallic clang.

"This is just a holding area," the chief explained. "We only keep people here overnight, two nights at the most. Then they go to the county jail. If they get convicted of something big — like murder — they get sent to the Maryland House of Corrections in Baltimore or out to the state prison in Hagerstown."

Two cells were empty, but the third was occupied. Jason Moody looked up nervously as our small posse trooped in. It was hard to tell his age, but he was somewhere between being a boy and a full-fledged adult. He was so skinny that I'd seen twigs with more muscle on them. His eyes had a sunken look and his hair was cut close to his scalp. He wore a T-shirt of dubious cleanliness; the armpits were stained yellow and there were several tiny rips in the fabric as if it had been perforated with buckshot. His jeans had a greasy sheen. His sneakers flopped because the police had confiscated the shoelaces.

"Okay, on your feet and down to the interview room," the chief ordered. "We have some people here who want to talk to you."

The kid knew the way because he slunk down the corridor with the chief behind him. I noticed the chief hadn't felt the need to bring extra guards with him, and it was easy to see why. The chief must have had at least a hundred pounds on the suspect. Any trouble and he could have backhanded this kid into the previous decade.

We entered a small, institutionalized room with white walls, folding metal chairs and a wood-grain laminated table. It was much nicer than I expected, although there was an unpleasant odor of stale sweat.

I couldn't help myself: "What, no bare light bulb and rubber hose?"

"We don't do that anymore, Professor," the chief said, giving me a wink that hinted there might indeed be a room like that just down the hall.

The suspect sat on one side of the table; the three of us took chairs on the other. There was no sign of a lawyer and nobody mentioned the need for one. Chief Wagner crossed his large arms on his chest and glowered at the suspect. "All right, Jason, tell these people what you were doing in the old man's yard."

"Excuse me," Agent Crockett interrupted. "If you don't mind, Chief, I would like to conduct this interview."

The chief shrugged. Agent Crockett produced a tiny digital recorder and placed it on the table. From the look on the chief's face you would have thought she had taken out a cobra. Agent Crockett's methods were apparently more formal than was usual in North Bay. She announced the date and time of the interview, then invited each of us to state our names for the record. The suspect went last.

"Jason Moody," he stated in a hoarse voice.

"You'll have to speak up," she said. "How old are you, Jason?"

"Nineteen."

"Does the name Hans Schmidt mean anything to you?"

"He's the old man that died."

"Jason, did you know Hans Schmidt?"

"Yes, I did. Kind of. He lived on the next street over. I've been in his store."

"You were arrested after digging in Mr. Schmidt's back yard, the day after he died during a robbery at his store. How did you come to be digging there?"

"I heard about how he buried stuff in his back yard," Jason said.

"Who told you that?"

Jason shrugged his thin shoulders. "It was just something everybody in the neighborhood knew, so I decided to see for myself. I figured it was money. I'd heard how sometimes old people buried money in the back yard because they didn't trust banks. Buried it in Mason jars, you know. He was dead so I figured he wouldn't need the money."

"So you went in his shed and got a shovel?"

"No, I brought one."

"How did you know where to dig?"

"Well, you can see Mr. Schmidt's backyard out my gran's kitchen window. I've seen him digging out there."

"What did you find?"

"No money, that's for sure. All I dug up was a couple of dead cats."

"Dead cats?"

"Everyone in the neighborhood said the old man hated cats and used to catch them and kill them. Guess they were right."

I was not a big fan of cats, but I didn't go around killing them. Suddenly I saw a whole different side of old Hans. Jason's story explained the fresh dirt I'd noticed in the back yard.

"You didn't find anything?"

"I was only there a few minutes before the police caught me."

"Did you ever go in Mr. Schmidt's house?" she asked.

"Nah." The kid shrugged. "But there was something weird about him."

"Why is that?"

"I mean, he killed all those cats, right? My gran always said to stay away from him when I was a kid. He wasn't like a friendly old guy or anything. He had that German accent and all, and we used to joke that he was some kind of old Nazi."

"Those were just jokes?"

"Yeah, you know how you say things about people." Jason paused, gazing absently at the digital recorder. "It's just talk."

CHIEF WAGNER STAYED BEHIND to lead the suspect back to the holding cell. We didn't wait for him. There was a cop on the other side of the barred door and he took his time buzzing the two of us through. I felt a great sense of relief upon seeing the door open. Perhaps I had a genetic response to being detained.

"Didn't go well, huh?" the cop asked. He laughed. "Maybe the chief will knock some sense into that kid."

We walked on, but in the hallway Agent Crockett's cell phone rang and she slipped into a corner to take the call. Chief Wagner found me there a minute later, still waiting.

"Learn anything?" he asked.

"Sounds like Hans Schmidt was full of surprises," I said.

"So is your partner," the chief said, nodding at Agent Crockett, who was now having what appeared to be a heated conversation on her end of the phone.

"She's a little hard to work with," I conceded, which from Chief Wagner's point of view was the understatement of the year.

"Better you than me, Professor." The chief clapped me on the shoulder and moved off, chuckling.

I thought about the interview with Jason Moody. He hadn't found anything, but I wondered if maybe he hadn't been digging in the right place. I recalled seeing a shovel in the back yard shed. I might just do a little digging on my own.

7

K ate drove me back to my car, which was still parked in Hans Schmidt's driveway. "We should stay overnight. First thing in the morning we can talk to some people who knew the victim," she said. "Do you think there are any motels in this town that don't rent rooms by the hour?"

"Our best bet would be over by the interstate."

"Good. Let's go pick up your car and drive out there."

Kate pulled up to the house. I got in my car and led the way out to the interchange. There were several choices of motels, and I picked the biggest one, a Hampton Inn that looked fairly new and rose three floors above the parking lot and adjacent truck stop.

"Lovely place," I remarked, getting out of the car. "If we're lucky, we can get an oceanfront room."

"Make that *rooms*," Agent Crockett said. "As in *your* room and *my* room."

"I thought we could share one and save the government money."

"Unlikely," she said. "However, I don't think having dinner together is out of the question."

That was good news. I'd only been kidding about sharing a room, just testing the waters to see how she reacted. I'd been starting to worry that OSI Agent Crockett was a completely cold fish. I cast a sideways look at her. She was attractive, no doubt about it. More striking than pretty. She was younger than I was, which may have been a factor in her earlier stand-offishness. As we crossed the parking lot, I caught her eyes sliding my way and had the uncanny sense that she was checking *me* out. I sucked in my stomach and stood up straighter.

Something there. I wasn't going to press my luck. The truth was that I had been off women since ending my disastrous affair with the co-ed. That had been what, a year ago? No, *two*. I was turning into the monk of Mob town.

We checked in. Agent Crockett put both rooms on her government credit card. Together, a one-night visit was costing United States taxpayers one hundred and eighty dollars plus change for accommodations that overlooked the interstate and the Dumpsters out back. At least the clerk gave me a free toothbrush and tiny tube of toothpaste when I asked.

"Now I know where the term highway robbery originated," I said. I noticed Agent Crockett was carrying an overnight bag. Even if she hadn't planned on staying here in North Bay, she was obviously a person who liked to be prepared. "You left that Nazi thing out in the car?"

"Yes."

"Good thinking. If it starts ticking or whirring, I don't think you want it in your room."

"You have an active imagination, Professor McCoy," Agent Crockett said.

"Mind if I borrow that?" I asked, pointing at the folder that held the surveillance photo the chief had given us.

"Go right ahead," she said. "See you back here in the lobby

at seven."

We got off at separate floors. The room had the usual two beds and TV bolted to the dresser top. I put the surveillance photo from the store robbery on the work table. I searched the grainy features once more, feeling a flicker of recognition I couldn't put my finger on.

I grabbed the remote and snapped on the TV just to have some background noise. Unlike Agent Crockett, I didn't have a change of clothes, but I took a shower anyway. The visit to the North Bay police station and to the late Hans Schmidt's house had left me feeling grubby. I shrugged back into my rumpled clothes and wondered what I had gotten myself into.

So far, Special Agent Kate Crockett struck me as a maverick. In my experience, the Special Investigations branch of the Department of Justice was a rather slow and lumbering organization caught up in dotting its legal i's and crossing its historical t's, a fact that had in the past proved frustrating to those seeking some measure of revenge for the Holocaust. You could prod and cajole, but the historians and lawyers and investigators of that agency did not move with any sense of urgency. Kate Crockett seemed driven in comparison.

I spent some time thinking over what we had found so far. The circumstances surrounding Hans Schmidt's death were a puzzle. Why had the robber been wearing a German uniform? What did the shrine in the old man's basement mean? My thoughts kept coming back to Kate. I was looking forward to dinner.

I made sure I was early getting to the lobby and got directions to a seafood restaurant from the desk clerk. Agent Crockett stepped out of the elevator at precisely seven o'clock.

"Let's go," she said. "I'm hungry enough to gnaw my way through the front door."

"Whoa. In that case, we'd better feed you. Crab cakes OK?"

"As long as you can get a drink with them."

8

The restaurant appeared to have started some years ago in a double-wide trailer. Now there was a tacked-on dining room built of mismatched windows and vinyl siding that overlooked a muddy tidal river out back. One good sign: the gravel parking lot was crowded.

"Well, it's got plenty of atmosphere," Agent Crockett said.

"In North Bay, I think the locals call this elegance."

Inside, the walls were decorated with the usual plastic crabs and fishnets found in cheap seafood restaurants. A few lobster pots and plastic lobsters were mixed in.

"I never knew there were lobsters in Chesapeake Bay," Agent Crockett remarked.

"There aren't any shrimp either, but I bet that's on the menu."

We lucked out and got a booth by a window. I had to admit the evening light gave the view of the river beyond a certain quaint charm if you tried not to be distracted by the sight of the restaurant's propane tanks out back.

The same might be said of Agent Crockett. She had

produced a fresh outfit from that overnight bag of hers and added a touch of makeup. The truth was that Agent Crockett was very pleasant to look at if you could get beyond her professional demeanor.

I offered her a package of cellophane-wrapped crackers from the plastic bowl on the table.

"Hors d'oevres," she said. "And individually wrapped. There's even one of those candles in a red jar on the table."

We both said, simultaneously, "Atmosphere," and laughed.

"You know, I do have a name," she said as she unwrapped her crackers. "It's Kate. I haven't heard you use it yet."

"I thought your name was 'Agent.' "

"Well, it's Kate over dinner." She smiled to show she was joking, but I wasn't so sure. So far, OSI Agent Kate Crockett had demonstrated that she took herself very seriously.

The waitress came, but Kate didn't bother to open the menu. "I'll have a crab cake dinner and a carafe of red wine," she said.

"I'll have the same but without the carafe."

The waitress took our menus, calling me "hon" as she did so, then hurried off. Kate slumped against the padded back of the bench seat. "So what's it like knowing your father was in a concentration camp? Tell me about that."

"There's a topic for light conversation over dinner if I ever heard one."

"I'm curious. And dinner isn't here yet."

"You've read my book."

"I know, but now I get to talk about it with the author."

"Where to begin? It was cold, most of the time he had no food. He was in his early thirties. His family was sent away . . ."

"Did they all die?"

"Yes. And they didn't just *die*. That's a terrible euphemism for what happened. They were murdered by the Nazis."

"Are you bitter about what happened to your father and your relatives? Are you bitter about the holocaust?"

"Bitter? You're *bitter* about missing your connecting flight. Even though all that happened sixty years ago, I don't think bitter begins to describe how I feel about what took place. The Nazis set out to exterminate an entire group of people. This is genocide that we're talking about. I think the best word to describe how I feel is hatred. I'm still full of hate. Twenty years ago I wanted to wipe out all the Germans."

"And now?"

I shrugged. "I wouldn't wipe out the ones who passed some sort of qualifying test in basic humanity."

"So you're half Jewish, half Irish."

"Even split. My father was a German Jew and my mother was an American nurse whose parents were Irish immigrants. They were both older when they had me. My mother was past forty. Dad was in his fifties. That's not so unusual now, but it was rare in the nineteen sixties. I was an only child. Of course, you know all that from the book. You also know I ended up being given my mother's last name, which was also unusual back then. No one ever explained it, but I think my father was ashamed by then of being a Jew. He was ashamed of what happened."

"I know this is probably on the book cover somewhere, but where did you go to school?"

"Loyola College in Baltimore."

"That's a Catholic school."

"Well, I suppose you could say I'm more Catholic than Jewish. My mother went to Mass every Sunday and took me with her. I don't ever recall my father going to synagogue. He was never very interested in religion. After the war, especially, he was so full of anger."

"Toward the Germans?"

"He was angry at the entire human race. He was angry at God too."

———

THE WINE CAME and I poured us both a glass.

"You've had some troubles of your own," Kate remarked.

"That's a nice way of saying you know I got fired from my teaching job."

"Fooling around with the undergraduates tends to be frowned upon these days."

"I know it sounds bad, but the situation was more complicated than that."

"Everything usually is," Kate said, a note of sarcasm slipping into her voice.

"Don't be judgmental. You don't know the details. I can give them to you sometime when we have absolutely nothing else to talk about. What about you? Don't you have any dark secrets? You must have grown up somewhere."

"I grew up in Connecticut," Kate said. "I went to school at the University of Virginia. I wanted to get away from home."

"Needed to escape from your parents?"

"My parents died when I was eight years old."

"I'm sorry to hear that," I said after a long, awkward pause. Kate took a gulp of wine, then another, before I managed to say, "That's tough for a kid to go through."

"It was. Sometimes at night I wake up and I still cry about it." She studied her wine glass, took another drink, then topped it off from the carafe. "You know, I don't think I've ever admitted that to anyone."

"I know something about loss," I said. "You can really only share that kind of emptiness with someone who has experienced it."

Kate nodded, went on. "My aunt and uncle raised me. It was really my Uncle Silas I needed to get away from, or at least to get out from under his shadow."

I raised my eyebrows as I made a sudden realization. "Your Uncle Silas? That wouldn't be Silas *Crockett*, would it? The former secretary of state?"

"Yes. That's my Uncle Silas."

I was a bit stunned. Back in the 1970s, Silas Crockett had been one of the most outspoken men in government. He was a regular on national TV. Time had moved on, a new generation had come to power in Washington, but for several years he had been one of the nation's most iconoclastic leaders. In all honestly, I hadn't even known he was still alive. "He's quite a man."

"Yes, he is. There was a time in my college years when I needed my own space, but I love him dearly and turn to him all the time for advice." Kate laughed. "My God, I certainly am telling you all sorts of personal information I don't normally share with anyone. I don't know why. It's strange, but I feel like I know you from reading your books."

"Then don't stop now. What was it like growing up as Silas Crockett's niece?"

"Never a dull moment. We had all the big names at our house and Uncle Silas always made a point of introducing me, even as a little girl. Of course, I'm too young to have met Kennedy. I always liked Jimmy Carter. We went looking for seashells on our beach when I was a kid."

"That must have been quite a childhood, meeting all those famous people."

"Yes, but Uncle Silas was always so at ease with everyone, like he was having one of the neighbors over for a drink. At the time, it never really sinks in that the person in the living room was famous from TV or the front page of the newspaper."

KATE REACHED FOR THE CARAFE, refilled her glass. Our dinners came and we stayed busy eating for a while. The crab cakes were filled with enough chunks of luscious backfin meat to satisfy any Marylander. "We must be hungry," Kate said between mouthfuls of crab cake. She sipped her wine.

"How did you end up working for OSI?" I asked once we had made some headway into our plates. "It seems like a strange choice for Silas Crockett's niece. I would think you would pursue a career in the state department or maybe even politics."

"It was all his doing that I got involved with OSI. At least indirectly. To make a long story short, he was at Nuremberg as a young lawyer during the Nazi trials. He told me such stories about it. He was one of the first to find Goering's body after the *Reichsmarshal* committed suicide, you know. He was very proud of helping to bring the Nazis to justice. I guess that fascination with the Nazis rubbed off on me, along with a healthy sense of outrage against injustice."

"That does sound like your uncle's influence."

"Yes, he's famous for being outraged about one thing or another, isn't he? He stands up for ideals."

"I would think that OSI is a dead-end job these days."

"It's true that nobody is banging down the door to work for OSI, at least not for the Nazi-hunting branch. In a few years there won't be any Nazi war criminals left. None that are under ninety, anyway."

"So why do it?"

Kate leaned toward me. The glassiness in her eyes told me that she'd had too much wine. "Before they're all gone I'd like to bring one of the really big names to justice. Maybe even Alois Brunner."

"So would I. But I'm sure they're all dead by now, Brunner

and all the rest," I said. "Most of the upper echelon SS leaders were in their thirties or forties when the war ended. Time itself would have caught up with them by now."

"Who knows?" Kate said. "If we hurry we might catch one of them yet."

9

In the parking lot Kate said, "I shouldn't be driving."

"Give me the keys. In my case, what's a little DWI on top of everything else?"

"God, you must think I'm a drunk," Kate said. Her breath was fragrant with wine. "I don't usually drink this much. I guess I got carried away."

"Don't worry about it," I said. The stars sparkled in the winter sky with a reassuring clarity and I told myself that I was sober enough to drive. "You have a lot on your mind. Everybody needs to let loose now and then."

We got in the car. The smell of the restaurant had settled into our clothes, stale grease and old cigarettes. I rolled down the window and let the crisp night air wash over us. My head felt clear now as I started the engine. The car was nicer than I expected for government issue, a black Chevrolet Malibu with all the bells and whistles. It was also fast, and when I hit the gas at a green light the big car leapt away from the intersection with a satisfying squeal of rubber on pavement.

"Take it easy," Kate said. "This baby has two hundred horsepower under the hood. And OSI would fire my ass if you wrecked my car."

"You could tell them you got carried away with the romance of it all. This town kind of reminds me of Paris after the war."

Kate laughed. "Like you were there."

"Sometimes I think I was because of all the history I've studied. You know that Hemingway always claimed to have captured Paris from the Germans?"

"Hemingway only got into the war because his wife nagged him into it."

I remembered something about Hemingway wanting to stay home and fish, which didn't seem like such a bad idea to me. "It's a strange thing, isn't it, to spend so much of your life dwelling on the past?"

"You mean pursuing Nazi war criminals?"

"Yeah. I mean, the war was sixty years ago. When do we let go?"

"Try asking Southerners when they're going to let go of the Civil War."

I laughed. "Like that's ever going to happen."

"The same with World War II. The Nazis gassed, starved or shot eleven million people and then systematically cremated them in ovens. That's a little hard for the world to put behind it."

"People forget," I said. "If history shows us anything it's that people always forget over time. Then we're doomed to do it all over again. We just repeat the same bloody mess."

Dinner left me feeling more upbeat than I'd been in a long time. We were on the trail of some kind of Nazi business and I've always enjoyed a good hunt. It also helped that I'd had about one glass of wine too many.

Then there was Kate. Just a few hours earlier I had been ready to write her off as just another career-minded cold fish. But now I wasn't so sure. One adjective that described her would be *edgy*. Something you couldn't put your finger on but that made you so excited you just wanted more. Books that kept you up nights were edgy. Good rock music was edgy. Kate was edgy.

She would be easy to fall for, I thought, if she ever let you. Kate was tough, and if her upbringing was a sign of anything, it was that she was a woman of the world. The niece of Silas Crockett wouldn't be anything less. I cast a secret glance at her profile in the passenger seat and weighed my chances. I would be fooling myself if I thought we were going to have more than a working partnership. She was out of my league, smart and rich and good-looking, not some co-ed or recent divorcee to be tricked into bed with the whiff of bookish notoriety. Nonetheless, I was looking forward to spending time with Kate. She was someone I wouldn't mind getting to know better.

"Let's drive by Hans's house," I said. "I want to check on something."

"I'm pretty sure he's still dead," Kate said. "Just don't get pulled over on the way, OK?"

It was a pleasure steering the powerful car through town, but I took it easy on the gas pedal. Kate wasn't the only one who'd drank her share of wine. The last thing I wanted was to get picked up by a North Bay cop. I felt sorry for Jason Moody back at the police station but that didn't mean I wanted to share a cell with him.

Most of the houses on Hans Schmidt's street were dark except for the blue flicker of TV sets. The streetlights cast a yellow glow over the wintry brown lawns. This was a working man's neighborhood where everyone went to bed early. Not even a porch light was on at the dead man's house and the windows were black as the eye sockets of a skull. Our headlights flashed over a photocopied poster on a utility pole. I caught the grainy image of a cat beneath the word MISSING. I eased the car into the driveway.

"Now what?" Kate asked, a bit impatiently.

"I don't suppose you have a flashlight?"

"There's one in the trunk. What the hell are we doing here?"

"Let's go see what else Hans had buried in his backyard."

Looking around at the darkness, I was thinking that it would be helpful if we also had a gun. How did we know the robbery suspect had not chosen this night to return? Maybe he'd had unfinished business with the old man. In all their years of chasing Nazis, I knew that seldom had anyone from OSI felt himself or herself in physical danger from one of the alleged war criminals being investigated. Their elderly quarry posed little threat. This was one of the chief reasons that OSI personnel did not carry weapons. When there was potential for a confrontation, OSI called upon the local police or FBI field office for an escort. Most everything the OSI lawyers, investigators and historians did was at arm's length anyhow, whether it was conducting legal action or sifting through old documents.

Skinheads threatened OSI from time to time and sometimes the family members of the old men got angry, but for the most part the chase was a matter that culminated in the filing of paperwork and perhaps an anticlimactic courtroom procedure. It did not end in drawn weapons and doors being battered down, or with shovels and flashlights in dark back yards. Yet here we were.

We got out, our breath making frosty clouds in the dim glow of the streetlight. I walked around to the trunk and found one of those heavy mag lights favored by night watchmen because the flashlight can double as a club. We opted to navigate the dark yard by starlight, however, rather than attract the attention of the neighbors. The weight of the heavy flashlight clutched in my right hand was reassuring.

I eased open the shed door and snapped on the light just long enough to locate a shovel. In the backyard, I found the circle of scorched earth that had caught my attention the day before. I handed the mag light to Kate and started digging.

"Good a place as any," I said, forcing the blade of the shovel down through the top two inches of soil. Once I got started, the digging was easy. With a *thunk*, the shovel struck something that was not dirt. I widened the hole, then asked Kate to come closer with the flashlight. The beam revealed something wrapped in burlap. I got the blade under the bundle, lifted, and was greeted by a smell of decay that fouled the winter air.

"What the hell is it?" Kate asked.

"Let's find out." I put the bundle on the ground, and with Kate focusing the flashlight beam, used the point of the shovel to peel back the burlap. We saw fur, bone, two gaping holes in the rotting skull where eyes should have been, white teeth drawn back in a feline snarl. Kate gave a stifled cry and stepped away.

"One of Hans' more recent victims."

"He must have been a sick old bastard," Kate said.

I reburied the cat, taking my time to do it right, finally stepping on the dirt to press it down firmly. "You know how Dante had the idea that hell holds what we fear most? I hope Hans is down there right now with a bunch of alley cats the size of tigers."

"Let's go," Kate said. Her voice caught, and I realized she was shivering in the night air.

10

We drove back to the hotel in silence, both of us lost in our own thoughts. A Nazi shrine. Dead cats. Long-ago crimes. Not to mention that I was still shaken by the image of the upturned face of the robber on the surveillance video from the old man's store.

I got the bronze disk out of Kate's trunk and lugged it through the lobby to the hotel elevator without anyone so much as giving me a second look. The girl at the desk had long lashes, a fresh young face with a flush of red on her cheeks that must have brought her plenty of attention from the local boys. She didn't even glance up as I came by carrying the disk, which was surprisingly heavy.

Up in Kate's room, I took the disk out of the bag and put it on the table. The bronze surface felt smooth to the touch, almost soft, like a worn penny. Kate repositioned a floor lamp to give us more light. There was a kind of burnished beauty to the metal, giving it an ageless quality. This could be an artifact from some lost civilization, left behind in the ruins of Pompeii or abandoned in the fall of Rome. But this was a relic of the Third Reich. The first thing one noticed was the swastika and eagle, the symbol of Nazi Germany that standard bearers had carried in the huge rallies at Nuremberg in the 1930s. The symbols were framed inside a perfect three-sided triangle.

The disk might have some utilitarian purpose but it had also been made to be decorative, like an old-fashioned presentation sword. The Nazis had a penchant for giving the simplest objects a kind of martial beauty. Those fancy Nazi daggers still had razor sharp blades. What had this disk been meant to do?

"Maybe it's a bomb," Kate said, taking a step back. "Old Hans kept it under his basement. It's like he wanted it far away."

"Nobody would make a bomb this fancy." I tapped the disk with a cheap plastic pen from the bedside drawer. One thing for sure, the disk was not hollow.

"I'll have somebody take a look at it when I get back to D.C. OSI doesn't have a lab, but the FBI does. The only problem is that we might never see it again once they get their hands on it. This could be our one and only chance to get a good look at this thing." She rummaged around in her purse and brought out a Swiss Army knife, one of the hefty ones with about a million gadgets. "Here. Try to open it up."

I took the knife and snagged out the can opener tool. "This might work. What we've got here looks kind of like a giant can of tuna fish."

"I'd start with a screwdriver."

But there were no visible screws. My tuna fish can analogy wasn't far off. However, there wasn't so much as a seam to slide the tip of the screwdriver into. Nor were there any edges where I could find a purchase for the can opener tool. The bronze skin of the disk was of continuous construction, as if it had been cast in one piece. All I ended up doing was putting a few scratches on the metal. They gleamed like fire against the darker, tarnished surface. The disk was not meant to be opened easily, if at all. The only clues to its purpose were two small tabs set at opposite sides of the disk. Seen from the side, these tabs were at slightly different heights, reminding me of the tabs on the brake light bulbs for my old Volvo. When inserted into the light socket and turned, the tabs held the bulb securely in place.

"This thing is not going to open," I announced and handed back the Swiss Army knife.

"Now what?"

"Take some pictures of it in case you're right about the FBI guys not giving it back."

"Good idea." Kate dug into her purse again, produced a digital camera, and began taking photographs after putting a dollar bill on the table to give the object scale. When she was done, I picked up the disk and put it on the dresser next to the television so we could spread our notes on the table. Then I clicked on the TV to catch the 11 o'clock news. A news junkie needs his fix.

Kate was spreading a map on the table.

"Where do you think the robber would have gone next?" she asked. "From the convenience store, he probably headed out to this highway, Route 40. Where did he go from there?"

"Toward the interstate," I said, tracing my finger along the map.

"Well, that narrows it down," Kate said facetiously. "A few hours north on I-95 means Philadelphia, New York, Boston. If he went south, there's Baltimore, D.C., Richmond."

"In other words, he could be anywhere."

I flopped down in a chair and tried to click through the TV channels, but all I got was snow. With a sigh, I got up and walked over to the TV. I shoved the disk out of the way and leaned around behind the set to check the connections. It had been my experience that sometimes the cleaning people accidentally loosened a cable. Everything looked to be plugged in and suddenly I could hear the comforting drone of a CNN anchor going on about bombings in Israel.

"What did you just do?" Kate asked.

"I'm just checking the TV."

"No, I mean this." She came over and pushed the disk back toward the TV. The image disappeared into a flurry of snow again. She slid the disk away and there was CNN again.

"Radioactive?" I suggested.

"Electronic?"

"Either way, if I were you I wouldn't sleep with that damn thing in the room," I said. "Just in case. Give me your keys and I'll put it back in your trunk."

"Good idea." We put the disk back in the bag and she handed me the keys. "Just hang onto these. I've got another set. See you in the morning, OK?"

"Shouldn't we spend the night discussing the case or at least getting to know each other better?"

"Good night, Professor McCoy."

Agent Crockett closed the door in my face, but gently.

IN MY DREAM, the camp was draped in winter fog and paved with damp bricks. A tall barbed wire fence surrounded the muddy prison yard or *appelplatz* and there were guards in long blue-gray coats holding dogs on leashes. *Obersturmbannfuhrer* Konrad Radl watched from a tower, his chiseled Aryan features hard as iron, a half-smile playing on his lips. My father came toward me wearing a worn wool suit, looking warm, well-fed, not like the other prisoners. "You are well, my son?" He spoke German in a more educated manner than the camp guards. He held his hands out toward me, and I noticed that they were clean. "Perhaps I can help you."

The guard dogs began barking. Someone shouted in German: *"Raus! Raus!"*

That's when I woke up. The dream was so vivid that I was

disoriented when I awoke in a bed in the hotel room, having expected to find myself at Dachau. I was sweaty and my legs were tangled in the sheets. The digital clock beside the bed leered at me like an angry red eye. Four a.m.

The dream. It was not the first time I had dreamed of Dachau, or of my father. The dream always jolted me awake, heart pounding. Were the guards coming for me? It was irrational, I knew, but you didn't spend most of your life studying the Nazis without giving yourself a few nightmares.

It was true I knew a great deal about the Nazis. But how much did I really know about my father? The dream had spooked me, unsettled me. Deep down, I had always had questions about my father's time at the camp. Some things I had never got around to asking, and he never got around to telling. Was the dream trying to show me something that deep down I already knew? Even all these years later, my father remained something of a mystery to me. Strange, isn't it, how you could live with someone for years and still feel like you didn't really know him? My father, sitting at the kitchen table, working the grime out from under his fingernails — his mind off somewhere a thousand miles away and decades ago. He was in a place known only to him, a place he would allow no one else to glimpse. I wished I had known him as a young man. I liked to think we might have been friends.

Maybe because it was late, I recalled how once when I was a boy my father had stayed up several nights designing a garage to go at the end of the driveway, next to our bungalow. He was not a carpenter, so he had hired the work done. But he designed it. Working at the kitchen table, night after night under the old-fashioned florescent ring, he drew the plans with graph paper and a ruler. I could still hear the scratch of his pencil, the faint rubber odor of the eraser.

"I'm sure the contractor has some good plans to choose from," said my mother, busy at the sink. "It's only a garage."

"It's a *building*," he replied, as if that explained everything.

Long after midnight I heard his heavy step on the stairs, finally coming to bed. At the time I'd felt sorry for him, working so hard. Night after night he worked on the plans, graduating from the graph paper to large sheets on which he carefully drew his plans with a ruler and pencil and cheap plastic angle. Now I understood that the simple act of creation had been a pleasure for him, a reminder of who he had been so many years before. After his death, I'd found his first sketches of the garage between the pages of one of the Dachau journals, tucked away like money or love letters.

The air in the hotel room was overheated, so hot and dry it rasped in my throat. I was sweating under the blanket. The stuffy room felt like a prison cell. Leaving the lights off, I got up and swept back the drapes covering the window. The parking lot was dappled in pools of light and dark and beyond it were black woods and fields. A shadowy figure passed among the cars, lingered by my Volvo, and then was gone.

I tried to blink the bleariness out of my eyes, wondering if I was seeing things or if this was some remnant of my dream. My heart raced. I pressed my face to the window to get a better view of the parking lot but nothing stirred. Then I realized I was standing there in my boxer shorts and nothing else, peering out.

The room, so hot a moment ago, felt cold. Shivering, I dragged the covers off the bed and wrapped them around me, then sat down at the table. The photo made from the surveillance video was still there, the harsh face glaring up at me. With a start, I realized *this* was why I'd had a nightmare about the camps. My mind had been trying to tell me something I didn't want to believe. Grainy though it was, I knew now there was no mistaking that face. I had studied it a hundred times, stared at it again and again while doing research or proofreading the galleys of my books. An icy pit formed in my belly.

I pulled the chair around to face the window. A false dawn was already coloring the sky as I waited for morning. Keeping watch.

11

"So this is where the old man worked?" Kate wondered out loud. "It's not much of a going concern."

We were standing in front of Victory Industrial, a plant that had once created vast amounts of munitions for the United States military. Now the cavernous plant was boarded up, with rotting plywood across the windows and Virginia creeper growing in thick blankets up the old brick walls. Even the name was faded, spelled out in ten-foot high white letters on the side of the building, the "V" a bit larger than the others. As we watched, a stray cat crept through a space between the boards covering a doorway and slunk away through the dead weeds. Maybe it was my imagination, but an odor of dry rot and mold mingled with an acrid gunpowder smell drifted out after the cat. There were several other large, vacant buildings lining the street, which appeared to be the brownfields area of North Bay.

"Kate, did you see anything weird late last night?" I asked, trying to sound casual. "I mean, you didn't go back out to the parking lot for anything, did you?"

"No, I crashed as soon as you left. Why?"

"Nothing important."

Agent Crockett studied my face. "What's the matter? You look awfully pale this morning. What, did you see a ghost last night?"

She wasn't far wrong about me seeing a ghost. The bad dream had left me spooked, but once the sun came up I still hadn't changed my mind about the face in the surveillance photo. By the light of day it seemed insane just thinking it, much less saying it out loud yet. "You're not going to believe this, but the man I saw on the tape bore a remarkable resemblance to SS *Obersturmbannfuhrer* Konrad Radl."

Kate's silence seemed to prove what I'd been worried about all along, which was that she would think I was crazy. Finally, she spoke. "He was the commandant at Dachau, wasn't he? Where your father was a prisoner." She really *had* read my books. "Radl's been dead a long time. Sometimes we see what we want to see."

"Why would I *want* to see Radl?" I asked.

"We've had a lot of cases at OSI over the years where a holocaust survivor will report seeing a camp guard on the street. Sometimes the man — or woman — is the right age. Every now and then it's someone who is far too young, but he resembles someone's tormentor. Even when the age is right, ninety-nine percent of the time it turns out to be nothing."

"You're telling me it's psychological," I said. "The need for closure." It saddened me to think of someone living out the long decades after the war always searching the crowd for an SS guard.

"OK, I agree that it looks like him," Kate said. "But we both know Radl hasn't been seen since 1945. Most likely he was killed fighting during the final days of the war or maybe the Russians got him. You say as much in your book. Even if he had lived, he would be an old, old man."

"No, he would be dead by now, even if he had escaped Germany," I said. "Radl was born in 1898. He was forty-seven when the war ended. He'd have to be more than one hundred years old, and the last time I checked centenarians generally don't shuffle off to the corner convenience store wearing jackboots."

"So it's not Radl."

"Of course it's not," I said, knowing I sounded defensive even to my own ears. "It's someone who looks like him."

"Let's chew on that one, Professor. I'm sure there's some logical explanation," Kate said, turning her attention back to the huge vacant building. "At one time this must have been quite an operation."

"During World War Two and right through the nineteen fifties, this place was going in three shifts around the clock," I said. "A good portion of the ordnance dropped on Germany and Korea was made right here."

"How did you get to be such an expert?"

I waved a brochure at her. "I picked this up in the hotel lobby. It's a brief history of the town of North Bay, including its hey-day as a World War II munitions center. Oh, and did you know George Washington slept here, too?"

"That man got around," she said, then nodded at the vacant plant. "Any ideas where we can find someone who used to work here?"

We hadn't expected to find the plant boarded up but had been hoping someone working there still remembered Hans Schmidt, even though he had been retired for nearly fifteen years. First thing that morning we banged on doors up and down his street but nobody seemed to associate much with the old man aside from the occasional neighborly wave. A couple of people mentioned disappearing cats. We were hoping someone at Victory Industrial might know more.

I nodded toward the building next door, which, judging by

the cars in the lot, was occupied. A large sign out front proclaimed it as the offices of *The North Bay Republican.*

"Somebody at the local paper probably knows something about Victory Industrial," I said.

"Just as long as they don't figure out why we're asking. The last thing we need is for the local press to go nuts with a story about how the Department of Justice is investigating Hans Schmidt as a Nazi."

WE GOT past the receptionist in the lobby and were admitted to the newsroom, which more closely resembled a frat house for journalists rather than an actual place of business—it was one of the reasons I'd always had a soft spot for newspapers. Reporters and editors always had been helpful to me in doing my research. Sadly enough, the Internet was quickly sending newspapers the way of typewriters, drive-in movies and phone books. Clutter stretched wall to wall, with piles of yellowed newspapers functioning as privacy screens between the reporter's desks. No one seemed in any hurry to clear away the empty pizza boxes, soda bottles and coffee cups. A television on a high shelf was tuned to *Fox News*, the sound muted.

The reporters were mostly just out of college and new to the area — none of them had a clue that the empty building next door used to be one of the nation's key munitions producers. The kids tried to be helpful but they didn't know much.

Kate and I were about to leave when one young Horace Greeley suggested we go talk to Carl in the pressroom. "He might know something about it," the young reporter said. "He's been here since, like, they still used typewriters."

"What's a typewriter?" I asked.

"Well, you know, before computers," the reporter said helpfully. "Like they typed stories on them and stuff."

Somehow, I didn't think this kid was *New York Times* material, but for all I knew he was the star reporter at *The North Bay Republican*. We thanked the young man for his help and went in search of Carl through a rabbit warren of hallways that led to the printing presses. We could hear them churning somewhere deep within the building.

Carl turned out to be an amiable old man with thick glasses and a blue mechanic's uniform. He sat in a neat office next to the churning press and we had a hard time making ourselves understood until Carl got up and closed the door. The effect was like rolling up the windows of a car hurtling down the interstate.

"Soundproof," he explained. "Now, what can I do for you?"

"We're trying to get some information about the Victory Industrial plant next door," Kate said.

"Well, you came to the right person. I worked there for twenty years, right up until it closed back in nineteen eighty-five." He smiled broadly. "Then I just walked next door and asked for a job here."

"Did you know a man there named Hans Schmidt?" Kate asked.

"Hans? Sure I did." The smile left his face. "This must be about the robbery."

"It is." Kate explained who we were. "We're trying to learn something more about Hans and what he did at Victory. I assume he worked on the production line."

"Hans? Well, he started on the line, after the war. But they didn't keep him there. He retired as the comptroller of the whole company. Worked his way up."

Kate looked as surprised as I felt. "Comptroller?"

"Sure, he was a whiz with numbers. Could add and subtract in his head like nobody's business."

"Do you know what he did in the war?" I asked. Carl was old enough that he didn't need to ask which one.

"Hans said he was a mechanic with the Krauts. He said he didn't want to be in the army but he didn't have much choice." Carl gave a snort that could be interpreted as a laugh. "Sounds like a lot of American guys I know. Anyhow, that was all ancient history as far as anyone at the plant was concerned. Most guys who were in the war just wanted to put it behind them at that point, at least in those days. Forgive and forget."

"What about you?" I asked. "Are you a vet?"

"Korea." He grinned. "Spent the winter of fifty-two freezing my keester off."

"What kind of man was Hans Schmidt?" Kate asked. "Was he quiet or outgoing?"

Carl shrugged. "Hans was all right. He ran around with a few women back in his younger days but he never did get married. Hans liked to tell a joke or two, usually a dirty one," he said, giving Kate an apologetic look. He was from a more decorous generation when it came to speaking in front of women. "He used to come out Friday nights and have a couple beers after work. Not a big drinker. Aside from his accent, you wouldn't know he was German. Besides, knowing numbers the way he did there was never any language barrier or anything like that. Old Hans. Damn shame he had to die like that."

"Would you know any of his friends?"

Carl shook his head. "Most of them would be gone, anyhow. Time caught up with them."

CHIEF WAGNER WAS WAITING for us out in the parking lot with one of his officers.

"You're determined, I'll give you that," the chief said, leaning against an unmarked police cruiser, his heavy arms folded across his chest. It was a little unnerving that he had known to find us at the local newspaper. I doubted that much happened in North Bay that Chief Wagner didn't know about. I had to wonder if maybe the chief knew more about Hans Schmidt than he was letting on.

"I believe in doing a thorough investigation," Kate replied. "I'm not interested in sweeping anything under the rug." The wind seemed to catch her words and make them snap like a whip.

"Let's you and me get something straight," Wagner said, moving toward Kate. Almost unconsciously, I took a step forward as well and the North Bay cop did the same, both of us hanging back like seconds at a duel. "This is *my* town. Don't tell me how to do my job."

"The victim had his blood type tattooed under his arm, which was typical procedure for Nazi SS personnel," Kate said. "Did you know he was the comptroller at Victory Industrial and that he was good with money?"

"You're trying to make the crime match your crazy theories, not the other way around," Wagner insisted. "Look at the facts. Goddamn you people. Who do you think you are?"

"I'm in the business of justice, Chief," Kate said. "Same as you."

Wagner shook his head. "Oh, I understand how a federal investigator thinks the police in little ol' North Bay have their head up their ass, but I'm not talking about that."

"What do you mean?"

"You people," the chief repeated. "Jews."

The cop at Wagner's elbow spoke up. "C'mon, Chief," he said. "That's enough."

Kate couldn't have looked more stunned if Wagner had hit her over the head with a menorah. "Just for the record, Chief Wagner, I'm not Jewish."

"Doesn't matter what you are or aren't. Who do you think runs the Office of Special Investigations?"

"I have no idea, Chief Wagner. Why don't you tell me?"

The chief hesitated, as if realizing he had already gone too far. But I had heard him loud and clear. The word *Jews* had seemed to hang in the winter air, too heavy to be carried off by the wind.

Kate stared at him a moment as if deciding to say what was really on her mind, then shook her head. "This is like talking to the wall. Professor McCoy and I are getting out of here."

The chief turned to the cop beside him. "You got that copy of the surveillance video?"

The cop nodded, handed off a computer disk to the chief, who in turn gave it to Kate.

We started to get in the car. Standing there with the door open, Kate looked back toward Wagner. "Hey, Chief. *Shalom.* You know what that means? It's Yiddish for 'Up yours.' "

She got in and slammed the door.

"*Begorra*," I said, sliding into the passenger seat. Through the windshield I could see that Chief Wagner's face was turning a deep red, and I doubted it was from the cold. "You know what that means? It's Irish for 'Are you nuts?' And *Shalom* is Hebrew, by the way."

"Whatever," Kate said, then stomped on the gas.

12

A fter our encounter with the police chief, our investigation in North Bay was over. We checked out of our rooms at the motel and went our separate ways. Kate promised to stay in touch. I didn't have to wait long. She got me on the cell phone as soon as I was coming out of the Fort McHenry Tunnel on I-95.

"I'm almost back in D.C.," she said.

"You drive fast."

"Is there any other way? Listen, I'm going to drop the beacon off with my friends at the FBI. They'll be able to look at the thing in their lab. Then at OSI I'll have the whole immigration database here and I can figure out who this Hans Schmidt really is, or at least who he claimed to be when he came into the country."

"While you're at it, you might have somebody look into his finances," I said. "His old co-worker said he was good with money. I'll bet it wasn't an idle pastime."

"Okay, I've got my to-do list. What about yours?"

I laughed. "Right now, all I plan on doing is finding some

dinner and getting the bad smell from North Bay out of my nose."

"Well, don't take too long doing it," Kate said. "As far as I'm concerned you're still on the payroll. Make yourself useful."

"What do you want me to do?"

"You're the famous Nazi expert," Kate said. "Figure it out."

I went for a walk as soon as I got home, trying to decide what to do next. Kate's remark rankled; it was as if she was trying to make the lack of progress my fault. It was true that we had found a few clues in North Bay, but had left with more questions than answers. A bronze disk decorated with a swastika and eagle. A solitary old man who was good with figures. A secret basement shrine to the Third Reich. Video that showed a man who looked a lot like fugitive Nazi Konrad Radl looking decades younger. *What did it all mean?* I wondered if maybe Agent Crockett had taken me on to be a convenient scapegoat if the investigation went nowhere.

I turned up the collar of my leather jacket against the wind off the harbor. I always did my best thinking when I was in motion somehow and right now I had a lot to ponder.

So where did we go from here? Kate was right about one thing; I *was* the famous Nazi expert. I had written books and countless articles on the subject. But that didn't mean I had all the answers. At the moment, all we seemed to have about Hans Schmidt were questions.

On Pratt Street, crazy-eyed homeless men sheltered in the doorways of the office buildings and hotels. Thumping rock and roll spilled out from a tavern. A funky low-tide smell drifted in from the harbor, carried on a chill breeze that rubbed my cheeks like a stiff towel. Nightfall was quickly approaching. In the red-brick shadow of the Orioles' ballpark, a light rail train whisked by. The sidewalks felt gritty and muddy under-foot because there was street work being done and in places plywood had temporarily replaced the concrete. The hollow sound of wood beneath my feet was like a throwback to when this section of the city had been a grungy dockside neighborhood. Back in the days before the Civil War, I would have passed slave pens and public auctions where whole families were sold to work plantations in the Deep South. Misery ran deep on these city streets.

But that was then, this was now. Baltimore was home. I took comfort in the constant motion of the city around me, glad to be anonymous, no longer a target and outsider as I had been in North Bay. Chief Wagner's words kept ringing in my ears: *You people. Jews.* Those words had shown his true colors. Prejudice often bubbled just beneath the surface of people and situations. Men such as Chief Wagner hated Jews or blacks or Asians, but they usually kept their bigotry hidden. Heat them up, get them angry, and hatred exploded from their very pores.

Sometimes that hatred could be harnessed. Adolf Hitler, for one, had understood the unifying aspect of hatred. It gave the Germans a common enemy. The genius of it was that Germany's poverty, unemployment and political misery was not the fault of the Germans themselves, but of the Jews. Hitler had been a true believer. Hunkered in his bunker as Berlin was reduced to rubble by Russian artillery, he had dictated these words as part of his last testament: *Centuries will pass but from the ruins of our cities and cultural monuments our hatred will be renewed for those who are responsible, the people to whom we owe all this — the international Jewry and its supporters.* The final words of a madman and hate monger in denial, but also one who understood how to use hatred as a political tool.

Not for the first time, I wondered how my father must have felt watching his country, his co-workers, and finally even his friends and neighbors set their minds against him. *Jew.* Like it was a dirty word. I felt some of the old bitterness well up inside me, an urge to somehow settle the score. *Let it go,* my father used to say when he saw the anger rising off me like heat from a skillet. *You can't answer hatred with hatred, Bram.* And yet deep down I knew hatred and frustration had consumed him at the very end, rotting him from the inside out. The doctors called it cancer, but I knew better.

My father was simply trying to warn me against making the same mistakes. Such is the way of fathers and sons, although the sons rarely listen.

I wandered up Charles Street next, walking uphill away from the harbor until I felt myself calm down. The evening rush was mostly over, the sidewalks beginning to empty out. My belly rumbled and I realized I had not eaten since breakfast in North Bay. At the bottom of Charles Street I found a Chinese carryout place and picked up an order of lo mein, wonton soup and shrimp rolls, then headed home. I went in through the parking garage because I wanted to swing by my car to pick up some notes to read while I ate.

The garage at the complex takes up the first two floors. It was dark outside by now so the only illumination came from pale yellow lights that cast a wan, sickly glow on row upon row of cars. The garage smelled strongly of motor oil and damp concrete. The space felt cavernous, empty.

Then I saw them in the shadows. Two figures back along the wall. Not talking or getting into a car. Just waiting. At the sound of my footsteps they came out into the sickly yellow light.

Skinheads.

They had a feral wildness about them like stray dogs. The bigger one had a spider web tattoo crawling up his neck and there was something not right about his eyes. Too close together or maybe the pupils open too wide. Drugs? Whatever the reason, he looked crazed. I noticed the other one hung back. He looked hard and square, like a concrete block. The ridges of his skull gleamed in the pale light. Both wore the skinhead uniform of blue jeans and white T-shirts under their leather jackets. What I really noticed were their boots. They had on black work boots, steel-toed and thick-soled. Good for stomping.

"Can I help you?" I asked, still hoping this must all be a mistake. Giving them an out. I felt ridiculous carrying my warm paper bag filled with Chinese food. The sour odor of steamed cabbage wafted out. "If you're looking for the exit it's right over there, down the ramp."

"Abraham McCoy, the Jew lover," said the skinhead with the spider tattoo. It was a statement, not a question. He held up his right hand and extended his middle finger, almost poking it at me. "You're a fucking Jew lover."

The rational thing would have been to run, make some noise, and hope that someone called for help. If I had just turned and run for it, I could have gotten away.

But the sight of these two ugly subhumans made me angry. Rage slid into me like a white-hot knife but I held it inside me, burning and waiting.

"You know the thing about skinheads?" My voice was steady. "Deep down inside, they're all faggots."

That was throwing gasoline on the fire. They stepped closer.

"Jew lover," the big one snarled at me. "Traitor to the Aryan race. You must be punished."

"Tough guys," I said. "Two against one in a parking garage."

"How is that any different from writing a book of lies?" the big one asked. He smiled. So maybe he wasn't as dumb as I thought.

It wasn't the first time I had been threatened. Some neo-Nazi groups used my book *Leaders of the Third Reich* as a kind of Bible, an inspiration. They were appalled to discover *Journey of Hope* and the condemnation of the Third Reich on its pages. If they scratched a little deeper they could find an article or two I had written about old Nazi criminals being brought to justice.

That made me a traitor in their warped minds.

The two of them stood there, ready to attack. Their shaved heads and hollow eyes looked all the more menacing in the dim yellow light. Somewhere, a car door slammed and an engine started, but it was too far away to do any good.

"I got Chinese," I said, opening the paper sack. "Anybody want some?"

In one smooth motion I threw the hot wonton soup in Spider Boy's face. He howled in surprise. While his eyes were still shut I gave him a side kick that knocked him clean into a new silver Lexus. He got right back up, but he left a dent. The car alarm wailed.

The second skinhead swung a wild fist at me. I stopped the worst of it with a high block then twisted away as he tried to knee me in the groin. With his body off balance I got hold of an arm and flipped him neatly to the concrete floor. He landed on his back with a solid *whump*. Then I did something I had practiced hundreds of times, but never actually done to any of my sparring partners over the years. Still holding onto the arm, I kicked it. The arm snapped backwards at the elbow. He screamed. For good measure I went to one knee and drove my own elbow into his face. Blood spurted.

One down. Spider Boy reminded me he was still there by kicking me in the back of the head with one of those work boots. The air around me lit up with stars and bursts of color and my skull rang like a bell. Instinctively, I rolled and took the next kick in the shoulder. Another landed on my ribs and knocked the breath out of me. Then I was scurrying away between two parked cars.

The dirty little secret about tae kwan do is that it's not much good in a street fight beyond the first few seconds. If someone gets in close and starts punching or gets you on the ground and starts stomping, you're in trouble.

I retreated around a bumper, shook my head to clear the

static out of my vision. A little harder and that kick would have knocked me out cold. I shouldn't have turned my back on him.

He chased me but I managed to keep the car between us.

"Asshole, asshole, you're gonna die!" he shouted.

Spider Boy was quick. He tried to corner me against the wall, but I slipped out into the open where I took up a guardian stance. One foot forward, one back, hands ready for high block, low block.

"Think you're the only one who knows that shit?" he asked, taking up his own stance. With a roar, he charged at me.

He knew a little martial arts, a sort of half-assed form of Ninjitsu. I was a few pounds heavier and an inch or two taller, but youth was on his side. And he was strong enough and I was hurting enough for him to be dangerous. He had a side kick that with the heavy boots would cave in my ribs if he connected. I stopped the first kick with a low block. The next time I pinned his boot to my body, then paralyzed his leg with an elbow to his knee.

I let go. He stumbled, head down, still swinging. A fist caught me on the cheekbone and my head snapped back. He hit me again, going for my belly, and I twisted enough that the punch landed on the rim of my rib cage. If he backed me against one of the concrete pillars I would be in real trouble. He knew that too and he put his head down like a bull to charge. That's when I took a chance.

I rocked back on my left foot and snapped a front kick at his face. It connected so hard that his whole body flipped backwards. Then I pivoted and gave him another kick that threw him against the tall side of an SUV. He slid down, tried to regain his feet. I punched him in the head twice and he slumped to the floor.

He was defeated. Down and out. I should have left him alone and gotten the hell out of there.

Instead, I wanted to get even. I wanted to make him hurt. I

grabbed a leg and dragged him away from the SUV. Spider Boy was damn heavy and his head bounced on the concrete. He was still conscious but in no shape to protest. I took his right arm and put the elbow on his chest, so that the wrist and hand ramped down to the concrete floor. Taking his hand, I tucked in all the fingers except the middle one, the *fuck you* finger, which I extended its full length. I stood up and held my foot poised above, ready to stomp down. I almost stopped myself. *What was I doing?* Then I thought of Chief Wagner, and the Nazi face tilted toward the security camera like he was looking right at me. Spider Boy hissing at me: *Jew lover.*

I grunted as I stamped my foot down, feeling like I was trying to crush the world. The finger broke with a wet snap. Spider Boy cried out, pulling his injured hand toward him and cradling it on his chest like a mother holds a baby.

I looked around. The second skinhead was sitting up, holding his broken, useless arm in his lap and avoiding my eyes. His face looked blue, then yellow as the headlights of the Lexus flashed on and off and the alarm continued to wail.

I was still quivering with anger. My racing heart skipped a beat and I forced myself to breathe slowly. I had defended myself. I had gotten even with these skinhead assholes. And I had gotten lucky. It should have been me down on the concrete, broken and bleeding. So why didn't I feel something like triumph?

I found my sack of Chinese food on the floor. The wonton soup was splashed everywhere, leaving greasy stains on the floor. The lo mein container had burst open and some was spilled on the concrete. The glistening brown noodles with their strands of green looked like slimy intestines. The stink of sour cabbage rose up from the steaming mess. I wasn't so hungry anymore, so I turned and walked quickly away.

13
————

Back at my condo, I double-locked the door, poured two inches of Bushmills into a glass, and stretched out on the couch with the whiskey within reach. I didn't expect to fall asleep, but the next thing I knew the phone woke me up. The sky beyond the windows was still dark, although I was so stiff that I knew I had been sleeping for a while. My head ached from the alcohol and my ears still rang faintly from the skinhead's boots.

"McCoy, are you there?" Kate said to the answering machine. "Pick up the goddamn telephone."

Every muscle felt tight as beef jerky as I shifted on the couch and reached for the portable phone on the floor. "Ouch."

"What?"

"Nothing. What's up?"

"You need to get down here to Washington," Kate said. "I'm learning all sorts of interesting information about our friend Hans."

"Like what?"

"For starters, we know who he really is," she said.

"Was."

"Whatever. We also have all his SS records."

"How did you figure out his real name?" I wondered.

"You'll never believe this one, but the North Bay police found some documents while going through the house again."

"You're kidding. I thought those guys had had it with us."

"It wasn't the chief who called. It was one of his lieutenants who wanted to let me know that not everybody in North Bay has his head up his ass."

"What about the disk?" I croaked into the phone.

"I gave it to my friends at the FBI to look at." She paused. "Have you been drinking? You sound like shit."

"It's a long story."

"In that case, tell me when you get here." Kate hung up.

One eye was puffy from the fight in the parking garage, so the clock on my VCR/DVD machine was blurry. Four a.m.? Either Agent Crockett was getting an early start, or she had never stopped. Slowly, I managed to sit up. God, I hurt. I was too old to be fighting skinheads in dark parking garages.

I seemed to hear the wet snap again of Spider Boy's finger breaking. I felt ashamed for having gone too far. The skinheads thought they invented violence, but they were wrong. Jews had been slaughtering their enemies in desert battles two thousand years ago. Irish warriors mad with battle lust had killed with spears and swords in forgotten battles century after century. No, the skinheads were amateurs when it came to violence or cruelty. In my case, it might even be genetic.

Both of my attackers had been young, hardly more than teen-agers. What was wrong with me? What had I done? I might tell myself it was self-defense, but I could have run or called out for help. The truth was, I had wanted to fight them. Seeing them defeated, I felt pity. *That* seemed like a weakness. Would they have felt the same way? I was doubly disgusted, both by what I had done in anger and also by my own pity. *Never be a victim*, I had once vowed, angry that my father had been one — that an entire race had allowed itself to be victimized. And yet, if you were truly human, there was no escaping the sorrow you felt even for your enemies. I realized I was cursing my own humanity.

I stumbled into the bathroom to assess the damage. Looking in the mirror, I took stock: puffy eye, swollen lip, bruise along my right cheekbone. Headache from Spider Boy's boot aggravated by too much Bushmills on an empty stomach. I stripped down. In the mirror I could see my torso covered with purple bruises like rotting fruit. No wonder it hurt to take a deep breath. All things considered, it could have been much worse. Like, I could have been dead. I popped a couple of Advil and got into the shower, turned it up as hot as it would go. Heat and ibuprofen would help. It was a good two hours before sunrise, and from Kate's phone call I guessed that it was going to be a very long day.

———

BEFORE THE SUN came up I was on an AMTRAK train to Washington. My bruised face drew more than a few stares from the early morning travelers.

Out the window, the gray light did little to soften the scenery. The train swept past crumbling overpasses covered with graffiti. Brown winter vines crawled over piles of railroad ties. The tracks looked rusty and decayed. Whole villages of cardboard boxes and filthy blankets crowded the underpasses. America the beautiful, I thought. My head throbbed. I needed caffeine.

I subjected myself to a grinning dining car attendant long enough to buy a coffee and danish.

"Rough night, buddy?" he asked.

"I walked into a door," I said. "Two of them."

Lurching back to my seat, ignoring the looks I was getting, I swallowed two more ibuprofen tablets and drank the bitter railroad coffee. I had brought along some reading materials, including my own files on Konrad Radl. When writing *Leaders of the Third Reich* I had kept a file folder on each and every person profiled in the book, then began to fill it as I gathered information. It was a wide-ranging mixture of sources. There were clippings from German newspapers, snapshots, handwritten notes I had gathered during interviews with those who had known the Reich's leaders. In some cases, I had interviewed the men themselves.

After years of gathering notes and interviews, I began to write. I blended all this information into profiles of the leaders that went beyond the facts and tried to get at their hearts. What drove them to become what they were? My goal had been to write about each leader as if I were writing a newspaper profile. Some of the entries for obscure officers or government officials were pages long and revealed how crucial some of these men had been to Nazi policy or to the outcome of battles. They were the unsung henchmen of the Third Reich. I had started out wanting to hate these men. Instead, I became intrigued by them. They were complicated brutes. So many were kind husbands, good fathers and devoted sons. They loved their country, even if they could not love Hitler. These Nazi leaders had been incapable of demanding less than excellence from themselves and the men they commanded.

And yet they were monsters. In the case of the SS, excellence meant efficiently rounding up and killing Europe's Jews and other enemies of the Third Reich.

My book of profiles was an approach that had not been taken before. Readers had found some of the men fascinating.

Right around the 50th anniversary of the end of World War II, *Leaders of the Third Reich* became a bestseller.

I was lucky in my youthful success. I had come late to the game and was much younger than most authors who had made a career of writing about World War II — who might have fought in it. My first interviews had been done in the early 1980s. I had begun this project when I was very young and been fortunate in some of my interviewees, who had indulged an eager schoolboy while turning down professional journalists and authors.

It still chilled me that many of the elderly leaders of the Third Reich I talked to were so charming. For the most part they were a tall, distinguished-looking bunch, well-educated and urbane. Sitting in cafes with them or even in their living rooms having coffee it was hard to imagine them as the monsters they were.

This explained the sympathetic tone that came through my pages. It was why skinheads and neo-Nazis thrilled to *Leaders of the Third Reich*. Surely the author of such a book must see things their way . . . which was why they felt betrayed when they read *Journey of Hope*. I had not written the first book to glorify the Nazis, but I had made these monsters human, maybe even showed a glimmer of empathy toward them. It was both the best and worst quality of my book.

I opened my briefcase and took out the folder on Konrad Radl. It made a thick bundle on my knees. The loose pages had been turned so many times that the edges of the papers were rounded and softened, like the pages of a favorite, well-read book.

If there were any secrets or insight into Radl in these pages, I surely would have found them by now. Yet it wouldn't hurt to take one more look. Sipping from my coffee, I began to flip through my notes.

Born in 1897 near the small city of Freiburg to a wealthy

family. The Radls were not aristocrats — not the barons or
counts that Hitler courted — but they were an old and distinguished family with a history of military service. He was not a
Goering or a Heydrich or a Rommel but he was one of the
subalterns who carried out the bidding of the Third Reich. In
other words, he was part of the madness and the darkness.

Radl rose quickly through the Nazi ranks. He saw combat,
first in the invasion of Poland and then in the long, brutal fight
against the Russians. A sniper shot him one winter morning
through the legs at Stalingrad and he lay all day in the snow,
stranded in no-man's land, being used as bait. He had already
seen how the Russian snipers would kill one man after another
who went to help fallen comrades, especially officers.

Radl ordered that no man should try to rescue him, then
chewed his gloved hand to keep from moaning in agony. Radl
bled into the snow until the wound froze, then crawled back to
the German lines under cover of darkness. Frostbitten and
badly wounded, he had still managed to direct his men in a
nighttime attack that destroyed the sniper's nest and opened a
hole in the Russian lines. As a result, the Germans captured a
large portion of the city. Radl was awarded the Iron Cross for
valor.

Because of his wounds, his combat career was over. He was
flown to Germany to recover in a hospital in the Fatherland.
Meanwhile, the Germans lost not only Stalingrad but all of
Russia. Just as Napoleon had been crushed more than a
century before by the Russian winter, so too were the Germans
defeated.

Radl's wounds had ultimately spared his life. But the defeat
in Russia would cost Hitler the war. Too much German blood
had been spilled, too much materiel was lost. Raging like a
wounded bear, Mother Russia continued to claw at the
Germans' Eastern Front. Then came D-Day and the Allied
invasion of Europe. Even those who truly believed in the

warped dream of the Third Reich could see that defeat was inevitable.

But Radl was out of the fight. He had been sent to become commandant of the Dachau concentration camp.

Oddly enough, for a man so driven by duty, he spent little time there. Most of the details of running the camp were left to subordinates. Radl spent most of his post-combat service traveling. He was away from the camp for long periods and when there he was seldom seen.

During the Dachau trial in 1947, the United States military tried 40 SS men and Jewish *Kapos* for war crimes. Not all were big fish. But all had committed acts of special cruelty against Jews, political prisoners and Russian POWs at Dachau. The SS had been especially harsh toward the Russian prisoners, many of whom were not older than seventeen or eighteen. Hundreds were murdered each week. Most were lined up in the prison yard and shot, but many were hanged in a basement-like facility lined with iron hooks along the walls. The Russian soldiers were made to stand on chairs, a short length of rope was looped around their necks from the iron hooks, and then the chairs were kicked out, one by one. They strangled slowly, their legs kicking, while the SS executioners stood by and smoked cigarettes. The bodies were taken down and the next batch of boys was brought in to be hanged using the same ropes and hooks.

All the SS men tried were found guilty, most receiving prison sentences. The camp adjutant who ran Dachau in Radl's absence was hanged in 1947 at Spandau prison, his body buried in a numbered but otherwise unmarked grave in a cemetery still closed to the public today, lest it become a shrine to neo-Nazis.

Radl was found guilty *in absentia* and sentenced to be hanged. Oddly, given the detailed accounts of Dachau by witnesses and SS personnel during the trial, Radl's name was rarely mentioned. It became apparent that the day-to-day operation of the camp was largely left to others.

To my mind, it was one of the great mysteries about Radl. He was not a man to dodge his responsibilities. He was a man *consumed* by the necessity of duty. So what had kept him so busy in the final months of the war?

The last known whereabouts of Konrad Radl were in Berlin in April 1945. He was nowhere near Dachau. And then he simply disappeared. He was not one of the more famous, senior Nazi leaders and so his face was not readily recognized. Still, there were enough who knew him from Dachau as their jailor and tormentor. There had been occasional "sightings" of Radl in Europe and South America in the decades after the war but nothing concrete. The most likely fate of Konrad Radl was that he had been swept up in the turmoil of the final weeks of the war and been killed in the last desperate fighting or he really had escaped to die of old age in some South American backwater. That someone who looked so much like him had managed to turn up on a convenience store security video in the town of North Bay was almost unthinkable. And yet . . . I could tell myself it was some trick of the light, but I knew what I had seen, crazy as it seemed.

I turned to some pages marked with a Post-It note and began to read.

RADL WAS A MOST exact and particular man. His boots were always shined and his uniform was spotless. I had never seen him without the Iron Cross at his throat. He was very proud of that medal. With his black SS uniform, he cut an imposing and intimidating figure. The Russian campaign, all that cold and then the recovery from his wounds, had left him ghostly pale. His pallor could at times make him appear frightening and otherwordly, like a spirit.

He was a soldier first and foremost, but he had talent as well as an administrator. He seemed to see all aspects of a project at once, all the small problems that would typically arise, and was able to solve them before they interfered with the whole.

At most times in the camp he was cold and remote. His orders were followed immediately and without question. I have seen him order prisoners shot for a disturbance in one barrack and in the next breath order more fuel for the stoves of another barrack that held political prisoners — there were a number of Germans at the camp who had been journalists or outspoken against the Nazi party and Radl seemed to have some pity toward them. For the concerns of the Jews and Russians he had only that ghostly, impassive face.

In his office, away from the eyes of the prisoners and his men, he was an engaging conversationalist. Sometimes we discussed music or architecture. He was a man who loved ideas and actually had quite a creative imagination although he strove to conceal it beneath an exterior that appeared efficient and unmoved. He strove to be the perfect soldier.

Having known him, I would say that Radl was neither cruel nor kind. What he lacked was that quality so basic in most humans, the simple capacity to feel compassion for men whom he did not believe were his equals. Despite his intelligence and creativity, something in his soul was dead. Maybe it had frozen in the Russian winter. It was this lack of compassion more than any other quality that made him a monster.

THESE WORDS WERE INCLUDED in the profile of Radl in my book, and they were from the very first interview I had undertaken on what would become a very long project. I was maybe sixteen years old and the interview had been conducted at our kitchen table.

The man who had spoken those words was my father.

When I asked how he had managed to talk with Radl in his office, my father had fallen quiet for a long time, inspecting his hands and picking at the grease under his fingernails.

Finally, he cleared his throat and spoke: "It just so happens that I was no ordinary prisoner."

14

"What happened to you?" asked Kate, meeting me at the entrance of the Department of Justice complex on Pennsylvania Avenue and clipping a visitor's badge to the lapel of my tweed jacket. I had worn it so that I would look sufficiently scholarly.

"I fell down some steps."

She frowned, took my right hand as if to shake it, then turned it over and examined it. "Did you use karate on the steps on the way down? I would say the bruises on the edges of your hands are consistent with the use of martial arts."

"I've had some training in tae kwon do."

"You're full of surprises, aren't you? Now, tell me what really happened."

I filled her in on the fight in the parking garage — leaving out the part about breaking fingers. When I finished, Kate seemed a little stunned. She didn't say much except, "That's awful. Jesus. Are you sure you're OK?"

"If I pass out during any meetings, don't take it personally."

"You are so not funny right now, Professor."

She turned and led me to an elevator, which we took to the

ninth floor and the Office of Special Investigations. Although I
was well aware of OSI, I had never actually been there. The
office was founded in 1979 as the Nazi-hunting unit of the
Department of Justice, although "Nazi hunter" was a term OSI
preferred to avoid. Back then, OSI was on track to having a
short life, simply because new leads on Nazi war criminals
were running out and the old ones met with literal dead ends.
Hunting Nazi war criminals was territory that had been well-
plowed by Simon Wiesenthal and other Holocaust survivors.
Then, around 1990, there came a windfall for Nazi hunters
everywhere. The Iron Curtain fell. Along with the end of
communism in Europe came access to World War II records in
former Soviet bloc countries. As it turned out, the Soviets and
their minions had carefully guarded these records kept by the
Soviet Union's most bitter enemy. For OSI, those newfound
records were like water in a desert.

Sorting through these records was not easy. At least one OSI
investigator taught himself Polish, Lithuanian, Hungarian and
rudimentary Russian — he was already fluent in German —
and took several trips to these nations that had been under
Nazi occupation. There, he pored over boxes of documents
sour with decay and dust, searching for clues. The Germans
had been formidable record-keepers, requiring that soldiers
sign even for boxes of bullets. Sometimes, those bullets had
been used to kill Jews or the *intelligentsia* of a particular occupied region. By linking simple records of munitions against the
dates of known massacres, OSI investigators developed a list of
suspected SS collaborators. These names were then paired
against United States immigration and naturalization records.
It was a slow and tedious process with odds of one in one
hundred thousand that one of the names in question would
appear. But from time to time, names churned up like matching
dice on a blackjack table.

Many of these war criminals were not German, but were

ethnic Hungarians or Lithuanians who had sided with the occupiers. They had lied about their wartime activities and settled around the Eastern European communities in Chicago and Detroit and Milwaukee, as well as other now-faded industrial cities. OSI had prosecuted most of its cases in Chicago, where it kept a small satellite office of two lawyers, a para-legal and a secretary. So far, OSI had successfully prosecuted one hundred former Nazi war criminals in the past twenty-five years. The United States could not prosecute these old Nazis for crimes that took place outside the nation's borders. Consequently, the intent of OSI was not to imprison anyone, but to deny them freedom in another way. Most of those convicted of war crimes were stripped of citizenship and deported. Another fifty cases were currently under investigation. It was more than enough to keep the twenty-eight OSI staff members busy.

Since 2001, OSI had been given an added mission. Teaming up with the Department of Homeland Secuirty, OSI was being charged with investigating a newer generation of human rights violators now living in the United States as citizens. These were mostly war criminals from the former Yugoslavia, Rwaanda and other African nations, even Cambodia. The new mission had created tension at OSI because some staff members saw it conflicting with the unfinished business of World War II while others saw the new mission as the path toward job security and twenty-first century relevance.

Stepping off the elevator, I found that the office space occupied by OSI was much fancier than I expected. Not posh by any means, but the matching desks and office furniture appeared new and every work area we passed had either a new laptop or a computer with an LCD screen. Strictly high-end. Still, the office had touches that reminded me of academia: large maps on the walls marked with colored push-pins, bookshelves overflowing with leather-bound volumes, a pipe-rack visible on one desk. Most of the staff members were historians or lawyers like

Kate. They traveled a great deal. They dwelled in the past and treated the present as a consequence of what had come before.

Kate must have noticed my roving eye.

"Your tax dollars at work," she said. "They keep throwing Homeland Security money at us."

Apparently, Agent Kate Crockett had gone far at OSI. She had an actual office with her nameplate on the wall beside her door. The door had an opaque window of etched glass. On the door itself was a bumper sticker decal featuring the Superman emblem — only Kate's said "Superbitch" at the bottom.

"What's with that?" I asked, stopping outside the door.

"One of my co-workers — hell, maybe it was a group project — slipped that onto my desk one day. I guess it was somebody's little way of dropping me a hint that I should tone it down a bit. So I stuck it on my door for all the world to see. I'm proud of it."

"To hell with 'em if they can't take a joke, right?"

"Something like that."

"So what did you bring me all the way up here to tell me?"

"First, I want you to meet the rest of the team."

"Team?"

Kate opened the door to reveal two people in her office, a young man with lots of gel in his short-cropped hair and a woman who looked like a New Age librarian in a long dress and dangly earrings. Kate's so-called team was huddled around her desk, poring over piles of computer printouts and well-thumbed file folders spilling documents and photographs. They looked up when I entered but didn't bother to get to their feet. There was a weariness about all three, as if they had been poring over these records for a long time. A box of stale doughnuts exuded a sticky sweet smell.

Kate made introductions. "Professor McCoy, this is Dustin Granger," she said, putting her hand in a proprietary fashion on the shoulder of an eager-looking young man, as if to indicate he was a star pupil. "He's an assistant investigator here."

"I read your books," Dustin said, jumping to his feet and grabbing for my hand. "They were just awesome."

I thanked him and Kate nodded at the other woman. "This is Eleanor Riggs, one of our computer-based researchers."

The woman gave me the kind of nod that techno wizards reserve for lesser mortals. She was dressed all in black, with chunky black-framed eyeglasses that reminded me of Clark Kent's—somehow nerdy and hip at the same time.

The last thing I had expected was a team. Apparently this investigation was getting hot in a hurry. There was an awkward pause in the room and I felt like someone who had walked into the middle of a conversation. I was the outsider; these three worked together every day. "Kate tells me you've found some interesting information about the victim," I said, hoping to break the ice.

Kate spoke up. "For starters, we know that Hans Schmidt was quite a wealthy man."

I was surprised. "I saw where he lived. The house was nice enough, but it wasn't exactly a palace."

"Well, our friend lived very modestly considering he had a net worth of close to two million dollars."

"Two million? Pretty good for a guy who crunched numbers at a munitions plant for a living."

"He made some smart investments," Eleanor said. "His IRS records showed he reported only a modest income from his pension, but he owned a fair amount of real estate. He had the convenience store and his own home, as well as several rental properties."

"If he had so much money, why live so modestly?" the young man asked. I noticed that Dustin wore a shirt and tie, and trousers with a razor-sharp crease. He made he feel stodgy in my tweed sport coat and flannel pants. "He could have afforded a better house."

"People see money as security, Dustin. For someone of his

generation, it must have been reassuring to know he had a nice nest egg."

"I'm thinking that someone with money could be a target for blackmail," Eleanor said. "Maybe the person at the store was threatening to reveal his true past."

Kate nodded. "That explains the heart attack," she agreed.

I thought about that. Someone would need to have something really good on you to hand over that kind of money. I wasn't sure that being involved in the SS in a minor way was enough. "Even if his past could get him deported, I doubt that the old man was all that worried. Two million dollars is a lot of money. Maybe not a fortune, but considering his age, he could still have taken his money and lived out the rest of his days in a nice, warm tropical country far beyond the reach of United States law. He didn't have any family ties to keep him here — or any friends, from the sound of it."

There was a quick knock, then the door to Kate's office opened and a forty-something man popped his head in. He surveyed the four of us like a teacher who had just caught a group of kids smoking in the boys' room. He might as well have worn a badge that screamed *administrator.* He seemed surprised to see Kate.

"Oh, hi," he said, meeting her eyes briefly before he seemed to become intensely interested in the framed photographs and certificates on the office walls. "I thought you were still in the field."

"I'm back here now doing some follow ups," she said, crossing her arms on her chest. "What can I do for you, George?"

"I'm looking for Eleanor, actually," he said, his gaze settling on the computer whiz. "I thought she was using your office. Eleanor, when you're done here I've got some records I need you to run down."

"She's working with me on an investigation. You know that." The accusatory tone in Kate's voice made it crack like a whip.

George snapped right back. "What, hassling old geezers at the nursing home again?"

"This is an important case." Now Kate sounded exasperated. "If you don't get something concrete in a day or two, Eleanor is back with me." He was almost shouting now.

"We need more time than that!"

"Time? Time is what you don't have. Just remember that in about ten years none of you will have a job — not tracking geriatric fugitives, at least," he said. "They'll all be dead."

"OK, George, we get the message. You need Eleanor. We don't need to have a discussion of departmental philosophy right now. We all know how you feel. But Nazi crimes are just as important as more recent war crimes OSI is working on."

"You know what your problem is, Kate? You're too caught up in the past. You — oh, never mind." He shook his head as if in disgust, then shut the door behind him.

"Who was that asshole?" I asked. Eleanor gave me a slight smile for my choice of words, while Dustin looked away and cleared his throat. I wondered what was really going on — those two had been ready to go at each other like cat and dog. It seemed like more than a turf war to me.

"George Foster." Kate rolled her eyes. "As you probably gathered, he thinks bringing Nazi war criminals to justice is a waste of resources for the Office of Special Investigations. He has his sights set on the next generation of war crimes from Yugoslavia, Rwanda, Iraq. He sees it as job security."

"That's a great attitude," I said sarcastically. "Doesn't he know the books are still open on a lot of these Nazi crimes?"

"King George," Eleanor said, glancing around at her co-workers and obviously sharing an inside joke. "He likes to lord it over us underlings."

"The name fits," I said, "considering that he does seem like a royal pain in the ass."

"Oooh, I like this guy," Eleanor said. "You're going to fit right in."

Kate didn't look as amused. "That goddamn George," she said, shaking her head. She sighed. "Unfortunately, he's also our boss. If we don't get some results, he's going to break up the team. So I suggest we get to work, people."

DUSTIN AND ELEANOR went to get coffee, leaving Kate to brief me about what they had found so far on Hans Schmidt.

"OK, so the guy was pretending to be something he wasn't," I said. "Will the real Hans Schmidt please stand up."

Kate handed me a thick file. "He's right here."

The folder held page after page of documents and forms. "Why don't you sum it up for me."

"Well, it's all pretty standard procedure to start with. We go through immigration and naturalization records from that time period, looking for variations on the spellings on the list of wanted Nazi war criminals. It sounds tedious, but we have computer software that does most of the sifting."

"The name Hans Schmidt seems to be a likely suspect."

"Exactly. The computer program matches up the two lists of names — one of immigrants from that time, the other of known war criminals — trying to find similarities. You would be surprised how many times these guys simply changed a few letters or Anglicized their names in hopes of slipping through immigration."

"A lot of them did."

"Yes. The truth is that nobody was looking very hard. The war was over and U.S. immigration officials weren't being too particular about who let in. This was before computers, so record-keeping was more localized. It was fairly easy for a former soldier to claim to be someone else. There was no real way to determine his actual identity. Documents from Europe were easily forged. The war left a lot of confusion in its wake, with entire countries in chaos. In most cases, immigration and naturalization officials simply relied on the signed statements of the individuals involved."

"And these were some of the last people on whose word you would want to rely."

"True. Anyhow, no matches turned up for our particular Hans Schmidt."

"I thought you told me you knew who he was."

Kate smiled. "His name was Juozas Juknys." She produced a computer printout and showed me the name. "Juknys was on the list of wanted Nazi war criminals."

"What?" I was stunned.

"Our old man was far more clever than we thought. He wasn't German at all, although he had chosen a name to make us think that. *Hans Schmidt.* Actually, he was a native of Lithuania."

"How do you know his real name?"

"The police in North Bay started to catalog that collection of artifacts in the old man's basement. They found one of those fireproof boxes down in the shrine," Kate said. "Inside were photos of Hans taken years ago. The North Bay police found several documents with the name Juozas Juknys on them, including a military commission. I think it's pretty safe that we can make the leap that the old man held onto a few items from his past life."

"Right," I said. "If he wasn't Juknys, why else would he have kept those things hidden away all these years?"

Even with the name the North Bay police had found, there was a time before the fall of the Iron Curtain when the OSI investigation would have hit a wall at that point. However, OSI investigators now had a bonanza of former Soviet bloc records at their disposal. I looked at the paperwork Kate had produced. In March 1947, a man named Hans Schmidt applied in Stuttgart for a nonpreference quota immigration visa.

"What you're saying is that Juknys transformed himself into Hans Schmidt," I said, catching on. I read over the notes the team had so far. "He presented documents, including a police record from Stuttgart listing a birthplace and birthdate, a record from the Vatican official in Germany listing the same information, a Lithuanian ID card also listing the information and a certificate from the Lithuanian Ex-Political Prisoners Nazi Victims Central Committee, which further verified his name and birthdate and indicated that he had been persecuted by the Gestapo."

"All of it false," Kate said. "He lied through his teeth and he must have had some powerful friends to provide the forged documentation. He also claimed to have been a farm worker." Kate handed me another sheet of paper, this one summarizing the wartime activities of Juozas Juknys.

"So he failed to mention that he had actually been a bank employee and then supervised a factory during the Nazi occupation of Lithuania," I said, skimming the document. Something else caught my eye. "He was also affiliated with the SS *Einsatzkommandos*. Son of a bitch."

"Keep reading, it only gets better."

Juozas Juknys, who through various false documents would transform himself into Hans Schmidt, was actually far different from the simple farm worker who claimed to be a devout Catholic targeted by the Gestapo for his anti-Nazi leanings. He entered military service in 1938 and graduated from cadet school. By 1940 he was a lieutenant. He resigned to become a manager of the Bank of Lithuania in Kedainiai. In June 1941 Germany invaded the Soviet Union and troops soon reached Lithuania.

For some in that conquered nation, Nazi occupation was a nightmare. SS troops began to round up every Jew they could find. Most were murdered. Those who survived were used for forced labor. Local citizens who opposed the Nazis met a similar fate.

For men such as Juozas Juknys, the arrival of German forces must have felt like opportunity. He was well-educated and fluent in German. Considering his easy acceptance by the invaders, one of his parents or grandparents may have been an ethnic German, although the record was unclear on that. In any case, with his military background and prominent banking position, Juknys quickly became a favorite of the Nazi invaders. They put him in charge of a factory. Then when SS *Einsatzkom mandos* had been overwhelmed with the number of Jews they found to round up and murder, they recruited local leaders such as Juknys to help. The former military officer headed up a group of Nazi collaborators and former members of the Lithuanian paramilitary organization known as the *Sauliai* or Riflemen's Association. They went to work helping the SS kill Jews.

"My God," I said. "He must have been one of the leaders of the Kedainiai massacre. The time frame is right."

"You won't find that on his application for a visa."

"No wonder," I said, putting down the document. There were no details in this report about what happened at Kedainiai, but I knew enough about it. Years ago I had interviewed one of the survivors for an article. "There were actually two separate massacres, both in the summer of nineteen forty-one. First, SS *Einsatzkommandos* with help from Nazi collaborators rounded up more than one hundred former Communists or Soviet government officials. They were taken by truck to the forest, where they were ordered into a large pit and shot. If you were someone like Juknys, a great way to settle the score with old rivals was to accuse them of being communists. It's not like there were any trials. His word to the Nazis would have been enough."

"What about the second massacre?"

"That one was bigger," I explained. "It took place at the end of August. All the Jews in the city had already been forced into living in a ghetto where the Nazis could keep them contained. At the end of August, the Nazis and their collaborators forced them out and took them all to a farm outside the city. They were taken to a large pit and ordered to undress. Then the Nazis and Lithuanians shot them. More than two thousand men, women and children were murdered. The Germans ordered dirt shoveled over the bleeding, naked bodies. Some of the Jews were still alive, wounded, in agony. They were buried alive."

It was quiet for a long time in the office.

"Juozas Juknys must have done a good job there," Kate said finally, handing me one last document.

"So here's the link and an explanation of how Juknys got out of Lithuania and became Hans Schmidt," I said after reading it. "In late nineteen forty-four because of his banking and money management skills he was sent to Berlin —"

"— and was assigned to work with Konrad Radl," Kate said.

"I'll be damned," I said, thinking about the face on the surveillance video. Radl's face. Or someone who looked an awful lot like him.

We were both trying to absorb the information in the documents we had just read when someone rapped at the door. Eager young Dustin Granger poked his head inside. "We just saw it on the Associated Press website and thought you should know," he said. "There's been another incident."

15

Ten minutes later Kate and I were in the hallway, headed for the elevator and the parking garage. The victim was in Connecticut, about six hours away if traffic was not bad. We could have flown, but with the time it took to get through airport security these days, driving seemed to be the better option.

George Foster ran into us on the way out. He made a show of looking at his watch, the supervisor's universal sign that you are a) late for work b) getting back from a long lunch or c) leaving early. The guy wasn't even my boss and he had me feeling guilty.

"It's barely one p.m.," Foster said. "Don't tell me you're cutting out of here."

"There's been another incident, George," Kate replied. "We think it may be related to the one in Maryland."

"You've got to be kidding. How?"

"The victim was shot in the head with a German Luger by someone wearing an SS uniform," she said.

Kate had then chosen that inopportune time to introduce me. Foster had a grip like a vise, but his flesh had an unpleasant, clammy feel. His eyes flashed from me to Kate as we shook hands. He wore a nice-looking charcoal gray suit, a white shirt, and a tie decorated with miniature American flags. He regarded my sport coat and jeans, not to mention my bruised face, with a dubious look.

"Professor McCoy. It's nice to finally meet you. You're something of a legend around OSI."

"Really? As it turns out, so are you."

Foster's eyes flicked to Kate. "I guess the troops have been talking me up," he said. "In any case, I'm sorry you had to witness that shouting match."

"I hope you didn't really mean what you said," I replied. "With an attitude like that, it's amazing OSI has caught any Nazis at all."

"Oh, we catch our share," he said defensively. "The point I was making — maybe a little too heatedly earlier — is that OSI has to evolve. Our department's resources are better spent on documenting actual war criminals whether they're Nazis or Yugoslavs or Rwaandans. We need to spend our time on paper trails, Professor McCoy, not haunting nursing homes or chasing down bad guys out of an *X-Files* or *Twilight Zone* episode."

With a twinge, I realized Kate must have told him about the image on the store's security camera. Now it was my turn to be defensive. "I know it's crazy, but the man on that surveillance video bears a strong resemblance to Konrad Radl."

"Who was last seen in nineteen forty-five." Foster clapped me on the shoulder. He must have seen the look on my face, because he took his hand away as fast as if he had touched a hot skillet. "Hey, don't worry about it. Over at the FBI they get two or three calls a week from somebody who just saw Elvis at the supermarket."

"I am well aware it can't actually *be* Radl," I said, although I wasn't sure of any such thing. Not exactly. I could feel my face turning red. At that point I was about two seconds away from choking Foster with his silly patriotic necktie.

Kate touched my arm. "We were just leaving, George. I'll give you a full report as soon as we get there."

Foster stared at her as if waiting for Kate to say something more, then shook his head and walked off. It was as if the guy had studied a manual on the body lingo bosses used to let you know they were not pleased.

Even by the time we got to Kate's car, my blood pressure was still coming down from boil to simmer. Watching the world outside spin past at 70 mph on the beltway I remarked, "Your boss is kind of a prick."

"He has some issues," Kate agreed.

"Apparently he's not much on the whole idea of bringing Nazi war criminals to justice."

"I have to admit he sort of has a point. Why are we chasing down old Nazis who are just going to be dead soon enough?"

"You mean, why can't we just let them die in peace?" I said. "Why make them look over their shoulders now all these years later, just because they murdered a few hundred or a few thousand children and women?"

Kate was somber. "When you put it that way it all seems so clear."

"It's about justice," I said. "And on a personal level it's about revenge. Your supervisor needs to be reminded of what happened. He ought to take a walk through the Holocaust museum to refresh his memory. It's just up the street from your building. My God, don't take pity on the Nazis just because they are old men. Don't give up on bringing them to justice, Kate. They're monsters who made human beings into soap, for Christ sake."

"You're shouting," Kate said. "Please tell me you're not going to shout all the way to Connecticut. Remember that you're supposed to be mad at George Foster, not me. We're on the same side here."

"Actually, I was only planning to shout as far as northern New Jersey and then adopt a strident tone for the rest of the trip."

Kate sighed. "The problem with George Foster is that although he won't admit it, he knows it's worth pursuing the remaining Nazi war criminals. However, what he's doing is going out of his way to belittle me and my efforts. You see, despite the 'Super Bitch' sticker on my office door there has been some talk about me moving up the Department of Justice food chain in a couple more years, in all likelihood being promoted over King George."

"Ah. He sees you as a rival."

"Exactly. Which means he does what he can to undermine me. Office politics. The guy has been there for eighteen years and I've been there for eight. He considers me to be an upstart who hasn't paid her dues. And who knows? If he can make me look bad enough maybe the powers that be will promote George instead and leave me chasing after old men in wheelchairs."

"Would that be so bad? The wheelchairs make them easier to catch."

Kate shot me a withering look. "Well, you've got to admit that catching Nazi war criminals is not a growth industry. The possibilities shrink year by year. Ten, fifteen years out and it's pretty much a done business."

"Which leaves you where?"

"Maybe in a dead-end career. If I move up in OSI, there's a whole new world of hate crimes out there and a promotion would put me in charge of some of those investigations. Skinheads, Rwanda, Serbian war lords, Iraq, cross burnings, beltway snipers, you name it. Not to mention plenty of hatred to come from countries and groups no one's even heard of yet."

"That's a cheerful thought," I said. "You're saying that war crimes and atrocities are a growth industry."

"Sadly enough, I guess I am saying that. Meanwhile, I'm happy enough catching Nazis. Plus there's one more little thing you should know about George." Kate hesitated. "Honestly, I don't know why I'm telling you this, but it seems relevant to the situation. George and I had a relationship for about six months and then I dumped him. Needless to say, he hates me on all sorts of levels."

"You and George Foster, huh? I guess there's no accounting for taste."

"Shit happens, McCoy."

The argument between them back in Kate's office now made more sense. There had been an undercurrent of something more than professional disagreement. I had to smile as I wondered about my own chances of picking up where George left off. A strong woman might be just what I needed. "So it's safe to say you like older men?"

Kate scrutinized my face a moment. "Go to hell," she said. "I mean, *you're* one to talk. I thought you had a thing for younger women."

She had me there. "That makes us a perfect pair."

"In your dreams," Kate said, stomping on the accelerator.

"You're going to get a ticket," I warned.

"I can't get a ticket," she said. "I'm a federal investigator on official business."

"We could have flown," I pointed out.

"This is faster."

Kate had a point. OSI did not have a jet at its disposal. In the time it would have taken us to get our tickets at Baltimore-Washington International we were already across the Delaware Memorial Bridge.

Somewhere in the vicinity of the Molly Pitcher rest stop on

the Jersey Turnpike, Kate's cell phone rang. She listened a moment before thanking the caller and hanging up.

"That was Dustin," she said. "The victim's name is Joe Miller. I wonder if it's really that obvious."

"Joe — Joseph — J-o-s-e-f. Miller is almost certainly Mueller. Unless he was trying to throw us off the trail like our friend Hans and was someone altogether different." Rather than create a new identity, the less creative Nazi war criminals had often done nothing more than Anglicize their names, with varying degrees of success. Working in their favor had been the fact that back in the late 1940s and early 1950s, our immigration officials had not been all that vigilant. Besides, we were suddenly more worried about communists than Nazis, one bogeyman replaced by another at the outset of the Cold War.

"Maybe we should run that name through the computer," Kate said. "I can call Eleanor back at the office."

"And risk getting King George further pissed off? Nah. Let's see what we come up with first."

I looked out the window at the Great American Landscape flickering past the window. When in a car, I often liked to pretend that I was a first-time visitor to the United States. I imagined that there I was in my rental car, fresh from the airport. What would be my impression of America? Massive highways, gas-guzzling SUVs, litter-strewn roadsides, swampy winter fields beyond, tract housing, gloomy warehouses. Hardly encouraging sights. I was not a pessimist about America. It really was the best country in the world. But sometimes I wished we would take a little more pride in ourselves.

Mostly, instead of talking, Kate drove. *Fast.* The Malibu could *move.* There are two ways to deal with New York City on an East Coast road trip: through the city on I-95 and the George Washington Bridge or around the Big Apple, crossing the Hudson River further north.

"I hate New York," Kate said when she told me she was

opting for the second route. "Try putting *that* on a bumper sticker."

AT THE WALT WHITMAN rest stop on the New Jersey Turnpike: "Who *do* you think we saw on the surveillance video?"

"I don't know." Kate pondered the question as she dodged around two big trucks. "Some guy who looked like a Nazi."

"It can't be Radl," I said. "Not unless he traveled through time."

To my surprise, Kate seemed to give serious thought to the idea that Radl had hitchhiked through quantum foam or a wormhole or whatever. "The Germans didn't have the technology for that in nineteen forty-five," she finally said. "*We* don't have the technology for that now. We know time travel does not exist."

"Do we?"

"I've never been to Iowa but I know it exists because I've met people from there. Have you ever met someone from the future? Time travel is just a theory."

"Maybe the Germans didn't know any better," I said. "Maybe they tried anyway."

AT THE ENTRANCE to the Garden State Parkway, Kate asked: "Do you get in a lot of fights like the one in the parking garage?"

"Not if I can help it. The truth is, I got lucky. I think those guys would have killed me, given half a chance. My ears are still ringing from getting kicked in the head."

"Jesus, McCoy. Did you get yourself checked out or anything? You could have a concussion."

"I'm all right. Seeing double has been kind of interesting."

She shook her head in disgust. "Men and their macho bullshit."

"I'll bet your ex-boyfriend George Foster would have gone to the ER."

Kate reddened. "I *knew* I never should have told you about me and George." She was quiet a moment before continuing. "You know, he did go to the ER from work once because a cup of extremely hot coffee spilled in his lap."

"How did that happen?"

"Well, I happened to be *holding* the cup of coffee at the time. It, uh, slipped."

"Remind me not to get you mad if you're holding a cup of coffee."

"That's nothing," Kate said. "George was lucky I wasn't holding scissors. I might have cut off something important."

AT THE TAPPAN ZEE BRIDGE Kate asked: "What was her name?"

"Who?"

"Don't be dense, Professor McCoy," Kate said. "The student you had an affair with."

"Deirdre."

"How very Irish."

"Actually, I think she was Scottish somewhere along the line. She had a sort of emotional stinginess about her, to be sure."

"Did you love her?" Kate asked.

"What is this, an interrogation?"

"It's just a question."

"Then . . . no," I said slowly. "I don't suppose I did love her. I mean, I was fond of her; we cared for each other, obviously. But love? We were both having an adventure. I think dating her professor gave her a kind of *panache* with her friends."

"And it probably made all those middle-aged female professors at your college wonder what they'd been missing."

"Hey, don't get the idea that Deirdre was some doe-eyed co-ed that I seduced. And she was a consenting adult. She was twenty-one and she knew exactly what she was doing."

"You sound so much like a typical male asshole right now," Kate said.

"Well, one small factor in our relationship was that Deirdre was using me to get back at her parents. 'Mom, Dad, I met this great guy at college. He's my history professor.' Something along those lines. You have to admit it's not what most parents want to hear."

"Did it get back at them?"

"A little too well," I said. "Her father was a state senator at the time and chairman of the senate finance committee. Needless to say, our college saw some budget funds cut for the next fiscal year."

"Needless to say, your days were numbered," Kate said.

"Well, they did let me finish out the year. But there was a faculty ethics commission hearing rife with a lot of sanctimonious indignation and my contract was not renewed. I had tenure — otherwise they wouldn't have bothered with the whole kangaroo court exercise — but in the end I had to go."

"Was it hard to give up teaching?"

I thought about that. "Not really. To be honest, I was never a great teacher. What I did miss was *this*. Being on the go. Back when I was making my living as a freelance writer, I'd be lying if I called myself an impartial journalist. Mostly I was interested in tracking down these old Nazi dinosaurs before the last of them turns to dust and escapes justice."

"We can always hope they'll burn in hell," Kate said.

"Why leave that to chance? Let them suffer a little in what's left of this life. Besides, I don't know that I believe in heaven or hell. But if there is a hell, there's a special place reserved in it for men like Konrad Radl."

"What about Deirdre?" Kate asked. "Do you miss her?"

"I don't miss *her*, but I miss certain aspects of our relationship, if you know what I mean."

Keeping one hand on the wheel, Kate punched my arm. "Spoken like a true male pig," she said, but she was smiling, which just goes to show that women love a rogue, no matter what they say. "So what happened to Deirdre after her professor dumped her? Something like that's not easy to live with on a small campus. I'll bet she had to transfer."

"Not Dierdre. She's kind of shameless that way. I think she knew it made the faculty a little afraid of her. At a college, the faculty is supposed to be in charge, but she had a kind of power over them after that. She had a proven reputation as a temptress."

"All because you broke ranks," Kate said.

"Is that what they're calling it these days? And here I thought I was just a dirty old man."

Kate did not reply. I got the sense that she was reserving judgment, at least for now. In the matter of Deirdre, I had decided some time ago not to judge myself. Just about everyone had already done that for me. Besides, I had learned that if you spent too much time worrying about your mistakes you could end up like a snake swallowing its tail, caught up in an endless circle as you digested yourself over and over again.

AT THE SIDE of the road on I-84 in Connecticut after being pulled over by a trooper who frowned upon speeding through the Constitution State's countryside, Kate said: "I hope this bastard gets with the program or I'm going to make it my hobby to make sure he never sees his pension." Kate glared into the rear-view mirror at the trooper.

"Hey, I told you some state trooper was going to pull you over."

"Eighty-five is *not* that fast."

"Try telling that to Mr. Mirrored Sunglasses when he comes back with your driver's license and registration."

"He wasn't very impressed by my Department of Justice credentials, was he?" Kate slumped in her seat. "Maybe I should have joined the FBI instead. Nobody ever gives speeding tickets to FBI agents."

16

Kate parked behind the crime scene van and we ducked under the yellow caution tape. I was stiff from the long ride, not to mention still aching from my encounter with the skinheads back at the parking garage in Baltimore. I was expecting a chilly reception from the local police, like the one we had received in North Bay, but to my surprise the uniformed officer who met us in the driveway actually seemed glad to see us.

"Headquarters told us you were coming," he said. He eyed Kate the way any red-blooded man would, perhaps a little taken aback that this federal investigator was a dish. Was that a twinge of protectiveness I felt, or simple jealousy? Then his eyes flashed from me to Kate and back again, appraising the situation. Whatever else, I'd bet this guy was a good cop.

"You're Bram McCoy, huh? I read your book," the cop said. "My wife got it for me for my birthday and I almost didn't read it, you know, with a name like *Journey of Hope*. Sounded a little too touchy-feely to me. But I've got to tell you I couldn't put it down. It was damn good."

"Thank you."

"I'm Jewish, you know. I felt like I was there every step of the way. Some books stay with you and that was one of them. Your old man was amazing."

I nodded. "It's my father's book as much as mine."

"Written anything else lately?"

"I'm between projects at the moment," I said, hating how stuffy that sounded. I tried again. "The truth is that I need a good subject to write about."

"How about this?" he asked, nodding at the house behind him. "Some guy in a German uniform shows up on an old man's doorstep and blows him away. Now, there's got to be some kind of story there."

"That's what we're trying to figure out."

"Join the club," he said. "We'll have to use the back door."

We walked around and went in through the kitchen. The room was dated right down to the wallpaper patterned with the words *Spirit of '76* and images of drums and eagles. With a pang of memory, I recalled our own kitchen growing up. The wallpaper had a seashell pattern, though we lived nowhere near the sea. My mother had picked it out. My father had put it up meticulously, aligning every curve of shell, each grain of sand. The air smelled of lemon-scented dish soap. And another smell that I couldn't quite identify.

The cop led us to where two crime scene techs were working in the living room. The front door opened directly into the room, where two big Lazy Boy chairs huddled around a large TV. One wall was taken up by a fireplace, above which hung a copy of a Renoir painting. The mantel overflowed with family photographs in silver and gold frames. Not a speck of dust anywhere.

What caught my eye next was the huge stain of dried blood on the linoleum near the front door.

"Head wound," the local cop explained. "They bleed like a son of a bitch. He got shot right between the eyes."

Before he left us with the crime scene techs, the cop paused in the kitchen doorway.

"You know, in my opinion as someone of the Hebrew persuasion, we should have dropped the nuke on Berlin, not Hiroshima. But we wouldn't do that because the Germans were too much like us. So we went after the yellow people." On that note, he went back to his post out front.

The techs were less talkative than the first cop, but only because they were preoccupied with their work. Neither one of them seemed to know much about the victim.

"Try two houses down," one of them said. "I understand that's where the widow is staying."

"You mean he was married?"

"Fifty years, from what I heard." The tech gave a short laugh. "You'd think that would have killed him a long time ago."

We left the gory scene in the kitchen and headed toward the front door. In the living room, the uniformed cop was standing by a front window, watching the street and keeping out of the cold. He looked up. "I hope you catch the son of a bitch, Professor," he said. "If there's some wannabe Nazi running around killing people, you need to nail his Aryan ass."

"I'M NOT sure how much I can help," said Hazel Miller. Joe Miller's widow sat at the kitchen table of her sister's house two doors down, clutching a cup of lukewarm milky tea in her wrinkled hands. The milk was starting to separate, forming swirls in the tea mug. I guessed she was around seventy-five.

Kate began: "This must be a terrible shock, Mrs. Miller."

"Yes," she said. "It's really the last way I thought Joe would be taken from me. You know, when you get old you expect

other things to happen but not something like this. *Murdered.*
My God."

"The police are doing all they can," Kate said. She meant it
to be comforting, but it sounded hollow. I was sure the sight of
the blood-stained kitchen floor flashed in all our minds.

Mrs. Miller nodded. She was a pretty woman, not quite
overtaken by old age. Her hair still had a touch of blond among
the gray. She wore a bit of lipstick, which seemed odd under
the circumstances, but it could have been an old habit. The rest
of her face was wan and colorless, like cardboard left in the
rain.

"The police don't know what happened. Maybe federal
investigators like yourselves can help." She sighed. "You'll have
to forgive me. At this point I'm all cried out. I'm trying to make
some sense of all this."

"I understand, Mrs. Miller," Kate said.

"Please, call me Hazel."

The sister hovered protectively, ready to shoo us away from
Hazel. "I told you we should have moved years ago," she
harped, fussing about the kitchen. "Next week Bill and I are
putting our house up for sale. Let the spics have it. They can
have the whole damn neighborhood."

"I suppose I'll sell too," Hazel said. "Joe would never do it.
He simply refused. I know it's not much, but he took pride in
that house, working on it all those years. But now that he's gone
I can't live there, not after what happened."

"Do you have any idea why someone would want to kill
your husband?" I asked.

"She's already been through all of this with the police," the
sister said sharply. "I don't see why you're asking her again."

"Hazel, the fact that witnesses described seeing a man in a
military uniform at your house around the time of your
husband's death is very unusual," I said, pointedly ignoring the
sister. "As you probably know by now, there was an incident

very similar to this one just five days ago in Maryland. The victim was also around your husband's age."

"There's crazy people everywhere," the sister said. "I still say it was the spics that did it."

Hazel was staring into her teacup, but it seemed to me that she now looked even more troubled. "I didn't know about the other one."

Kate and I exchanged a look. So, no one had told Hazel about the death of Hans Schmidt. I wasn't surprised. She had enough worries of her own without being burdened by the details of a crime that had taken place hundreds of miles away and wasn't necessarily related.

"I don't know what to think," Hazel said, finally looking up and meeting my gaze. I noticed for the first time that she had unexpectedly intense blue eyes. *Very Aryan,* I thought uneasily as I met her steady gaze. "None of it makes any sense."

"Do you have anyone else besides your sister?" Kate asked, looking genuinely concerned.

"No, no children, if that's what you mean," Hazel said, dropping her eyes back to her teacup. "Just the two of us."

The sister got up, explaining that she had some phone calls to make. "Funeral arrangements," she explained. "And we'll have to get some eats in for after the service."

Hazel winced at the words and watched her sister go. Through the doorway, we could just see the sister's thick legs going up the stairs. Then Hazel got up from the table and closed the kitchen door.

"My husband had secrets," she said in a soft voice. "There were things about him I still don't understand."

17

———

Hazel reached into a pocket of her sweater and took out an aged photograph. The edges of the snapshot were worn and there was a crease across the middle where the picture had been folded. The photograph was decades old, faded to a brown-and-white sepia tone.

"I can't show you this in front of my sister," she explained. "I'm not even sure I should show it to the two of *you*. But it may help catch whoever is responsible for doing this to Joe."

In the photograph were four young men. Three wore SS uniforms with the Death's Head emblem just visible as a white dot on their collars and the peaks of their caps. The landscape around them was bleak and wintry. They stood in front of a compound surrounded by a tall barb wire fence. The fourth man wore a suit and stood apart from the three soldiers. He was older than the SS men, his features more haggard.

I stared at the photograph. Hazel continued to speak but I didn't hear a word.

"Are you all right?" Kate asked. "Don't tell me you just saw another ghost."

"It must be my week for ghosts." My hands shook. *It wasn't possible.* I knew the face of the civilian all too well. It was the same face that had squinted down at greasy fingernails all those evenings in our kitchen. The face of the man who put on work clothes every day and went off to a job he thought beneath him. The face of my father.

Kate noticed me staring. "Who is it?" she asked.

"I'll tell you later." I looked up at Hazel. "Where did you get this?"

Kate gave me an exasperated look. "She just told us. Weren't you listening?"

Hazel explained again for my benefit. "Years ago I was painting our bedroom and I had to move the dresser away from the wall. To make it easier I took the drawers out. This photograph was taped to the bottom of one of Joe's dresser drawers. When I asked him about it, he said somebody else must have put it there."

"How could that be?"

"Well, we didn't have much money when we were starting out and we bought used furniture. Whoever owned the furniture before us could have put it there." She shrugged. "I had no reason to think anything else. Joe took the photograph and made a show of throwing it out. But when I looked later it wasn't in the trash."

"You suspected something then?"

"Well, he kept it, didn't he? Later on, I found the picture and took a closer look." She tapped a finger on the man in the center of the photograph. "That's Joe in the middle."

"What did you do?"

Hazel's eyes were focused on the picture. "Such a handsome man, my Joe. He and I weren't always old, you know. We were once young and strong. Even a little good looking. We loved each other a great deal." She sighed again. "It took me six months to bring the photo up. I was afraid that the truth would ruin our marriage and the good life we had with each other. But how can happiness be built on a lie? I had to know."

"Those are German uniforms," I said. "He was a member of the SS. They ran the concentration camps."

"Buchenwald," she said. "Dachau. I know."

My belly clenched as she named the camps. *Dachau.* No wonder my father was in the photograph. But he was supposed to be a prisoner. What was he doing in civilian clothes, having his photograph taken with a trio of SS guards? He had never told me about that. I thought of my father at the kitchen table as I interviewed him when I was a teenager, scribbling notes on a legal pad. He had told me he had a few special privileges because he was part of a work crew. Seeing the photograph now, I had to wonder what else my father had left out.

"Bram?"

I realized Kate must have asked me a question, but I had not heard. I was more interested in asking a few questions of my own. I looked up at Hazel Miller. "Your husband told you about Dachau and all the rest?"

"Everything," she said. "Or almost everything. He was very troubled by the past and what he had done, especially as he grew older."

"I don't understand," Kate said. "How did he come to be in the United States?"

"He lied to get into the country," Hazel said. "That was in 1948. He used a false name and false paperwork. The immigration officials did not scrutinize him very hard. They were looking for the important war criminals and Joe had simply been a soldier. Everyone was eager to put the war in the past."

"How did he meet you?"

"After the war there were a lot of manufacturing jobs in Waterbury. We met working at Scovill. He told me he was drafted into the Wehrmacht — the regular Germany army — and had served in France and Belgium at the end of the war."

"May we keep this for now?" Kate said, touching the photograph.

"If it helps, of course you may."

"What did your neighbors think of having a German soldier in their midst?" I asked. "There must have been some resentment."

"You wouldn't know it now, but things were good here. Everyone was making plenty of money. The houses were new, the whole street was filled with young families and young couples. It was a good life." Hazel shrugged. "Nobody talked about the war much. At least, not the fighting. People seemed to understand that Joe had simply been caught up in it and didn't have much choice. Not so different from a lot of young men from here. And there was the fact that he left Germany. He became an American citizen."

"But all that time he had a secret that he kept even from you."

She nodded. "I didn't know the truth until after I found the photograph. He told me he was proud at the time to have served the Reich, but as the years passed he began to doubt himself."

"You never told anyone?"

"Of course not. How do you explain something like that? You don't tell people your husband was a guard at a Nazi death camp. And then in the nineteen eighties the Justice Department began to persecute old men like my husband for things that had happened a long time in the past."

Across the table, I felt Kate shift in her chair, but she did not jump to the defense of the Justice Department. Hazel Miller had made an interesting choice of words. *Persecute.* In Hazel's mind, her Nazi husband was a victim.

Kate asked, "What did you think of your husband's past? Could you forgive him for something like that?"

I wanted to kick her under the table. In the courtroom this would have raised an objection as badgering the witness.

"He lied to me in the beginning, of course. I forgave him because he told the truth and I could understand why he lied. But there was more to it than that. What he had done tormented his conscience. He was truly sorry for what had happened. It even gave him nightmares."

"Nightmares?" Kate sounded incredulous, but I knew that nightmares were not all that surprising, even for an SS killer. One of the reasons the Nazis had adopted the gas chambers was because SS troops began to break down when required to shoot so many Jews, especially women and children. Gassing was far more impersonal, and efficient. The Germans had always approved of efficiency.

The ceiling creaked as Hazel's sister walked overhead. All three of us looked up, afraid she was eavesdropping. We all knew this was not the sort of conversation that should ever be revealed to Hazel's family. Then we heard the muffled sound of the sister chattering on the telephone.

"She must never know. She would never understand," Hazel said quietly, as if to herself. Then Hazel looked up from her tea, her eyes even more intensely blue.

"For the fifty years we were married, Joe often woke up to the same nightmare. Not every night, just once in a while. And the older he got the more often he had nightmares. What sense does that make? I knew he was dreaming about the war, but after I found out the truth about his past he told me about the massacre."

Kate reached out and touched the old woman's hand. "Tell us about it, Hazel."

"It was in the winter of nineteen forty, not long after the Germans invaded Poland. Joe was sent to a town outside Krakow. He was practically a boy, really. He was part of a unit that rounded

up what you would call the educated and middle-class people of
the town, doctors, teachers, businessmen. They were the natural
leaders in the community, I suppose, and they didn't like the Nazis.
The Germans marched whole families out to the woods beyond
town — men, women and little children — then lined them up and
shot them in the snow. There were several hundred bodies tangled
together. By the time they were done it was getting dark and Joe
and the others were forced to spend the night. They camped out in
the woods. The dead were scattered nearby. Only not all of them
were dead. There were little children the parents had tried to
protect by using their own bodies as shields, and the children were
calling out and crying, some of them badly wounded."

"My God," Kate said. She was pale.

I glanced at Hazel, whose lower lip was trembling, then
looked away. I stared at the kitchen wall, but what I was seeing
was a cold winter's woods in Poland, blood on the snow. Somewhere, a child whimpered. *Papa?* Answered by a harsh voice in
guttural German: *Gibe ruh!* Quiet! And then the crack of a
pistol. Silence louder than the gunshot. The young SS
murderer Josef Mueller turning away. *That photo. I had to be
wrong about Hazel's photo. It wasn't possible. My father wasn't one
of them.* I shook my head to clear it as Hazel continued to
confess her husband's sins.

"Joe explained that the bodies of the dead shifted during
the night. An arm moved, a leg twitched. They listened to that
all night, along with the crying."

"What happened?"

Hazel was crying softly now. "In the morning, when it was
light, the captain who was with them ordered them to shoot
anyone left alive. Some of the children were still struggling and
they were shot. Most of the other wounded had tried to crawl
away and they froze to death among the trees during the night."
She took a napkin from a holder on the table and swiped at her
eyes. "That's what Joe had nightmares about."

It had grown very quiet in the kitchen. Hazel sniffed. I should have touched her shoulder, tried to comfort her in some way. But I could not bring myself to move.

Finally I asked, "Hazel, why do you think your husband was killed?"

"I don't know. Obviously, because the killer was seen wearing a German uniform, it must have had something to do with the war."

"Was anything taken?" Kate said. "Money?"

"Money? We didn't have any money. Not enough, anyway, or we would have moved out of this neighborhood years ago."

"Anything else?"

"I was out at the optometrist getting my eyeglasses fixed. I suppose if I'd been here, I'd be dead too."

We all let that sink in for a moment.

"Hazel, did your husband have some kind of bronze disk with a swastika on it?" Kate asked.

"Why, yes," she said, surprised. "We called it 'The Hubcap.' It was something Joe brought back from the war. We called it The Hubcap because it looked like one."

"Did the intruder take it?"

"I don't know. It's gone. Joe kept it on a shelf in the garage, and it's missing now. The thief left other stuff, but he took that."

We talked for a few more minutes around the kitchen table, then stood to leave Hazel to her tea, her haunted past, and her sister, who had finally re-appeared in the kitchen, looking angry now that Hazel was weeping softly.

"Can't you see she's had enough?" she demanded. She placed herself between us and Hazel.

"We'll be leaving now," Kate said. We both headed for the door.

A sort of strangled cry from Hazel stopped us in the doorway.

"Don't think badly of him," she said, drying her eyes and

standing to face us. "He tried to live a good life, to do good deeds after what he had been before."

"We're not here today to judge," Kate replied.

Hazel gave her a bitter smile. "No, but if poor Joe was still alive you would only have come to arrest him." By now, the sister was staring at her wide-eyed but Hazel silenced her with a look. "You've asked so many questions today but now I want to ask one of you."

"Of course."

"Joe tried to live a good life so that one day in the afterlife he might be forgiven. Do you think good deeds can ever outweigh the sins of the past? Do you think God will forgive him?"

Kate looked at Hazel, then turned to me for help. This was a question for a philosopher or a college professor, not a Justice Department investigator. I was ready with an answer because I hadn't studied the Holocaust for so many years without having asked myself the same question.

"You're talking about redemption, Hazel. For all our sakes, I hope it's possible."

She nodded sadly and sank back into her chair.

We showed ourselves out.

I n the car, Kate took out the photograph Hazel Miller had given us.

"The soldier in the middle is Joe Miller," she said. "Recognize the one on the right?"

"Hans Schmidt," I replied without hesitation. "Much younger, of course, but there's no mistaking him."

"That must be the ghost you saw," Kate said.

"Yeah."

"So who are the two guys on the left, the soldier and the civilian?"

"The soldier is probably the next victim."

"I was afraid you were going to say that," Kate said. "Because that's just what I was thinking. Too bad we don't know who he is or where he might be. What about the civilian?"

"Probably nobody," I said, trying to keep my voice steady. It was *somebody*, all right, but I wasn't ready to tell Kate that was my father photographed with a bunch of Nazis. I was still trying to absorb that information. "The soldiers are the key to whatever is going on here."

Fighting to keep my hands steady, I look the photograph

from Kate and flipped it over. The back was blank. The crease down the center was curious and I wondered if Hazel's husband had been forced to fold up the photograph in order to hide it. We could ask Hazel about that later. Otherwise, there were no clues.

"Unfortunately, the two men who could tell us the name of the third soldier are dead," I pointed out.

"Keep coming up with brilliant observations like that, Professor, and I might have to reconsider keeping you on the payroll."

"Well, you could always release the image of the third man in the photograph to the media, saying he's a wanted Nazi war criminal. It would be all over television and the Internet within hours. The media would eat that up. 'Nazi war criminal sought.' Someone may recognize him even all these years later. Some faces are very distinctive."

"OK, I might keep you on the payroll after all."

"I try to earn my keep."

Kate started the car. "You know, we're not that far from my uncle's house. It's right on the ocean and it has plenty of room. And Uncle Silas knows a thing or two about Nazis. He used to visit Goering and Albert Speer in their cells at Nuremberg."

"How far?"

"An hour." Kate smiled. "Maybe forty-five minutes if I drive fast."

"Pedal to the metal," I said.

In the side view mirror I caught a glimpse of a black Chevrolet following us up the exit ramp onto I-83. *Hmm.* There were about a million black Chevies on the road. The case was starting to make me paranoid.

KATE *DID* DRIVE FAST. We made two stops, one for coffee and another to make several copies of the photograph Hazel Miller had given us. A couple of times I thought I saw the black Chevrolet again, but maybe it was just my mind playing tricks on me. Who would have followed us all the way from Water-bury? Exactly forty-five minutes later, we were entering the town of Branford on Connecticut's coast. A winter's twilight was falling and we were caught in the evening commuter traffic. Red tail lights winked at us far into the distance.

"You're awfully quiet," Kate said.

"Just thinking." I'd been staring at the photo as if it might give up some secret, but all that happened was that my eyes began to hurt. The thoughts I'd had were not ones I was about to share with Kate. Not yet, at least.

I felt stiff and tired after riding in a car most of the day. Kate steadfastly refused to let me drive her government vehicle. She claimed I wasn't authorized, which was true; but more than that, Kate was a woman who wanted to be in the driver's seat.

My bladder ached from drinking too much rest stop coffee and my teeth felt furry from eating most of a box of doughnuts. I was looking forward to stretching my legs.

"You know what I can't imagine," Kate said, "is how Hazel kept that kind of secret to herself for so many years."

"She loved him. People are driven to do all sorts of ends for love."

"But her husband was a murderer, for God's sake."

"Maybe after she found out the truth, it still wasn't enough to give up what she had."

"What do you mean?"

"Her husband, the house, being part of a community," I said. "Some people are willing to trade high ideals for the sake of hanging on to what they have. It's about survival. I can understand that."

"What an odd thing to say, coming from the author of *Journey of Hope*."

"Why? Have you ever faced the possibility of losing every-thing, maybe even your life or the lives of your loved ones, unless you were willing to bend your personal moral code?"

Kate considered that a moment. "No," she finally said, powering past a slower car. "I suppose I haven't faced that test before. How about you?"

I thought about the photograph Hazel Miller had given us. "No, but I think I know people who have," I said. "Survival is our most powerful human instinct."

"If I were Hazel, I would have left him a long time ago," Kate said.

"Of course, there is another possible reason why Hazel kept quiet all those years," I said. "Deep down, maybe she didn't think what he did was all that wrong."

"You told Hazel Miller that you believe in redemption," Kate said. "Is that really true?"

"I was trying to ease an old woman's pain, Kate. I do believe in redemption, but not for someone like Joe Miller. He murdered children. He shot them in the snow after killing their parents. How do you overlook that?" I paused. "How does *God*?"

We drove for a while in silence. Kate turned off at the next exit and immediately the traffic-clogged commuter route was replaced by a tranquil New England country road. In the fading light I could see Cape Cod-style houses with wood-shingle siding lining the roadside. Here, closer to the coast, it had snowed recently and the countryside was dusted white. Windows glowed pleasantly with warm yellow light. Beside me, I could sense Kate relax after the long drive.

"Home?" I asked.

"Home."

The road grew narrow and became shadowed with bare winter trees. Sand spilled onto the blacktop. I rolled down the window and smelled ocean air.

Kate slowed the car and pulled into a long driveway with

entrance pillars made of smooth beach stones mortared together. The house ahead was sprawling and low-slung like a villa. I could hear surf crashing in the distance. Kate had called ahead, and an outside light winked on at our approach.

"Brace yourself," she warned. "You're about to meet Uncle Silas."

19

The sprawling waterfront estate was named Rock Bottom, a double-entendre that matched the dry sense of humor of its owner. As a successful young lawyer, Silas Crockett had purchased fifteen acres on Branford Bay for next to nothing years ago when the village was a simple summer retreat far removed from New York. It would be hard now to put a price tag on such a unique property and its long stretch of rocky beach dusted now with snow, but I guessed it must be worth millions.

A figure advanced out of the shadows beyond the spotlights. He was just a silhouette, but I could make out the trademark hank of white hair and the tall, gaunt figure. Just as I had seen on television, he leaned forward slightly as if forging ahead into a perpetual storm. Silas Crocket wasn't known for doing anything the easy way or for avoiding controversy.

Without a word, he went to Kate and caught her in a bone-crushing hug. Then he stepped back and held Kate at arm's length, studying her with a smile on his face.

Kate nodded in my direction. "Uncle Silas, this is Bram McCoy. He's a writer and a history professor."

Silas took my hand and gripped it. *Hard*. He stood up straight and to my surprise, he was taller than me by an inch or two. "History. Really. Some of the greatest lies ever written are in history books."

"Winston Churchill?" I asked.

"No," he said, still holding my hand. It felt like my fingers were locked in a vise. Hard to believe the man was deep into his eighties, maybe even coming up on ninety. "That's an original Silas Crockett witticism. Consider it yours for free, Professor McCoy. It's about goddamn time somebody started quoting me. I'm certainly old enough, and plenty wise enough."

"Uncle Silas, Bram is helping me with an investigation."

Silas finally released me and turned to Kate. "So that's what's troubling you."

"Is it that obvious?"

"Why else would you come to see me? Well, time enough later to explain your investigation," he said. "How have you been?"

"Good," she said. "Not much different from how I was when we talked last week."

"That was on the telephone," Silas said. "Does that really count as talking when family is involved? No matter. Now you're here. And you've brought a friend."

"A colleague," Kate said.

"Some of my best friends have been my colleagues," he said. "So have some of my worst enemies, now that I think about it. Come inside, both of you."

We followed him indoors. The house offered welcome warmth after the wind off the bay.

"First things first," Silas said. "Kate and I prefer scotch, so I hope you aren't one of these white wine sippers or worse yet, a mineral water fanatic."

"Scotch is fine. Just make sure you leave the bottle within reach."

Silas chuckled. "We'll see about that. I don't share my favorite double malt with just anyone, Professor McCoy."

The house had a kind of wide central corridor, off of which several rooms were located. As Kate had explained, Rock Bottom had begun as a simple cottage and been added on to time and again until it had achieved the New England equivalent of a sprawling villa. Each room and hallway was filled to overflowing with art and artifacts collected over a lifetime. Rock Bottom was a masculine place that smelled of cherry pipe tobacco and salt. I leaned closer to a particularly vivid seascape and squinted at the canvas. An original Homer Winslow. The furniture tended toward a British Colonial style, with lots of dark, carved wood and rattan. Every room seemed to contain leather chairs and sofas weathered by the sea air. The glass eyes of a Rocky Mountain sheep glared at me in one room, the eyes of a cougar in another. Swords and ancient battle spears hung from the walls, along with oil paintings darkened by age.

I knew that the likes of the Kennedys and Kissinger and even Margaret Thatcher had wandered these same rooms. Distinguished ghosts, indeed. Beyond the windows, I could hear waves crashing on the beach. This was a house of spirits and history.

We walked into the biggest room I had seen so far. A fire roared in a beach stone fireplace and the lights were low so that through the tall floor-to-ceiling windows I could see all the way to Long Island Sound. The old man handed me a glass of scotch. It tasted as if it dated back to the days of Sir Walter Scott.

"What an incredible house," I said.

"It suits an old man," he said. "I'm told it started out as a two-room cottage that the previous owner built mainly out of lumber that washed up on the beach. I've always liked the New England parsimony of that legend."

"You shouldn't be here all alone," Kate said.

"What, because I'm an old man? I have the housekeeper here all day and a handyman who lives in his own house within shouting distance. My neighbors are very nosy. I'm sure if I collapse on the beach, I won't lay there for more than an hour or two."

"Uncle Silas —"

He dismissed her concerns with a wave of his scotch glass. "Don't worry about me, my dear. I've had a long life and I will come to a quick end soon. Until then, I plan on living out the rest of my days on my own terms, as should we all."

"No one ever could tell you what to do," Kate said. "Not even Betty."

"Your aunt was the only one who ever came close," Silas said. A wave of sadness seemed to wash over him, and then just as quickly was gone. "God, how I miss that woman. If there's one good thing about death, it's that I may get to see her again if I'm lucky. How about you, Professor? Do you believe in the afterlife?"

"I'm not sure," I said. "But I'm in no hurry to find out."

"Oh, I like this one, Kate. He's much livelier than any of the others."

"Uncle Silas, please." Kate's face actually reddened, which I hadn't thought was possible. She shot me an apologetic glance. "He thinks he can get away with comments like that because he's old."

Silas laughed. "At this point in my life, I've earned the right to be nosy and brash. But I haven't forgotten how to be a good host. You two must be hungry. There's a nice clam chowder simmering on the stove. I know that down your way they prefer oyster stew and I have to admit I had a love affair with the stuff in my Washington days, back when the Chesapeake Bay actually had oysters. All that cream and butter. Absolutely delicious. Clam chowder is far humbler but it's perfect for a winter's night."

"Did you dig the clams yourself?" I asked.

"I walk out to dig them on the flats at low tide," he said. "It's how I get my exercise, though some say I've done enough muckraking for one lifetime."

"Why don't I get us some chowder?" Kate said, and disappeared through a doorway. I was a bit surprised because I had a hard time imagining Kate doing anything even remotely domestic. I had a feeling she would do just about anything for her uncle.

Silas topped off our glasses. For such an old man he had a quick way of moving, so that if you blinked he was already halfway across the room. His skin was tanned and leathery from time spent outdoors. He wore deerskin loafers, black wool slacks and a dark gray turtleneck sweater that for some reason made him resemble an explorer from one of those Antarctic explorers from a nineteenth-century expedition.

Age is not kind to most women, but some men look all the more striking and distinguished as they grow older. Silas Crockett was like some movie star's portrayal of himself. He had always looked so fierce on television, whether answering reporters' questions at a White House press conference or crossing swords on a Sunday morning talk show.

I was especially struck by his eyes. They were dark and deep-set, vaguely disturbing even now, hardly mellowed by age. Then I realized what it was: the old man did not wear eyeglasses. It had been a long time since I had seen an octogenarian without horn rims.

The old man cleared his throat and leaned forward in his chair, making the leather creak. He suddenly looked very serious. "While Kate is in the kitchen, Bram, we have time for a little man-to-man talk. What are your intentions toward my niece?"

My swallow of scotch went off course. I coughed as the fiery stuff burned a new path down my windpipe. "My intentions?"

"For your sake, I hope your intentions are honorable." The old man glared at me a long moment. Then he smiled. "Gotcha."

"You had me going there," I said uncomfortably.

The humor drained out of his eyes until they were as hard and dark as beach stones. "Let me tell you something, Bram. Kate is all the family I have left. I love that girl. I would go to the ends of the earth for her even now, old man that I am. That's just a little something to keep in mind."

Kate walked in. "Uncle Silas, leave poor Bram alone. It's no wonder I'm still single. He's been doing that to every guy I've brought home since I was sixteen."

"Is that what I am?" I asked, getting a mental picture of a parade of rejected men running the gauntlet at Rock Bottom. An image flashed in my head of the "Superbitch" emblem on her office door. "Just another guy you're bringing home?"

"Now, now, I didn't mean to start a lovers' quarrel," Silas said, getting to his feet. "Let's eat."

Lovers' quarrel? Kate and I exchanged a look at that one. I could see that we were both wondering how we felt about it. The *lover* part, not the *quarrel* part.

"Uncle Silas, Professor McCoy and I are simply working together," Kate said, trailing him into the dining room. "Nothing more."

"I'm a man of the world," Silas said. "And I can tell you that men and women will never simply *work* together. It's also why we need to get women out of the military."

"Now you're being an old school chauvinist," Kate said.

He sat down to his bowl of chowder and poured us all a glass of wine. "My dear, I may be a chauvinist. But I resent being called 'old school.' " He grinned. "I'm more like *Classics Illustrated.*"

Kate rolled her eyes.

20

A fter dinner, back in the great room with the roaring fireplace and a view of the bay, Silas poured three large cognacs. "I come from the smoking and drinking generation," he explained. "I gave up cigarettes when I turned seventy-five, but I think the booze is keeping me alive at this point."

Kate got up and dimmed the lights, so that the room was lit only by the glow from the fireplace. We could see the water flashing in the moonlight and the iridescence of the surf breaking on the rocky shore. Cognac in hand, I believe I could have sat there for eternity, admiring the view.

"Now tell me what's on your mind," the old man said.

"Uncle Silas, we came here because you were part of the International Military Tribunal at Nuremberg," Kate said. "You actually interviewed some of the Nazis."

"I can't say it was a pleasure," he said, sipping his cognac. "Some will tell you that being assigned to the Interrogations Division was something of a plum job, but talking with those Nazis was like feeding caged tigers with your bare hands and wondering if you were ever going to get your hand back. It was especially disturbing because on the surface they didn't *seem* like monsters. They were cultured men, even clever. The closest comparison I can make would be to Dr. Hannibal Lecter in that *Silence of the Lambs* film. You might enjoy a witty conversation with him, but given half a chance you knew he would eat your liver."

"Uncle Silas!"

The old man shrugged and sipped from the snifter. "Not all the Nazis were brought to justice by the IMT at Nuremberg. Thousands of SS men or men affiliated with the SS in Nazi-occupied nations simply faded into the fabric of war-torn Europe. These are the men OSI tracks down now. Of course, you know all this.

"Then there were the big fish. Hitler himself committed suicide in April nineteen forty-five because he didn't want to be captured. Smart move, because at that point in Berlin the Russians would have gotten him. The Reds snapped up a few others but the Allies ended up with most of the real leaders. Goering, of course, ate a cyanide pill in his cell and died."

"Some got away."

"Oh, yes. Adolf Eichman, Josef Mengele, Alois Brunner and Konrad Radl were the more famous ones. The Israelis eventually caught up with Eichman, and then he was put on trial and hanged for his war crimes. Mengele, a real monster who carried out pseudo medical experiments on Jewish children, went to Argentina. By all accounts he drowned while swimming in the ocean in nineteen eighty-seven. I don't know about Brunner and Radl."

"Brunner is believed to be living in Syria."

"My God. I didn't know that." Silas laughed. "It must be true that only the good die young. The desert must agree with him. He must be older than I am. Still, nobody knows what happened to Colonel Radl. He simply disappeared. One of the great mysteries of the war."

Kate shot me a look. "Uncle Silas, we want you to watch something."

She had a copy of the surveillance video from the store in North Bay. She clicked on her uncle's flat-screen television and popped a disk into the DVD player.

Silas leaned closer, squinted at the grainy image. "Good lord. Is that who I think it is?"

"That would be impossible," Kate said. "But it's certainly someone who looks like him."

"Radl." Silas nodded. "I recognize his face. It was everywhere at Nuremberg when we thought the trail might still be hot. Of course, no one had the surveillance capabilities or intelligence network that we have today. When was this taken?"

"Two days ago in a small town in Maryland, at a convenience store where a former SS corporal died of a heart attack during a robbery. The man on the tape is the suspect."

"A man wearing a uniform just like this one committed a murder yesterday in Waterbury," I added. "That's where we drove from."

Silas remained captivated by the image on his television screen. He played it back again. "Remarkable."

As we watched the scene in the convenience store acted out again silently in black and white, winter's chill seemed to sweep through the room. I caught myself shivering and took a large drink of cognac. It burned going down, but in a good way, like when you step into a hot tub.

Silas watched the sequence through one more time, then flicked off the television. He sat staring at the blank screen.

"Nobody believes that it's really him," I said. "It's impossible."

"Uncle Silas?"

Silas shook his head in disbelief and sipped his cognac.

"Tell him about the disks," I suggested.

Kate nodded. Silas stared into space and appeared to be

only half-listening, perhaps letting his thoughts drift back more than half a century to what had happened at Nuremberg. "The first victim had a shrine to the Nazis in his basement," Kate said. "Flags. A portrait of Hitler. Daggers. A strange bronze disk. You name it."

Silas raised an eyebrow. "Tell me about the beacon."

Kate looked surprised. "What did you call it?"

"A beacon. Some sort of radio device enclosed in a seamless circular housing emblazoned with a swastika and the Reich's eagle."

"How would you know what the disk looked like?"

The old man sighed. "I may have been a lawyer at Nuremberg, but I had friends involved in intelligence work. The OSS. Sometimes our jobs crossed paths."

"But I don't understand. How could someone have known about these disks — beacons — all those years ago?"

"Those were heady and confusing times," Silas said. "No one knew the extent of the so-called Final Solution, but the details began to come to light and we were all horrified. There were a lot of crazy rumors going around. Almost every day a new cache of documents was turning up or a secret testing ground was found for some Nazi super weapon. There was a lot of speculation about what had really happened to Hitler and members of the upper echelon who disappeared."

"Hitler committed suicide in Berlin," Kate said. "We all know that."

Silas shrugged. "The Russians got to his bunker first. Someone had reportedly made a half-assed attempt to burn his body but it wasn't done properly. As a general rule, the Germans were very meticulous about carrying out direct orders from the Fuhrer, even if it was his final wish. The very fact that the body was not properly incinerated seems suspicious."

"This sounds like some kind of conspiracy theory," Kate said. "Hitler died in his bunker like a coward, even while some soldiers were still fighting for their Fatherland. Hitler cheated everyone. End of story."

"Ah, but you see, the Allies never had actual proof that Adolf Hitler was dead. A good lawyer always seeks proof. There wasn't any in this case."

"He was just one man," Kate said. "And Germany was smashed."

"Then there were the rumors about the missing divisions," he said.

"What?"

"We had a good idea of German troop strength and the numbers of Wehrmacht and SS giving themselves up fell far short. It didn't seem possible that the Germans had lost millions of men on the Eastern Front, though battles like Stalingrad would explain what happened to so many troops. Compared to American losses in both Europe and the Pacific, the German death toll was hard to grasp. Still, the confusion over German losses on the Eastern Front also created an opportunity to conceal the whereabouts of several divisions."

"Where would they be?" I asked. The idea of a whole German army hiding out somewhere in 1945 sounded absurd.

"Dead, probably. Buried in the frozen mud of the Eastern Front or captured by the Russians and worked to death in Stalin's labor camps. Stalin, you know, killed something like twenty million of his own people, which makes the Nazis seem like dilettantes," Silas said. "Anyhow, there was some concern about the German troop numbers not adding up. You see, the United States had recently undertaken some interesting experiments in regards to moving and concealing large numbers of troops. The results were disastrous. But what if the Germans had tried the same thing and with more success?"

Kate and I looked at each other, bewildered. "Uncle Silas, we have no clue what you're talking about."

"It's classified information from sixty years ago, but I

suppose it's all right to share it. Stuff of legend at this point, really. Supposedly, the Germans built some kind of time machine. Project Time Reich."

"You mean even while the Germans knew they were losing the war, they were trying to engineer some kind of Fourth Reich?" Kate asked. "That's ridiculous."

Silas's dark eyes flashed at his niece. "Oh really? Then I suppose it's just an interesting coincidence that Colonel Konrad Radl was in charge of the project."

21

We went to bed after midnight. An ocean wind had sprung up over the bay, a real howler, and surf crashed on the beach. With the house so close to the bay and swathed in the darkness of the grounds, it felt like we were at the edge of the world.

Old Silas may have been proud of New England thrift, but he kept his sprawling house comfortably warm. It was something I was glad of as I slid under the quilt in one of the guest rooms, listening to the wind tug at the shutters and eaves. It had been my experience that houses along the water were constantly buffeted and battered by winds and storms. Hardly the ideal location for a house. In most New England towns people had the good sense in the olden days to build inland to be sheltered from the weather. Shore property was left to poor fishermen and vacationers.

My brain was swimming in a nice, warm layer of cognac. Kate had stopped after the first snifter but the old man and I kept pace with each other as he recounted some of his war stories. Silas Crockett had never toted a rifle or driven a tank, but as part of the International Military Tribunal he had been armed with a briefcase. Nonetheless, he and the rest of the Allies had carved up Europe even faster than Hitler.

Although the evening had been pleasant, the jocularity was somewhat forced as the night grew deeper and the storm outside picked up. We all sensed our unease and tried to ignore it, but all the same that didn't make it go away. It felt like ghosts from the past stalked the night.

Time Reich.

Konrad Radl.

Kate had guessed correctly that her uncle might know something about Time Reich and the mystery surrounding the fall of the Third Reich. Silas had told us what he knew about Time Reich, which wasn't much, only that the attempt to create a time machine was another desperate effort by the Nazi scientists to forge a super weapon.

I thought about the secret I had kept from Kate. What would she think if I told her my father had been photographed in the company of war criminals? I had not yet worked through it myself. I was trying to understand.

I took out the copy of the photograph I had made during one of our stops on the drive from Waterbury and looked at it again. The photograph that Joe Miller's widow, Hazel, had given us showed four men, three of them in SS uniforms. Two of the soldiers were dead. The third soldier would likely be targeted by the killer, who, somehow, was able to find these men more than half a century later.

The duplicated image was blurry, but it was clear enough for me to make out the faces. The two dead men stood on the right, the third soldier stood on the left. The tall, dark-haired man on the end, standing apart from the others and not smiling, wore civilian clothes and seemed to be appraising the photographer.

My father. My father working with the SS.

Looking at the photograph now, it felt like the world as I

knew it had been dumped out on the floor like a bowl of marbles, rolling in every direction. I switched off the lamp and lay in bed, listening to the wind howl. The cognac had made me pleasantly high, but now it was starting to give me a headache. Best thing to do was sleep it off. The last thing I wanted to do was think too much and let the truth about my father come crashing down on me. Some things were better analyzed by the light of day with a clear head.

I was starting to drift off when a sound in the hall brought me back to the present. Someone scratched at the door as if reluctant to knock. The door opened and closed. Whoever it was had slipped inside.

"Hey, you still awake?" Kate whispered.

"Yeah." I propped myself up in bed and Kate sat on the edge of the mattress. It was not a situation I had expected. I asked myself how I felt about Kate sitting on my bed and decided I liked it. The fact that we were in her uncle's guest bedroom also made it kind of sneaky, like we were teenagers doing something naughty. "For a second there, I was worried it was your Uncle Silas."

"He's not that lonely, believe me."

"What about you? Couldn't sleep?"

"Something like that," she said. "Actually, I had a question."

"You wandered down here in the dead of night to ask me a question? Pardon me if I sound disappointed."

"It's important."

"I'm sure."

She gave her head a toss, flinging her long brown hair out of her face. Considering that she normally wore her hair pulled back, it was a surprisingly intimate gesture. "I want to know why you're really doing this. Helping with the investigation, I mean."

I was surprised. "You mean you don't know? Then ask yourself why you're doing it, and I'm sure it's not for the great pay and federal pension twenty years down the road."

"Tell me."

"This could take a while," I said. "You might want to make yourself more comfortable here under the covers with me."

She clutched at her bathrobe and smiled. "That's not why I'm here. Now tell me."

"I hate Nazis," I said. "I'd hitchhike to Siberia if I thought I could catch the last one. I'm also fascinated by them. I've tried being a college professor, and the truth is that I wasn't a very good one. I'll admit I was kind of half-hearted when it came to teaching. That thing with the undergraduate was really just an excuse to get rid of me for other reasons, mainly malfeasance in the classroom. I'm helping you because I would give almost anything to catch someone like Konrad Radl, or at least solve the mystery of what happened to him. You really came in here to ask me that?"

"Yes," she said. "I couldn't sleep. I guess that coming here made me wonder what the hell I'm doing with my life, and I needed to know if I was the only crazy one."

"You're not. Now, if you're not going to stay, go the hell back to bed so we can both get some sleep."

Kate smiled, tousled my hair. "Good night." She went out into the hall and shut the door behind her. Somewhere above the wind outside I thought I heard the whine of a boat engine out on the bay. That struck me as odd. It was too late at night and too rough for some fisherman to be out.

I burrowed under the covers. Maybe I was getting old, but I was kind of relieved Kate was gone. All of Silas's cognac had made me sleepy. And I couldn't quite get around that "Super-bitch" thing. You had to admit it wasn't the sexiest nickname.

Still, I thought about trailing after her. The downside of that was I didn't know which room was hers and the thought of wandering into the old man's boudoir by mistake conjured up all sorts of unpleasant scenarios. My irresponsible self spoke up and said, 'Bram, you deserve for your tallywhacker to dry up and fall off, often as you put it to any use.' My mature and sensible self simply yawned and pulled the quilt up to my chin.

I was just drifting off when I heard Kate's voice next to the bed again. "Bram." Her hand touched my shoulder. "I think there's someone outside."

22

"What do you mean someone's outside? Like a prowler?"

"On the way back to my room I went through the living room and there was a light out on the bay, which was odd in the middle of winter. The light came right up on the beach. I halfway thought I was seeing things until a few minutes later I saw someone walk right past the window."

Fully awake now, I flung back the covers and grabbed for my pants. "Let's not freak out just yet. Maybe it's your uncle's groundskeeper or something."

"What, Paul? He's got better sense than to be out on the bay tonight, and if he wanted to come in the house he would just walk right in. He's like family."

"Call the police."

Kate grabbed for the phone beside the bed and punched in 9-1-1. She looked blankly at the phone a second, then slammed it down. "Phone's dead."

"Either your uncle forgot to pay the phone bill or somebody cut the lines. Where's your cell phone?"

"Back in my room."

"Let's get it. Now."

We went out in the hall. If the phone had not been dead, I would have been the first to admit we were overreacting. Our conversation with Silas about the horrors of the Nazi past and the fact that we had just investigated two murders had admittedly left us spooked. The storm outside didn't help.

Kate and I left the lights off. It was a big house, but not so big that we couldn't hear someone rattling the doorknob in the kitchen.

"Did you hear that?" Kate demanded, sounding scared. That disturbed me more than anything, because Kate was not a person who frightened easily. "He's trying to get in!"

"Does this place have an alarm system?"

"Yes, but it's connected to the phone lines."

"Come on, let's get to your room."

We raced down the dark hallway. The problem with big houses is that it takes a while to get from one place to the next. Not to mention that I kept bumping into things in the dark.

Behind us we heard breaking glass.

"Go on," I said. "Call for help with your cell phone, then go to your uncle's room. I'll see what he wants."

"Bram —

"*Go.*"

I was trying to act calm for Kate's sake, but my heart was pounding. Who the hell was breaking into the house? I was sure the intruder hadn't picked tonight to get even with Silas Crockett for some decades-old political slight. That left two possibilities. First, that the intruder had something to do with my run-in with the skinheads in Baltimore last night. If that was the case, we had a chance against some neo-Nazi with a shaved head. But how would they have found me here? The second possibility was that this guy was coming after us because of the Time Reich investigation. That scenario was far scarier.

At the other end of the long hall, I heard the creak of footsteps. *He's in the house.* The salt smell of the bay blew in through the shattered window. Looking around, I saw one of Silas's antique swords on the wall and grabbed it down. The old broadsword was damn heavy, its edge pitted and dull as a butter knife, but it was the only weapon at hand. I stepped into a darkened doorway and waited, wondering if the thudding of my heart would be enough to give me away. My mind flashed back to East Berlin and my youthful foolishness playing Nazi hunter, dodging down dark alleys a step ahead of what were then the communist authorities. That had been nothing like this. I grasped the sword in both hands and held it high overhead.

Seconds later, I heard breathing that wasn't my own, then the sound of stealthy footsteps on the long oriental carpet runner. I gripped the sword harder and forced myself to believe that this was for real.

"Bram, where the hell are you?" Kate shouted from down the hall.

I realized she must be standing in the hallway, silhouetted in the half-light. A dark figure materialized in front of me, raised what appeared to be a pistol, and leveled it at Kate.

"Get down!" I shouted, then swung the sword like I was trying to split firewood. I was swinging at his head but he threw up an arm to block the blade. He grunted as the dull edge connected.

If I'd been faster or if the blade had been sharp I would have killed him. Instead, the shadow before me began to turn, the pistol seeking a new target. I swung again, the heavy blade striking the gun barrel and filling the hallway with the clash of steel on steel. The gun went off. The muzzle flash stabbed down and buried itself in the hall carpet. My ears rang.

Dropping the sword, I grabbed at his torso and tried to take him down. But to my surprise he was slippery. *Wet suit,* I thought. I couldn't get a good grip. He stepped back in a perfect defensive move that threw me off balance and I fell on the carpet in a heap. So much for my martial arts skills.

Instead of turning and running he hit me in the head with the barrel of the pistol. *Hard.* I saw white stars like some cartoon character and found myself on the floor, but my vision wasn't so blurry that I couldn't see Kate down the hall taking up a perfect shooting stance, feet spread, handgun held shoulder high with arms slightly bent. I hugged the floor as she fired over my head.

Blam. Blam. Pause. *Blam. Blam.*

The noise in the hallway was deafening. When the shooting stopped, I scrambled toward Kate, expecting at any second for the intruder's pistol to blow the top of my head off. I reached Kate and both of us ducked into the room. A shot ripped out at the same instant, the *whunk* of a bullet tearing into the door frame.

Crouching near the floor now, Kate peered out the door, then fired several shots down the hall. We heard a grunt of pain and surprise.

"He's running!" she shouted. We piled into the hallway. The lights came on and I blinked savagely in the sudden brightness.

Silas was standing behind us, aiming a double-barreled shotgun. Not a hair was out of place and he was wearing a smoking jacket and silk slippers. I had no doubt that he would have coolly shot whoever came through the bedroom door.

Behind him, French doors faced the lawn and beach. It was a dark night, but I could make out an even darker figure running toward the beach. He was outlined against the snow.

"Give me the gun!" I shouted at Silas, grabbing for the shotgun. I got the French doors unlocked and sprinted across the lawn.

A light appeared, and then the sharp whine of a Jet Ski engine. Already, the craft was bucking against the waves toward the bay. The wind was like a wall but I battered against it. I ran out into the water, slogging up to my knees, then my waist. At first it seemed like I might have a chance of catching him, but then the engine whined louder and the stern light shot away.

The shotgun was useless at that range but I fired both barrels anyway, hoping the sight of the twin muzzle flashes would give him something to think about, if nothing else. Frustrated, I watched the lights of the Jet Ski grow smaller and finally become a pinpoint racing across the bay.

Then I realized I was standing up to my armpits in the cold ocean. I could feel my blood turning to sludge. I waded back toward shore, freezing now, the wind cutting like a razor on my wet skin. Barefoot, I followed my tracks back across the snow. Kate and Silas were in the bedroom, watching through the open French doors.

"Got away," I tried to explain, my teeth chattering.

"Jesus, get in the house," Kate said. "Are you out of your mind, chasing him like that? What were you going to do, swim after him?"

"Kate, never mind that," Silas said, taking charge. "He needs to get warm immediately. I'll put him in the shower, you go wait for the police. They ought to be here any minute."

By then I was shivering so badly out of a combination of fear, anger and simple hypothermia that I allowed myself to be guided across the room by an octogenarian and pushed unceremoniously into a large shower stall. His sinewy old hands fiddled with the faucet and soon hot, steamy water was pouring over me.

"Warm up," he said over the streaming water. "When you're ready, put on some of my clothes and meet us in the kitchen. We need to figure out what just happened."

I pulled off my shirt and let the hot water flood over me, running over my head, across my shoulders and down my chilled body. The wet fabric of my slacks clung to my legs. My feet felt completely numb.

I stood in the shower a long while, letting my body warm up and my thudding heart calm down. There were still about two quarts of adrenalin pumping through my system. I must have lost track of time because Kate's voice just beyond the shower stall startled me enough to set my heart pounding all over again.

"Goddammit," I said. "What are you trying to do, give me a heart attack?"

"That was a stupid thing to do," she said. "Running after the guy, chasing him clear into the ocean. If he had bothered to stop and fire one shot, he probably would have killed you."

"If he had stopped, I would have killed him with your uncle's shotgun."

"Men," she said. "You've always got to be so macho."

"Do you mind?" I said. "I'm trying to take a shower here. You'd better go wait with your uncle."

"The police are already here. He's talking to them in the kitchen."

"I'll be out in a minute." I put my head under again, felt the hot water course over me.

She yanked back the shower curtain. "OK, Professor, that's enough with the shower already. We've got work to do."

I turned off the water and she threw a towel at me. "Close your eyes," I said, then stripped off my soaking-wet pants and wrapped myself in the towel.

I walked over to Silas's wardrobe and pulled out dry boxer shorts, socks, khakis and a T-shirt. Silas and I were basically the same size and the clothes were a pretty good fit. I couldn't help but notice that his clothes were much finer than mine.

Meanwhile, Kate was pacing the room, walking to the French doors and looking out toward the dark sea. She tugged at the doors to make certain they were locked. Then she swung out the cylinder on a sturdy looking .38 special revolver, emptied the spent cartridges, reloaded, and locked the cylinder back in place. Her hands shook, but she handled the gun with familiarity, and it occurred to me that Kate was full of surprises. I wanted to ask her about the gun, but I was worried that if I startled her just then by so much as opening my mouth she might shoot me.

Instead, I found one of the old man's turtleneck sweaters and pulled it on.

Kate was watching me. "That's spooky," she said. "Now that you're wearing his clothes, you kind of look like him, forty-plus years younger."

"There's only one Silas Crockett," I pointed out.

"Thank God for that," Kate said. Then: "Who was he?"

I had been wondering the same thing. The intruder who had broken into the house wasn't some cat burglar or strung-out skinhead. He had come to Silas's house with a deadly purpose in mind. This could only have had something to do with the deaths of the two former Nazis we were investigating. Had the intruder come to stop us or to find something? The beacon was safe at an FBI lab in Washington. Had the intruder wanted that? We had stumbled upon something that was far more dangerous than either Kate or I knew.

Whoever the intruder was, he had come prepared with a gun, a wetsuit and a Jet Ski. This had taken some planning. Maybe I was wrong about the skinheads. Perhaps they were better organized than I thought. After I fended off the two attackers in the garage, they may have decided to send someone with more skill to get the job done. These groups had connections to all sorts of paramilitary types.

I thought about the Chevy I had glimpsed behind us as we left Waterbury. Had we been followed here?

What I said to Kate was: "To hell if I know who just tried to kill us."

23

I n the kitchen, Silas was sitting at the head of the table as if presiding over a conference. Three police officers sat in chairs, all of them fidgeting with cups of coffee. They glanced up at me, then went back to studying their coffee. The local police appeared more puzzled than anything else. This was beyond their scope of experience in chasing teenagers off the beach for drinking beer.

"We can put a patrol car out front, if that makes you feel better," one of the cops offered.

"He came in off the water," Kate said, sounding exasperated.

Silas smiled politely, but he looked pained by the conversation with the local police. "This is my niece's colleague, Professor Abraham McCoy," he said, introducing me. "He chased whoever it was across the lawn with my shotgun. While you talk to him, I'm just going to make a phone call."

The old man excused himself and the three cops turned their attention to me. Apparently, they had already interviewed Kate and Silas.

"Any idea who might have done this?" the senior cop asked.

"I'm really not sure," I said, keeping my theories to myself. "Whoever it was came with a clear intention of doing harm."

"Like an assassin," the youngest cop suggested, which earned him stern looks from his colleagues.

"Exactly like an assassin," I agreed. "I hit him pretty hard with a broadsword, and then he opened fire on Agent Crockett in the bedroom hallway. She apparently wounded him with her own weapon. Then I chased him down to the beach and fired two shots at him with a twelve-gauge."

The cops were looking at me wide-eyed.

"Hell, that sounds like more fireworks than we had on the Fourth of July," the young cop said.

"Hey, Pete, why don't you go wait outside for the guys from the state police crime lab?" the older cop suggested. Reluctantly, the young town cop got up from the table.

"You mean you haven't even dusted for fingerprints?" Kate asked in disbelief.

"We're going to let the state police team from Hartford do that," he said.

"It won't matter," I said. "I got a good look at him when I hit him with the sword. He was wearing a wetsuit and what appeared to be Neoprene gloves. You won't find any fingerprints."

"Then I'll tell Paul to board it up," Silas announced, marching back into the kitchen ahead of a large and beefy man carrying a Skilsaw and a tool belt. "The intruder broke a window to get in and it's damn cold out tonight."

The Branford cop said: "I don't know —"

"It'll be all right," Silas said firmly, settling the matter. "Board it up, Paul. It's getting cold in the house."

I got up from the table and went outside to help Silas's handyman wrestle a sheet of plywood across the broken window. Because of the wind, it was a two-man job. In the light from the outdoor floodlights, Paul deftly measured and cut the plywood with his cordless circular saw and I held the sheet in place while he drove screws through the plywood into the window frame. My father had always been handy around the house but I had never picked up any of his skills, although I knew enough to hold a sheet of plywood in place on a windy night. Mostly, I guess dad had tried to teach me when I was fourteen or fifteen, at a time when I really wasn't interested in learning anything from him. Too bad I hadn't listened. But I had only wanted to hear his stories about Nazis, not how to measure and saw and nail.

I wasn't all that interested in learning carpentry skills. What I really wanted was to get a close-up look at the handyman to make sure he hadn't been the guy in the wetsuit. I quickly ruled him out. Paul was a burly man with hands like catchers' mitts and a belly that he used skillfully to pin the plywood in place until it could be screwed down. Our attacker had been fit and trim.

"Has Silas had any trouble lately, any threats or anything?" I asked, blowing on my numb fingers.

"He's got kind of this running feud with the neighbors about their dog," Paul said. "But I don't think anyone would try to kill him over trying to keep their dog from shitting on the lawn."

"Probably not. Actually, I was thinking on a bigger scale. Any unresolved political grudges? You'd know about that kind of thing. You're around here every day."

"No, nothing like that. Mr. Crockett has been out of the spotlight for a while. He doesn't even get many visitors anymore."

Pete, the young cop, found us out back. "Hey, is that your Malibu out front?" he asked.

"Aren't you supposed to be watching for the state guys?" I asked.

"They're not here yet," he said. "Anyway, I thought I better tell you that your car is trashed."

"What?"

"Yeah. Whoever that guy was, he must have paid a visit to your car before he tried to break into the house."

I left Paul to put the finishing touches on the plywood and walked out front with the cop.

He wasn't kidding about the car. The side window was smashed, the trunk open. It looked as if a tornado had touched down just on the car.

"He slashed the seats too," Pete said.

I peered inside. Sure enough, a knife had been taken to the seats, exposing the foam inside. The glove box was open and the contents were now scattered on the passenger seat and floorboards. A few papers fluttered away across the lawn, ghostly on the crusted snow. Even the tires were flat, each punctured with a sharp blade.

"Nice car," the young cop said. "I can't understand why anyone would trash it like that. Doesn't make sense."

"Sure it does," I said. "He was looking for something."

The young cop seemed surprised. "Like what?"

I shrugged. "Who knows? Maybe a forgotten secret from the Third Reich."

"You mean, like, Hitler?"

That's when the crime scene guys drove up.

THE TWO STATE police crime lab techs were not happy with Paul and me for putting up plywood across the broken window but they dusted for fingerprints anyway. They grumbled about being rousted out of bed, but Silas Crockett was a *somebody*, so investigating a crime at his personal home was not something that could be put off until morning. I tried to explain about the intruder wearing gloves, but the state techs ignored me so I went back to the kitchen to pour myself a coffee and maybe a cognac too.

The Branford cops were still there, filling out some paperwork but making noises like they were getting ready to leave. I noticed that they treated Silas with a great deal of deference. Silas Crockett was a personal friend of the last four presidents of the United States. He was also rich as Midas. If you wanted to remain employed by the town of Branford and collect your pension, you had better treat him right.

And there were some new arrivals. Two very professional-looking types were setting up shop in the kitchen. One was white, the other African-American. Both had hair cut so short you could see the sheen of their scalps. They weren't especially tall, but they were broad through the shoulders and chest, all muscle and meat like some aggressive breed of dog. Definitely ex-military types or even CIA. Now I understood why Silas had excused himself to make a phone call about an hour ago.

The two watchdogs gave me a quick look-over when I walked in, sizing me up, then went back to unloading some gear from black duffel bags. A pair of night-vision goggles appeared. Then a submachine gun and a very nasty looking assault shotgun. It was a far more impressive arsenal than a dull broadsword and a skeet gun. Neither of these guys said much, and frankly, they made me nervous.

The crime scene guys had finished up in the living room and they passed through the kitchen on the way to examining the hallway. They did a double-take at the sight of the weaponry, mumbled something, and disappeared toward the bedrooms.

The Branford cops made their exit, talking louder than necessary and making repeated promises to be back first thing in the morning.

Silas motioned Kate and me out of the room and followed.

He didn't bother to explain who the two gentlemen in the kitchen were and we didn't ask.

Paul had finished boarding up the window and was in the living room sweeping up the broken glass. He had also rekindled the fireplace. Silas went and stood by it, soaking up the heat, and Paul shoved a leather chair close so the old man could sit.

"Thank you, Paul," Silas said. "We can worry about repairs in the morning."

The handyman gave us a nod and went out.

"What a night," Kate said. I could see that all her nervous energy had flared off and she was running on fumes. I think we all were at that point.

"This is a serious matter," said Silas, slumped in the chair and looking every bit of his advanced age. "Someone came into my house with the clear intent to do harm."

Kate sat on the floor beside the chair and touched her uncle's arm. "He wasn't after you," Kate said.

"Don't you think I already know that?" Silas snapped, some of his old fire returning. "You two have stumbled onto something very dangerous. You need to get to the bottom of it and find out what the hell this is all about."

"I could turn this whole investigation over to someone else in my office," Kate said. "I'm not the only investigator at OSI."

No," said Silas with finality. "When did a Crockett ever run from a fight? We crush our enemies and gnaw their bones. And that's just what you're going to do."

I brought the old man a cognac and he smiled gratefully. He drank it down, then pulled a throw blanket across himself, making it clear he planned to sleep in the chair by the fire. Kate curled into another chair. I stretched out on the leather sofa. The room was filled with the creak and groan of leather and the popping of the fire. Outside, wind still gnawed at the house. The fact that there were two armed men on guard duty in the kitchen made me feel more nervous than secure, but at least we wouldn't have to worry about a repeat performance of what had happened earlier that night. I thought I was too keyed up to sleep, but I surprised myself by drifting off.

Right before I went out, I had a final thought: whoever had attacked us had gotten away, and he would be back. Not tonight, and not necessarily at Rock Bottom, but something Kate and I had found was worth killing for. I slipped into an uneasy sleep, haunted by the stuff of nightmares.

24

T V crews arrived during the night and were now parked out front on the road, but the house was too far back for them to see much of anything. It seemed that an attack on the former secretary of state was still considered newsworthy.

The wind had blown in wet weather. Stinging rain mixed with fat balls of sleet pelted the media corps, who huddled miserably inside their vans and rental cars, clutching cups of lukewarm coffee. Paul went down and shut the gate just in case any of the reporters got up enough nerve to actually knock on the front door. A state police trooper arrived and parked in front of the gate, promising to arrest anyone who set foot on Silas Crockett's property.

The one car to make it through belonged to the Branford police chief, who looked even more anxious than he had at Silas's kitchen table last night. We gathered around the table again for another conference.

"We found a Jet Ski this morning washed up on the beach in Green's Cove," the chief said.

"Where's that?" I asked.

"About five miles by car, maybe a mile by water."

"You think maybe Kate wounded him badly enough that he fell off and drowned?" Silas asked.

The chief shook his head. "There wasn't enough blood for that here in the house or in the snow leading down to the beach. He probably had just a scratch."

"I could have sworn I hit him pretty hard. I was so close."

"Look, I was on the Boston police for twenty years before coming down here. I saw my share of shootings. I've seen gunfights where twenty rounds get fired with everybody within ten yards of each other and nobody gets hit." His eyes slid to Kate to check her reaction. Seeing her nod, he went on. "What you see on TV with these great shots is, well, it's a television show."

"Maybe you got him," I said.

"Maybe, maybe not," Kate said. "There are a lot of roads that go right down to the beach. I think what he probably did was ditch the Jet Ski and get to a car he had parked somewhere. Or somebody picked him up. He could be anywhere by now."

"Did you try to track down where the Jet Ski came from?" I asked.

"It was stolen from a dock in Green's Cove. A lot of people around here have them. We tracked the registration. The owner didn't know it was missing until I called this morning."

"In other words, the Jet Ski is a dead end," Kate said.

"Looks like it."

I stood up and paced the room, wondering about what the chief had said. What it all came down to was that we really didn't have any idea who had invaded the house, or why.

"The chief and I have already talked about this and we agree that the police are going to hold a press conference later," Silas said. "I told them to say someone broke in but they were frightened off and no one was hurt."

"I don't think it's any secret at this point that shots were fired," Kate said. "But we need to downplay that. If one of the reporters asks about it — and I'm sure one of them will — we need to say that no one was shot. That smothers the fire before it can start burning."

The police chief nodded. "No problem."

"What are we doing next?" I wanted to know. "There's no point in staying here."

"There's someone you need to see in Washington," Silas said.

"Who?"

"He works for ONR."

"What's that?" I asked.

Silas gave the police chief an affable smile. "Would you excuse us, please? Maybe you and my niece can work out some of the details of what you'll say to the media."

We slipped out of the kitchen and left Kate to entertain the chief.

"Office of Naval Research," Silas explained, once we were alone "There are some things he needs to tell you . . . and show you . . . about Time Reich."

"So the government actually knew what the Germans were up to?"

Silas shrugged. "They built rockets and jet planes ahead of us, made nerve gas and crematoriums and created codes we couldn't crack. Why wouldn't they have attempted to travel through time as well?"

"You're telling me they succeeded?"

"No one really knows that, Bram. But there's the possibility that they had some success. I think that in light of recent events we really have to consider that the Germans did at least dabble in time travel."

I shook my head. "I don't know. Time travel? Think about it."

"Yes," said Silas. "Think about it."

Kate came out of the kitchen and found us. "I think the chief is all set. He just left. He knows what to say, as long as he doesn't slip up. He's nervous. Talking in front of a camera isn't something he does every day. Maybe you ought to do this, Uncle Silas."

"Me? Never. This is a police matter. Meanwhile, let's go check on the barbarians at the gate, shall we?"

We went outside. The media people in the distance saw us and there was a flurry of action among the white news vans sprouting antennae and satellite dishes. From this distance I could see a lot of bundled-up people clutching take-out cups of coffee to keep warm. Umbrellas popped like black dandelions at the far side of the wintry lawn, keeping off the rain and sleet. All eyes were on us and I shoved my hands into my pockets to keep from waving. I wondered if this was how the elk and bison felt at Yellowstone Park during the height of tourist season.

"Well, it's pretty clear we're not going anywhere in *that*," I said, nodding at Kate's damaged car. "But we'll need to get to the airport somehow."

I noticed the old man glance questioningly at Kate, but she wouldn't meet his gaze. "You can take my vehicle," he offered. "I have a Hummer in the garage."

"Thanks, but a plane would get us there faster," I said. "Maybe you can have Paul run us up to Hartford. What is that, about forty-five minutes from here?"

Kate appeared to be studiously ignoring both of us while listening intently at the same time. I didn't have a clue what was going on. "Kate doesn't fly," Silas said.

"You don't fly?" This surprised me because Kate seemed so fearless. Just last night I had watched this woman shoot it out with the man who had broken into her uncle's house. "As in, you don't like planes?"

"No."

"But you've been to Europe —"

"*QE II*," she said.

"You know, I used to have a terrible fear of heights. Got dizzy and everything. Then I realized that I really wasn't afraid of falling at all. It was the landing part that bothered me."

"Are you trying to make me feel better, McCoy, or are you just trying to annoy me?"

"Don't get mad about it," I said, continuing to goad her. There was something enjoyable about ruffling her feathers. Some juvenile part of me liked to see her all hot and bothered. I don't know why I was so surprised that she didn't like to fly. I guess I just hadn't expected Kate to have any phobias or similar chinks in her armor. And then I remembered having dinner in North Bay, how she had told me. *My parents died in a plane crash.* "Oh. Listen, I'm an idiot."

"Is that a confession or an apology?" Kate walked toward the garage door, which was starting to go up. As the door lifted, it revealed a new Hummer SUV gleaming darkly under the garage light. The big vehicle hunkered like a beast, knobby tires brushing the concrete like the knuckles of a gorilla.

"Okay, we hit the road on one condition," I said.

"What's that?"

"I get to drive."

25

S
ex would be at the top of any man's list of good things. Closely followed by a cold beer on a hot day. The tug of a fish on your line. War movies. A big fat pizza. Also pretty high on that list would be a jet black Hummer with a big engine and plenty of attitude. The huge tires churned through the icy slush on the roads along the Connecticut coast. The stereo wasn't bad, either, although Silas Crockett's collection of big band CDs left something to be desired. Glen Miller wasn't my idea of driving music. If we saw a music store near the highway, I vowed to pull off and buy some tunes for the road: Nirvana, old school Led Zeppelin, maybe even some Metallica.

"Sweet," I said, rolling past other drivers in their puny cars.

"Give me a break," Kate said. "You sound like you're in high school."

"I wish I'd *had* this baby back in high school. It would have been a chick magnet. Actually, I'm surprised your uncle drives one. I figured him for a Cadillac man."

"Silas likes to be different," Kate said. "He's also got this latent macho thing going."

"That explains the antique guns and swords on the walls."

"He's very into the warrior myth. He even re-reads *Beowulf* from time to time, just for fun. He has a signed copy of the Seamus Heaney translation."

"Silas does seem to have more weapons than some museums," I admitted. "But that doesn't explain how *you* came to have a gun last night. OSI agents don't carry sidearms. And you knew how to use it. You're just full of surprises, aren't you?"

"Uncle Silas taught me how to shoot it years ago. Sometimes when I stayed at Rock Bottom by myself I've gotten a little spooked and the gun gave me some peace of mind. I keep it in a drawer beside the bed."

"It came in handy last night."

"Sure did," said Kate. "That's why I've got it in my purse right now."

"Oh boy. Have you got a permit for that thing?"

"At the moment I'm not worried about that particular detail."

We passed a Ford Expedition and the people inside flashed us an envious look. Compared to the Hummer, the Ford looked like someone's imitation of tough, like a biker jacket made out of pleather. I glanced in the rearview mirror and caught myself grinning.

"What makes women happy?" I asked.

"What do you mean?"

"You know, finding a really good sale at the mall, eating ice cream, having babies."

"Ugh. Give me a break."

"I'm serious. What makes women happy?"

"Well . . . relationships, I suppose. Not the male-female thing necessarily but just having good friends, deep conversations. And then I would have to say chocolate. That's pretty universal. I'm not much into shopping personally but that does make a lot of women happy. The baby thing sounds good until you're up at three a.m. changing diapers."

"Sounds like you're speaking from experience," I said.

"Some of my friends have dropped out of their careers to do the family thing and I can pretty much tell you there's not a single one who doesn't wonder if she's made a mistake."

"That's bleak."

"No, it's society," Kate said. "We measure our self-worth in terms of careers, what we've accomplished and how much money we make. Raising babies is for welfare mothers. Or soccer moms, which is just another kind of ghetto. If you enjoy staying home and raising your children, everybody thinks there's something wrong with you."

"Listening to you, it's a wonder the human race has continued."

"Believe me, it probably wouldn't have if it hadn't been for sex. There's always a down side to anything good. Like chocolate. It makes you fat."

"And the downside of sex?" I asked.

"It makes you pregnant. Which leads to changing diapers in the middle of the night."

"Unnhh."

"That's what men do when you violate their comfort zone in conversation," Kate said. "They say 'unnhh' and get all quiet. Even college professors."

"Not if they're driving a fifty-thousand-dollar Hummer," I said, and mashed down the gas pedal. Dirty gray slush covered the roads but traffic hadn't slowed down. New England drivers were used to this mess. Later, as we headed down I-95, we talked about the investigation. Both of us had the feeling that this thing was getting out of control.

"I can't believe someone broke into Uncle Silas's house last night and tried to kill us. The question is, who was it and what did he want?"

"He went over your car pretty thoroughly. He was looking for something. When he didn't find it there he came after us."

"But what did he *want*?"

"I don't know," I said. "Maybe he wanted the disk we took from Hans Schmidt's house. Maybe he was coming after me, or you, or both of us."

"There is another possibility," Kate said. "The photograph we got from Hazel Miller."

"That thought had crossed my mind," I said.

"How would anyone else know about it?" Kate asked.

"The killer knew where to find Joe Miller. He knew the man's history. He might have known about the photograph too." I slowed the Hummer down, slipped across a couple of lanes toward an exit coming up. "Look, there's something I need to tell you that's going to blow your mind."

"What?"

"We've got to get off the highway first."

I drove down the exit, not even bothering to check the sign to see where we were headed. What I was about to tell Kate wasn't something you tried to explain while negotiating I-95 at seventy-fives miles per hour. The shoulder widened out and I pulled over. Sleet popped against the windshield.

"Okay, what's such a big deal?"

"Look at the photo again."

She took it out of the glove box. "What am I looking for?"

"See the men in the photograph? We know Hans Schmidt, we know Joe Miller. We don't know who the third Nazi is. But we do know the fourth man in civilian clothes, the one wearing the suit."

"You figured it out?" Kate was instantly excited. "Bram, that's wonderful. Who is it?"

"He's my father."

Kate laughed. "Very funny. Now tell me who it is."

When I didn't answer, Kate stopped laughing.

"That's impossible," she said. "How could that be? Your

father was a concentration camp inmate. What would he be doing in the photograph?"

"Don't think I haven't wondered about that. I thought I could be wrong about the picture. But it's him, all right."

"You're imagining things," she said.

"No, I'm not. That's my father in the photograph. I can tell you he definitely was not a Nazi. He hated the Nazis. But the photograph answers a lot of questions about my father."

"It seems to me this would only create more."

"Yes and no. I always wondered how he survived the camp, Kate. He was there for years. Think about it. It was cold all the time, there wasn't enough to eat, people got sick. But look at him, for God's sake. He's wearing a ratty old suit but it's not a camp uniform. The soldiers are standing a little apart from him. Look at the body language in the photograph — they don't consider him an equal, but there's still a kind of respect."

"He was a *Kapo*," she said, using the term for Jews who had become the jailors of their own people in exchange for favored treatment, such as better food. A *Kapo* was something like a trustee in prison, an inmate given special privileges for carrying out some essential duty, like running the prison kitchen. In the camps, *Kapos* were reviled as traitors by the other inmates. They were often even more cruel than the SS guards.

"Not a *Kapo*. They were mostly thugs with sticks anyway, and that wasn't my father. He was an educated man. He was an engineer, a building designer. There were a lot of Jews like him who maybe did the accounts or the office work or even the plumbing. They were useful to the Germans, a class of prisoners who stayed alive by using their skills to help their SS captors."

"My God," she said, getting it now. "He *worked* for them. He worked for these men in the photograph. What did he do for them?"

"He helped them do more than build barracks," I said. "Dad

was an engineer. Judging by the identity of two of the SS men in the photograph, I'd have to say he helped them build something to do with Time Reich."

Kate appeared even more shocked than I expected. She spent a long time just looking out the window. "But what about your book?" she finally asked. "*Journey of Hope* is such a beautiful book. It's all about your father's struggle to survive the camps and the lives of the others there. He writes about daily life at Dachau. It's all so vivid."

"I'm trying to come to grips with the journals and with *Journey of Hope*. He wrote the truth about camp life." I realized I was getting defensive and softened my tone. "The fact is, Kate, that I've always wondered about the journals. My father never wrote about being hungry or sick, but he does describe many times how he gave food away or nursed others. I always questioned how he had extra food when everyone around him was starving, or how he not only obtained some rudimentary medicines but never seemed to get sick much himself. He never explained. But you see, that makes sense in a way. If he was working on some secret project for the Nazis, he couldn't write about it in his journal. He had no privacy. If one of the camp guards found the journal and saw him writing about Time Reich, he would have been shot."

"So he left it out," Kate said.

"The Nazis would have killed not just him if they found that in the journals, they might have killed everyone in his barrack too. You know what they were like. Bloodthirsty thugs, every last one of them. He had to leave it out." I realized I was defending my old man. Defending what he had done.

"But didn't he tell you later?"

"No, not really," I said. "He just told me that he helped the Germans build barracks for Russian prisoners, so in return he got some special treatment. I always sensed there was something more to it than that, but he refused to talk about it. I think he was ashamed. He felt that what he had done was wrong."

"But he did it to survive."

I gave her a sharp look. "Does that make it right?"

"We weren't there. It's not right that we should judge what your father did to stay alive."

"There's something else you should know. The journals are ... edited."

"What do you mean?"

"Dad wrote a lot. Filling up those pages was all that he had to do. There was far too much to include, so when I was editing the book I focused on certain aspects of the journals. I included what I thought was the message of the journals. I focused on life in the camps, the people there, survival and hope."

"I know," she said, her voice sad. "I've read it, Bram. More than once."

"So you see, there were parts I left out. Dad wrote a lot about the SS officers at the camp. Apparently, he had spent enough time with them to get to know some of them fairly well. He wrote a lot about Konrad Radl, as a matter of fact."

"There's not much of that in the book," Kate said, her tone accusatory.

"There wasn't room. We're talking about stacks of journals, all boiled down to a three-hundred-page book."

"Jesus, McCoy. This is really spooky. Your father being in the photo like that. You're freaking me out."

"You think *you're* freaked out? How do you think I feel?"

"We need to go talk about Time Reich with this ONR researcher my uncle knows," Kate said. "And then we're going to go back and read the journals again. Now that we know about Time Reich and Konrad Radl, there might be some clue in the journal that didn't make it into *Journey of Hope*. It may be something you've completely forgotten about."

Kate was thinking more clearly than I was, but then, she

wasn't dealing with the realization that her father might have been a Nazi collaborator. Looking at my father's journals again was a good idea.

"Thank you," I said, then leaned over and kissed her. I think I caught us both by surprise. When Kate didn't move away from me, I kissed her again.

"Wow," Kate said when we both came up for air. "I wasn't expecting that, but it was nice."

"I've been waiting to do that for a long time," I said.

Her cell phone chirped. For all we knew it could have been ringing for a while. "What timing," she said. "The story of my life."

Kate flipped it open, rolled her eyes at the number. "I understand that you're wondering where I've been, George," she said into the phone. "And if you don't know, it's a pretty good guess you haven't been watching CNN."

While Kate was on her cell phone, I got us back on the highway. She hung up with her boss and immediately made another call. This time, she mostly listened.

"How's George?" I asked once she'd hung up.

"Not happy, from the sound of it," she said. "He reminded me that the clock is ticking, so I called Dustin, who filled me in on the rest. Dustin saw the news, by the way. Everyone in the office is suddenly interested in this investigation and they're pitching in, trying to run down names and make any connections they can. It's something of a mutiny. Dustin said King George is having spasms over it."

"Ah, office politics," I said. "I'm glad to hear that in-fighting and turf wars aren't limited to academia. Now what?"

"Drive," Kate said. "We need to find out about Project Time Reich."

26

W e were just getting to the top of the New Jersey Turnpike when Kate said, "Tell me about your father. What was he like?"

"You read the book," I answered, shifting in the seat of the Hummer. The sleet had changed over to rain and the wipers sluiced it off the wide windshield. Driving had become easier now that the roads were just wet. "Aside from a few major details he left out, like working on Time Reich and possibly being a Nazi collaborator, I think you should already have a pretty good feel for his personality."

"The book is all words on paper," Kate said. "What if we were in a room with him right now? It might help us figure out what's going on."

"What do you want me to say, Kate? It turns out that maybe I didn't know him that well. My father was a complicated person. He lived surrounded by ghosts and memories of his childhood in Germany and of his dead friends and family who were murdered by the Nazis. Those are scars you don't see, of course, but the fact is that he lived his life completely out of context after the war. His childhood home was gone, all his friends. He wouldn't even go back to visit because nobody would be there. Basically, his past had been erased. Think about what that does to a person."

"What happened to him right after the war ended?"

"He was in the hospital for a while. At the end of the war he became very sick. That's supposedly why he stopped his journal."

"Imagine, all those years and all that time in the camp and then he got sick."

"That happened to a lot of the people in the camps. Especially at the end. The Germans practically stopped feeding them. He had dysentery and then pneumonia. Healthy, my father was six two and about one hundred and ninety pounds. He only weighed about one hundred and twenty pounds by the time he made it to an Allied hospital."

"Skin and bones."

"My mother saved him. She sat him up in bed and gave him beef broth a spoonful at a time. He was her favorite patient."

"Why him?"

"Who knows? He wasn't like the other refugees. He spoke English, he was educated and he had this dry sense of humor. He could be very funny when he wanted to be, which wasn't often. But I can see him charming her even from his hospital bed. He was that kind of man. All those American GIs running around and she chose my father, the concentration camp survivor. The day he left the hospital, they got married."

"So it was love at first sight in the hospital? How romantic. It sounds like *A Farewell to Arms*."

"Don't forget that Hemingway didn't write a happy ending for that story. The same could be said for my mother and father. You see, he never really forgave my mother for saving him. Not deep down."

"What do you mean?"

"You know how some cultures have a philosophy that if you

save someone's life, you are responsible for that life forever? I think my father felt that way about my mother. He felt beholden somehow and he didn't like that. It's complicated, all mixed up with a big dose of survivor's guilt, but basically what it comes down to is that he was a proud man."

"What happened after they got married?"

"My mother was his ticket to America. The marriage certificate made him an instant citizen. Needless to say, her family was a little put off by this tall, charming European. They were all what you'd call shanty Irish. Uneducated, working class people. Their daughter went off to have adventures in the war and look who she came home with."

Kate laughed. "And he was a Jew, to boot. That must have blown their minds."

"Well, the fact is that he abandoned his religion. I suppose that after you've suffered through what he did you either become a true believer or you learn to hate God. My father fell into the second category."

"That must have unsettled those Irish Catholics even more."

"Religion never became an issue. He tried hard to forget about the past and leave it behind. I think he was ashamed. That's the reason why my legal name is McCoy, not Baumann." I sighed. "That means 'builder' in German, by the way."

"But you're also Abraham," she pointed out.

"His father's name. He had a lot of respect for his father — my grandfather. Abraham didn't survive the war."

"What did your father do for work?"

"He took a job in a factory that made parts for cranes. After a few years he worked his way up to foreman of the three-to-eleven shift."

"But he was an engineer," she said. "He designed entire buildings in Europe."

"He had to take what he could get. All the good jobs went to the boys coming home from the war. Nobody was interested in giving a good job to a Jew from Germany, whether or not he had a degree in engineering."

"That alone could make a man bitter."

"At first I think it did," I said. "By the time I came along he had simply given up and accepted his fate. But there was some part of him that always thought he was better than what he did. You know, he wore a shirt and tie to work every day and then changed into work clothes at the factory. Sometimes in the winter he just wore coveralls over his good clothes. He would come home and scrub his hands and under the nails, getting all the dirt out from under them. They were rough hands from handling tools and steel all day, but they were clean."

"He must have been a proud man," Kate said. "How did your family survive on his salary? It couldn't have been much."

I laughed. Here we were, driving down the road in her uncle's gas-guzzling luxury vehicle. "Rich people. They haven't got a clue."

"Okay," Kate grumped at me. "I get the message. Still, it couldn't have been easy."

"There used to be a time in America when you could live just fine on a blue-collar job. My mother continued to work as a nurse. They had enough money to get by and then some. It was a different generation. They never had color TV, never had cable or a credit card balance. They made do with less their whole lives."

"Then you came along."

"Yes." I smiled. "I suppose I was quite a surprise to them. They were married twenty years without any children and suddenly they were parents more than two decades after the war. It was a rude awakening. My mother liked to call me their little atomic bomb."

Kate laughed. "I guess that's another way of saying you were an accident."

"You should do that more often," I told her.

"Do what?"

"Laugh. I like the sound of it."

"I've always been the serious kind." She sighed. "You were lucky to know your parents. It's not something to take for granted."

"No, I suppose not. And I do miss them. My mother was such a peaceful person. Calm and relaxed. I'm sure she was a wonderful nurse. She died two weeks after she retired. One day she said she was tired, so she fixed herself a cup of tea and sat down in the living room to watch TV. She closed her eyes and never woke up. Massive stroke."

"Peaceful," Kate agreed. "And your father?"

I shook my head. "Toward the end he became obsessed about the war. He started reading all the newspapers he could and clipping out articles about Nazis who had turned up over the years. He started files full of clippings about them all."

"And the journals?"

"He started to type up what he had written all those years ago in the journals. By then his hands were so knotted with arthritis that I started to help him. Pretty soon I was completely drawn into them, as obsessed as he was with the Nazis. We used to sit around the kitchen table and speculate about what had happened to this one or that one. Konrad Radl was always the one he talked about the most. I edited *Journey of Hope* and wrote the introduction, but it's really my father's story. People forget that."

"He died before it was published."

"Yes. He was a hollow shell by then, eaten up by hatred as much as cancer. When he died he weighed even less than he had when the Americans liberated the camp. He had tried to forgive the Nazis, even tried to forgive God for what had happened, but he couldn't. For him, I think the worst part of dying was not being able to forgive. Now it all makes more sense."

"What does?"

"Why he couldn't forgive," I said. "It was because he had never forgiven himself. You saw the photograph. He helped them, Kate. Whatever this Time Reich project was all about, he helped them. In his own mind he had sinned as much as any Nazi."

"I read the book. I know what he went through, even if he never mentions Time Reich. He did it to survive."

"Yes, but he knew he was selling out the future. He was helping the Nazis conduct their goddamn experiment so he could have a warm meal at night. He must have known he was making a bargain with the devil."

27

C aptain Roy Howard, United States Navy retired, lived on a tree-lined neighborhood in Arlington, Virginia. The real estate boom had sent home prices here skyrocketing. What was once a modest neighborhood of families, government managers and teachers was now filled with lawyers, deputy directors of governmental agencies and business executives. It was a pricey street for a retired Naval researcher living on a pension. The man who answered the door was younger than I expected, maybe late sixties, not some decrepit retiree. Kate had called him from the road, but hadn't gone into detail about what we wanted.

"I ought to move," Roy Howard grumped. "All the yuppies have ruined the neighborhood. You don't even see any kids riding bikes anymore. Everybody works so much to pay off these big mortgages that they can't afford kids."

"Or maybe they just don't want kids," Kate said.

"Who wouldn't want kids?" Howard asked. "That's a damn selfish notion, if you ask me. There's a little thing called the human race to think about. Our whole reason for existence is to create more humans, not to build up our 401K portfolios or lease the latest BMW."

"You're a philosopher," I said. "I should have expected as much from a friend of Silas Crockett's."

Howard laughed. "I'm an historian, Professor McCoy, just like you. Now ask yourself, what good is our past without the promise of the future?"

" 'And so we beat on, boats against the tide, borne back ceaselessly into the past.' "

"Ha! Scott Fitzgerald. It's so refreshing to meet people nowadays who've read more than the back of a cereal box."

Captain Howard looked more like a scholar than a Navy officer, even a retired one: tweed coat, corduroy slacks, gray hair that was a bit too long and that looked as if he cut it himself. He smoked a pipe and had a habit of jabbing the pipe stem at you to make a point. Except when he smiled, however, it was hard to tell what he was thinking behind his peppery, clipped beard.

The captain invited us in. From the outside, the house was a nondescript 1960s ranch. But it was furnished with a cozy mix of antiques, old leather furniture and rattan chairs, along with Asian pieces most likely collected during overseas duty. Overall, it was a house vastly different from Rock Bottom, but Roy Howard was not a multi-millionaire political power broker like Silas Crockett. The house had a pleasantly musty smell of old books and pipe tobacco, like some shop you discovered on a side street in nearby Old Town Alexandria. Framed photographs of what I took to be his children and grandchildren crowded the fireplace mantel in the small living room.

"Have a seat," he said, indicating an old sofa. He settled into an overstuffed armchair. The coffee table between us was stacked high with history books. *History of Warships, 1812: Rediscovering Chesapeake Bay's Forgotten War* and *The U-Boat Offensive, 1914-1945.* I had the feeling that Captain Howard knew the difference between a stern and a bow, not to mention a cruiser and a battleship. One title in particular caught my eye. The book was called *Dark Arts: The Search for Cloaking Devices on Land and Sea*. According to the name on the book jacket, the author was sitting across from us.

"I'm forgetting my manners," he said. "If my wife were home, she'd be giving me a stern look just about now, but fortunately she's volunteering down at the hospital auxiliary. Tea? Coffee?"

"None for me, thanks," I said. "I already had my week's allotment of caffeine during the drive down here."

"No thank you," Kate said.

"Well, I know you didn't come all this way for a cup of coffee." He puffed his pipe, flashing teeth stained the color of old ivory. "Now, what can I do for you?"

"My Uncle Silas sent us here, Captain Howard," Kate said. "There's no point beating around the bush. We're interested in Project Time Reich."

Instantly, a change seemed to come over the old man. The warm affability with which he had greeted us was replaced with a guarded look that came down across his face like a window shade. He clenched his pipe stem firmly between his teeth as he spoke. "Time Reich?" he asked. His expression was neutral behind his beard. "I haven't heard that one in a long while."

"Silas said you would know something about it," Kate insisted.

Howard made a show of re-lighting his pipe, although I suspected that he was just buying time to frame a response. Once or twice I caught him assessing us with shrewd eyes. Obviously, the mention of Time Reich had set off some alarm for him. Deep down, I had been hoping that this business about time travel was all some mistake, a crackpot rumor that had survived from the tumultuous final days of the Second World War.

Captain Howard puffed at his pipe, filling the room with a sweet cherry smell. Finally, he nodded as if he had reached some decision and asked, "Is that your vehicle out front, that great big monstrosity?"

"It belongs to Silas, but we drove it down from Connecticut," Kate said.

"Looks like there's plenty of room," he said. "You can drive us out to the graveyard."

"Graveyard?"

"Sure," he said, smiling around his pipe stem in a way that wasn't altogether reassuring. "It's where I take all my friends."

———

"How much did Silas tell you about Time Reich?" Captain Howard asked, once we were in the Hummer.

"Only that there was a German research program that investigated the possibility of time travel," I said. "I have to admit that it sounds pretty far-fetched."

"Why are you interested in that?"

"It's quite a story, actually," I said, but hesitated before I went on. If I told him the truth, he might think we were crazy. On the other hand, if I concocted some kind of story, I had the feeling that Captain Howard would sniff us out. I glanced over at Kate, who gave me a nod. *What the hell*, I thought. The worst Howard could do was have someone from the nearest mental health facility come pick us up.

"You want to get off at the next exit," he said. "Then we take 295 north for six miles and get off at Route 32."

"Four days ago there was a robbery in a small town at the top of the bay," I said. "The suspect was wearing what appeared to be an SS uniform. The robbery victim died of a heart attack. Two days ago, another man was killed in Connecticut by someone wearing the same kind of uniform."

"You think the crimes are related?"

"Both victims were also former SS soldiers. Not only do we think the murders are related, but we think the killer may be a German SS officer named Konrad Radl."

"Radl? I've heard of him. He'd have to be what — eighty, ninety years old?"

"Radl was born in eighteen ninety-eight," Kate said. "That would make him one hundred and eight."

Then Captain Howard got it. "Good Lord! This is why you want to know about Time Reich. You *actually* think Radl traveled through time."

"No, of course not. That would be crazy," Kate said as she guided the Hummer deftly through traffic. "Look, we'll understand if you want us to take you home again."

"Sweetheart, of all the research joints in the world, you had to walk into this one." The captain laughed. "Lucky for you, Silas knew just where to send you."

"THE GERMANS WERE MORE TECHNOLOGICALLY advanced than us in many areas," Captain Howard explained. "For instance, from an engineering standpoint, they already had the Autobahn. Just imagine, a superhighway much like the one we're on right now in existence back in the 1930s. There was nothing like it then in the United States. Eisenhower saw the roads the Germans had built and when he became president, we started building superhighways of our own. The strategy at the time was to get people to move away from the population centers in case of nuclear war with the Russians. It ended up being a cold war military strategy that really changed the landscape of the United States. But Eisenhower got the idea from Hitler's autobahns.

"It wasn't just highways, of course. The Germans developed

Sarin nerve gas long before us. They had a radio code our greatest minds couldn't solve until we stole one of their Enigma machines. They possessed rocket-propelled missile delivery systems and more highly developed radar. And mind you, this was all done in the days before computers."

"We had the atom bomb," Kate said defensively, as if the captain had wounded her sense of national pride. "The Manhattan Project."

"Ah, yes, now *there's* an invention to take pride in," Captain Howard said. "We Americans came up with the means to destroy humanity. To be fair, the Germans were close to inventing the A-bomb too. If they'd had another year, possibly six months, they would have had a bomb and no doubt would have used it on the Russians. They saw the Russians as subhuman and therefore worthy of atomic incineration, much as Americans perceived the Japanese. We never would have dropped the bomb on Berlin."

"The bottom line is that the Germans lost the war," Kate said. "Excuse me if I'm skeptical about Nazi superiority."

"Hitler lost the war in nineteen forty-one when he invaded Russia," the captain said. "He repeated the same mistake made by Napoleon Bonaparte. The only reason he held out so long was that he hoped some super weapon would sweep Germany to victory. His strategy wasn't that far off the mark. Did you know that the Germans had jet fighters at the end of the war?"

"Jet fighters?" Kate said.

"Yes. They were just beginning production of true jet fighters such as the Messerschmitt Me two six two interceptor that could fly one hundred miles per hour *faster* than our best fighters and was more maneuverable. If the Germans had been able to bring them into play a few months earlier the Luftwaffe would have dominated the skies over Europe, not the Allies."

"You almost sound like you're rooting for them," Kate said.

"I'm just explaining the facts," Captain Howard said. "Down

through the ages, technology always has been the key to military victory. Nazi Germany is often portrayed as being a sort of Dark Age that settled over Germany. While it's true that Hitler discouraged most forms of political and artistic creative thinking, he encouraged the sciences and paved the way for them with almost unlimited funding. History gets written by the winners, but it's not always accurate."

"What about the kind of twisted 'science' that monsters like Josef Mengele carried out on children in the concentration camps?" Kate's voice rose a notch and I could tell she was losing her patience with the captain's apparent praise for the technological accomplishments of the Third Reich. Kate was always spoiling for a fight, just like her uncle in his prime. She was gripping the steering wheel so hard that her knuckles were white. "That wasn't science. That was torture and murder."

"There's no defending someone like Mengele," Captain Howard agreed. "He's always been a poster child for anti-Nazi propaganda. You know what they say about one bad apple."

"I can't believe you actually think this way," Kate said. I could tell Kate was getting upset because she was speeding again.

"Werner Von Braun helped send V-2 rockets to London but that was conveniently forgiven because he shaved a decade off our space program. The Nazis gave him his start, but because our side shanghaied him after the war he's held up as a hero for school kids even today," the captain said, taking out his pipe and jabbing the stem at Kate. "It's all in how you spin it, my dear. Now, don't get me wrong. I'm not praising Hitler. All I'm saying is that at some point you have to ignore the larger purpose of the Nazis and look at their technological capabilities objectively. The entire scientific community of Nazi Germany was not made up of madmen, even if the country was led by one."

"Rockets, jets, atomic experiments," I said, summing it up

and eager to get off the philosophical aspects before Kate got too worked up. "I guess it's no stretch of the imagination that the Nazis might have experimented with time travel as well."

"Why not? Our government certainly did."

"What are you talking about?" Kate said. "Time travel?"

"Let me tell you about an experiment undertaken in 1944," he said. "What's amazing is that it did actually succeed to some extent. But at the same time, it was such a disaster that it was never attempted again."

"What happened?"

"You've heard of the Philadelphia Experiment?" he asked.

"Sure," I said. "Movie stuff. Science fiction."

"Yes and no. The truth is, experiments really were carried out during the war in an effort to create a huge cloaking device using powerful electromagnetic fields. Cloaking devices are something I've made a careful study of over the years."

"Your book," I said.

"Exactly. It's hardly a bestseller — not like your book — but it represents years of research into a legitimate military strategy of cloaking devices. Of course, I'm pretty sure the only people who actually read books like mine are other retired Navy officers."

"Okay, this is where you're losing me," said Kate. "You're going to have to explain what a cloaking device is."

"It's a fancy way of saying camouflage," he said. "That's an ancient tactic used in hunting and war, employed by everything from insects and animals to the Greeks who hid inside the Trojan horse. American Indians draped themselves in buffalo hides or wolf skins to creep closer to buffalo herds for the hunt. Some breeds of shaggy dogs such as the Puli were intended to blend in with flocks of sheep. When the wolves came down from the hills to eat the sheep, they got a nasty surprise. These are all cloaking devices. You outfox your enemy or prey by either appearing to be something you aren't or by disappearing altogether."

"I'm getting the picture," Kate said.

"Now, what I've described are very ancient forms of cloaking devices. The problem is that in modern warfare, it's not enough to disguise your warplane or warship visually. With radar and other forms of surveillance, you need to disguise yourself electronically. As a result, the search for the ship or plane that's 'invisible' to enemy radar has become a kind of Holy Grail in modern warfare."

"I thought that's just what the Stealth bomber did," I said.

"Yes," the captain said. "The Stealth is the perfect example of that. It makes use of metal alloys in its skin that absorb radar waves. Nothing is reflected, so nothing appears on the enemy's radar screen. It's not perfectly invisible because some enemy nations have advanced radar that can detect the Stealth bomber, but it's very close to the ideal. There are also radar-jamming techniques, although these aren't quite the same as cloaking devices."

"But the Stealth bomber is an airplane," Kate said. "How would you hide an entire ship?"

"You want to get off up here," the captain said, jabbing his pipe stem at the windshield and the looming exit sign. Then he went on to answer her question. "Ships have never successfully been made invisible to radar. That's because the kind of alloy used to shield an airplane from radar doesn't really work with, say, an Aegis-class destroyer. There is simply too much surface area to cover, too many irregular structural features that are difficult to disguise with a radar-absorbent alloy."

"But I thought the Philadelphia Experiment had something to do with creating electro-magnetic fields," I said.

"It did. The Navy was attempting to generate an electro-magnetic field that was powerful enough not only to hide the ship from radar, but also to remove it from sight altogether by altering the spectrum of visible light. It was to be the ultimate cloaking device."

"Excuse me," said Kate. "But what does this have to do with time travel?"

Captain Howard smiled. "The problem with the experiment was that it worked too well. Not only did the ship disappear from view, but also it apparently traveled through time and space."

"Sounds like something from an episode of *The Twilight Zone*," Kate said.

"There's a lot of controversy about what actually happened," the captain agreed. "Remember, this experiment occurred during wartime under the utmost secrecy, so records of the experiment are hard to come by even today. Some of us have seen bits and pieces over the years. Officially, the position of the Office of Naval Research is that the experiment never really happened. That's not true, of course. One of the chief physicists involved in the experiment was none other than Albert Einstein."

"Einstein? I didn't know that."

"You're telling us that the experiment worked?" Kate asked.

"Quite the opposite. It was a terrible failure because it spiraled out of control. The full force of the electromagnetic fields was very destructive, almost as if the ship had been cooked inside a giant microwave oven. There was a terrific burst of energy. Some men died outright, while others became fused with the metal hull of the ship. Thankfully, those poor bastards didn't live long. Other men simply disappeared, and a handful of sailors possibly traveled through space-time. There's some confusion about that. In any case, there's little doubt that they ended up far from where they started out that day. There are even claims that the ship itself was transported briefly to another location, but I've never been sure about that."

"Why the cover-up?"

"A lot of men died and it had to be explained away. Men died all through the war because of secret military experiments involving everything from radiation to mustard gas trials. That's not what the families were told because nobody wanted to hear that. It also didn't help that Einstein himself was sickened by the carnage and refused to have anything else to do with the project."

"What does this have to do with Time Reich?" Kate wondered.

"I've told you about the Philadelphia Experiment to make a point, which is that if the United States conducted an experiment like this and had some limited success, don't be surprised if the Germans attempted something similar. What if they were slightly more advanced than us in this field as well and learned just enough about the physics involved to make it work?"

"Impossible," Kate said.

"Don't be so sure." Captain Howard smiled as we drove up to a gate where two sentries carrying automatic weapons came out to meet us. "Let's go have a look."

28

The Commodore Joshua Barney Naval Yard and Restoration Facility operated by the Office of Naval Research occupied nearly one hundred acres just south of Annapolis, Maryland. Several large buildings dotted the property, and all the buildings were connected by roadways or expansive parking areas filled with abandoned boats and aircraft. The facility was surrounded by a tall chain-link fence topped with razor wire.

"Welcome to the graveyard," Captain Howard said.

Retired or not, the captain must have been a regular visitor because one of the guards greeted him by name.

"New wheels?" the sentry asked, looking over the Hummer, admiration plain in his eyes. "Where's that old Buick of yours, sir?"

"These are some colleagues of mine," Howard explained. "I want to show them some of the restoration projects we have going on."

The sentry hesitated. "I don't know, sir. You know how they're getting about unauthorized visitors."

"Next thing you know you'll have to be an admiral or a senator to get into this place," Captain Howard said. "Hey, did you see last night's game? The 'Skins really pulled it off in the last quarter."

"If they'd gotten their act together in the first quarter they could've won," the sentry said. His eyes wandered toward Kate, taking her in. It was a good bet that Kate's was not the sort of face he was used to seeing at the Navy restoration facility. The guard and Captain Howard talked a minute about what apparently had been a very bad game the week before.

"We'll see how they do this week," Howard said.

"We shoulda made it to the playoffs," the sentry griped.

"Maybe next year," the captain said.

The two men waited a beat, then burst out laughing. I knew that Redskins fans had a streak of self-deprecating humor, which helped when your team hadn't had a good season in years. The sentry stepped back, wishing us a good visit. The second, more serious guard waved us through the gate.

"It takes a certain kind of fortitude to be a Redskins fan," the captain said, wiping tears of laughter out of his eyes. He had really cracked himself up. It also wasn't lost on me that the captain had slipped us past the sentries.

"I thought you said this was a restoration facility," I said. "Why the armed guards?"

"Can't be too careful these days," the captain said. "Some of the artifacts here are actually quite valuable in and of themselves. We have Civil War vessels, World War II vessels — people are crazy enough about both those topics to break in to get themselves a souvenir."

"This isn't truly a research facility?"

"No, you wouldn't have simply driven into a Naval research facility as easily as that," Howard said. "What goes on here is strictly mothballing, restoration and hands-on historical research. Hardly matters of national security. It's a graveyard for vessels and aircraft that are no longer useful to anyone."

He wasn't kidding about it being a graveyard. The place had an air of ruin. We drove past rows of river patrol gunboats from the Vietnam era, several ancient helicopters and what appeared to be a mini-submarine. The paint on all the equipment was faded from the sun or streaked with rust.

Captain Howard directed us to one of the larger warehouse buildings. Like the others, it was built entirely of corrugated steel and didn't have a single window. The structure was two stories tall and hundreds of feet long, painted a dull gray that matched the watery winter sky.

"This is where we keep the good stuff we don't want to rust away," he explained. "We have a few smaller wooden vessels in here, electronics, and various odds and ends."

We got out of the Hummer and Captain Howard led us to a small steel door in the side of the building, then let us in by punching a code into a keypad. A few security lights gave the interior a yellow glow. He flicked a switch that turned on a long string of overheard lights leading down the length of the building. It wasn't exactly bright, but it was enough to navigate the walkways between piles of electronic devices, odd bits of machinery and mysterious stacks of wooden crates. It reminded me of a mad scientist's basement. The air smelled of damp concrete and rust.

"It's so dark in here," Kate said. "How do you see anything?"

"This is primarily a storage area," he explained. "We move projects to one of the restoration or research buildings to work on them. We can also set up portable work lights when necessary."

He went to a cabinet and took out three hard hats and a powerful Maglite. "Best put these on," he said. "I'm breaking enough rules as it is, so we don't want anyone to break a head on top of that."

He also handed me a portable halogen work light, comprised of a shoulder-high flexible arm atop a fold-out base. Then he flicked on the Maglite and we started down a pathway through the piles of crates and equipment.

"What is all this stuff?" I asked.

"Honestly, we don't even know what's in some of these wooden crates," he said. "You know that scene from *Raiders of the Lost Ark* when we know the Ark of the Covenant is safely hidden when it disappears into a government warehouse filled with wooden crates? Well, this place is a lot like that."

"You mean the Ark of the Covenant might be hidden in here?"

Captain Howard chuckled. "Nothing that dramatic, I'm sure. Most of the crates contain old electronics nobody knew what else to do with. Sometimes there's a crate of old K-rations mixed in. Or champagne that got lost on the way to some general's headquarters. When things get dull around here, we pop open a crate. It's like a treasure hunt."

"What are we looking for?"

"Follow me."

We walked for what seemed like miles through narrow corridors between the piled detritus of naval history. The flashlight burned with a clear, steady light, but Captain Howard played it around the cavernous space as he walked, so that the shadows of the skeletal machines seemed to move and leap as if they were things alive. We climbed some stairs, our footsteps ringing on metal treads, reaching a loft that contained yet more stacks of equipment.

Finally, at what seemed to be the farthest corner from where we had begun, Captain Howard stopped. He fiddled with the Maglite until it cast a wide beam, and then shined it on what appeared to be a collection of old wires, tubing and black steel. At the center of it all was a seat that could have come from a fighter plane, complete with a harness to strap in the occupant. The entire contraption resembled the framework of a stripped-down dune buggy or Volkswagen that rested on metal struts instead of wheels. The air around us hummed from the dim sodium lights overhead.

"Let's set up the work light and take a closer look," the captain said.

We unfolded the legs of the light and found an outlet to plug it in. The halogen bulb cast a surprising amount of light, but it was discordantly silver-white, like the brilliant burst of a strobe or flashbulb, and cast harsh shadows. The machine in front of us appeared black and sinister, sprouting thick rubber wires like the head of a Medusa.

"What is it?" I asked.

"Don't tell me you don't recognize a time machine when you see one," Captain Howard said. "It's not one of ours, by the way. It's German."

Kate stepped closer and touched it. I fought the urge to warn her not to, reminding myself that this was just a machine. But the damned thing looked so sinister.

Kate's fingers traced the outline of a dust-covered symbol. I could see it too. An eagle gripping a swastika, framed by a triangle.

"Just like the one on the disk," she said.

"What disk?" Captain Howard asked. Kate described the bronze disk that had turned up in Hans Schmidt's basement. Howard nodded and started to say something, then seemed to think better of it.

"Does this thing work?" I asked.

The captain nodded at the seat. "Go ahead and take it for a test drive."

"No thanks."

"As far as we can tell, this was a prototype. We have no idea whether or not it was ever tested — on humans, at least."

"I'm sure if the Germans had wanted a human test subject,

they would have found someone wearing a Star of David," I said, shuddering at the thought of being forced into that seat.

"This is the only one that exists?" Kate asked.

"The Russians beat us into many of the German military labs and they took the lion's share of these experimental devices," Captain Howard said. "We have to assume they got one, unless this was the only prototype."

"But could it have worked?" Kate asked.

"It's hard to know without testing it," the captain said. "Whatever calibrations had been done have surely been jarred out of position during transport all those years ago."

"Not only that," I said, pointing out areas where the wiring had been ripped away from some part of the machine that was no longer there, "but it looks as if someone took some of the vital parts. Kind of like taking the distributor cap out of your car to make sure no one drives off with it."

"Someone gutted it," Howard agreed. "We don't know if it was the Germans or Russians, but whoever it was did not want some parts of the machine to fall into our hands."

"Can't you just plug it in or something and see what happens?" Kate asked.

"It's not that simple. As far as we can tell, this machine requires a tremendous amount of energy. An extension cord on a twenty-amp circuit isn't going to cut it. This machine would probably require the output of a small generating station . . . or maybe even the energy of a nuclear explosion. It's hard to say."

"If it needs that much juice running through it, I say we test it on somebody we don't like," I said.

The captain stood for a long while staring at the machine. The black framework surrounded it like a steel rib cage. For the first time, I noticed the huge copper wires coiled like snakes all around its base. I could see what he meant about the enormous amount of electricity needed to power the thing.

"I've thought a lot about this machine over the years," the captain continued. "There's a sort of antennae; in many ways it seems to be set up almost like a giant radio transmitter. What you have to ask yourselves is this: if someone sixty years ago had found a cell phone with a dead battery, how would he ever really understand what it was for or even if it worked? Without someone to explain it or any written instructions, a cell phone would simply be a mysterious collection of plastic and electronics. It would be a source of wonder, a curiosity, but it would remain a mystery. Sixty years ago, no one would have believed you could make a digital cell phone call or send a fax. How can you send a piece of paper over a telephone wire? And yet now we do it without a second thought."

"You can't send a fax through time," Kate pointed out.

"Actually, you can," the captain said. "At least in theory. How much do you know about quantum physics?"

"I thought you said the Germans were experimenting with radio waves."

"True," the captain said. "But like our own Philadelphia experiment, I think they stumbled upon quantum foam."

"What's that?" Kate wondered.

"Wormholes," I said. You don't serve on a college faculty without picking up a little science here and there. "Fluctuations in the fabric of space-time."

"Thank you, Professor. It seems you know something about sub-atomic physics."

"Only that it may be possible to travel through time or even to other dimensions at the subatomic level. It's only theoretical."

"Excuse me," Kate said. She was looking at us as if she thought the captain and I had lost our minds. "But would you two please explain what you're talking about?"

"Quantum foam is what binds the universe together at the

tiniest levels," the captain said. "It's basically energy, but I think it's more helpful to imagine quantum foam as being like the sea. To give you an idea of the scale we're talking about here, plankton might represent electrons, fish are atoms and whales are molecules. That's how vast quantum foam is compared to matter."

"Hold on," Kate said. "I'm still trying to wrap my mind around this. Okay, I get that we're surrounded by a sea of energy and matter."

"Now imagine that there are currents in this energy sea, tides and whirlpools as powerful as any in our actual oceans," Captain Howard continued. "These are the wormholes professor McCoy mentioned. If you throw a message in a bottle into just the right place in the sea, it might wash up on the shores of a different continent."

"This is all very interesting, Captain Howard, but I don't see what this has to do with Time Reich," Kate said.

"The Nazis were tossing messages in bottles into the quantum foam sea," the captain said. "Even if they didn't understand it, they knew they had stumbled onto something. The disastrous Philadelphia Experiment frightened off our own physicists, but it's just possible that the Germans somehow hitched a ride on the tides that flow through space-time."

"I thought you said they were experimenting with radio waves."

Captain Howard nodded toward the sinister-looking chair. "Whoever sat in that device was vaporized. What if they were consequently transmitted through space-time?"

"Faxed to the future," I said.

Kate approached the machine and ran her hands over the controls. There was a panel with a series of levers and toggle switches labeled in German. "There's nothing here anyone could use for a setting," she said. "How would you know where you were sending someone?"

"That's a good question. There may have been some controlling device that was removed. The best answer I've been able to come up with is that there is no setting."

"What?" Kate sounded baffled.

Looking over the machine, I was beginning to get the idea. This wasn't something out of a science fiction movie where you punched in a date and sent someone to the future. You would never be able to send someone to a specific location. How would you ever send someone to Hans Schmidt's house, for instance? You can send a fax, but to receive it you needed a fax machine on the other end.

"I think I know how they could do this," I said.

The captain was smiling. "Go on," he said, and I had the thought that he had figured it out a long time ago. We had confirmed his theory when we had shown up on his doorstep with our wild story.

"It's a transmitter," I said. "And every transmitter requires a receiver. It really *isn't* much different from a cell phone or a radio or a fax machine."

"You mean, it's like how you can't hear a radio broadcast without a radio," Kate said, getting it.

"Exactly. The Nazis set this up to transmit to a receiver."

Kate thought a moment, then grabbed my arm. "The disk," she said.

"The disk traveled through time," I said. "Actual time. Real time. It's designed to pick up the signal sent back in nineteen forty-five."

"It's rather brilliant," Captain Howard said. "You send your receiver through real time, then turn it on to connect with the past. The disk you described might actually be a beacon for a time machine."

"You wouldn't catch me volunteering to be sent through time," I said.

"The Nazis were desperate enough to try anything as their

world crumbled around them," the captain said. "If you were planning to commit suicide anyway, why not do so with the possibility that you might pop up in the future? It's one of the reasons people have adopted cryogenics. They freeze themselves after death in hopes that there will be a cure in the future for whatever ails them."

"Who would they have sent in this thing?"

"Try some of the big fish who have never been found," I said. "Radl, Mueller, maybe even Hitler himself."

"Come on, Bram," Kate said. "You don't really believe that."

"But consider this," Howard said. "Whether the actual science works or not, Project Time Reich has some powerful symbolism. What other historical figure can you think of whose 'second coming' is being awaited by millions of faithful followers?"

"Jesus Christ," Kate said. The way she said it, the name sounded like an epithet.

"Exactly," Captain Howard said. "It's no wonder the government has kept this under wraps for so many years."

Kate's cell phone rang. Kate looked startled, as if afraid to touch it, now that technology had taken a darker turn.

"Go ahead and answer it," I said. "Maybe it's Hitler, letting you know he's on his way."

As Kate took the call, checking in with Dustin, I looked over the machine once again. The metal framework felt cold and somehow brutal to my fingertips. Cannons felt this way, and so did axe blades. I wondered what other hands had touched that same metalwork. The very idea of time travel was madness, and yet Captain Howard made it sound plausible.

Still touching the machine, I thought about all the energy that had once coursed through it all those decades ago. I imagined that the metal suddenly felt hot and my hand flinched away.

A time machine.

Was it possible that Konrad Radl had hurtled through quantum foam, summoned by a bronze beacon bearing a swastika and eagle? Was he the only one, or had others tried to come through time?

My stomach turned cold at the thought.

29

Back at OSI, we stepped out of the elevator and came face-to-face with George Foster. He had a coat over his arm and his briefcase in hand.

"We've been watching the news all day," he said, putting the briefcase down to touch Kate's arm. "Thank God you're all right."

"It was pretty crazy," Kate agreed. She glanced at his hand, obviously embarrassed by her supervisor's display of emotion. Seeing them together now, and knowing their history, it was plain that Foster still had feelings for her. Kate shrugged his hand away and Foster's face clouded.

He wasn't a bad-looking guy—Kate deserved some credit for not having completely bad taste. Foster was a little over six feet tall, and trim from regular trips to the gym. But there was something grim and humorless about him. He would be slow to laugh, I thought, and quick to do the bureaucratic dirty work that kept a department running. He was also good at holding a grudge against Kate.

"Your team has been scrambling all day and it looks like they're gearing up to go all night." He paused. "Just so long as they don't go overboard on the comp time. Those extra hours are hell on the budget."

"I thought the saying was that Justice never sleeps," I said.

Foster seemed to acknowledge me for the first time. His eyes slid from me to Kate and he smirked. "When Justice does sleep, I bet it's in your bed," he said.

My right hand bunched into a fist. Kate grabbed my arm. George stepped around us into the elevator. The doors began to whisk shut but Foster caught them with his briefcase. "You may want to know that I'll be sending a memo to Elliot Nusbaum just to keep him updated about how his star investigator is pursuing a Nazi time traveler."

"George, you wouldn't —"

But the elevator was gone.

"That son of a bitch," Kate said. "He's trying to make me look like a fool."

"If we're lucky, maybe the elevator will crash on the way down."

"Got a pair of cable cutters handy?"

"I should have decked him when I had the chance."

"Believe me, George would like nothing better than for you to punch him out or give him a good shove. Are you kidding? Then he gets to blame me for bringing in cowboys like you as consultants. He'd risk a bloody nose if it got me in hot water."

"But it sure would have felt good."

"You might get your chance yet."

On the rest of the floor, people were busy wrapping up their day, making that last phone call, checking their e-mail, writing 'to-do' lists for the morning. Back in the Office of Special Investigations' Nazi-hunting branch, however, it appeared that things were just getting started. The very air seemed to be electric. I recognized Kate's eager young assistant, Dustin, and the computer guru Eleanor, bent over her monitor. There were three other people I didn't recognize from my last visit, one woman and two men both wearing white shirts with the sleeves rolled up and loosened neckties. "Hate crimes guys," Kate whispered by way of explanation. "There's been a rash of black churches being set on fire down south."

"It's about time you got here," Dustin cried, leaping up at the sight of Kate and looking concerned. "We've all been worried sick."

The poor kid really did sound shaken up. I noticed, too, the way his eyes slid over me before he gave me a wooden nod. I was thinking that maybe Dustin had a bit of a crush on Kate. In the space of five minutes, I had run into two jealous men at the Office of Special Investigations — one of them a spurned ex-lover, which is always the worst kind — and I hadn't even had the pleasure of doing anything to earn their jealousy except spend time with Agent Crockett.

"Oh, Dustin, you're so sweet," she said. "Fortunately, nobody got hurt. The bastard who broke in got away. They found his Jet Ski washed up nearby, so with any luck he drowned. It's possible that I winged him."

"You shot at him?" Dustin's mouth fell open. "The TV news didn't say anything about shooting."

"Well, the intruder started it," Kate said. "He shot at me, I shot at him. Professor McCoy also shot at him — that's after he hit him with an antique Scottish broadsword."

"Kate, remind me never to go into the field with you," Eleanor said, glancing up from her computer.

"We haven't been doing anything nearly that exciting," Dustin said, looking crestfallen. "Just going through the records again, looking for anything we missed."

While Kate and her team talked shop, I went in search of a soda machine. Normally I avoid the stuff but I was feeling tired and felt that a dose of caffeine and sugar might just do the trick. I'd already had so much coffee I felt like one more sip of the stuff would put me off it forever.

I found a vending machine, fed it some change, and a Coke *thunked* down. I popped the top and went wandering through the corridors, back toward the OSI section of the floor. They had given me a laminated pass that I wore on a lanyard around my neck so no one bothered me as I poked from room to room.

When I got back to Kate's office the only person there was Eleanor, still hard at work. She had turned off the lights and the glow from the screen reflected off her eyeglasses.

"Hello," I said. "You know, if I didn't know better I'd say you were hiding in here."

"Not hiding, exactly," she said. "More like being anti-social. Besides, I needed to get away from Kate for a while. She's a little wound up."

"Being shot at tends to do that to a person," I said. "Other than that minor detail, I'd say she's having the time of her life."

Eleanor shook her head and gave me a grim smile. She was actually kind of attractive in a bookish, librarian sort of way. "Kate is under a lot of pressure. She puts *herself* under a lot of pressure."

"She's tough," I said.

"You're one to talk. You're a college professor, but Kate told me how you beat up some skinheads, and then chased that guy who broke into her Uncle Silas's house with a shotgun. I'll bet you would have killed him if you'd caught up with him."

"Probably. Unless he killed me first. If my luck had been better I would have split his skull open instead," I said. "Unfortunately, I'm a little rusty handling a broadsword, although you'd think it would be an ancestral talent, at least on my Irish side."

"I also know how you went into East Germany back in the late eighties while the Iron Curtain was still up and tracked down Hermann Ubrecht. You found him and interviewed him for a story published in *Rolling Stone* magazine. I read it today in their archives." She shrugged. "Not a bad article."

Ubrecht had been one of Heinrich Himmler's young under-studies. During the war, Ubrecht had helped Himmler design his "final solution" to the Jewish problem. Some even credited Ubrecht with coming up with the idea for crematoriums to burn the remains of Jews gassed in the camps.

"I was young and foolish back then," I said. "The East German officials would have given me plenty of trouble if they had caught me. Ubrecht had a lot of friends. They were not happy with me after the article was published. They thought I had taken advantage of an old man. A few even offered to make sure I never lived a long life myself."

"But you pulled it off and revealed him to the world," she said. "I saw what you wrote. My God, he was *bragging* about what he had done. You described how he lived, where he lived. I heard that what you'd written caught the attention of the Israelis. There was even some talk of the Mossad snatching him out, but it was too risky politically."

"So far, I haven't been as lucky tracking down our latest Nazi," I pointed out.

"You really think it's Konrad Radl?" Eleanor asked.

"We both know that's not possible," I said, although, in the back of my mind, I was thinking of the time machine Captain Howard had shown us. "But it sure looks like Radl on that surveillance video."

Eleanor reached her arms high overhead in a lazy stretch that reminded me of a cat, then pulled herself back to the computer and started tapping at the keys. "That's what I started to wonder. I've searched several databases trying to find more information about Radl. Aside from his service records with the SS there's really not much. He disappears in nineteen forty-five."

"Tell me something I don't already know."

"I keep forgetting that you wrote a whole book about the Nazis," she said. "References to your book turn up quite a bit on the Internet, you know. There have been a few Radl sightings, or I should say, reported sightings. One in Germany in sixty-four, one in the United States in eighty-three, and three sightings in Argentina. The most recent was Buenos Aires in nineteen ninety-nine."

That last sighting was news to me. "It couldn't have been him," I said. "Radl would have been more than one hundred years old at that point. As for the earlier sightings in Germany and the United States, it's hard to say. If he wasn't caught up in the confusion of Germany's last days and killed, maybe he did manage to live out his life without being discovered."

Eleanor readjusted her glasses. "The sightings in Argentina caught my attention. A lot of Nazis fled there after the war. Even today there's a strong German community in Argentina, with something like twenty thousand people of direct German descent. That doesn't make them all Nazis, of course."

"What did you find out about Radl?"

Eleanor smiled, an expression that made her look even more like a very satisfied cat. "My Spanish is as rusty as your broadsword skills, but there's not much about Konrad Radl. Then I got the bright idea to do a general Internet search for Konrad Radl, something anybody could do, like punching in your own name just to see what comes up."

"Googling yourself, in other words," I said. "That seems a little obvious. Don't tell me you cracked the case by surfing the internet."

"Hang on, I'm getting to that," Eleanor said. "I hit a few references to your book again, that kind of thing. Then I decided to run a search engine that does some serious heavy lifting. You'd better have a look at this. Seeing is believing."

I looked over Eleanor's shoulder. The screen showed a search engine like Google, only this one was called Enigma.

"What's Enigma?" I asked. "I've never heard of that."

"It's a search engine for a database operated by intelligence-gathering organizations," she explained. "It's named after the infamous Nazi code-writing machine, coincidentally. You need a password to get into it because it's a subscription only-type deal mainly for law enforcement organizations."

She selected "images" and typed in *Konrad Radl*. Then she clicked on *search*. The Justice Department computer screen filled with twelve thumbnail-sized images. Six were black-and-white photographs of Konrad Radl from the Nazi era. Five were of people who had the unfortunate bad luck to share the surname of one of World War II's most-wanted war criminals, though not all had the first name Konrad. Like a Google search, Enigma dredged up anything that was a close match, if not exact. The final hit was a color photograph of Radl. But even from the thumbnail image, something did not seem right.

"Color?" I said. "I didn't know any color photographs of Radl were in existence."

"That's only the beginning," Eleanor said. "Hold on."

She clicked on the color image. On the screen, up popped a website in Spanish with an Argentinean URL. There was our guy, the color photograph version of Radl, wearing a camouflage uniform. Only there was a problem. Two big problems, as far as I could see.

"I know enough Spanish to get the gist of this," I said, leaning toward the screen and reading some of the text. "I don't get it. What's this got to do with Konrad Radl? This guy looks like him but as far as I can tell this is some kind of web site for the Argentinean military."

"You've got that right," Eleanor said. "I've been poking around on the site. I can puzzle out some of the Spanish. Basically, this is the website for what in Argentina is the equivalent of our Army Rangers. Real gung-ho guys, hard core macho men. I don't think this is an official web site or anything. It's macho-man stuff like who in the unit just climbed some big mountain in the Andes, who just did a triathlon, that kind of thing."

"And this Radl is one of them?" The guy in the photo appeared to have just finished with some rappelling, judging by the coil of rope over one shoulder.

"Going by the web site, he would seem to be."

"From the photo, he looks just like the old Nazi must have looked when he was late thirties, early forties."

"Bingo," Eleanor said. She smiled again. "After I found this website, I made some calls. What if I were to tell you that what you're seeing is a family resemblance? As it turns out, you're looking at your Nazi's grandson, Stefan Radl."

"I'll be damned."

"Now tell me, Professor. You're an old pro at tracking down Nazis. What's the first rule of any investigation?"

"There's no such thing as coincidence." I thought about it for about half a minute. "I wonder what the weather's like in Buenos Aires this time of year?"

"It's summer. I know that much."

Eleanor printed out the web page on her screen and we hustled down to Kate's office. Dustin was with her. She was slumped behind her desk, drinking from a tall cup of coffee, and I thought about what Eleanor had said about Kate being under a lot of pressure. I hadn't noticed it before, or maybe it was just the light from the overhead fixtures, but Kate's skin was a shade too pale. The smell of the coffee made my stomach churn. I didn't know how she could drink any more of that stuff.

"This would explain a lot," Kate said, once Eleanor showed her the printout. "I wish we had thought of it sooner. But Buenos Aires is pretty far from Rock Bottom. Why would Radl's grandson be mixed up in all this?"

"We don't know for sure that the grandson had anything to do with it," I said, worried that we were jumping to conclusions.

"But it makes a lot more sense that we saw Stefan Radl on the surveillance video rather than a time traveler."

"You're not seriously suggesting that someone traveled through time?" Dustin asked.

I waited for Kate to say something, but she didn't reply to Dustin's comment. Instead, she and I exchanged a look. *Were we suggesting that Radl had traveled through time?* What Kate finally said instead was, "Someone has to go to Argentina to see if we can talk with the grandson." Her voice sounded weary.

I turned to Dustin. "Grab your passport, kid. This is your big chance. You and I are taking a trip."

30

Argentina

Arturo Valdez was whip thin with a sharp voice to match. "You are the Americans?" he asked, his voice so loud that people at the Buenos Aires airport turned to stare. Valdez wore an army uniform with short sleeves and shoes polished to a mirror finish. The heels clicked on the tile floor as he approached us.

"I represent the Office of Special Investigations of the United States Department of Justice," Dustin said, trying to sound just as official himself. Rumpled from the long flight and looking more like a college intern than a government official, he was hard to take seriously.

Valdez turned to me. "I have a car waiting," he said. "Would you prefer to go to your hotel first or directly to see Major Radl?"

"Radl first, if you please," I said.

Valdez nodded and started off at a brisk pace toward the airport entrance. Behind him, Dustin was rushing to explain the purpose of our visit. He may as well have saved his breath, because Valdez knew who we were and why we were in his country. We had not arrived in Argentina unannounced. Back in D.C., Kate had made the arrangements. I suspected that her Uncle Silas had called in a few favors on this one to ensure that the Argentinean authorities cooperated.

Cooperation was not the same as a warm welcome. Back when the Third Reich had been crumbling, refugee Nazis had streamed into Argentina by the thousands, greeted with open arms by the Peron government. That was because the ousted Germans, French and Eastern European Nazi collaborators brought their stolen wealth. Argentina was a haven far beyond the reach of the International Military Tribunal or the United States government. These Nazis were never punished for their crimes. Even now, that influx of Nazi influence cast a long shadow across the decades. Modern Argentina was not eager to be reminded of its past, but it was also beholden to it.

Outside, Valdez opened the car door for me. Argentina had only been a democracy since 1983 and had not yet shed its class system. Valdez figured I was someone important and had acted accordingly; considering that I was nothing more than a disgraced college professor, I had certainly fooled him. I also felt a guilty pleasure that his obvious deference toward me was aggravating Dustin to no end. Poor kid.

"I know Major Radl well," Valdez said. "He is a well-respected officer in our special forces. I can't imagine why you've come all this way to talk with him."

"He may not know himself," I explained.

It was summer in Argentina, here on the other side of the equator, and the air conditioning in the car felt good after the stuffy confines of the plane and the heat in the airport. Minutes later we were heading out of the city, Valdez silent on the front seat beside the driver.

"Where the hell are we going exactly?" Dustin asked in a voice that wasn't much more than a whisper. He looked tired and nervous, deflated after our less-than-friendly greeting in the airport.

"We're going wherever they're taking us," I said. "Our tour guide here promises that Major Radl will be there."

Dustin seemed satisfied with that answer and he stared out the window. Like Dustin, I had never been to Argentina, but the scenery passed my eyes in a blur. I was too busy trying to imagine the conversation we were about to have with Stefan Radl.

We didn't have to wait long. In less than an hour we arrived at a home in the suburbs outside Buenos Aires. It was a ranch-style house with a roof of red clay tiles. The only landscaping consisted of spiny bushes planted in the stone mulch around the foundation. The stucco walls reminded me of a retiree's dream house in Florida, but from what we had seen on the drive from the airport it was clear that this was a solidly middle-class home.

No sooner had our car pulled up than the front door opened and a man stood in the doorway, waiting for us. His features were difficult to make out in the shadows, but I had an overall impression of a tall, blond-haired man.

Valdez started to get out. "Wait here," I told him.

"I am authorized to accompany you wherever you go in our country," Valdez said haughtily.

I would have argued with him, but the twelve-hour flight had sapped my energy. "Suit yourself," I said. "But don't blame me if you don't like what you hear."

Stefan Radl greeted us at the door. All I could do was stare. At first glance he was the mirror image of his infamous grand-

father. The differences soon became apparent. Konrad Radl
had had a rounder face, while his grandson's visage was longer
and more angular. But there was something of the wolf in the
faces of both men. Taller than me by an inch or two, Radl was
lean and muscular. He was not wearing a uniform, but had on
chinos, leather loafers, and one of the colorful rayon shirts,
worn outside the belt, that seemed to be in fashion here. He
was very tan, which contrasted with his crystalline blue eyes
and hair that at a distance looked white as an old man's. Up
close, his hair was a platinum blond like desert sand.

Dustin rushed up and explained who he was and why we
were there. Valdez didn't say much, but I noticed he was
respectful toward Radl. The man was an officer in the Argentine Special Forces, an elite unit. I was the last to be introduced
and Radl kept throwing wary glances in my direction. I noticed
a heavy bandage on his right arm.

His grip when he took my hand was strong and the skin
calloused. *All that climbing*, I thought. Radl did not let go right
away but took a long look into my face.

"Abraham McCoy, the famous Nazi hunter," he said.

"Stefan Radl, grandson of the famous Nazi."

Radl smiled at that. "Come in. I cleared away the swastikas
especially for your visit."

In the living room, we met his wife, a pretty blond who
looked uncertainly from her husband's face to mine, then went
into the kitchen to make coffee. We sat down, except for Valdez,
who stood stiffly to one side with his hat tucked under his arm.

"You've come a long way to hear about my grandfather,"
Radl said in perfect, but lightly accented English. "Unfortunately, there's not much I can tell you. I never met the man.
Most of what I know comes from Professor McCoy's fascinating
novel about the leaders of the Third Reich."

"It's non-fiction, actually."

"Oh? I wouldn't have thought so."

Dustin started to open his mouth, but I cut him off with a look. I hadn't come halfway across the world to let some kid do the talking for me. Radl had been facing the two of us, but now he shifted in his chair so that he looked at me directly.

"We came to find out about you," I said. "Have you visited the United States recently, Major Radl?"

"I was there less than two weeks ago for a conference in Washington," he said. "I used to go more often to do some climbing in your Rockies, but flying these days is hardly worth the trouble, with all the security. Why do you ask?"

"That wound on your arm – how did you get it?"

"A climbing accident."

"I'm sorry to hear that."

I recalled how hard I had swung the old broadsword at the intruder. If Radl had been our attacker at Rock Bottom, he was lucky he still had an arm. "There have been two deaths in the last week that the Office of Special Investigations is looking into."

"Should I call my lawyer?" Radl's smile was a touch conde-scending. "You do realize that I am beyond the reach of any American laws."

"The deaths involved former SS soldiers," I said. "We have someone on video who looks remarkably like you at the scene of a fatal robbery."

"Lieutenant Valdez, perhaps you could help my wife with the coffee things," Radl said, all traces of a smile gone from his lips. Obediently, Valdez disappeared into the kitchen. "You think I was responsible?"

"As I said, the person on the surveillance video looks like you. However, you weren't the first person who came to mind when I saw you on the tape. I was thinking of your grandfather."

"My grandfather?" Radl asked. Some shadow passed across his blue eyes then.

"*Obersturmbannführer* Konrad Radl, an officer in the Waffen SS," Dustin said.

"I'm familiar with who my grandfather was, thank you," Radl snapped. "You can't seriously believe he had anything to do with these murders. He's been dead for sixty years."

"I know what I saw on the security tape," I said quietly. "Of course, since it can't possibly be your grandfather, you came to mind."

"America is a dangerous place, Professor McCoy. Did you know that more than three hundred people were murdered last year in Baltimore, the city in which you live? That's more than were murdered in all of Argentina."

"Do you know what happened to your grandfather?" I asked.

Major Radl picked up a metal carabineer on his coffee table and toyed with it absently. His fingers were strong and dexterous. Looking at him now, I was certain that if it had been Stefan Radl who broke into Rock Bottom intent on killing us, then Kate, Silas and I would not have survived. "My grandfather disappeared during the war."

"Did your father ever tell you about him?"

"My father was very young when they fled Germany. He died six years ago."

"What about your grandmother? She must have reminisced."

"Always the journalist, aren't you? You Americans and your precious freedom of the press. In Argentina, fortunately, we have laws against that." Radl snapped the carabineer open and shut thoughtfully, over and over again. "My grandmother grieved for him all the rest of her days. She once told me she had seen him as she might see a dead man when he left for

Russia. He was changed when he came back, she said, cold as winter."

"He was one of the most-wanted war criminals," I said. "Are you sure he didn't survive the war and live out his life quietly here in Argentina?"

Major Radl shook his head, then said with an air of assurance, "Nothing that romantic, I'm afraid. He most certainly died in the final days of the war, probably in April nineteen forty-five."

"There's no documentation," Dustin said.

Keeping my eyes on Stefan Radl's face, I asked, "What do you know about Project Time Reich?"

Radl simply stared at me for a long time. "An honest question deserves an honest answer, Professor McCoy."

Radl glanced toward the kitchen as if to make certain that his wife — or perhaps more importantly, Valdez — was still occupied. "A long time ago, when I was still just a boy, a man came to our house to see my father. They spoke German, but I understood enough of it. The man questioned my father about a bronze disk which he was convinced had come with our family from Germany."

"A bronze disk?" I slid forward on the soft cushions of the sofa.

Radl gave me one of his thin smiles. "Does that sound familiar, Professor?"

"Why should it?"

"Come now, I thought we had agreed to be honest with each other. You see, when I was in Washington I read about the robbery attempt in the newspaper and I was curious. When I heard about the second incident, I took it upon myself to call your Office of Special Investigations and ask for details."

"You did *what*?" I couldn't believe what I was hearing. "Someone told you about the disk we found?"

"I was given a few details by a very helpful young man who

was glad to assist a police officer," Radl said, smiling at Dustin. "At least, that is how I represented myself."

Dustin stared at him. "You?"

"Go on," I said.

Radl leaned forward. The intensity of his blue eyes was electric. "You *know* who you saw on that security video, Professor. I can assure you that it was not me. And if it was not me, then who do you think it must be?"

"Impossible," I insisted, although the enormity of what Stefan Radl had just said was beginning to sink in.

"Have you ever been a soldier, Professor McCoy?"

"No. I have not."

"I know something about a soldier's life. A soldier does his duty. My grandfather served the Fatherland. As an officer in the SS who wore the Knight's Cross, he was a man *consumed* by duty. I just want you to understand the forces you are up against. This is not the classroom or a book, Professor. This is something *real*."

Mrs. Radl entered then with the coffee. Valdez followed behind, bearing a tray laden with cups, saucers and cookies. Dustin looked from me to Radl, but both of us had fallen silent. The major set the carabineer back on the coffee table with a deliberate motion. Awkwardly, we worked our way through a cup of coffee, commenting on nothing more than the weather. When we finally stood to make our goodbyes, Radl didn't offer his hand to anyone.

"Thank you for your time, Major," I said.

Radl fixed me with a cold look. "My grandfather would let nothing stand in the way of duty. He did not believe in failure. You would do well to remember that, Professor McCoy."

We drove back to the city in silence. Night was coming on, and I felt exhaustion tugging on my very bones. Watching the sun go down on this foreign land that had harbored the worst of the Nazis, I felt a cold chill at the base of my spine, convinced that Radl had not told us everything he knew. What secrets had he held back? Valdez didn't say a word, but there was a faint smile on his face as if he thought Major Radl had given Dustin and me our comeuppance.

Valdez and the driver dropped us at our hotel. Valdez got out to open the car door for us. "So you came all this way to bother Major Radl about his grandfather," he said. "The man has been dead for six decades. It seems to me to me that you were sent on a fool's errand."

I didn't have a snappy comeback for that one.

Dustin was helping the driver get our luggage out of the trunk. Valdez retreated into the car without another word and drove away. I grabbed my suitcase and trudged into the lobby.

There was some confusion at the front desk, with Dustin and I ending up in the same room, which apparently was the last one available. I was too tired to argue with the hotel clerk in my broken Spanish. Upstairs, I chucked my suitcase on the bed and called down to room service. They understood the word *cerveza* well enough and sent up half a dozen bottles crammed into a bucket of ice. The beer was good and cold, the bottle caps thoughtfully cracked halfway, so I gave the man who delivered them a tip that left him grinning. Dustin had stretched out on his own bed without bothering to take off his shoes. I handed him a beer.

"I am *so* beat," said Dustin, who had been unusually quiet since Stefan Radl's revelation regarding the helpful young man at OSI who had given him details about the case. "I don't know if it's jet lag or meeting up with that Nazi creep today, but I feel like I got hit with a truck."

"A Panzer tank is more like it," I said.

"He played me, all right. He got me to tell him about the case."

"Don't worry about it," I said. "I've got the feeling Stefan Radl has played a lot of people. He seems awfully smart."

"Was it worth coming all this way?"

"I'm not sure," I said. "Radl isn't telling us the whole story."

"We could go back tomorrow and talk to him again."

"It wouldn't do any good. He knows we can't touch him."

Dustin sipped his beer, but I could tell something was bugging him. "You think I'm an amateur, don't you?" he finally said. "You wouldn't even let me say a word today to Major Radl or that Valdez character. I'm the one who works for OSI, not you."

The comment took me by surprise. When I thought back on it, I *had* been kind of short toward Dustin. What sort of professor would act like that? Some mentor I made. I *had* tried to make him feel better about having been duped by Radl over the phone.

"I asked you to come to Argentina, didn't I? You're doing fine. It's just that you're a kid. Hell, you're so young I'm jealous of you." I wanted to add that the likes of Major Radl did not suffer young fools, but instead I said, "Radl felt more comfortable talking with someone closer to his own age."

Dustin nodded—he seemed to accept that. He took a long drink. "Are you going to tell Kate that Radl tricked me?"

"No," I said. "I'll let you do that. You're the one who works for OSI, remember?"

"I feel like I let her down," he said.

"Believe me, Kate will respect that you told her yourself."

Dustin nodded, thinking it over. "I guess you're right. The thing with Kate is, I know she's my boss, and she's a little older, but I also think she's pretty hot. Let's say we're just a couple of guys talking here. You know what I mean?"

"I think I do." I had to wonder if Dustin was truly confiding in me, or was he trying to send me a message, as in, *hands off.* At the moment, I was too tired to think about subtle meanings. With a sigh, I changed the subject. "There's a lot of nightlife in this city, Dustin. They've even got whorehouses, if you're interested. God only knows what some girl here would do for an extra twenty bucks."

"I'm too exhausted for that," Dustin said a little too quickly. "Mind if I have another beer?"

"Youth is wasted on the young," I said, and handed him a cold bottle.

31

Washington

Dustin's cell phone rang as soon as we stepped off the plane Sunday night in Baltimore. While he answered, I went in search of caffeine.

"That was Kate," he said when I came back with two coffees. "She thinks she knows the identity of the third soldier in the photograph."

"That's great news."

"The only problem is that he's been dead for six weeks."

"That's going to make him a little hard to interview," I said.

I was glad to hear that Kate had made some progress in our absence. I felt that Dustin and I had returned from Argentina with nothing but more questions, chief among them being who had killed Joe Miller and frightened Hans Schmidt to death, and who looked enough like Colonel Radl to bear more than a passing resemblance on the security video. There remained the possibility that Stefan Radl had lied to us and was the actual killer. He might even have attacked us at Rock Bottom. It took no great leap of the imagination to see him as a murderer. But what would be his motive?

Dustin didn't say much on the taxi ride to OSI, probably because he nodded off. We rushed directly to Kate's office and gave her the disappointing news that while Stefan Radl was the spitting image of his grandfather, he claimed that he hadn't murdered anyone.

"Tell me what you found out about the third soldier," I said when it was Kate's turn to update us.

She turned to Eleanor.

"There was an unusual break-in in Delaware," Eleanor said. "I found it on the website for the local TV station. A man wearing a German World War II uniform forced his way into a house in a town called Elsmere. The homeowner wrestled with the guy, who got away."

"Sounds like our Nazi."

"There's more," said Eleanor. "I was wondering: why that house? So I made a few phone calls and got the street address, then checked state-of-Delaware tax records. The house was owned by a man named Peter Geiger."

"Nice work," I said. "There's only one problem, right?"

"I guess you heard the news," Eleanor said. She handed me a copy of Peter Geiger's obituary. "It's from the local newspaper. Evidently, he died several weeks ago from natural causes. Records show the house is still in the family, so whoever broke into the house evidently was fighting with a family member."

"As far as the family knows, nothing was taken," Kate chimed in.

"How do you know?"

Eleanor gave me one of her feline grins. "I called the house this afternoon and spoke to the late Mr. Geiger's son."

What the obituary failed to mention, but which Eleanor had found in a newspaper clipping with the headline "SS

Soldier's Funeral Becomes Neo-Nazi Spectacle," was the fact
that Geiger's funeral had been well-attended by various skinhead organizations. The reporter described how they had
raised their hands in a Nazi salute as the old man's casket was
lowered into the ground.

"Why didn't you deport him?" I asked. "He never should
have been allowed into this country in the first place."

"Nobody knew about him," Eleanor said. "His name wasn't
on our watch list."

Even all these years after the end of World War II, the
Justice Department maintained a list of more than twenty thousand suspected Nazi war criminals. The list was issued to all
customs and immigration officials, who were under orders to
arrest anyone on the list who tried to enter — or leave — the
United States.

"How is that possible?" I asked.

"Chances are that Peter Geiger wasn't his real name," Kate
explained.

"We do have the immigration records for Geiger," Eleanor
said. She recited from her notes: "Peter Geiger, born nineteen
twenty-one. He joined the Wehrmacht and served in Holland,
then was called back for the battle of Berlin. He survived and
surrendered to American forces. After the war, he was briefly in
a detention camp, then applied for entrance to the United
States."

"That's all very interesting," Kate said. "But pointless if
Geiger was simply an alias."

"So who was he?"

"We'll have to find out. Eleanor?"

"I'll start cross-referencing Peter Geiger against the SS
service records we acquired from former Soviet bloc countries,"
the researcher said. "With luck, the database will have some
record of who he was before he became Geiger."

"It wouldn't hurt to go speak with his family," Kate said.

"Elsmere, Delaware. It's more or less a blue collar suburb of Philadelphia. How far away is it?"

"It's a good two-hour drive," Eleanor said. "I looked it up on the map. It's a straight shot up I-95."

Kate looked at me, and from her expression I could tell what her next question was going to be. "Are you up for it?" she asked.

I glanced at my watch. "It's almost seven. With a two-hour drive, I can't see us banging on the doors of respectable citizens after nine o'clock at night. That's too late."

"First thing in the morning, then," Kate said, sounding almost grateful to put it off. I realized how exhausted we all were; weariness hung on all our shoulders like chain mail. The flight to Argentina, the attack on Rock Bottom, even our field trip to the ONR graveyard were beginning to take their toll.

"I could go with you," Dustin offered. He looked so eager, like a Boy Scout. "You and I could go on this one, Kate, if Professor McCoy is too tired."

Kate hesitated. "I think the professor and I have got this covered, Dustin. See if you can help Eleanor dig up something more on Geiger."

"I'll never get any experience if I don't get out into the field," Dustin said, not ready to give up. "You just sent me to Argentina, so what's a trip to Delaware? The Nazi we're looking for has been dead for weeks, anyway."

"All right," she said, relenting. "You can come with us. Be here at seven a.m. Stragglers get left behind."

With that, Kate grabbed a stack of paperwork threatening to topple off her desk and headed out the door, saying, "C'mon, Professor. We have some work to do."

"Is that what they're calling it these days?" said Eleanor, smiling like a Cheshire cat.

Kate shot her a look, then started down the hallway with me in tow.

"I've been thinking," said Kate. "I'd like to see your father's journals. He was at Dachau with Hans Schmidt. Did he ever write about Schmidt?"

"I'm not sure," I said. "Not that I know of."

"That's why I think we should go take a look."

"Right now?"

"No time like the present."

"All right. If you think you're up for it."

We took the elevator down to the garage. However, instead of turning toward where we had left the Hummer, Kate went to a small cinderblock office where a lone, uniformed man sat. A sign on his door said: "Transportation." Several vehicles were parked nearby, including a jet-black Malibu that caught my eye.

"We need new wheels," she said before ducking into the office. "I'm not taking Uncle Silas's Hummer to Delaware tomorrow morning. We've already put enough miles on it in the service of Uncle Sam."

"Fine by me," I said. "Just so long as we don't have to drive my old bucket of bolts."

We entered the cramped office that smelled of damp concrete and car exhaust. "Hi Ben," she said. "We need a car."

"What's wrong with the one you got?" he asked, raising one eyebrow. He had that suffer-no-fools attitude common to ER admission nurses, motor vehicle employees and high school teachers. Ben acted as if he'd had his lifetime fill of excuses and tales of woe.

"My car was slightly damaged," Kate explained, using the honey version of her voice. "It's in Connecticut right now."

"I may have seen something on the news about that," Ben admitted. "Trouble is, I don't have any cars to give you right now. A transportation van, maybe, but not a car."

"How about that one there?" Kate said, nodding toward the black Malibu.

"That car was just assigned," he said. "It's not part of the motor pool."

"Whose car is it?"

"George Foster's."

"Oh. He mentioned he was getting a new car." Kate took out her cell phone, turned away, and chatted for a moment. "I have George on the phone now. He says it's all right if I use the car as long as I only have it a couple of days."

"I don't know —"

She held the cell phone toward him. "Do you want to speak with him?"

From the look on the man's face, I could see he wanted no part of talking to Foster. "If he says it's all right, that's good enough for me."

Kate said goodbye and got off the phone. She signed a couple sheets of paperwork, and then the motor pool operator handed her a set of keys.

"Don't bang it up," he said. "This baby cost a bundle. It's got leather seats, performance suspension, a turbocharger, two hundred and ten horsepower."

"I'll be careful," she said.

Driving away, I asked: "Who did you really call?"

"My answering machine at home."

"You're going to get that poor guy in trouble."

"George doesn't have that kind of clout. He's just good at making life miserable for his co-workers in OSI."

We got our bags out of the Hummer and put them in the trunk of the Malibu. After what had happened to her car at Rock Bottom, I wondered about leaving the Hummer in the garage, but Kate explained that her uncle's vehicle would be just fine where it was.

"What kind of idiot would try to steal a vehicle from the Department of Justice parking garage? This place has so much security it makes Fort Knox look like a drive-through bank at a shopping center."

"You have a point."

Kate steered the car through the city streets and got us out onto I-495, the famous Washington "beltway" that divided the world of those in the know from the rest of the nation "beyond the beltway." Then we exited onto I-95 north toward Baltimore. The car was fast and Kate handled it recklessly, flying up the entrance ramp like she was merging into a NASCAR race and then cutting from lane to lane.

"This baby moves," she said.

"King George is not going to be happy when he finds out you drove off with his new wheels."

"He's not happy with me anyway, so what's the difference?"

"Men don't like it when you mess with their wheels."

"What does he need a car for, anyhow?" Kate asked bitterly, punching the Malibu into a space between two tractor trailers, then weaving around as she hunted for an open lane. "His idea of field work is going to meetings across town. He ought to take the metro."

32

W e were halfway back to Baltimore when Kate growled something like *Aargghh* and jabbed at the car stereo until she figured out how to turn it on. "That George really pisses me off," she said, fiddling with the tuner until she found a station playing Prince's "Purple Rain" and turned it up.

Like me, Kate was a closet fan of '80s music, the era when both of us had graduated from high school, even if I was at the earlier end of the decade. "What pisses me off even more is that we almost got killed the other night. I haven't even had time to think about that until now."

If Kate's hands hadn't been on the steering wheel, I was pretty sure they would be shaking. "That's the kind of thinking that you can use one of two ways," I said. "You can let it make everything that much sweeter, or it can make you afraid to get out of bed in the morning."

"You've been there before, huh?"

"Nobody chases monsters without having a few bad days," I said, then touched her shoulder. "You okay?"

"I'm okay now," she said. "It's more my dreams that I'm worried about."

Traffic was light this time of night. Even on the highway, the night felt primal. Cold and darkness pressed against us beyond the windshield, red taillights winking in the night like animal eyes. Neither of us said much. Kate gunned the car down the I-395 ramp into downtown Baltimore. We passed the gray hulk of the Ravens stadium and then the brick enormity of Oriole Park at Camden Yards. I told her to turn right and we headed toward the harbor area where my condo perched near the waterfront. We passed the usual homeless guys on the corners, then headed toward my building and turned into the parking garage entrance.

"Keep your eyes open," I said. "This is where I got my bruises three nights ago and I don't want a repeat performance."

We moved through the garage, toward the elevators. Kate was jumpy and nervous, symptoms of too much caffeine and not enough sleep, not to mention bad memories of what had taken place at Rock Bottom. She clutched her handbag under her left arm; I didn't recall her ever carrying a handbag before. I had a pretty good idea that Kate's well-oiled .38 Special was in there. If there were more skinheads waiting in the shadows, they wisely kept out of sight.

We rode up in the elevator. Tired as I was, it was only just beginning to sink in that Kate had come to my place. There was a legitimate excuse, of course, which was that we had decided we needed to review my father's journals. However, Kate hadn't made any mention of a need to return to Washington tonight, which meant that she was either getting a hotel room in Baltimore or planning to stay at my place. Normally I wouldn't mind the second option, but the truth was that Kate scared me a little. She was somebody I could fall for. And we would be continuing to work with each other, at least for the next few days. Was I ready for this? Was I reading too much into her coming here? It wouldn't be the first time I had misread a situation. Then again, Kate hadn't asked if I had a couch.

I let us in, then carefully locked and bolted the door behind us. Kate walked through the door and gave the condo a quick appraisal.

"Your place looks like a big office with some furniture and a kitchen thrown in," she announced. She walked toward the windows. "Wow. Nice view of the harbor."

"I paid extra for that. Believe me."

Kate plunked down in my worn leather sofa. It felt strange to have someone else in the condo. With just me in it, the space always felt comfortable. Now, it seemed cramped, like your car does when you're not used to passengers. I hardly knew where to sit in my own living room. "I like this," she said, bouncing on the sofa. "Just the kind of place to curl up with a book and a drink."

It was also good for sleeping on, but I didn't mention that yet. Then Kate was up again and examining the bookshelves, which was when I realized that she was as nervous as I was. Kate hadn't come here with a plan. She ran her fingers over the spines. Books clung to the shelves, jammed in every which way, old leather-bound editions squeezed in next to cheap paperbacks.

"And I thought I read a lot," Kate said. "I'd say you've got me beat, Professor."

"Before you came along and got me hunting Nazis again, let's just say I had some time on my hands for reading."

She picked up a paperback with a glitzy cover. "Paperback thrillers?"

"A guilty pleasure," I said.

"I know. Mine is reading *People* magazine. It's trash, but every now and then they have a photo of Ryan Reynolds in a swimsuit."

"And here I thought you were more of a Tom Cruise kind of girl."

"When I was in high school I thought he was cute dancing around in his underwear in *Risky Business*, but he hasn't done it for me since then." Kate moved on to an antique barrister's bookcase with glass doors. "These aren't books, are they?" she asked, squinting at the notebooks lining the shelves. "They look like old papers, like you've saved a bunch of school assignments."

"Those are my father's journals," I said.

She touched the doors. "No dust. You still read them, don't you?"

"Yes."

"Are these all your father's?"

"No. Just the top shelf. Since *Journey of Hope* came out, people are always sending me other journals and diaries. Some are photocopies, some are originals."

"What are you going to do with all of them? It looks like you have the makings of another book here."

"I don't know that I want to make a career out of compiling other people's journals. My father's were personal. The others I'm safekeeping for now."

"May I?"

Reluctantly, I nodded. I felt like I was letting her into a very private place. Kate opened the doors and pulled out one of the journals from the top shelf at random. It was battered and yellow with age but the notebook had a strong binding. She opened it and frowned.

"I'm afraid my German isn't very good," she admitted. "I can maybe order a beer or ask how to get to the train station, but that's about it. Would you read it to me?"

I took the book and gazed down at my father's familiar handwriting. Each line was neat and orderly, squaring off perfectly with the line above and below it. This was the hand of an engineer, a man who worried about details. And therein was the power of his journals. The writing stood out not so much for its literary merits but because of the descriptions of life at Dachau, that hell on earth where the Germans had sculpted *Arbeit Macht Frei* on the iron gates. The motto was a taunt and a threat all at once: *Work will set you free.*

I began to read, translating for Kate as I went:

MORNING DAWNED GRAY AND COLD. *A freezing drizzle fell and coated the barbed wire and clots of frozen mud with ice. The guards came and unlocked the doors for the morning apfel. Even with the doors open it remained dark inside the barracks. No one moved quickly enough and the damp and cold had put the guards in a foul mood.*

"It stinks in here!" the soldiers shouted in disgust. "Stinking kikes!"

The smell only fueled the soldiers' anger the way an awkward boy sets off a schoolyard bully. And it did stink. An odor of onions and unwashed bodies and the smell of despair like rotting meat.

In their bulky wet uniforms and helmets each soldier looked inhuman. The angry guards sent in two kapos with sticks to drive the slower ones out. We hated the kapos, Jews who were even more cruel than the Nazis, having turned on their own people for a few more scraps of bread each day.

We stumbled out into the cold and were counted. Even though I had my own small room in the prison barracks, I was not exempt from the morning roll-taking and if I didn't move fast enough a kapo would lay a stick across my back. There were new faces each day and old ones gone. But it was only the numbers that the Nazi guards cared about. When we came in from the morning apfel there was the smell hanging in the barracks like a fog. Did we smell like that? It made us ashamed and to keep from being overcome with self-loathing I had to remind myself that the Nazis had done this to the Jews; it was not by choice.

I remembered how there was a time when I loved mornings and the promise they held of a new day. It was hard now to greet a new day with anything like joy. I think many of us would have preferred to have died quietly in the night, in our sleep, rather than bear the indignity of a new day. But they beat us with sticks and drove us out. We stumbled into the cold morning and were counted.

KATE WAS quiet for a long time after I finished reading. "My God," she finally said. "How does someone survive something like that?"

"One gray morning at a time, I suppose. At least, that's how my old man survived."

"I don't remember reading that passage in *Journey of Hope*."

"It's not in the book," I said. "Look at the shelf. He filled up dozens of journals. There were so many mornings he wrote about. Narrowing it down to the material needed for a published book was like pulling out my fingernails."

"You know, it doesn't always take a time machine to travel through time. Your father's words are still being read sixty years after he wrote them. The Germans may have tried to invent time travel, but your father actually did it, in a way."

"My father would have liked that idea. He was very proud of having outlasted the Nazis in the end."

"What about the rest of the journals? Do you think there is some clue in them to help us today? You're saying he was at Dachau with these Nazis, Hans Schmidt and Josef Mueller. Didn't he ever write about them?"

I thought about that, sweeping my hand along the length of the shelf, touching the faded spines of the notebooks. "I'm not sure. There are so many journals. In the past I always read them with an eye toward understanding what life was like in the camp, but not for any projects my father may have been working on for the Germans."

"Maybe you need to take another look. It could be like English class. You don't see a theme or symbolism in a story until the professor points it out."

"I'm the one who's supposed to be the professor," I reminded Kate. "I think I would have noticed if time travel was mentioned in my father's journals. That's something that's kind of hard to miss."

"He probably wouldn't have known about Time Reich," Kate said. "He wouldn't have known the real purpose behind what the Germans were having him do. He only would have seen a part of it. It's the perfect cut-out."

"You might be right. But even if my father did know about Time Reich, he couldn't have written about it openly. As a prisoner at the camp, his journals could be seized at any time. The SS guards would have shot him in a minute if they'd thought he was writing about their secret project."

"Do you have these journals indexed somehow, or maybe transcribed?"

"No, nothing that organized, I'm afraid. The best I've done is put them in chronological order on the shelves."

"In that case," Kate said, "we have our work cut out for us."

"You're not kidding." What I didn't point out was that for Kate, these were just pages out of history, with all the emotion of documents in a court case. But for me, these were my father's words haunting me out of the past. I never would be able to skim through the journals. It would be like Kate trying to flip through the pages of a family photo album and not get caught up in some reminiscence. How did you hurry through handwritten journals describing four years of pain and suffering at Dachau? There were places where my father had pressed so hard that his pencil left indentations in the paper, as if he had been carving furrows. These were not words to be taken lightly.

Kate got to work, flipping through the journals in hopes of seeing some mention of Time Reich, Colonel Radl, Josef

Mueller, Peter Geiger or even wily old Juozas Juknys, who would go on to re-invent himself as Hans Schmidt. Her German was not comprehensive, but it was good enough to pick out key words and meanings. Loose pages and my own notes inserted between them fluttered out as she rifled through the journals. It was like she was scattering my memories across the living room carpet. In her excitement, she grabbed up another journal and flipped it open too hard. The sixty-year-old cardboard spine cracked, sending loose pages spinning to the floor.

"I wish you would be more careful," I said, resisting the urge to pry the notebook out of her hands and return it to the safety of the bookcase.

"Are you *sure* your father never wrote about Juozas Juknys or any of the rest?" Kate asked, continuing to flip the pages of the broken journal with abandon. "If he had his picture taken with those SS men, surely he must have known them."

"He might have mentioned them," I said. "Better keep looking. But go easy on the notebooks, will you?"

I lost track of how long we sat there, going through the pages. When I finally looked up, my eyes blurry as I tried to focus on the clock face, it was a few minutes past eleven.

In compiling *Journey of Hope*, I had found some passages that simply did not fit. The book was about a survivor's journey through the hell that had been Nazi Germany's concentration camps. Some of my father's entries felt out of context with that theme. There were times when he dwelt on some family matter or a job he had done before the war. Any editor faced the same problem when he had too much material to fit into the pages of a book.

Kate was still plowing through the shelves, although the pile of handwritten journals on the floor now outnumbered the remaining books. With the end in sight, Kate seemed to work even faster. She grabbed another book from the shelf and whipped it open. I winced as she did it, and with good reason;

the leather spine cracked at the rough handling, leaving the cover dangling by a flap of dry rotted leather.

"Goddammit, Kate, I asked you to take it easy," I snapped, more anger in my voice than I'd meant to show. Seeing the journal damaged seemed to wrench something inside me.

"All right, I'm sorry," Kate said, sounding angry right back. We were both running on fumes. "But it's nothing a little tape can't fix."

She held the book up to better examine the damage, flexing the cover back and inspecting the cracked spine.

"Just give it to me," I said, reaching for the journal.

"Hold on," she said, peering at the binding. "What's this?"

From between the cloth binding that held the pages together and the leather spine was a pocket of space, the same space created in any hardcover book when you open the cover. Now that the spine was broken, we could see several sheets of paper stuffed inside, pages that had been carefully folded to about the thickness of a Popsicle stick and then slid into the space. The spine must have cracked away not just because of Kate's rough handling, but also from the pressure of the hidden pages.

Using her fingertips, Kate tugged out the yellowed pages and unfolded them. Written on thin wartime paper, they came apart at the worn creases but it was easy enough to tape them back together. Kate patched the pages with trembling hands, then handed them to me and asked, "What do they say?"

Quickly, I scanned the sheets of paper, wondering why my father would have hidden them. I'd found things tucked away between the pages before, but never anything hidden so carefully.

Now, reading what my father had written so many years ago, I was amazed to see that the passage described a visit from a guard named Otto Friedrich to my father's room in the prisoners' barracks. Friedrich was mentioned in *Journey of Hope*. He was a guard who had a peculiar relationship with my father, friendly at times but threatening at others. You might call him your typical psychopath, not an uncommon trait in an SS camp guard. I recalled that Friedrich had seemed amused by my father. I began to read.

33

I was just settling in for the evening when Friedrich came into the room. It was dark out, past curfew for the prisoners, but Friedrich was an SS sergeant so he could do as he pleased. He held the door open longer than necessary so that the little bit of heat in the room rushed out and was replaced by the cold, wet night air. I did not want him here but I had little choice. All day long I had to endure Friedrich and the other Nazis. I hoped for at least a few hours to myself at night to write in my journal and think my own thoughts.

"Nice place you have here, Herr Baumann," he said, for it is always his habit to be formal with me. Still, even as he said it, a small smile flitted across his heavy face.

"It keeps the rain off," I replied.

He laughed harder than necessary and that made me uneasy.

"Herr Baumann, always the humorist," he said, and took one of my chairs, turned it around and sat straddling it. Seeing him sit made me feel easier, if wary. "Such a smart man, an educated man. Unlike myself. You've actually read all these books, haven't you?"

The room holds a few small shelves of books, hardly the library I'd had at home, but an incredible luxury compared to what prisoners had. Working for Radl had its privileges if not its rewards.

Friedrich went on: *"It must make you bitter deep down to know that an educated man such as yourself is being held captive by the likes of me. I'm sure you would gladly trade places."* This was a dangerous remark and I passed it off with a shrug. He sat studying me with that half-smile on his face, the kind of look the wolf used while contemplating the sheep. *"Herr Baumann, always so careful. Always watching."*

"Would you like a game of chess to pass the time, Sergeant Friedrich?" I asked, trying to sound friendly. *"Sometimes at night I play a game against myself. It would be better to have an actual person sitting across from me."*

"Nein, nein," he said, still amused. He lit a cigarette. *"Never play chess against a Juden. And a smart one at that. An SS man needs to feel superior, and what would happen if I lost? I might be forced to shoot you."* He patted the Luger in its holster.

"Then perhaps we'd better not play chess," I said.

Friedrich laughed. *"You are not so bad, Herr Baumann. I hate Jews, but in your case I am willing make an exception."*

"Thank you, Sergeant Friedrich."

"Stupid, isn't it, for you to accept such a compliment from me? But that is the way of the world right now."

"Yes," I agreed. *"Do not think that I ever forget for one moment that I am your captive and you are my jailor."*

For the length of a heartbeat, he looked angry, sucking deeply on his cigarette. Another prisoner would have been shot for such a remark. I had seen men killed for less. I wondered if I had made a mistake, if he would draw that Luger now, order me out into the muddy prison yard, and shoot me.

Then he shrugged it off. It was then that I knew Friedrich wanted something from me. *"Tell me, Herr Baumann. You are no fool. You have read all these books. You have seen something of the world. Do you believe a man can travel through time?"*

"What?"

"You mean you don't know about the experiment?"

"Time travel?"

"Yes, the project we are working on. The bunker you are helping to build. Colonel Radl intends to send a man through time."

"I was told we were building a bunker for members of the high command from Munich."

"You were misled, Herr Baumann."

Of course. Now it made sense. But I had only seen my portion of the project. Had Radl sent Friedrich as some kind of test? Perhaps the colonel wanted to see how much I really knew.

"To travel through time," I said. "That would be something."

"But can it be done, Herr Baumann?" Sergeant Friedrich leaned forward, intent on my answer.

"Anything is possible, I suppose." After all, he was asking a man whose world had been turned upside down.

"Radl won't send me, you know," Friedrich said, tossing down the stub of his cigarette and grinding it into the floor with the toe of a muddy boot. "The colonel wants me to grow into an old man and wait in the future for whomever he will send through time."

"You have your duty," I said. I tried to smile, still wondering what was going on. "Who knows what the future will bring?"

Friedrich stood. "Then my duty is to grow old. I'll travel into the future the old-fashioned way, not aboard some time machine."

"There are worse things than growing old."

Friedrich glared. "Who wants to grow into an old man and die, Herr Baumann? Not me. Once again you may wish you could trade places with me because you don't need to be one of these degenerate gypsy fortune tellers to know what your future holds, Herr Baumann, and it's not old age."

And with that, he went out into the night.

After Friedrich was gone, I sat up for a long time tinkering with the chess board. The lights had been shut off in the main prisoner barracks but the guards left me alone with my candle. Their special prisoner. Their builder.

Sleep did not come easily. Maybe Friedrich had come because he *did simply want to know my opinion. But he had warned and threatened me all at once. When this project was finished and Colonel Radl no longer had a use for me, Friedrich would likely be the one to put his pistol to my head and pull the trigger.*

34

W hen I finished, I passed the open journal to Kate. After a few minutes she looked up and said, "I feel like we're the ones who just stepped into a time machine. There's the guard telling your father about Time Reich. He was sent into the future to become on old man."

A thought occurred to me. "Wait a minute. Think about the photo we got from Hazel Miller. Who's in it? Hans Schmidt. Joe Miller. My father. Who do you think the fourth man is?"

Kate nodded. "*Unterscharfuhrer* Otto Friedrich."

"I have a hunch that when we show that photo to Geiger's relatives tomorrow, they're going to recognize their grandfather."

"Peter Geiger and Otto Friedrich, one and the same?" Kate nodded in agreement. "It's worth a shot."

She grabbed up her cell phone and put a call in to Dustin and Eleanor, who were still at OSI going through the database. They reported no luck so far. Kate told them to see if they could find anything on Otto Friedrich, gave them my fax number, then hung up.

Kate rubbed her eyes. "I'm so tired I can't even think straight."

I was tired, too, but I wasn't ready to quit. "My father knew about Time Reich," I said. "He knew about it but he did nothing to stop it. My God, he even helped build the thing. Some journey of hope."

"Don't be so hard on him," she said. "His first job was to survive. He had to help them build it. He had no choice."

"We always have a choice. My father chose to help the Nazis."

I looked at the clock. Somehow, it was now nearly midnight. From my window, the lights of Baltimore twinkled and bobbed on the black waters of the harbor. This was not tourist season, so the streets were largely deserted. It was as if we had the whole city to ourselves. Volume after volume of the journals were open and strewn around us where we had dipped into them, trying to find anything that might be related to Time Reich or offer a clue about the whereabouts of Konrad Radl. The smell of musty paper made my nose wrinkle. Someplace in there it held a lingering smell of the camps at Dachau: stale air, unwashed bodies, spoiled food, fear. We had stuck Post-It notes to the relevant pages but even after hours of reading there were precious few yellow flags. "I don't know if we're getting anywhere with this," I finally said. "We haven't come across anything definitive."

Kate shrugged. "That's the way it works sometimes. But we do know that your father wasn't masterminding the plan. Obviously, he was working with the Germans, but he didn't really know what they were building. Not until Otto Friedrich told him."

"I don't think he really had any idea," I agreed. "But my father was a smart man. He must have known something was going on."

"Maybe he did but he made a point never to write about it,"

Kate said. "You yourself said writing about Time Reich would have gotten him shot."

"So you think he left it out? Like ignoring the elephant in the living room?"

"Or in this case, the SS guard with the Luger to your head."

"It's possible he left it out."

Kate picked up a copy of *Journey of Hope* and opened the book to the last page. "You know, I've always thought the last line was somewhat cryptic," she said. " 'Behind hope lies everything.' What does that mean?"

"Well, it's supposed to be inspirational, like saying 'Tomorrow is a new day' or 'Think positive thoughts.' "

"Can you show me where it says that in the journals?"

"Sure."

It took me a few minutes, but there it was. Strangely, I could almost hear my father's voice saying it. Even stranger was the fact that my father was not one given to uttering inspirational phrases. It simply wasn't in his personality. He had been more the sort of person who survived by keeping his head down. A pragmatist.

It suddenly struck me that maybe I had selected the wrong title for the book.

"Good Lord," I said. "Maybe I should have called this thing *Dachau One Day at a Time*."

Kate was looking at the journal entry. It was the very last entry of the very last page.

"This isn't the last journal."

"Sure it is," I said. "At least, it's the last one I have."

"But look how it ends," she said. "He's writing about the poor rations in one paragraph, and then he's writing 'Behind hope lies everything.' It doesn't make sense."

"Maybe he went back and added it later."

"That's possible," Kate agreed. "But then where's the description of the last days of the camp, the liberation? It would be like me keeping a journal of my many failed relationships and then ending it with 'And then one day along came Mr. Right.' That's cheating the reader out of the whole story."

"I don't know why it ends this way."

"Don't you see? It's a message. Your father is sending us a message."

"Sure he is. He's telling us to be hopeful."

"No, he's not." Kate shook her head. "Didn't you read your own book? It's not a story about hope. I mean, not really. It's a story about hanging in there, about survival in a world that's gone to hell."

"Then what does the message mean?"

Kate looked stumped. "I don't know."

"And why wouldn't he have told me if there was more?"

"Maybe he wanted you to figure that out for yourself," Kate said. "He knew you would, when the time came. But right now, my brain is too tired to think anymore."

"Time to give it a rest, then. How about a beer?"

"You won't have to twist my arm."

I went to the refrigerator, my mind still back in 1945. Looking through my father's journals had really sent my mind whirling. It was also a reminder of how little had actually made it into *Journey of Hope*. The question was, where were we headed with all this?

When I came back in with the beers, Kate was still sitting on the floor. I turned on the stereo, some old U2. The thumping rock beat dispelled any lingering ghosts of the past.

"I hope you're not thinking of driving back to D.C. tonight?" I asked.

"Well, I hate to impose . . . I could get a hotel room."

"Don't bother with that," I said. "It's already after midnight. What's the point of going to a hotel now? There's plenty of room."

She reached for her cell phone and left a message for

Dustin to meet us in Delaware instead of at OSI in the morning. Considering he hadn't answered the phone himself, I hoped it meant he had the good sense to be getting some sleep. Tomorrow promised to be a busy day.

"We may not have figured out who's killing off these old Nazis or why, but we certainly made some progress tonight," I said. "Coming here was a good idea."

Discovering the hidden pages wasn't the only good thing, I thought, watching Kate settle back on her elbows, the beer bottle at her fingertips. It was as laid back as I had ever seen Kate Crockett look.

"What?" she asked, catching me looking at her.

"I don't know how to proceed here."

"Proceed?" She tried to sound puzzled, but she flashed me a playful smile.

"Do I kiss you? Attempt to get you into my bed? Or is that just a really bad idea?"

"I'm not one of your students, Professor. There's no code of conduct to follow."

"All the more reason that I'm worried about messing this up."

I got up and sat down on the floor next to Kate, beer bottle dangling from one hand as I rested my arms on my knees. Mentally, I was still weighing the pros and cons of sleeping with my new professional colleague and I had the sense that Kate was doing the same.

Letting the scales tip toward abandon, I leaned over and kissed her. It could have been a one-time kiss, something she shook off with a smile, a shake of her head, and a swig of beer. But Kate kissed me back. She had made up her mind too.

We kissed slowly, tentatively, with plenty of stopping points built in like emergency exits. We didn't use them. Kate rolled onto her back on the floor and I hovered over her, unbuttoning her blouse, while she busily worked my belt buckle, both of us fumbling at each other now like a couple of horny teenagers. Our clothes came off in a series of clumsy tugs. I unsnapped her bra to reveal her firm, high breasts, then bent to take one of her nipples between my teeth, feeling it harden at my touch. Kate gasped and arched her back to press herself harder against me. Her skin felt so soft. My fingers trailed down Kate's smooth belly into her triangle of dark hair. Kate put her hand on top of mine.

"This seems like the start of something dangerous," she said. "Are we sure we want to do this?"

"It's been a long time since I felt this sure about anything."

"That's just what I wanted to hear," she said.

I LISTENED to Kate's steady breathing, the city lights from the windows playing over our bodies, feeling more content than I had in years. Was it because of Kate? Or was it because I was finally beginning to learn the truth about my father? The morning was only going to bring more questions about Time Reich, not to mention the problem of waking up next to the woman who was technically my boss. But it was too late to think, and I was too tired. I reached for a throw blanket and pulled it over us. And then, blessedly, for the first time in several nights, I fell into a dreamless sleep.

35

In the morning, Kate was already up when I woke. I smelled coffee. She was at the kitchen counter, reading a fax. She wore one of my long-sleeved shirts, her hair still tousled from the pillow. She seemed to be giving the sheet of paper more attention than necessary. This was one of those awkward moments when, in the light of day, we were both wondering whether the other person thought we had made a mistake the night before.

"Good morning." I leaned over and kissed her, sliding my hand up her bare thigh and discovering that she was naked beneath the shirt.

"Mmmm." She kissed me back. No doubts in that kiss. "I made coffee, but I couldn't find anything worth eating around here."

"I haven't been to the store for a couple of days."

"Looks more like it's been a couple of years," she said. "The only food you have in your cabinets is a can of Ravioli, a jar of olives and some Ramen noodles. Maybe you were going to whip up something really special with all that one of these days?"

"I live a five-minute walk from any kind of food you could want," I said. "I was thinking about going across the street for a box of doughnuts. You prefer jelly or crullers? I like those squishy ones with the white icing and rainbow sprinkles on top."

Kate shook her head, but she was smiling. "You are a piece of work."

I opened a cabinet, found a mug, poured a cup of coffee. Kate slid the sheet of paper toward me across the counter.

"Dustin sent it first thing," she said. "It's what we have on your father's friend, Otto Friedrich."

"I would hardly call them friends. But could Friedrich be one and the same as Peter Geiger?"

"Dustin and Eleanor couldn't find any connection. We won't know until we show that photo to the relatives."

"You didn't phone that in until after midnight. Did those two sleep at the office?"

"As a matter of fact, they did."

"So what's his story?"

"Friedrich was born in 1921 in Romania to ethnic German parents. He joined the SS in January 1943 and served as an armed guard at three concentration camps," Kate said, reading from Dustin's report. "He spent the first few months of 1943 at the Gross-Rosen camp, helping guard about 100,000 Jews, Poles, Russians, Ukrainians, Gypsies and Jehovah's Witnesses. They were used as slave labor in a nearby stone quarry. About 1,500 died while he was a guard there. Apparently, the SS guards were fond of shooting the prisoners who could no longer swing a pick or push a wheelbarrow."

"Dustin dug all this up?"

"It's in his report," Kate said. "From Gross-Rosen, Friedrich went to the Dyhenfurth camp in August nineteen forty-three. Actually, it's rather romantic. He got married there and he and his wife had a child."

"How nice," I said. "But what's his connection with Dachau?"

"It's right here. In late nineteen forty-four he was sent to Dachau."

"What then?"

"That's all Dustin wrote, and I would guess that's pretty much the end of the official service record. The Third Reich only lasted a few more months and if Friedrich was working on a top-secret project I doubt that would have been noted in his service records."

"My guess is that he ditched his uniform and got the hell out of Dodge just before our troops showed up," I said. "Somewhere along the line, he must have obtained fake identification papers, which he used to apply for a visa."

"This is madness," Kate said. "Here's an SS war criminal who worked on a time travel project for the Nazis and we not only let him into this country, but he's been flaunting his Nazi past. It's in his obituary, for God's sake: 'During World War II, Mr. Geiger was proud to have served the Third Reich as a soldier in the SS, holding the rank of sergeant or SS-*Unterscharfuhrer*.'"

"You can't deport a dead man," I pointed out. "There was nothing to hide anymore. This obituary is for someone named Peter Geiger, not Otto Friedrich. We don't know for certain that he's our man."

"We'll find out soon enough." Kate slid off the kitchen stool, showing a flash of thigh beneath the shirt tail. "I'm going to take a shower. If your bathroom is anything like your kitchen cabinets, I'm wondering if I'm going to find soap and clean towels."

"Maybe I'd better help you look."

Halfway across the living room, Kate shed the shirt, letting it flutter to the floor. We made love in the shower as the hot, soapy water ran over us. Any thought that last night had been a mistake, just a one-night stand between lonely co-workers, swirled away like the water down the drain.

—————

ELSMERE, Delaware, had grown up in the shadow of Wilmington, a city known for corporate headquarters, for the wealthy duPont family and for being the one-time home of F. Scott Fitzgerald. None of that wealth had touched this blue-collar community. This was the city's original suburb, springing up as cheap housing for factory workers in the days just after World War II.

Peter Geiger's house was a tiny ranch covered in faded aluminum siding. A battered minivan with bald tires was parked in the stub of driveway.

A ragged brown rosebush by the front door was the only attempt at landscaping and its bare branches were studded with thorns that we tried to avoid as we went up the front steps. Even from outside the house smelled like an old ashtray.

"Geiger must have died of lung cancer."

"The obituary said it was natural causes." Kate glanced back toward the street. "Dustin isn't here yet. But I don't think we should wait."

I banged on the door. Despite the minivan in the driveway, it was hard to know if we were going to get an answer. I knocked again. Finally, there was a sound of heavy footsteps moving toward the door, which was then jerked open.

"Yeah?" asked the large man who stood in the doorway, wearing a black T-shirt and blue jeans.

"Mr. Geiger, we're from the United States Department of Justice," Kate said. "We'd like to ask you a few questions about your father."

"I thought maybe you were more of those Nazis," the big man said, then stepped aside. Geiger was fiftyish, which made him too young to be the son the SS sergeant had fathered in Germany. He had a shaved head big as a cannonball and round shoulders. Not fat so much as barrel-chested. An intruder would have had his hands full wrestling this man. In the fresh winter air, the house breathed out a greasy smell of stale cigarettes and bacon. The Allman Brothers played on the radio.

"Your father had a lot of visitors?" Kate asked.

"I keep telling them dad's dead. Been dead and gone a month. They come by to hear dad tell his stories. Most of them are assholes, if you want to know the truth." Geiger talked too loud, like he was a little deaf. The radio was now playing AC/DC.

"We'd like to ask you a few questions about your father. May we come in?"

"I guess so," he said, stepping out of the doorway to let us pass.

Geiger's son introduced himself as Eric. I searched his face for some resemblance to the soldier in the old photograph. Something about the eyes reminded me of the SS man, but beyond that it was hard to say. I thought of my father's journal and felt a twinge of anger building in my stomach. Maybe some fear too. Fathers and sons, still caught up in the past.

We followed him into the living room. Faded curtains covered the windows. An enormous Nazi flag decorated the wall above the sofa. The bright colors had faded and what had once been white was stained tobacco brown.

Geiger shoved aside a stack of newspapers to make a place for us on the plaid sofa. The cushions sagged. The air in here was sour, and not just from cigarettes, as if a pot of sauerkraut had burned on the stove and maybe the litter box needed emptying too. I thought about the passage in my father's journals that described how Otto Friedrich had been bitter about not being chosen to travel through time. No wonder. He must have had an idea of the old age that awaited him.

"I don't get many visitors," Geiger said, settling down on a loveseat across from us. "A few Nazi assholes come around because they didn't get the news that dad is dead. It's not like the neighbors stop by because it's mostly just Orientals and Mexicans living here now."

"So why not move?" I asked. Like the Millers in Waterbury, Eric Geiger's world had changed around him.

He shrugged. "I just moved back here, as a matter of fact. My old man left me the house and it was better than my apartment in the city. I live free, not counting taxes and utilities. I know it's a mess and the place could use a good airing out, but I've only been here a couple weeks, trying to move in and all that in between working. I work the second shift down at the chemical plant in Delaware City. I'd sell the house, if I thought I could get anything for it. But who the hell would buy this place?"

"Mr. Geiger, we would like to ask you about your father's past," Kate said. "Did he talk much about it?"

"Oh, sure. He liked to tell how he had seen Hitler once, at some big rally. So close he could have touched him. *Der Fuhrer*. He thought Adolf Hitler was one hell of a great leader."

"What about you?"

"Hell, the Bush family was in office almost as long as Hitler. He was just an unfortunate blip in history, if you ask me. But I'm not German, like my dad. I'm American."

"But you didn't try to hide your father's past. You put it in his obituary."

Eric Geiger shrugged. "It's what he wanted. He was proud of being in the SS. You know, they were the best of the best, Hitler's crack troops. Real believers. Not like the Wehrmacht, the regular German army. Dad was always down on the Wehrmacht. He claimed they lost the war because they couldn't beat the Russians at Stalingrad."

"He didn't try to keep his past a secret?"

"Maybe at first, but not in the last twenty years. Once ma died I guess he felt free to talk about the past. And talk and talk. Word got around. Later on, as dad got older, he started getting these nut jobs coming here who wanted to know what it had been like, being in the SS. Skinheads and gun collectors and types like that. They wanted to hear how he had killed Jews. All that attention kind of built him up, you know. He got to be real proud of what he'd done during the war. He also collected all sorts of Nazi shit — guns and medals and uniforms. These nuts who came around were always trying to buy it off him."

"Did your father ever mention being at Dachau, the concentration camp?"

"Like I said, he used to brag about shooting Jews and Russians there, but I think he made a lot of it up."

"Made it up?" Kate sounded incredulous.

"You know, like an Old West gunfighter exaggerating how many cowboys he gunned down. Maybe dad did kill a couple of people, I don't know. It was a *war*. But the way he talked, you'd think he'd wiped out thousands of people all by himself. Mostly I think it was bullshit. An old man telling stories."

"I hate to tell you this, Mr. Geiger, but we believe your father was telling the truth," Kate said gently. "He was involved in genocide."

"Maybe, maybe not. But my old man is dead now, so who cares? Listen, I don't mean to be rude or nothin' because you two seem like decent people, but you caught me at a bad time. I'm getting ready to go in to work. You're welcome to come back later or give me a call."

Geiger started to get off the love seat. We still had too many questions to let him go that easily. I held out a copy of the photo we had taken from Hazel Miller. Geiger took it in one of his big hands, stared at it for a long moment, and then guffawed. "That's the old man! Where did you get this?"

"It was taken at Dachau, Mr. Geiger, sometime in late forty-four or forty-five."

"Who are these other men with him?"

"The two SS men are Juozas Juknys and Josef Mueller," Kate said, not bothering to mention that they both had died in the last few days. "The civilian is Michael Baumann. Did your father ever mention any of those names?"

"No," Geiger said, handing the photograph back. "Look, that's all real interesting, but it was a long time ago."

"Did your father ever tell you that he was married in Germany during the war?" Kate asked. "He had a son."

Geiger collapsed back onto the loveseat so hard it was as if Kate had punched him. "A wife and kid? Hell no, he never mentioned that."

"Our records show he had a family in Germany," Kate said. "Your father also entered this country using an alias. His real name was Otto Friedrich."

"How do I know you're not making all this up?"

"Trust me, Mr. Geiger. We're here from the United States Department of Justice. We don't tell lies, but we seek out people who do."

"I've got a brother," Geiger said. "I'll be goddamned."

He sat staring at the floor, his heavy shoulders drooping. It occurred to me that my father had kept almost as many secrets as Otto Friedrich. Here we were, two sons, trying to understand what our fathers had done long before we were born. "My old man never said a word about being married before. That sly son of a bitch. No wonder he didn't mind telling everyone he was a Nazi, if he wasn't even using his real name.

"Did he ever mention something called Time Reich?" I asked, not wanting to give Geiger time to collect his thoughts. He looked so shaken that I hoped he would forget to lie. "Or a man named Konrad Radl?"

"Colonel Radl, the big Nazi who got away? I heard all about

him from dad. Radl was the commandant at Dachau. Dad always said Radl was still alive, hiding out."

"What about Time Reich?"

"I never heard him talk about that. If you mean *Third* Reich, that's a different story. Not a goddamn day went by that I didn't hear about *that*."

Kate and I exchanged looks. This was turning out to be a dead end.

"Why did you leave that flag on the wall?" I asked in an effort to keep Geiger talking.

"It was dad's. He always said it was from the rally he'd been to at Nuremberg. He was real proud of that flag. It's been there since I was a kid." Eric Geiger gave a snort that could be interpreted as a laugh. "Other families had paintings from Sears hanging in the living room, but we had a Nazi flag. I've seen it so many times I kind of don't see it anymore, if you know what I mean? Give me a minute."

Geiger got up and returned with the kitchen waste basket. He ripped down the flag and stuffed it into the trash. "That's that," he said. "Most of the rest of his stuff I sold."

"What kind of stuff?"

"Guns, uniforms, medals. A buddy of mine put a lot of it on the Internet and the guns mostly went to private dealers and collectors who started calling here when they found out dad died."

"But it was your father's. Most people like to keep the things that belonged to their parents. You sold it?"

"I'm not exactly sentimental about my old man. To tell you the truth, I need the money," Geiger said, spreading his big hands until he was holding empty air. "People pay a lot for all that Nazi memorabilia, and money don't come easy in this world. I'm not real attached to the Nazi stuff. Kind of creepy, if you ask me."

It was a long shot, but I asked: "Did your father have a disk with a swastika and eagle on it, about eighteen inches across, made out of bronze?"

Geiger gave me an odd look. "Sure, he had a disk like that. Some bastard tried to steal it from me on Sunday night."

Kate and I flicked our eyes at each other. "What happened Sunday night?" she asked.

"This guy came by about nine o'clock wearing a German uniform—"

"A *German* uniform?"

"I know, I know." Geiger shook his head in disbelief, a half smile on his lips. "It sounds weird, but he's not the first asshole to come by the house to see dad with a uniform on. A lot of these Nazi nuts, they love their uniforms. He comes by looking for dad, and when I tell him my old man was dead, he starts in on this disk. He described it, and I remembered it. Only he called it a beacon. 'Where's the beacon?' he asked, getting all excited. I told him to get out, but he ignored me and started tearing the house apart. Crazy son of a bitch."

"What happened?"

"I tried to throw him out, grabbed him around the waist, you know, and the next thing I know I've got an elbow in the gut and I'm on the ground. He was tougher than he looked. Then he started waving a gun around. 'Try that again and I'll shoot you,' he said. I told him I sold the goddamn beacon. He cussed me out and left. The son of a bitch. That was the kind of Nazi-lover my father idealized. Imagine that. I even called the police because the guy kind of shook me up."

"What did this man look like?" I asked

"He was about six feet tall, in pretty good shape."

"Blond hair, blue eyes?"

Geiger shook his head. "No, he had dark brown hair and dark eyes."

Kate and I exchanged a look. One thing for sure, whoever had barged into Geiger's home was not Stefan Radl.

"Who did you sell the beacon to?" Kate asked.

"It was with a bunch of stuff I gave to a dealer from Philadelphia to unload for me. He's got a shop in the city. I told that to this crazy Nazi. And I told your people when you called this morning."

"We never called you, Mr. Geiger." Kate sounded puzzled.

Geiger shrugged. "Somebody called me and said they were from the Department of Justice, just like you, and wanted to know who lived here since my father was dead. We started talking, and I told him how I'd pretty much cleaned out the house, including my collection, and hauled it to the dealer."

"Do you remember his name?"

"Dusty somebody. He sounded young on the phone."

"We know him," Kate said. "He works for OSI."

"He said he was going to talk to the dealer to see if he still had the disk," Geiger went on.

"Not if somebody else already got there," Kate said, half to herself. "That was three days ago."

"Not much danger of that," Geiger said. "The store is closed Mondays and Tuesdays. Today would be the first day it was open since that Nazi freak came by the house."

We left Geiger so he could get ready for work. Back in the car, Kate took out her cell phone.

"Dustin should have called," she said. "This is such a rookie thing to do, not checking in, goddamn him." She glared at the phone, then hurled it into the back seat. "I don't believe this. The battery is dead. I meant to charge it last night but I was a little goddamn *distracted*, McCoy, thanks to you."

"Use my phone."

Kate punched in a number, listened, then hung up. "No answer. Let's just hope Dustin doesn't do anything stupid."

36

I n five minutes we were back on I-95 headed north toward Philadelphia. Traffic was light and Kate dodged around the cars and trucks that were going too slow.

"Try Dustin again," she said.

I hit redial. "No answer. It says the cell phone customer is not available."

"Damnit, Dustin."

"He's trying to prove himself," I said. "Let's just hope he remembers that the people we're dealing with are not sweethearts."

"In case you haven't notice, Professor, that's why I'm speed-ing," Kate said, sounding anxious. She smacked the horn at a slow car in the fast lane. "I don't want Dustin to get in over his head."

Not for the first time, it seemed to me that this investigation was spinning out of control. Nothing had made sense since

Hazel Miller had produced the photograph from Dachau. Then came the attack at Rock Bottom. It was true I had hunted down a few Nazis in my day, but they were mostly like toothless old crocodiles — ugly, prone to snap at you, but relatively harmless. Finding them was mainly a business of following paper trails. Once I had found these ancient reptiles it was my job to interview them, not bring them to justice.

"Do you think maybe it's time to call in the cavalry?" I wondered.

"I hate to tell you this, Professor, but we *are* the cavalry."

"*Us?* I was thinking more along the lines of well-groomed young men with dark suits and guns. The FBI, in other words. And failing that, I'd settle for the local police."

"Look where the local police got us in North Bay."

"C'mon, Kate, Barney Fife looked good compared to the North Bay cops. But this is Philadelphia. There's an FBI bureau office."

"And what do I tell them?" Kate asked. "That I need help solving a Nazi time travel case?"

"Just tell them we need help," I said.

"It's not that simple," Kate said. "Let's get to this militaria dealer in Philly first, then see what happens. Maybe Dustin is waiting for us there."

THE SHOP WAS CALLED Military Matters and it was located near the corner of Broad and South streets, not far from center city Philadelphia. I was expecting a dingy Army surplus store, but Military Matters turned out to be a pleasant and well-lighted place. Rich paneling covered the walls and bright track lighting gave an almost festive air to the drab collection of weapons, uniforms and military paraphernalia. The proprietor was a talkative man who turned out to be a retired history professor from a community college in New Jersey. An instrumental version of *When Johnny Comes Marching Home Again* – heavy on the flutes – played softly from hidden speakers.

"If I didn't have a pension I probably couldn't survive doing this," he admitted. "To make good money in this business you have to be a real wheeler-dealer or a little shady. You've got to be willing to tell people that their great-great grandpa's Civil War sword is only worth a hundred bucks, then turn around and sell it for a couple thousand."

I gave a low whistle. "I've seen them for less on eBay."

"You'd be crazy to buy something like that online. There's no authenticity," he said. He came around from behind the cash register, tugging on white cotton gloves as he went, then reached for a sword suspended from pegs on the wall. "Look at this beauty. Leather grip wrapped with wire, thirty-six inch blade, single fuller, with C.S.A. worked into the guard. It was made by the College Hill Arsenal in Richmond, most likely in 1862. This is the genuine article. The stories this sword could tell. Seeing is believing, my friend."

"How much?"

"I'll let you have it for two thousand and that would be giving it away."

"That's giving it away?"

"I'll throw in a scabbard if that helps."

"You get a lot of World War II items in here?" I asked as he replaced the sword with something like reverence.

"Oh, yeah. World War II is very hot right now. There are a lot of guys whose fathers or maybe grandfathers were in the war. They've heard the stories, but they want something tangible from the war. I think Hollywood has made the war popular all over again with *Saving Private Ryan* and *Band of Brothers* and all that."

"What about Nazi items?" I asked.

"Ah." He grinned. "That's where the real money is. Flags, SS daggers, basically anything with a swastika on it is worth serious money. That's really good for business because a lot of that can't even be advertised on the big Internet sites. *Verboten.* Nazi memorabilia gives shops like mine a boost."

"Why do you think people are so drawn to it?"

He shrugged. "Who knows? Doesn't make sense, does it? I mean, the Nazis were the bad guys but everybody wants something from the Germans. It's partly a perverse fascination. But there are plenty of people who want a genuine flag or dagger because they *liked* the Nazis. I can spot those guys as soon as they walk in the door. To them, it's almost a religious relic, like a Catholic owning a piece of some dead saint's robe."

Next to me, I sensed Kate growing impatient. *The Star-Spangled Banner* was now playing, heavy on the horns. I turned to Kate, giving her the floor.

"We're looking for two things," said Kate, diving right in. "First, we believe one of our colleagues was here today, maybe just a short time ago —"

"Sure was," the shop owner said. "Young fellow from the Department of Justice? He was here an hour ago, asking after some Nazi memorabilia, just like you."

"Was he looking for a bronze disk decorated with a swastika?"

"Yes, a disk." His eyes looked thoughtful behind the thick glasses. "The disk was a curious thing; it almost seemed electronic, or maybe ceremonial. I'd never seen anything quite like it before and I've been collecting all my life."

"Why am I getting the feeling that we're about two steps behind?" I asked.

"As a matter of fact, you are. I sold the disk a few days ago to a collector from Delaware."

"We'll need his name and address," Kate said.

The dealer's face, so genial a moment ago, took on a wary expression. He hesitated before answering. "I'm not sure I should give it to you," he said. "A lot of the people I deal with are very private. I don't think he would want me giving it out to just anyone."

"We're not just anyone," Kate reminded him. "We're investigators with the United States Department of Justice."

The proprietor looked less than impressed. "The kid who was in here this morning pulled the official government business routine on me too, although he hardly looked old enough to be a Boy Scout."

"But you gave him the information," Kate pressed.

"He talked me into it," the dealer admitted. "Look, I was just trying to help him out. He was so eager, you know? I used to love it when I had students like that. Anyway, I probably shouldn't have done it."

"If you gave him the address, you can give it to us."

With a sigh, the proprietor reached under the counter and produced a box filled with index cards. It resembled the system my mother once used to keep track of her recipes. He took out a card, copied down the address on a slip of paper, and handed it to Kate.

"You know, I don't want to seem like a smart Alec or like I'm uncooperative, but you people need to get your act together," the dealer said.

"What are you talking about?" From Kate's tone of voice I could tell she was running out of patience with the man, especially now that she had what she wanted.

"You're all investigators, right? Maybe you ought to try working together. I gave you two the address of the buyer. I gave it to that kid this morning and I gave it to that FBI guy too. Nobody can say I haven't been cooperative."

"What FBI guy?" Kate asked.

"The one who came in the shop asking about that same disk."

Kate and I exchanged glances. *Uh oh,* I thought. "What did he look like?"

"Tall, late thirties, dark hair."

I froze. Definitely not Dustin. "You told him who bought the disk?"

"Sure, just like I'm telling you. He was FBI."

"Damnit," Kate said.

"I thought you were all on the same team," the dealer said, looking confused. But he caught on quickly, nodding as if to himself. "He wasn't FBI."

"No, he wasn't."

"Then who was he?"

I could see that Kate wasn't going to tell him, but I thought he deserved to know. "We're not really sure, but he's not FBI. He might even be some kind of neo-Nazi."

"Weird. He had on a suit and everything, just like you expect FBI agents to wear. He even flashed some kind of ID at me but I didn't pay much attention."

"How long ago was this?" Kate asked.

"About an hour after the young man came in. Why?"

But Kate was already rushing out the door with me close behind.

37

"That's Dustin's car," said Kate, pulling in behind the government-issued vehicle parked at the address given to us by the memorabilia dealer.

"I don't like this," I said, feeling spooked. The house was in a neighborhood of upscale older homes built of stone, white clapboard siding and slate roofs. Mature trees and shrubbery screened one house from the next, even in winter. Through the trees beyond the houses was the slate gray water of the Christina River. The back yard sloped toward a boat house and dock, where two speed boats were tied up. "You can hardly see from one house to the next. It's too isolated. *Now* do you think you should call in the cavalry? You could get the City of Wilmington police out here. Or call the FBI. This is what OSI is supposed to do, call for backup."

"I don't have enough to go on yet," she said. "For all we know, Dustin is in there having coffee. Let's just knock on the door and see what happens, okay?"

We got out and crossed the lawn. The neighborhood was quiet except for the crunch of stray leaves under our feet and the distant noise of traffic. Somewhere among the bare trees a crow was cawing, the sound harsh and piercing on the winter air. I wanted in the worst way to see Dustin suddenly open the front door ahead of us, wearing his goofy grin and running a hand through the thick mass of his gelled hair. But there was no one in sight.

Kate cleared her throat and it sounded loud as a rusty door hinge. "I don't like this," she said. "It feels too quiet."

I knocked on the door. No answer. I raised my eyebrows at Kate, who gave me a nod, and then I pressed the brass latch.

"Hello?" Kate called as we stepped inside. The silence was the kind that comes from someone holding his breath. Kate reached inside her handbag and took out the revolver she had put to good use at Rock Bottom.

"You've been carrying that around all this time?" I whispered.

"Insurance." She called out again as she stepped inside, "Anybody home?"

I've never carried a gun, but this was one of those times I wished I did. I looked around for some kind of weapon but there wasn't so much as a flower vase. There was hardly ever a broadsword handy when you needed one.

We crept forward. On the walls of the foyer were several prints of World War II combat planes. I noticed an alarm console in the living room, the clear plastic cover flipped down, as if someone had disarmed it or maybe tried to press the panic button. Floorboards creaked underfoot as we crossed the foyer into the dining room. Glancing toward the kitchen, I saw a gummy crimson pool at the edge of the floor.

"Bram?"

"I see it." I rushed into the kitchen, hoping that we wouldn't find Dustin's body lying there. The man on the kitchen floor had his feet together, arms at his sides as if he were standing at attention. He looked to be around fifty. Blood puddled around his head. The coffee carafe was shattered on the floor. He must have been fixing breakfast because lumps of gray, overcooked scrambled eggs were scattered everywhere. On the counter, an English muffin was slathered with congealed butter.

I bent over the body. The bullet hole was no bigger than a nickel, right in the middle of his forehead. The wound was purple at the edges. With a sickening feeling, I realized that the chunks on the floor were not eggs at all but gobs of brain matter. If this was the militaria collector, someone had shot him as he was about to pour coffee.

"Oh my God," Kate said. "We need to find Dustin. We know he's here. *Dustin?*"

Someone groaned.

"This way." Kate rushed toward the sound.

We found Dustin in the combination mud and laundry room, slumped beside the back door. He was barely conscious. His entire torso was covered in blood. My stomach felt hot at the sight and I fought down the urge to vomit.

"Oh, Dustin." Kate put the gun down on the floor and crouched beside the young man. "What did he do to you?"

A deep slash began high on Dustin's rib cage and angled across his belly. Blood soaked his blue dress shirt. Another deep cut on his left forearm bled much more freely. His right hand was tucked under his left armpit.

I groped at his neck for a pulse. His flesh felt rubbery and cold, like a doll's. The carotid vein pulsed faintly. I noticed a deep puncture wound under one eye.

I looked at Kate. "We've got to stop the bleeding, and I mean *now*," I said. "The slash on his arm might have cut an artery. Grab a dish towel, anything."

"C'mon, Dustin. Hang in there."

Dustin's eyes fluttered open. His voice was barely a whisper.

"I hid the disk," he said. "He wanted it but I wouldn't... look... dryer..."

Dustin's head slumped. His right arm shifted and I could see a bloody stump where a finger had been cut away. My heart skipped a beat.

Behind me, I heard kitchen drawers pulled open. Kate was back in seconds with clean dish cloths and a roll of duct tape. She put her gun down. "I'll try to close the wound. You wrap it."

Kate used her fingers to force the edges of the wound together. I slapped on a dish cloth, wrapped the duct tape around it. Tight. Then I raised the arm above Dustin's head and got a good grip high up on his bicep, using my thumb to clamp down on the big artery there. The bleeding slowed as the blood was forced to move uphill through the restricted artery. We wrapped more cloth and tape around the stump of his finger.

"The cut on his arm looks like a defensive wound," I said. "He managed to block the knife just enough to keep it from going right to his heart. That's where the attacker was trying to stick the blade, right between his ribs."

"He cut off Dustin's *finger*. We've got to catch him, Bram. We've got to."

"He could be anywhere by now, Kate."

"But there was someone else in the house when we came in. You felt it too, didn't you?"

"Yes," I said, my voice hushed as I remembered that sense of someone holding his breath. The thought made my scalp itch.

"For all we know he's still in the house."

"I'm calling the police now, Kate. We need to let them handle this."

"Okay."

One-handed, I used Kate's cell phone to call 911. The blood made my hands slippery, so it wasn't easy tapping out the three digits. The dispatcher sounded oddly calm when I told her there was one man dead and that we needed an ambulance for a stabbing victim.

I was still on the phone when Kate announced there was a police car out front. "That was fast," I said. Then I remembered the alarm box in the front of the house. Maybe someone had managed to hit the panic button.

"He's taking his sweet old time," Kate said. "Probably figures it's another false alarm."

She practically dragged the police officer through the door and explained the situation. I could hear him coming through the house, that creak of leather and swish of polyester uniform that cops have. He passed the body without comment. In the mud room, he saw Dustin and said, "Aw, Jesus."

"Ambulance is on the way," I said.

The cop shook his head. "I dunno. Looks like he lost a lot of blood."

"Do me a favor, will you?" I asked the cop. "Come here and take over for a minute. We've got to keep pressure on this artery up here so he doesn't bleed out."

The cop produced a pair of surgical gloves from his utility belt and tugged them on. He was older than me, pudgy in the tight-fitting uniform. "Can't be too careful these days," he explained. "Hepatitis, HIV —"

"Yeah, yeah. Just keep the arm elevated, will you?"

Unlike the cop, I wasn't much worried about blood-borne diseases, but Dustin's blood was beginning to dry on me, turning sticky between my fingers and crusty in the wrinkles of my hands.

I went into the kitchen and ran water over my hands. Returning to the mud room, I stepped around the cop and Dustin, then opened the door of the clothes drier. A bronze disk was wedged inside. Dustin had nearly given his life to protect it. Maybe I had underestimated the kid.

I started to show Kate, but saw she was staring out the back door at the garage.

"What?"

"Someone's out there," she said, reaching for her gun.

"Who's out there?" the cop asked, still bent over Dustin.

Before Kate could answer, we heard a car engine start. And then the garage door began to go up.

38

"Officer, take care of him!"

Leaving Dustin with the city cop, we raced out the back door and ran toward the garage. Kate had her gun out but as soon as the door was up a BMW sedan burst from the dark interior with a screech of wheels.

She stood for an instant too long in the driveway, trying to get off a shot.

"Kate!" I grabbed her arm, pulling her out of the way of the speeding car.

We tumbled into the shrubs lining the asphalt, but not before I caught a glimpse of the driver in profile. Dark hair and dark eyes. Nobody I recognized.

Kate rolled and had her gun up but already the car was past us, heading out the driveway toward the street. Without a clear shot, she held her fire. Then the car squealed around the corner.

"Goddammit, Bram! I would've had him if you hadn't grabbed me."

"He was about to run you over."

"Let's go after him."

"I'll drive," I said. "You shoot."

We ran back to our car and I slid behind the wheel and hit the gas before Kate was even all the way in. She pulled the door shut and fumbled her seat belt as I gunned it down the street. Dustin's attacker had a head start but I could see his car at the top of the long, steep street that led back toward the highway. I slammed down the accelerator. The car hit a pothole, bounced badly, came back down.

We blew through the stop sign at the intersection with another neighborhood street, nearly clipping a station wagon. The woman behind the wheel stared, wide-eyed and mouth open in a scream we couldn't hear.

Dustin's attacker was already turning onto the busy highway. Somehow, he had gained on us. The light at the end of the street was red. I jammed the gas all the way to the floor. Don't let there be anybody coming. We went through the red light and skidded onto the highway.

"Jesus, Bram. You drive like a history professor."

"Hang on."

"Who the hell are we chasing? Do you think it's the same guy who attacked us at Rock Bottom?"

"I'd say the chances are pretty good. Let's catch him and get some answers."

Two lanes of traffic now in each direction. The street lined with doughnut shops and gas stations. I dodged the Malibu around somebody making a left turn, swerved around an old lady slowing to turn right. The speedometer touched eighty.

"He's turning onto the interstate," Kate warned. "Don't lose him."

"I've got him."

The Chevrolet was fast in a straight line but it didn't like curves. The tires thrummed in protest and I thought we were going over. Up ahead, the BMW accelerated into the curve like it was on rails. Why did American cars always handle like crap?

The ramp split. To the right was Interstate 95, to the left Interstate 495, which had been closed for construction on our way to Philadelphia. A big orange sign that said "CLOSED" was plastered across the I-495 entrance.

The BMW took it anyway. Yanking at the wheel, I steered our car onto the closed highway.

"Now we've got him," Kate said. "He's cornered."

"Don't forget that a cornered animal is the worst kind," I said.

"He's going to run out of road in about twenty seconds."

As the ramp curved around, we expected to see concrete Jersey barriers and the end of the road. But there were no barriers in sight. A few dump trucks and other construction vehicles were parked along the shoulder. Several men in orange vests jumped back as our two cars flashed past. Beyond the workers, the highway straightened out, four lanes of blacktop with nobody on it but us.

"Hang on," I said. "We're about to find out how fast this thing can go."

On any other road the BMW would have out driven us, but the Chevy was two hundred plus horsepower of good ol' American whomp ass.

Kate read my mind. "Floor it," she said.

The car hit ninety, edged toward one hundred, and started to get wobbly. Kate clutched the edges of her seat. My knuckles were white on the steering wheel. The other car wasn't getting any closer. I put my foot down harder.

"Back off, back off," she said. "This is crazy."

"He's going to run out of road any minute now."

"I can't believe I'm trusting my life to a history professor," she said.

"Hey, the deal was that I would drive and you would do the shooting. I'm holding up my end of the deal. What about you?"

"He's a little out of range."

Kate was right. Even with my foot jammed to the floor, we weren't getting any closer.

That's when I saw the flashing yellow lights ahead. No more road. I started to let up on the gas.

The BMW's brake lights winked and then the car spun around, heading right for us.

"I don't believe this," I said. "He wants to play chicken."

"Bram, turn the wheel."

"Hold on."

The distance between us shrank, both cars flying toward each other straight and swift as arrows.

"Bram!"

I spun the wheel to the left and the BMW brushed past. We must have touched because something went bouncing away with a metallic *ting, ting, ting.*

"We just lost part of the car," I said.

"What part?"

"Beats me. Let's just hope it wasn't anything important."

The only escape route was back the way we had come and the BMW had a head start. I got us turned around and saw, with relief, that a police car with flashing lights was blocking the entrance ramp far ahead. The other driver saw it too. He braked to a halt, then jumped out and ran for the side of the highway. I gunned the Chevy toward him but before we could cut him off, he was sprinting down an embankment covered with freshly graded earth. Still running, he bent at the waist and disappeared into a huge drainage pipe.

We stopped at the edge of the highway and got out. "I don't suppose you have a flashlight in the trunk."

"No," Kate said. "But neither does he."

"If we go in there, he can see us coming. We'll have daylight behind us. We won't be able to see him."

"We can't just let him get away," Kate said, starting toward the pipe. "Not after what he did to Dustin."

The concrete drainpipe was nearly five feet in diameter. A trickle of water from ditch at the bottom of the embankment ran into the pipe, forming a stream no more than three or four inches deep. Just enough to get our feet wet. I listened for a moment but didn't hear any splashing. Either he was too far away to be heard or he was waiting in the darkness to ambush us.

"Here goes," I said, and ducked inside. I'd gone about ten feet before I heard Kate start after me. My feet were already soaked.

"Bram, I think this is a really bad idea," Kate whispered behind me.

"Just be ready to shoot," I said. "Give me some warning and I'll duck."

I tried to pick up the pace, thinking we would never catch him at this speed. But it was hard to move any faster. I tried to straddle the stream of water and take steps without making a splash, so that our Nazi friend wouldn't have any warning that he was being pursued. The darkness seemed to have weight, clinging to my arms and legs and shoulders as I pushed through it, slowing me down. The darkness pressed closer. Who even knew we were down here? If he got lucky and shot us, we would be skeletons before anyone found our bodies. I could imagine the headline in the local paper: SKELETAL REMAINS FOUND IN DRAINPIPE.

Focus, I warned myself. Looking back over my shoulder, I could see Kate's silhouette a few feet behind me. The pipe entrance was shrinking. As long as we kept it in sight we had a way out. Ahead of us was only more darkness. And silence. Where the hell had he gone?

That's when I felt the breath of air on my cheek.

"Kate," I hissed. "There's something up ahead."

"Get down," she whispered in reply. "I'm going to nail his ass for what he did to Dustin. No way I can miss in here."

"I don't know what it is," I said. "But I don't think it's him."

"For God's sake, Bram, what is it, a troll? Let me shoot."

"No, I feel some sort of draft. Come on."

We went a little farther. To my right, a pipe branched off. Another trickle of water emptied into the pipe. The stream beneath our feet grew deeper and disappeared into blackness. At the end of the pipe on the right was a halo of winter light. Then a shadow appeared and the sound of splashing.

"This way," I whispered to Kate, starting up the feeder pipe after him. He was moving fast, already far ahead of us.

"We're losing him," Kate said.

"Run," I urged, but it wasn't easy. This pipe was smaller to the point of being claustrophobic, forcing us to crouch even more. There was no way to go quietly and the splashing we made sounded to my ears like a crowd. Up ahead, his silhouette passed across the pale disk of light that marked the pipe entrance, and then was gone.

"He's out of the pipe," I managed to pant.

"All he's got to do is waiting outside and pick us off as we come out."

"You want to turn around?"

"Hell, no."

We ran the rest of the distance, my back aching and thighs burning from the strain of holding myself bent over. The pipe seemed to go on forever. I remembered that when people have a near-death experience they describe going through a tunnel toward the light of eternity. I let my fingertips brush the rough concrete walls, felt the cold water rushing over the tops of my shoes and knew this was no near-death experience. Not yet, at least.

Nearly out of breath now, we approached the end of the pipe cautiously. No sign of the man we'd been chasing, unless, as Kate had suggested, he was waiting just outside the entrance.

Kate squeezed past me, the press of her body reminding me

of our encounter last night. It was a thought out of place with the surroundings, but there it was anyway. I knew what she was going to do. "Wait," I said, suddenly fearing to lose what I had only just discovered.

"There's no time," Kate said. "Better cover your ears."

She raised the revolver and fired. The noise in the pipe was insanely loud. My ears rang as I watched Kate run ahead, firing the handgun. *Pop, pop, pop.* We charged out into the light.

Outside there was only a deserted embankment. We struggled up it toward the interstate highway. There was a lot of traffic, and on the other side was a shopping center parking lot, packed to overflowing with cars.

"There!"

He stood just at the edge of the busy interstate. The man looked over his shoulder as if he had heard Kate's shout. We were closer now. He wore jeans and a brown leather jacket. He turned and started across the highway.

No way was he going to make it. Beside me, Kate gasped.

He was halfway across the northbound lane when a delivery truck going sixty or seventy miles per hour came out of nowhere and struck him. It seemed to happen in slow motion, like something unreal in a dream or in a movie. His body flew to one side and lay still.

39

Washington

First thing the next morning, George Foster called a staff meeting in the OSI conference room. Kate sat at the conference table along with a handful of other OSI investigators. She and Foster had argued. He wanted her off the investigation, but Kate had played too much of a role at this point to take her off the case, much less exclude her from the meeting. The rest of the room was crowded with various support staff who occupied chairs along the walls. I was late, so I slid into an empty chair just by the door. Eleanor came in and sat next to me.

The room was too small to comfortably accommodate so many people. Everyone was dressed for winter in sweaters and dark J.C. Penney suits. The air soon smelled of wool warmed by overheated bodies. I hoped I could stay awake. To that end I had gulped down some caffeine and my mouth was filled with the cloying taste of Coca Cola. No one joked, not after what had happened to Dustin Granger. There was a tension like the moment a falling platter hangs in the air before hitting the floor.

Foster fiddled with the projector he had attached to his own laptop so that his screen shone on the wall for all to see. He kept plugging and unplugging the same computer cables. I wasn't sure what was making Foster so uneasy: making sure everything was hooked up correctly, Kate's glaring presence or three well-groomed Justice Department higher-ups in the more expensive suits. They might have been FBI but no one bothered to introduce them and they did not introduce themselves, sitting in their own huddle, backs to the wall. All three had fat pens set out beside leather-trimmed portfolios.

I tried to catch Kate's eye, she was lost in her own thoughts. I knew she was upset about Dustin. She blamed herself for what had happened. Dustin had been taken to a trauma center in Delaware. Kate and I had hung around the hospital for most of the night. The doctors said he would pull through but there had been some times when things had been tough and go. His parents had flown up from Ohio and they were with him now.

Yesterday's events had been brutally violent, but we now knew so much more than we had. The mystery man who had run out into traffic and been killed turned out to be an unemployed Gulf War veteran named Jimmy Hall. He was thirty-six years old, with ties to various neo-Nazi groups—including one in Argentina led by Stefan Radl.

The police had already been to Hall's home in rural Pennsylvania. The computer they seized there had several emails from Radl that showed the two men had been in constant communication. The picture that emerged was of a deranged man who had been easily awed by Radl's Nazi pedigree and masterfully manipulated by the SS officer's grandson.

The emails and several receipts from gasoline stations and a motel proved it had been Hall who attacked us at Rock Bottom.

But it was Radl who suggested that he do it. The emails showed Radl was tired of us meddling, and that he thought it was important for Hall to get rid of us and try to get the beacon back at the same time. Hall had eagerly done whatever Radl asked him.

JUST AS FOSTER was about to get started with the meeting, a fourth man entered the room. He caused a kind of ripple effect as the people around the table struggled to their feet to greet him. I recognized the man, although we had never met. Elliot Nusbaum, director of OSI, moved with an easy grace. He nodded at the staff on the fringes, then his gaze settled on me for two beats. He looked puzzled, as if trying to recall my face. Then his eyes flitted away and he sat patiently, waiting for Foster to begin.

Eleanor leaned toward me. "The boss is here," she whispered. "George looks ready to have a cardiac."

"If he does, I'm not giving him CPR."

Foster had good reason to be nervous. As director of OSI, Nusbaum was just a few rungs down the ladder from the United States attorney general. A word from him could make or break a career. Even though OSI was a relatively small agency, Nusbaum kept his distance from most of the staff, preferring to let them do their jobs while he did his, which was to make sure OSI continued to prove its usefulness and to lobby Congress for continued funding. Every year he managed to get a bit more, which was no small achievement considering the shrinking ranks of OSI's quarry.

Foster squared his shoulders and signaled a start to the meeting by clearing his throat. "This has been a tough couple of days for us," he began. "OSI began investigating a case in which a previously unknown SS concentration camp guard was murdered. Within 48 hours, a second man with apparent links to the SS was killed. Then one of our agents and a consultant were attacked."

Several eyes turned toward Kate but Foster pointedly ignored her. He continued, "Just yesterday, while investigating this string of crimes, one of our young agents was assaulted and critically injured in the field, apparently by the suspect in these two other killings. This man, who has been identified as Jimmy Hall, died yesterday when he was struck by a vehicle. Consequently, our colleagues at the FBI have become involved in our investigation, which has moved far beyond the realm of the civil cases usually investigated by OSI."

My mind flashed to Dustin on the floor of the house in Delaware, his arms covered in blood and Kate trying to squeeze the knife wounds shut. I shook my head to clear it.

Like any good teacher, Foster was trying to refresh the collective memory of his class by summing up the situation so far, although it occurred to me that just about everyone in the room was already up to speed on the situation. I realized that Foster was summing up for Nusbaum, who was watching him with restless eyes. But even Nusbaum fidgeted in his seat as if to signal *get on with it*.

Foster touched the keyboard of his laptop. A larger-than-life, somewhat grainy black-and-white image of Konrad Radl leapt onto the wall. I recognized it instantly. It was cropped in close, but I knew the background behind Radl would have shown the camp yard at Dachau. I had used this same photograph in my book.

Foster touched another computer key and an image of Stefan Radl appeared on the wall. This was a color photograph, obviously more recent. The man wore a military uniform, but not the black, high-collared tunic of an SS officer. It was the same photograph Eleanor had found on the Internet.

"The more recent photograph shows Stefan Radl, who is the grandson of the SS officer shown," Foster said.

He touched his computer again and the two photographs appeared side by side. The resemblance was stunning, but on second look there were subtle contrasts between the two faces. People can look changed from one frame to the next in a series of photographs, but there seemed to be a more fundamental difference here. The black-and-white image showed a face that was gaunt by comparison to the man in the color image. It was a faced hollowed by stress and worry. Pools of shadow filled the hollows of his cheeks and the deep-set sockets of his eyes. The eyes in the color photograph were blue as ice in the tanned face. Stefan Radl was smiling, but the eyes remained cold. It was easy to imagine them sighting down the barrel of a pistol or deciding just where to cut with a kitchen knife.

I knew that the black-and-white photograph was taken in late 1944. Winter. The future bleak for Hitler's Germany. Radl was a true believer in the Third Reich, but he wasn't stupid. He must have known the end was near. In addition to the duties pressing around him, he must have considered his own fate. And he had his wife and children to consider. Was he already making arrangements for their safe transport to Argentina? When the end came, what should he do? Shoot himself, flee, take his chances with the Allied invaders . . . or even attempt to send himself through time? Those questions and more wore heavily on his face.

Radl would have been in the throes of his Time Reich project, with the Fuhrer himself calling daily to check on his progress. The Fuhrer's demands must have bordered on madness. Radl, in desperation, was forced to rely on his Jewish engineer, Michael Baumann, to help complete Time Reich. My father may have overhead one of those calls. The thought made the hairs at the back of my neck stand on end. *My father*, I thought. *The traitor*. For Radl's part, he wouldn't have dared to let anyone in Berlin know that he was relying on help from a Jewish engineer.

Nusbaum spoke up. "I'm not sure I understand the connection, Mr. Foster. Are you implying that we are still pursuing Konrad Radl? He would be a very old man by now, if he's even still living."

"Actually, sir, that *was* one agent's foolhardy theory," Foster said.

I glanced at Kate and saw her turning red at the remark. He had gone ahead and thrown Kate under the bus. Foster hadn't mentioned her by name, but that didn't matter. Everyone in the room knew he was talking about *her*. He had put in the knife. Now all he had to do was twist. Beside me, Eleanor stiffened. "We are still gathering information about this man here, the one in the color photograph, Stefan Radl."

"Actually, sir, we *have* gathered some additional information," Kate said, looking directly at Nusbaum. "Our preliminary findings are that Major Stefan Radl is an officer in the Argentine Special Forces and grandson of the Nazi war criminal. Two of our investigators recently interviewed him in person and denied any involvement in the case we've been investigating, but the emails found at Jimmy Hall's home show otherwise. One of our staff members contacted Radl this morning. Eleanor?"

Eleanor spoke up, sounding surprisingly authoritative. "One thing we do know is that Stefan Radl was not involved in yesterday's incident. I took the liberty of calling him at home. It was the middle of the night there. Considering that it's at least a twelve-hour flight to Buenos Aires, it would be physically impossible for him to have returned to Argentina in that time frame. I think it's safe to say that Mr. Hall was acting alone when he, uh, attacked our agent."

Another surprised murmur ran through the room. Foster

tried to redeem himself by taking charge of the meeting again, but was interrupted by Elliot Nusbaum.

"What's the connection between Konrad Radl and his grandson?" Nusbaum asked. "What's really going on here? The mission of OSI is to pursue war criminals, not their descendants."

I glanced at Kate, who offered nothing. Did she really want to look like a complete fool? But someone had to say it. Why not the crazy professor? I stood up and cleared my throat. "Project Time Reich."

In the quiet that followed, someone in one of the chairs along the wall snickered.

"Time Reich?" Nusbaum blinked rapidly and glanced from me to Foster, then back to me again. "I'm not familiar with that. But I do know of *you*, Professor McCoy. I've read your work. If you have a theory, I'm sure it's worthwhile."

Foster hurried to interrupt. "Time Reich was a wild goose chase pursued by Agent Crockett and Professor McCoy," he began. "It's just some crazy story —"

"Not quite," Kate cut him off. She kept her tone level-headed and matter-of-fact, not at all what you would expect from someone on a wild goose chase. "You see, sir, in late 1944 and early 1945 the Nazis built a prototype of a time machine. This is still classified information so not many details are available. However, the indications are that the Germans actually attempted time travel as part of their wartime research and development program."

Foster made a noise that sounded like "guffaw." One of the FBI agents snorted. But not Nusbaum. He touched his fingertips together to make a tent. He looked interested, and as far as Kate and I were concerned he was the only person in the room whose opinion mattered.

"Colonel Radl was in charge of the German's Time Reich program," Nusbaum guessed.

"Exactly, sir," Kate said, apparently surprised that the director of OSI made the connection so quickly.

Foster glanced from Nusbaum to Kate, then stammered, "This is outrageous. Agent Crockett has been insubordinate, taken my assigned vehicle without authorization, hired an outside contractor without prior approval and nearly gotten an inexperienced young agent killed."

"Go to hell, George!" Kate snarled.

She looked ready to launch herself across the conference table at Foster. Eleanor reached out and put a hand on Kate's arm.

"Whoa," somebody said from the chairs along the wall.

The others in the room looked shocked. Profanity and raised voices were not typical of high-level staff meetings.

Nusbaum stood up, taking charge. "I know that emotions are running high," the OSI director's tone was calm but firm. He was making it clear that he would brook no more outbursts, and also indicating that this was no longer George Foster's meeting. I had to wonder if Foster had just provided the nails for his own bureaucratic coffin. *Couldn't happen to a nicer guy.* "We've seen a promising young man badly injured and we are facing violence on a scale most of us are unaccustomed to at OSI. But I would like to remind everyone that all of us here are, first of all, professionals, and second of all, adults. We are not here today to assign blame but to seek solutions. No one in this room was responsible for the harm done to Dustin Granger. He was attacked by a criminal. Let's not forget that."

Foster tried to interrupt. "But sir —"

Nusbaum held up a hand. "I'm not through yet, Mr. Foster. I would like to test a theory on Ms. Crockett and Professor McCoy." He turned to Kate. "Do you believe SS Colonel Konrad Radl traveled through time to commit these acts of violence?"

"No," Kate said, glancing at me as she spoke. "We all know there's no such thing as time travel."

"Project Time Reich," Nusbaum said, tenting his fingers together again and touching them to his lips. "But why would Radl's grandson be involved?"

"We're not sure why," Kate said. "It could be some warped sense of family honor."

"It is difficult to say," Nusbaum agreed, spreading his hands wide. "The FBI is handling the murder investigations, but there is still a role OSI can play. Konrad Radl's case file has been open for all these long decades, and maybe now we can finally bring his victims closure by finding out what happened to him. One thing *is* for certain. You won't find the answers here."

Foster spoke up, sounding puzzled. "Where then?"

Nusbaum exchanged a look with Kate and me. The three of us knew, even if no one else in the room had grasped the answer yet.

"Germany," Kate said. "We have to go to Germany."

40

Dachau

A ghostly winter fog hung over the landscape. We could hear the steady *drip, drip, drip* of water off the skeletal branches of the trees and the eaves of the concrete and glass structures that made up the airport complex. The travel magazines would have you believe that Munich — *München* in German — was the land of *Oom-pah* bands, *lederhosen* and the *biergarten*, but all we could see was the bleak landscape.

"Guess it's the off season," I muttered.

"Yeah."

I glanced at Kate. She was pale enough to match the fog and stood like a zombie.

"You OK?"

"I'm better now that we're on the ground," she said. "But I'm already dreading the flight back."

"With any luck, Hitler will come back to life and overthrow the government first," I said.

"Thanks, Bram. You really know how to make a girl feel better."

"Sorry. It's just that this place makes me nervous, like wandering around the wrong neighborhood after dark."

"What place? The airport?"

"More like the whole country."

I found it hard to feel welcome in a modern nation that put six million fellow human beings to death in systematic fashion. Mass murder on that scale was like something out of a science fiction tale – or a horror novel. Sadly, the holocaust was all too true.

It didn't help that the first Germans we met getting off the plane were so stern and serious. German police in combat boots and flak jackets stood ready with machine guns slung over their shoulders. One held a large Rottweiler on a leash. These guys made American airport security personnel look like the late shift at McDonald's. A whole corps of hard-faced, unsmiling young men scrutinized passports. They waved us through without looking at our bags, one of which contained the bronze disk that Dustin had nearly given his life to protect. If it truly was a beacon, as Captain Howard had claimed, I hoped we would find some use for it here.

We had not gone through any official channels before coming here. There wasn't time, and it was better to keep a little thing like a time travel plot to yourself before you were sure of it. No point in OSI becoming the laughingstock of Europe. Better to check things out first and call in German authorities only as a last resort. Besides, with the current anti-American sentiments pervading Europe, the Germans might have hindered our investigation. Right-wing candidates had won the last election, following the shift in government that had taken place across Europe. Nobody here wanted Americans digging up their dirty little Nazi secrets. They were through with apologizing for the past.

We did have a car and a driver waiting for us. Although the United States Department of Justice did not have a field office in Munich, the U.S. Army's investigative branch did. They had agreed to help us out, which was a little unusual, but I thought I smelled Silas Crockett's hand in the deal. There was more than one general who owed his career to the former congressman and secretary of state.

We were met outside the airport by a fresh-faced young man who came running up and said, "Professor McCoy?"

"Who wants to know?"

He seemed a little put off by that, but Kate stepped forward. "I'm Agent Crockett from OSI. And you are?"

"Lieutenant Jimmy Dean."

"Like the sausage?" I asked.

"Yup."

I couldn't put my finger on it, but this kid might as well have worn a sign around his neck that said "American." What he wasn't wearing was a uniform, which I pointed out.

"We're under orders to wear civilian clothes off base," he said, tugging at his dark slacks and leather jacket. "Americans aren't real popular right now, especially with the change in government, and the feeling is that we should not antagonize the local population by wearing uniforms."

"Keep spouting double-speak like that and you'll go far in the hierarchy," I said, realizing that the long flight had left me cranky. It didn't help that being back in Germany had put me on edge.

"Sir?"

"Be nice," Kate warned me.

"Do you know what an oxymoron is?" I asked.

"Huh?"

"Let me give you an example. Military intelligence. *That's* an oxymoron."

Lieutenant Dean looked at me sternly, the beginnings of an insult beginning to register, then at Kate as if appealing for help. She shook her head. "Ignore him, Lieutenant. He's been under a lot of stress." Then: "Where's the car?"

"Right this way."

The lieutenant led us to a government-issue Ford four-door in a parking lot surrounded by sleek black BMWs and Mercedes Benz sedans. "I've been instructed to take you anywhere you need to go," Dean said, more confident now that he was behind the wheel. "Do you need to stop by the base?"

"No," I said. "We're going to Dachau."

"The town?"

"The concentration camp."

Only Germany could be so dark and dismal on a winter's day. Germany is located at a higher latitude than much of the United States and so its winter days are naturally darker and its nights longer. To make the weather even gloomier, the fog turned to drizzle as we left the city. Lieutenant Dean attempted some nervous small talk but gave it up when Kate and I insisted on answering in grunts and monosyllables. The car rolled on, each of us lost in our own thoughts.

What were we expecting to find? It was hard to say. Now, driving through the gloom, it suddenly seemed unlikely that we were going to unravel the mystery of Konrad Radl or the deaths of two former SS guards and the attack on Dustin. I also doubted that I was going to find any real answers about what my father had done to help the Nazis with Time Reich. But if there were answers or clues, it was clear we were going to discover them at Dachau and not at OSI headquarters back in Washington. Elliot Nusbaum had sensed that as well. Some immeasurable power had pulled us toward Germany and we had obeyed. Maybe it was the gloomy weather, but I also had the sense that something was going to happen.

"God help us," I said.

"What?" Kate's face whipped round toward me from the window. She was so lost in her own thoughts that the sound of my voice had startled her.

I studied her face for a moment, noticing the sharp eyes and grim set of her lips. Not for the first time, I thought she might be tougher than me. Was this really the woman I had made love to? It seemed a lifetime ago that she had spooned, naked, against me.

"Promise me one thing," I said.

"Sure."

"When this is over, take me sailing on Branford Bay. It's got to be a warm day with the sun shining and the ocean blue around us. I have this image of it in my mind. If something happens to me here, promise you'll spread my ashes on that bay. Don't let me be buried in the mud here in Germany."

"Don't be ridiculous."

"Promise?"

"Okay, okay." Kate looked at me intently. "You hate this place too, don't you?"

"Is it possible to hate a whole country?"

She looked out at the gray winterscape of Bavaria. "Don't hate Germany," she said. "Hate the Nazis."

"Whatever we need to know, we'll find it at Dachau," I said. "And then I can't wait to get the hell home."

DACHAU IS a suburban town just a short ride from Munich on the S-bahn and a slightly longer drive by car. Most tourists who have come to see Munich's famous beer halls and *Glockenspiel* never venture to Dachau. It is a pleasant, sprawling town filled with busy roads and could almost pass for an American suburb.

There are few signs pointing the way to the concentration camp. You need a map to find it. From the back seat, I guided Lieutenant Dean down street after street until we reached the entrance to the old camp. Just beyond the modern parking lot we glimpsed crumbling brick buildings and the remnants of a fenced topped with barbed wire.

"I hate this place," I said. "It's so damn creepy."

Kate reached for my hand. "Hang tough. We'll do this together."

Lieutenant Dean parked the Ford and Kate and I got out.

"What do you want me to do?" the lieutenant asked, leaning out the sedan's window.

"Sit here and wait for us," I said. "And keep an eye out for a guy who looks like the German tank commander from *Battle of the Bulge*."

As we walked away Kate asked: "Do you really think our Nazi might be here?"

"We knew to come here, didn't we? There's a good chance he had the same idea. We don't know what he was up to back home, but the one common thread is this place."

"Who is he?" Kate asked. "Do you think it really is Konrad Radl?"

"I don't know," I answered. "But I have a pretty good idea that we're going to find out, one way or another."

We walked on. I had been to Dachau before but no matter how many times I visited, I knew I would never get used to this place. The former concentration camp had a feel about it like the Gettysburg battlefield or even Valley Forge. The ground was full of ghosts. At Dachau, there is a visitor center and museum that attempt to describe what happened. Signs in German, English and French explain the exhibits of shoes and other camp artifacts. Black-and-white photographs show sad-eyed children with paper Stars of David pinned to their clothes. In later photographs the children are all gone but there are bunks filled with emaciated adults. Their faces are all hollow eyes and lips curling away from sunken teeth. Some of the men are so skeletal that it doesn't seem possible that they are still alive. Their bodies are merely parchment stretched over bones.

Kate had never seen any of this before and she lingered over the exhibits, fascinated by the sheer horror of them. She was no longer an investigator for OSI but a spectator, a citizen of the 21st century horrified by the sins of the past.

"This is awful," she said. "Let's go."

We walked outside, but it wasn't any better there. The museum wasn't crowded to begin with and it was such a bitter day that hardly anyone else ventured outdoors. The cold drizzle quickly soaked into our clothes.

"How did anyone survive here?" Kate wondered out loud.

"Most didn't," I said. "The Germans took a dim view of anyone surviving too long."

While the state-of-the-art museum was spotless, the sprawling acreage of the concentration camp itself looked run down. The Germans had a policy against restoring or maintaining any of the buildings or concentration camp facilities. Dachau and the remains of camps like it were left to fade away. No one wanted them preserved as shrines. The memory of what had happened there was enough. Dead weeds filled the spaces between the barracks and clung to the remaining fences. Mortar flaked from between the bricks. Wooden siding, sodden and green with moss, sagged away from the buildings.

"This is the yard where they shot the Russian prisoners," I said.

"You mean, on a daily basis?"

"I'd say so. It was a slaughter pen, especially toward the end of the war. The Nazis hated Jews, but they hated Russians even more, if that was possible."

Fog hung over the brown grass. A brick wall with faded whitewash was still pockmarked with bullet holes.

"I don't know what we're doing here, Bram," Kate said. She shivered. "It's like this place is haunted."

"There are a lot of uneasy spirits in this place," I agreed. "A lot of horror."

We walked on, past a row of crematoriums that, thankfully, had never been put to use, unlike the infamous facilities at Auschwitz and Bergen-Belsen concentration camps where still-living victims had sometimes been shoveled into the fires. Tell-tale greasy black smoke had hung above those camps.

Finally, we reached a row of single-story brick buildings that resembled chicken coops. They looked cold and damp, but far more substantial than the rotting wooden barracks we had passed. This was where the Nazis kept the more privileged prisoners.

Standing before the last unit, in front of a narrow wooden door, I couldn't bring myself to go in. On my one previous visit to Dachau years before, I hadn't been able to summon the courage to go inside then, either. As with the rooms of our minds, there are some that we are better off leaving unvisited.

"This is it, isn't it?" Kate asked. "This was where they kept your father."

Rather than answer, I swung the door open. There was no lock. The door creaked on rusty hinges. It struck me as strange that the modern German officials let visitors go where they pleased. Nothing was hidden anymore.

"Go ahead," Kate urged, in a voice she might have used to encourage a child.

I stepped inside. It was smaller than I expected, maybe 10 feet wide and twelve feet deep. The floor was made of wide, rough-cut lumber worn smooth and sheltered from decay. The ceiling was low, giving the room a claustrophobic feel, and I fought the urge to stoop over. A single window was set high in

the outside wall, filled with four blocks of glass rather than a
single pane. Light filtered in but you couldn't see out, or open
it. The bare, cramped room was nothing more than a monk's
cell.

"Your father had books here, a table and chair, and a bed,"
Kate said. "I wonder where all that's gone now?"

"The same place six million Jews went. It's all just gone."

I don't know what I expected as I stood in the room. Some
kind of revelation? All I knew was that I wanted to get out of
this cell and out of Germany. Give me America any day. We had
our share of racism and hatred but Americans never had built
ovens to cook the remains of a people they sought to eradicate.
Outside, through the open door, I could glimpse the yard
where the Russian prisoners were lined up and shot. My father
had described it vividly in his journals.

Kate was running her hands over the bricks, touching the
mortared grooves between them. Finally, crouched low against
the wall, she made a *hmmm* noise like she'd found something.
"What?" I asked.

"There's a brick here with something scratched on it."

I bent down to look. The window gave us just enough light
to see. "Where?"

"This brick. The word scratched on it must be in German.
What does it say?"

Faintly, I could make out the word etched into the damp
brick. *Hoffnung.* "Hope. It says *hope*."

"Do you remember the last entry in your father's journals?"
Kate sounded excited.

" 'Behind hope lies everything.' "

She took keys out of her pocket and began to dig at the
mortar. The metal grated against the old mortar like a saw
against bone.

"Let me try," I said. Taking the keys from her, I set to work
more carefully than Kate's frenzy. "Watch the door. We don't

need some German park ranger wandering in here right now thinking we're looking for Nazi relics."

Kate went to keep watch and I kept working the key into the mortar. A crack began to form around the brick. I got my fingers into the crack, feeling the grit work up painfully under my fingernails. Tugged. Grunted. Tugged again. Then the brick slid out like a drawer opening.

In the small, dark space behind the brick was a bundle of papers. The bundle was wrapped in oilcloth, possibly a corner cut from a German soldier's rain poncho. It was covered in dirt from its hiding place but remarkably dry. I slumped down against the wall, shook off the debris, set the bundle in my lap, and unwrapped it.

"Bram, what is it?" Kate's voice quivered with anticipation.

"I don't know yet. Give me a minute, for God's sake. And keep an eye out."

If some German had walked in just then and tried to take the bundle from me, I was sure I would have killed him. Fortunately, no one disturbed us.

In my lap, the covering fell away to reveal a small, leather-bound book. I recognized it instantly as another journal. Inside, the writing was in my father's hand. I flipped through the pages and a photograph fell out. At the sight of it, my breath caught in my throat. The photograph showed a smiling man and woman, well-dressed, with three children, a girl and two boys. The man held the hand of the youngest boy, a beautiful child who looked to be five or six years old. I could see at once that the older boy was my father. The man and woman were my grandparents, the girl and the young boy my aunt and uncle.

It was the only photograph I had ever seen of my German family. My father had survived but the Nazis had killed the others. The youngest, I remember my father telling me, had gone first. Their murders were just one more tragedy in the midst of the enormous horror that had been the Holocaust.

How could humans be so cruel? I studied the dead faces in the photograph, imagined the sharp crack of rifles in the yard outside as another row of Russian boys died. Then I remembered the snap of bones in the parking garage in Baltimore, where I had broken the skinhead's hand out of sheer cruelty. What kind of creature had God created when he made mankind? He had made a race of monsters.

Staring at the photograph, I knew that my father had left me a gift. He had given me the past that had been taken from him.

"Bram, are you all right?"

"Yeah," I croaked. Angrily, I swiped at my tears, leaving a smudge of grit on my cheeks. "Let's see what he had to say that was so important he hid it in the wall."

41

"It's about Time Reich," I said, skimming the first few pages of the document my father had risked his life to write. "It explains the whole program, how the Germans were trying to send some of their top people through time. It's exactly what we thought, if not worse. The Germans were hoping to send entire divisions through time, even Panzer tank units."

"That's madness," Kate said. "It could never work."

"The Germans were desperate. There were experiments. They tried it first on the Jews. Most everyone died. Then soldiers actually went into some kind of time machine like the one we saw at the ONR facility in Virginia and they disappeared."

"Just like the *USS Eldreth*. The Philadelphia Experiment."

"Yes," I said. "The Germans really tried it."

Kate paused. "Your father knew about it."

"He knew everything," I said. "He probably knew more than the Germans thought he did."

And just like that, my father was no longer an innocent victim. Now I understood why he had not told me about the hidden journal. He was ashamed of what it held. If it was never found, he must have thought, so be it. But my father had left clues. He knew me well enough to know that if I needed the journal, I would find it.

At first, he wrote that he had not understood what he was helping to build. Otto Friedrich's revelation had helped open his eyes. As I read deeper into the journal, I realized my father not only helped with Time Reich, he had been fascinated by it. The possibilities awed him. Never mind whether or not it would actually work.

His role had also been larger than he ever let on. He wasn't simply some humble minor player. He had designed the entire bunker where many of the beacons were kept. He had shaped it like an Egyptian pyramid that extended deep underground, growing ever wider at its base. Inside were supplies and beacons, waiting for the day when the Nazi leaders would arrive from the other side of time. He had overseen the construction, working both under the Nazis and with them — instructing them how to build the underground pyramid.

Now, I understood the special treatment. This was how he had survived the camp. How he had eaten well, been able to have his books and the dignity of his own quarters rather than a shared barrack with the masses. He lived better than many of the German officers. He was almost an equal of his captors.

But then, as I began to read his description of the last, terrifying day when they had finally finished Time Reich, I saw how far he had gone to survive.

WHEN I LOOKED into the faces of the guards that morning I knew something was going to happen. None of the guards would meet our eyes as we waited for the trucks and they would not touch us.

Normally, they helped some of the women onto the vehicles, but this morning the guards only stood off to the side and watched.

I noticed almost for the first time how young most of these guards were. Hardly more than boys. One or two of the guards carried submachine guns, which was something new. Mostly they were armed with old rifles, all the good ones having gone to the soldiers in Russia.

Sergeant Friedrich was the only one who seemed to be in a cheerful mood. "Guten morgen, Herr Baumann," he said, clapping me on the shoulder so hard that I staggered. "I trust you slept well. Was the feather bed to your liking in our little hotel? Did you enjoy the coffee?"

"All excellent as usual, Sergeant Friedrich," I said, playing along because it was wise to stay on Friedrich's good side, although the only hospitality I had experienced was a bitterly cold barrack and stale bread. The soldiers' rations were not much better. "The butter was especially sweet."

"Butter? Ha! That's a good one. I haven't tasted butter in years. I am going to miss your jokes, Herr Baumann."

Laughing, Friedrich moved on to supervise the loading of the other prisoners. In the truck, a young man I had played chess with several times exchanged a nervous look with me but we knew better than to break the rule about talking, not with two guards sitting at the end of each bench. We had all become good at picking up on the mood of our SS captors, in the same way insects trapped in a web sense the spider is coming.

The trucks drove out of the camp, the convoy winding its way toward the Wolf's Lair we had been building. Winter still hung in the air; we could see our breath, though the canvas top sheltered us from the wind. But there were signs of spring. Buds swelled on the trees and shoots of green showed through the brown leaves. The tree trunks blurred as the trucks picked up speed.

Across from me, one of the other prisoners could barely sit up. Whether he was sick or frightened, I could not say, but the men on either side of him held their companion firmly by the arms to keep him from falling forward. The young guards gripped their rifles so tightly that their knuckles showed white.

We reached the project site and jumped off the trucks. Usually, the laborers found their shovels waiting for them and shuffled off to work, while I took up my blueprints and other drawings. This morning, nothing waited for us. It was as if the site had been swept clean except for the peak of the pyramid. Even the prisoners whose minds were dull from hunger and cold finally noticed and began to look around nervously as if for an escape route, but there was none to be had. No one dared speak up because the guards all had their rifles in their hands, not slung over their shoulders as usual.

The guards started shouting for us to line up. We were all fright-ened, anxiously watching these heartless boys in their black SS uniforms. A staff car drove up after us and Colonel Radl got out. I had a bizarre hope that perhaps he was having us assembled because he wanted to thank us for our efforts. But Radl just nodded at one of the other officers and stood to one side as they marched us toward the pit where the construction debris had been thrown. The pit was cut into the frozen earth like a scar, filled with scraps of stone and wood. All the guards started shouting for us to get into the pit. Their faces looked so angry as their lips curled back, shouting, Schnell! Schnell! We all knew then what was coming.

I do not know what came over me. To defy the guards was to die; and yet not to defy them was to die as well. Colonel Radl stood just a few paces away and I took a step toward him. Instantly, a guard leveled a submachine gun at me. He could not have been older than sixteen.

"No," Radl said. "Let him come."

I walked up to the colonel. Radl's face might as well have been carved from wood, and I wondered if this was the same man with whom I had discussed architecture on several occasions in his office. He seemed changed. The others were going down to the pit but now several of the SS men were watching Radl and me, wondering what was going to happen.

"I built the Wolf's Lair for you," I said. "And this is how you would repay me. Where is your honor, Herr Radl?"

Radl seemed to look right through me. He unsnapped the holster of his pistol and I thought that he was going to shoot me right there in front of his soldiers. He drew his pistol, but instead of pointing it at me he handed it to Otto Friedrich, who had materialized beside me.

"I will take care of him, sir," the sergeant said almost gleefully. He took me firmly by the arm. "Come, Herr Baumann."

"No, Sergeant." Radl's blue eyes glittered. "Give Herr Baumann my pistol. If he wishes to live, he must shoot one of the other prisoners."

I could hardly believe what I had just heard. My legs felt so rubbery that I did not know if I could walk. Still holding me by the arm, Friedrich led me toward the pit. Most of the prisoners were already in the bottom, getting on their knees. The soldiers lined up on the rim, pointing their rifles down at the Jews there, men and women alike. A few men were waiting their turn to scramble down the steep bank and Friedrich pulled one of them aside. It was the young man I had ridden out with in the truck that morning.

"Get on your knees," Friedrich ordered him. The young man did as he was told. He let a single sob escape him, then knelt on the edge of the pit. I remembered that he had told me he had a wife before the war, but he did not know what had become of her. The sergeant pressed the pistol into my hand. "It's better if you shoot him in the back of the neck. Not as messy that way. And hard to miss. Go ahead."

My hand shook. I felt Radl's eyes on me. I willed myself to turn around and shoot him, but I knew I would be gunned down in an instant if I tried.

Friedrich took my wrist to steady my aim. "Do you want to live, Herr Baumann?" he whispered. "Don't be a fool. Pull the trigger, or I will have to shoot you."

Sergeant Friedrich's hand guided my own until the muzzle was pressed into the young man's neck near the base of the skull. My mind was so blank that I wondered if I had already been shot myself and was actually dead. I don't remember pulling the trigger. The recoil would have knocked me over if Friedrich had not been holding onto me. With his boot, he gave the body a shove so that it tumbled down into the pit.

"Congratulations, Herr Baumann," Colonel Radl called out, though I could barely hear him over the ringing in my ears from the pistol. "You are one of us now."

Then he gave the order to shoot and the guards poured fire down on the helpless prisoners in the pit. The machine gun bullets tore the clothes away from bodies like a strong wind. The shooting lasted several minutes. When it was done, Sergeant Friedrich climbed down with Radl's pistol and shot the ones who were still alive. Two or three of the youngest guards doubled over to retch. They were given shovels and made to start filling in the pit. After a while, a tractor with a plow blade came to finish the job. I rode back to camp in one of the empty trucks. They did not even bother to have a guard ride with me.

This is my final journal entry. March 5, 1945. Dachau.

───────

"It wasn't his fault," Kate said. "They made him do it. Your father had no choice."

"He was no better than them."

"No, don't you see? He wanted you to find this, Bram. It's his confession. All you can do is forgive him."

"I don't know if I can."

"But you do have to help him, Bram. Help him stop Radl. Don't you see? He was powerless to do anything then, but you can help him stop Radl now. We need to find the bunker."

"It's in the woods, Kate. North of here."

"How do you know?"

I opened the journal again. The description of the massacre was not actually the final entry. On the last few pages were several precisely drawn diagrams and sketches of the Wolf's Lair.

W e walked back out to the car, the bundle from behind the brick hidden under my coat. Like their counterparts at Gettysburg or Fort McHenry, the Germans who kept watch over Dachau frowned upon visitors taking away any piece of it.

Lieutenant Dean jumped out to open the door for Kate. She got in the back and I slid into the front passenger seat.

"What happened to you?" he asked, looking at me with concern. "You look like your best friend died."

"Something like that," I said. "Listen, do you know how to get to Freising?"

"That town way out in the woods? I think I can find it."

"Good."

The lieutenant guided the Ford through Dachau's streets, away from the concentration camp. After the visit to the camp, every building we passed felt sinister; every German face looked savage. Here and there on the side-walks or waiting to cross the street I saw old men or women who would have remembered the camp when it was actu-ally in operation. And yet they had gone on with their daily lives, oblivious to the horror. This was a town that had lived a lie, condoning through silence what took place at the camp.

Soon, Dachau fell away and the road entered open fields. Unlike American towns and cities with their endless suburbs, in Europe the transition between town and country was often abrupt. In this case, the fields began just past the last S-bahn station. It was far more expensive to own and drive a car in Europe, which consequently had not embraced the American version of suburbia. The empty winter countryside made me hate Germany all the more.

We could see tree-covered hills rising beyond the plain where the town was located. Lieutenant Dean seemed to be headed in that direction.

"How far?" I asked.

The young officer shrugged. "It's up in the hills, sir. I don't know how far exactly, but maybe just a few miles."

In back, Kate was unusually quiet. "What are you thinking?" I asked.

"We do know more about Time Reich," she said. "But I'm wondering what all this has to do with the deaths and attacks we've been investigating. What set them in motion after all these years?"

I glanced over at Lieutenant Dean, who was busy keeping his eyes on the road and his hands on the wheel. Like a good soldier, he was minding his own business.

"I'm not sure what we'll find," I said. "But if there is any explanation for what's been going on, I have a feeling we'll find it at the bunker."

"The Wolf's Lair," Kate said, giving it the name my father had in his journal. She shuddered.

As the road began to climb, the fields fell away and a thick forest sprang up. Not so much as a house was in sight. It never ceased to amaze me how a country as populated and modernized as Germany could maintain relatively untouched wild areas, but the outdoors was guarded jealousy here.

The day was already dark and foggy. Beneath the wintry trees just a few feet from the road the day receded into twilight. The woods were almost primeval. I knew this was the twenty-first century but I half expected to see wolves among the trees.

I turned my attention back to the map my father had drawn all those years ago. In typical engineer fashion, the map was meticulously detailed. Fortunately, the bunker did not appear to be located far off the road. We seemed to be on the same road to Freising my father had depicted on the map. All those years ago the road to a remote Bavarian village most likely had not been paved — or perhaps there was a tar-and-chip surface at best. In early spring the road would have been a muddy morass. But in winter the ruts would be frozen solid as concrete, a perfect surface for hauling in building materials and truckloads of slave labor to build the bunker.

"Freising two miles," Lieutenant Dean noted helpfully as we passed a road sign near an outcropping of gray rock that bulged from the trees.

"Pull over."

"Sir?"

"Stop the car, goddammit!"

"Yes, sir."

The lieutenant guided the Ford to the side of the road and shut off the engine. Kate and I got out. This time, I took the bronze disk with me, carrying it in a canvas rucksack. I wasn't sure yet how it was going to be useful even after bringing it all the way to Germany, but if this wasn't the time to put the disk to use, I didn't know when it would be. The woods around us hummed with stillness although in the distance we could hear another car somewhere on the mountain road below us.

"How do you know this is it?" Kate asked. "It's just a bunch of trees, unless I missed the sign back there that said 'Nazi bunker this way.'"

"See that outcropping?" I asked, pointing at a gray hulk of stone that rose beside the road. Then I held up the map. "These same rocks are noted on the map as a landmark. Now we just head west about one mile."

"Darn, and wouldn't you know I left my GPS at home."

Still seated in the car but with the window down, the lieutenant didn't let on as to whether or not he thought we were crazy. "Sir, what do you want me to do? Should I come with you?"

"You can sit right here, Lieutenant," Kate said in her full-bore authoritative voice, and I could tell she was getting fed up with the young officer's assumption that because I was the man that meant I was the one in charge. "If we need your assistance, we'll give you a shout."

"I doubt I'll hear you if you're a mile away in the woods," the lieutenant pointed out. To his credit there was not a trace of sarcasm in his tone.

"We'll shout really loud," Kate said. Then she stomped off into the trees. When I didn't follow right away she turned back to me and said impatiently, "Come on."

"You're heading east. We need to go west."

"What, was orienteering one of your electives in grad school?"

"No, but I used to be a Boy Scout. You can just see the sun through the clouds, so we need to go that way."

We headed into the woods, this time going in the right direction. Between the denseness of the trees and the dusky winter light, it seemed we were hardly off the road before the car disappeared from sight. The thought occurred to me that if we got turned around in the trees and lost our bearings we would be a long time walking out of the woods again. I might have been a Boy Scout, but I didn't tell Kate that I had never made it as far as getting my Eagle badge. I figured that as long as we forged straight ahead without taking any detours we should be all right.

"You'd think there would be some kind of road into this place," Kate said.

"Most of this would have been clear cut during the nineteen forties," I said. "I'll bet you could see the complex from the road back then. But the trees have all grown up. This isn't some ancient forest. Most of the trees here are fifty, maybe sixty years old. Whatever road bed was here has long since grown over."

"Then how do we find the bunker?" Kate asked. "Coming across it in these woods will be like finding a toothpick in a box of wooden matches."

"Just keep walking," I said. "I don't think it's going to be all that hard to find."

We kept going for maybe another twenty minutes, cutting back and forth between the trees, looking for some clue. I was trying hard to keep myself oriented so that we wouldn't lose track of where the road lay, but after crossing back and forth through the trees I was somewhat confused.

In the distance there was the pop of a gunshot. An echo rolled across the mountainside. Disturbed by the sudden noise, a pair of crows swept across the treetops, cawing in alarm. The birds were the only wildlife we had seen so far in these desolate woods.

I wasn't positive, but it sounded as if the shot had come from the direction of the road.

"What was that?" Kate asked, sounding worried.

"Probably just a hunter."

"You think so?"

"I don't know. Maybe a car backfired. All I know is that I want to find this goddamn bunker."

I stopped and took out the map again, but it was very rudimentary. When my father had drawn it there was a road leading to the bunker construction site. It would have been hard to envision the forest that eventually sprang up over the site and the shallow graves of his fellow Dachau prisoners.

"Admit it, Mr. Boy Scout. You don't have any idea if we're even looking in the right place."

"We are," I said stubbornly, stomping off through the woods. I shoved aside a long pine bough and nearly walked headlong into a pyramid of smooth stone rising from the forest floor.

43

"Oh my God," Kate exclaimed as she came running up. "We found it. But is this it? It's so *small*."

"This thing is like the tip of an iceberg," I said. "You only see this much of it up here but the rest of the structure is under the forest floor."

It was no wonder we hadn't seen the pyramid until we almost walked into it. The structure was hidden by several pines that had grown up around it. The peak rose ten or twelve feet above the forest floor. The stone sides were green and slick with moss. It was like coming across a relic from some lost civilization. I reached out and touched the cold stone.

Kate looked at the topmost stone, then at the mushy brown carpet of the forest floor. "If that's just the tip, it must be enormous." She began to walk around the stone structure. "Should we go in?"

"We didn't come all the way to Germany not to," I said. Whatever mysteries we were dealing with in the present were sure to be solved inside the bunker. "We've got to go in. Once we report this place to the German officials, they won't be letting anyone near this place. Including us."

I realized that my father bought his life by building this pyramid, although in all the years to come his life must have seemed like a lie to him. He had survived the concentration camp, but at what price?

"This is obviously a door of some kind," said Kate, walking around to the lichen-covered north face of the pyramid. Set flush against the stone, the door appeared to be made of thick iron, originally painted black, but faded now to a shade of gray streaked with rust. There was a circular depression in the center of the door, the sunken metal embossed with the symbol of an eagle gripping a swastika in its talons.

Kate shoved. Nothing happened, so she gave the door a karate kick. She grunted. Kicked again. Frustrated, she said, "You try it."

I got a running start and hit the door with my full weight. I was rewarded with a dull thud, not to mention a jarring pain in my shoulder. Flakes of rust showered my head and shoulders. "This door was probably built to withstand a bombing run," I pointed out. "We're not going to get very far trying to knock it down."

"How about a battering ram?" Kate asked, already scouring the forest floor for a suitable log. "If the two of us swing it, we might knock something loose."

I was sure it would take more than that to open the door. The door looked too sturdy, like the entrance to a bank vault. I stood for a moment studying it.

Stepping closer, I ran a finger inside the depression and found that it was grooved and slotted. Where had I seen something like this before? I wracked my brain before I remembered that a lens fit onto the body of a camera in much the same way, or even a smoke detector on its ceiling bracket. The front of the door was actually a lock mechanism. But where was the key?

"Wait a minute," I said, and stooped to pick up the rucksack containing the bronze disk. We had brought it all the way to Germany, so it must be good for something. "I've got an idea."

Whereas before the metallic disk had felt cold and lifeless, the beacon now felt as if it had an energy all its own. I could have sworn it felt warm to the touch even in the winter air.

"Look at the bottom," Kate said. "Those two tabs on the side. I thought they were just decorative."

"Let's find out," I said, dropping the rucksack onto the carpet of pine needles and placing the beacon onto the depression in the door. It didn't quite fit. I rotated the beacon one way, then another, like turning a steering wheel. All at once the beacon slipped into place as neatly as one bowl nests inside another. I turned it again and felt the satisfying click of the beacon locking into place. One more turn brought the eagle design right side up. Deep inside the thick door, something mechanical stirred.

A moment before there had only been a faded, rusty surface. Now the gleaming metal disk seemed to blaze forth, the eagle looking almost alive as it gripped the swastika in its talons. The pyramid itself, which had appeared abandoned and forgotten, had taken on new life. The woods around us seemed to have yet more still. Not so much as a breath of air stirred the branches and no birds sang, although I could have sworn that just a few minutes ago I had heard some hardy winter songbirds twittering in the treetops.

"Now what?" Kate asked.

"Now we go in."

"I don't see a doorknob."

"Push."

Kate pushed with her hands but nothing happened. I braced my legs, got a good grip, and shoved. Slowly, the door creaked open. As the crack widened, stale air rushed out of the bunker with a sighing sound and tickled our legs. It smelled like the air inside a musty basement or an attic trunk. Kate wrinkled her nose. "Ugh. I hope there's nobody dead down there."

The door was heavy, thick as the door of a bank vault, and even pushing with all our might we could only get it open a couple of feet. But that was enough to slip inside. Concrete steps led down into absolute darkness. The noise from our feet and our breathing tumbled down the steps and echoed, giving the impression that the space beneath us must be vast. I look a flashlight from my coat pocket and switched it on but the blackness swallowed up the beam.

"Bram, I don't know about this," Kate said. "I'm having second thoughts."

"Come on. You know me. I've got a reputation for going places I shouldn't."

"Maybe we ought to wait for some help here."

"Suit yourself." I started down the steps. Over my shoulder, I saw Kate give one last glance at the woods and then come after me.

The steps descended quickly. Light bulbs were set into the wall behind steel cages, but we had to rely on our flashlight. Then, from somewhere deep below us came the unmistakable growl of an engine turning over. The lights began to flicker.

"Bram, what the hell is going on?" Kate asked.

"It's a generator. The door triggered it somehow. There must be an automatic sensor."

"This is spooky. It's like this place is alive."

"Come on, just a few more steps," I urged. "Let's see where this takes us."

We found ourselves in a chamber. We had reached the first level. By now the light bulbs had come on completely. They were too old and too dim to throw out much light. But it was enough to see by. I switched off the flashlight.

The room around us was utilitarian, with no furniture other

than a few benches along the walls and a rack that might once have held rifles.

"Some kind of guard room?" Kate wondered.

We found the next set of stairs and descended further. Again, there was not much of note in the next level down. I looked around at the walls, thinking that my father had likely been one of the last people to look at them before the bunker was sealed up. We went down another level.

That's where we found the other disks. The beacons were arranged on pedestals in orderly rows, like brass buttons on a military dress uniform. At the very end was a beacon set further apart from the others. Sensing that this one must have some special significance, I took a step closer and flashed my light on it to get a better look. The beacon had a burnished patina of old silver. Like the others, it was decorated with an eagle and swastika. But the silver set it apart and this beacon was also more ornate, the symbols more finely engraved.

"Will you look at that," said Kate. "It's like a giant piece of jewelry."

What man would warrant a silver beacon? My scalp began to crawl.

"I've got a bad feeling about this one," I said, keeping the flashlight aimed at the disk. It was just a hunk of cold metal, but part of me was half afraid it would leap to life before my eyes. "That beacon must belong to somebody important."

"Who?"

"Why don't you see if there's a button you can press to turn that thing on, so we can find out."

"No thanks," she said. "Besides, it can't be a simple as that."

"No? Time Reich is real, Kate. It exists. We're standing in the middle of a goddamn Nazi science experiment."

"Jesus, Bram. Do you know what this means?"

"For starters, that maybe Hitler didn't commit suicide in

April nineteen forty-five. That maybe he's floating around somewhere in time."

"That's insane."

I flicked the beam of light around the chamber. Other rows of beacons waited, filling the cavernous space. It seemed beyond credibility, and yet here was the evidence, plain to see. *Legions of Nazi storm troopers?* The thought sent a shiver up my spine.

Behind me, Kate cried out.

44

A burst of light from a powerful flashlight blinded me. Before I could move, a dark figure appeared to block the doorway.

"How good of you to do all the work for me," said a voice in accented English.

"Who are you?" I demanded, although deep down I already knew the answer. This was the man we had sought across three continents.

"You mean you don't know?" the voice asked, amused. And then the flashlight beam shifted to illuminate his face. It was all I could do not to gasp.

Stefan Radl watched me in the cold glare from his own flashlight. I started toward him but a movement on the other side of the bright light stopped me.

"I have a weapon," he said. "The two of you will put your hands on your heads and go stand along the wall over there."

Kate looked toward me, her face pale. She was angry, I could tell, but also frightened. I gave my head a tiny shake to let Kate know she shouldn't try anything. We were at Radl's mercy now, and we both knew he had precious little of that. Briefly, I weighed the odds. It was two against one, but if we rushed Radl, he still had the advantage because he had the gun. Maybe against an amateur we would have stood a chance, but Radl was an experienced soldier. Kate and I would be dead before we took two steps.

"*Now*," he said harshly, barking it out like an order.

"Okay, okay," I said. "Don't shoot." I nodded at Kate and we backed toward the wall.

Hands on heads, held at gunpoint in the flashlight beam, I felt what it meant to be a prisoner, to be completely under someone else's control. A feeling of helplessness washed over me. *So this is what it felt like to be a Jew in Germany.* It could have been 1945 all over again. The thought that I was being held at gunpoint by a man who had traveled through time was almost too outlandish to comprehend.

"Very good," Radl said. "Now, if either one of you takes your hands off your head, I will shoot you both." On the other side of the flashlight, I could sense that Radl was smiling. He switched off the beam and I blinked, trying to get used again to the soft light cast by the bulbs along the walls. "Amazing, isn't it, that these lights work. You must admit it is rather impressive that they came on after more than sixty years."

"Why are you here?" Kate asked, her voice flat with anger. "What do you want?"

"The same thing as you," Radl said. "To find out if it's true. Project Time Reich, that is."

"You can't seriously believe it's possible that someone from the Third Reich traveled through time."

"Look around you," Radl said. "My grandfather helped to create all of this. Wouldn't it be interesting to set events in motion?"

"You're mad," Kate said. "Absolutely nuts."

"Come now, what is it you Americans are always saying? Think outside the box," Radl said. "Deep down, you're wondering. You want to know if it's possible. Let's find out together, shall we?"

He motioned us ahead with the pistol and we entered the room.

"How did you know we were here?" Kate asked.

"I followed you from Dachau," he said. "I was waiting for you there."

"What?"

"Where else could you have planned to go? Dachau was a natural starting point. It was only a matter of time before you found this place. As you know, the beacon opened the door. These beacons are useful things. They were intended not only as receivers to bring a man through time but also as keys to the door of the Wolf's Lair. It was a beacon that I lacked, and I hoped you might bring the one you took from Juozas Juknys's house. The old fool had gone and hidden it from me."

"So that was you in North Bay."

"Yes. It's not so far from Washington, where I did have some business. I told you about that trip."

Kate took a step toward him.

"Don't make me shoot you quite yet." He made a *tsk, tsk* sound and raised the pistol. I had started to let my hands drift down and my eyes roved around the room, looking for some kind of weapon. However, aside from the beacons there was little else in the room.

Radl waggled the pistol at me. "*Nein*, Professor. Keep your hands on your head or I really will shoot."

The casual way he said it convinced me he wasn't bluffing. He was a man who had made a career of weapons and violence. He probably planned to shoot us both anyway, but the longer we delayed him the better our chance of escape.

As if reading my thoughts, Kate asked, "What are you going to do with us?"

"Since you've come this far, I believe you've earned a tour,"

Radl said. "We will go down to some of the lower levels. You
two go first. I can only guess at all the dangers of the Wolf's
Lair. My grandfather would have taken precautions. If there are
any trip wires or booby traps, you will spring them first."

It should have occurred to me that the Nazis would have
rigged a few surprises for unwelcome visitors. I felt foolish for
not thinking of that sooner. "I'll go first," I said to Kate.

"How noble of you, Professor," Radl said.

There was just one door leading out and I moved toward it,
glad to be getting out of this room, one I had already come to
think of as a sinister sort of nest, a place where the beacons sat
waiting to hatch, like a snake's den or a spider's hidey hole. We
moved into a short hallway or landing, then down yet more
stairs. Electric lights cast a yellow glow on the damp concrete.
The hum of the Nazi generator was louder down here but
remained subdued. All sounds were strangely muffled in this
underground bunker. Even the air felt heavy, which made sense
— it was likely the atmosphere inside the bunker had gone
undisturbed all these decades.

The bunker's pyramidal shape became more apparent as we
moved deeper inside. The rooms grew larger, the walls seem-
ingly less sloped. Judging from the progression of the rooms, I
guessed there were five or six levels. What the Germans had
done was taken the ancient Egyptian concept of the pyramid,
with all its mystical powers, and created one beneath a
Teutonic forest. But where the Egyptian pyramids seemed
suited to their desert surroundings, an oasis that brought order
to the sandy wastes, the German version was dark and forbid-
ding as a cave, a lair for things better left alone.

At the bottom of the steps, the doorway was closed with a
steel hatch like one might see on a ship.

"Open it," Radl ordered. Behind me, I could hear him
retreating up the stairway. If there was a booby trap, it seemed
that he intended to be out of harm's way. When his voice came

again, it was noticeably more distant. Radl still blocked our only exit route. "Go ahead."

The steel door had a latch like an old refrigerator. I grabbed it with both hands and looked at Kate. "Here goes."

I half expected that we would disappear in a flash flame and whiff of cordite. But there was only a click as the door mechanism opened. The door swung open to reveal another dimly lighted room.

Radl was suddenly right behind us again, his gun at the ready. "This is it," he said, sounding excited. "It must be."

"What is it?"

"Go in. You will see soon enough."

We slipped into the room, Kate and I just ahead of Radl. I kept looking around for anything I could use for a weapon, or hoping for a moment when Radl would be distracted enough for me to try to take the gun. I sensed that Kate was waiting for the same chance. But Radl's gun never wavered. To attempt anything now would be suicide.

Where the chambers above us had been bare and Spartan, the one we entered now was almost sumptuous. The floor was paved in stone rather than concrete. Heavy, carved oak chairs and a massive oak table filled the center of the space, arranged for a meeting that had yet to take place. I swept my fingertips down the cool, polished surface of the table. The filtration system of the underground pyramid had not allowed so much as a speck of dust to gather. The cavernous space soared overhead, its vaulted ceiling nearly lost in shadow. A life-size oil painting of the Führer dominated one wall. Standing there under Hitler's penetrating gaze, I felt my skin crawl. In real life, the man must have been truly intimidating. What else to expect from a thug who hung his enemies on meat hooks? A huge Nazi banner covered another wall, the fabric still blood-red after these many decades, the background white as a blizzard, the black swastika like a burn mark. We had discovered a temple — and a tomb — to the Third Reich. I felt like a grave robber who had disturbed something better left alone.

Off to one side was a hulking metal contraption with a seat in the center, surrounded by coils and wires. Kate and I had seen its cousin at the Naval research facility near Washington.

Radl saw me staring. "That is the time machine," he said. "My grandfather left from this very place in nineteen forty-five."

He motioned us toward the wall beneath the banner. Expertly, he positioned us where he could keep us covered with the pistol while exploring the space.

The room grew brighter, or perhaps it was only our eyes becoming used to the dim light. Several marble pedestals loomed out of the gloom, rising four feet off the polished floor. Each held a bronze beacon, like a display in a museum.

"We are in the Wolf's Lair," Radl said. "This is where it all begins again."

"My God," Kate said, realization flooding over her. "You're talking about the birth of the Fourth Reich. That's madness."

Radl did not answer right away. He moved among the pillars, caressing the beacons one by one with the fingertips of his left hand. He might have been greeting old friends. The other hand continued to point the gun in our direction. A trip wire no thicker than a fishing line ran between the pedestals and Radl stepped over it carefully. He paused at the black pedestal that stood alone. On top of it rested a golden beacon. Even after all these years the metal remained untarnished, catching the light and reflecting it with a cold gleam.

"Adolf Hitler himself," I guessed.

Even Radl sounded awestruck. "Incredible, isn't it?"

It occurred to me that it didn't even matter whether or not Radl's grandfather had found the secret of time travel. The discovery that such a place as this Wolf's Lair existed was enough to set off a new wave of dangerous nationalism in

Germany. More and more, among the growing right-wing sentiments of Europe, Nazi Germany was being seen as a political
pinnacle rather than a low point. The beacons around us would
be a powerful symbol.

"These people are monsters," Kate blurted. "Your grandfather was a monster. They murdered all those helpless Russian
prisoners, women and children, Jews —"

"The Jews, the Jews, always the Jews!" Radl was shouting
now, his voice echoing in the chamber. "I am sick to death of
the Jews! My grandfather was a German soldier, not a
murderer."

I cast a glance at Kate, trying to give her my "keep your
mouth shut before you get us both shot" look. I got an angry
stare in return, as if this were all my fault. She took a step
toward him.

"Kate!" I grabbed her by the shoulder. Another step and she
would have tripped over the wire that snaked between the
pedestals.

Radl changed his grip on the pistol, holding it in a more
business-like way. "Maybe I could get rid of a Jew and a Jew-
lover right now."

Before Kate could come up with a witty rejoinder that
would prompt him to pull the trigger, I asked a question to
keep Radl talking, since he seemed to be in a mood to explain
himself. "I've been wondering about something," I began.
"Juozas Juknys died of a heart attack. Why did Jimmy Hall
shoot the other old man?"

"I ordered him to," Radl said.

My thoughts turned to the troubled veteran who had
attacked Dustin, and then died trying to escape us by running
across the interstate in Delaware. "And Hall did whatever you
said?"

"Jimmy Hall was star struck by my famous grandfather.
After he found me online, there was nothing he wouldn't do

once I asked. I told him there was no point in letting the other old man live. They had a saying on the Russian front, 'Dead men don't shoot you in the back.' He had done his duty to the Reich, so I told Jimmy Hall to kill him."

"Your grandfather could have hidden the beacons in Germany," Kate said. "Why did he have them smuggled into the United States?"

"He believed it would be easier to operate in your country than just about anywhere else. People would shrug them off as war souvenirs there, whereas here in Germany such Nazi relics would be seen as contraband. Americans have always been so trusting."

Radl had been pacing among the marble pedestals. Now he stopped and leveled his gun at Kate. In the wan light, every inch of him resembled one the cold SS killers he so admired. I shivered, thinking how my father must have felt, all those years ago, staring into German guns. I felt afraid and powerless. Yet also angry. As a young man I had vowed, *never be a victim.*

Beside me, I felt Kate grow tense as a coiled spring. I flicked my eyes at her, wondering what she was about to do. Radl must have sensed the change in her too, because he took a step back and gripped the pistol with both hands, bumping his elbow against one of the marble pedestals in the process.

That was all the opening Kate needed. With a grunt, she shoved one of the pedestals, which toppled, sending the disk it held crashing to the floor with about the same level of noise a metal garbage can lid made bouncing on concrete. The falling pillar struck another, setting off a chain reaction like collapsing dominos. Beacons clattered to the marble floor. In the confusion, Kate made a run for it.

Like some Nazi prison guard, Radl shouted an angry warning. "Halt!" He raised the pistol and fired. But Kate ducked and weaved, not allowing herself to be an easy target. She crashed into row after row of pillars. Radl did not seem like the kind of man who missed, but he was also busy dodging the pillars and beacons toppling around him. It all happened so fast I didn't have time to move. Radl fired again and Kate went down.

"No!" I cried and launched myself at Radl. He twisted in time to get off a shot. Something slashed against my side, burning like a hot coal, and I knew that I'd been hit.

45

The marble floor lurched up and slammed into me. Stunned, I lay there for a moment trying to get my breath.

Radl stood among the fallen pedestals and scattered beacons, pointing the pistol at me. He smiled absently, the way a hunter might as he squeezed the trigger for the killing shot. He took two steps toward me and put the barrel against my temple. I could feel the heat in the muzzle from the shots he had fired and the smell of gunpowder. I lashed out with my foot, missed Radl, and knocked over the black marble pedestal that held the golden disk. It crashed to the floor somewhere outside my field of vision.

Radl ground the muzzle deeper against my skull. "You are a fool, Professor," he said. "Why must you meddle in such things? You should have stayed at home, writing your history books."

I held my breath, thinking *this is what it's like to die. I'm sorry, Kate.*

Radl didn't know it yet, but I was taking him with me. His gun was still pressed to my skull as I took a step back and tripped the wire winding between the pedestals.

"No!" Radl cried. And then the walls exploded.

Something whistled as it clawed the air. Even with my limited military knowledge I guessed I must have set off an antipersonnel mine that sprayed the chamber with steel ball bearings designed to shred flesh with deadly force. Radl cried out and fell, his left arm streaming blood. He lost his grip on the pistol and it slid a few feet away.

My ears rang in the silence after the blast. I looked at Kate's crumpled form, hoping that the metallic spray from the mine had missed her. She hadn't moved since Radl shot her.

"You killed her," I said in disbelief.

Both of us looked at the gun on the floor at the same time. Radl was closer and he scrambled toward it, but he was hampered by his arm, which was a bloody pulp at the shoulder. But he was closer to the gun, the fingertips of his right hand almost touching it. I lashed out in time to kick the gun away and rolled to my feet.

"You win, Professor," Radl said, down on his hands and knees, his voice raspy with pain. "But let us not be foolish. There is more to the Wolf's Lair than the beacons. It is well provisioned in many ways. My grandfather made sure of that. Do you want riches, Professor? I can show you a vault filled with gold. Together, we can open it."

"You can keep your Nazi gold."

I reached down and picked up one of the beacons, then tested its heft. I got a good grip on it, one hand on each side, and stood over Radl. He looked up at me and I was reminded of the image from the security tape. I could tell from his face that he knew what was coming. His blue eyes radiated hatred.

"Clever Jew," he said in German. "Just like your father."

"This is for Kate, you Nazi son of a bitch."

I raised the disk over my head and swung it down hard as I could. There was a satisfying crunch of metal against bone.

Radl slumped to the marble floor. I wasn't sure if he was dead or just knocked out and I really didn't care. I ran to Kate.

She was still breathing. I moved her enough to see the bullet hole in her back. The red stain on her coat was no larger than my hand but it was spreading. "Kate, can you hear me?"

Her eyes flickered and she murmured something.

As I stood, my hands felt warm and wet. Kate's blood. The sight of it made my knees weak. It was hard to tell how badly she was hit, but she was slipping into shock. I had to get Kate help fast.

The floor around us was a litter of marble pedestals, some now cracked, and fallen beacons. Hitler's watchful eyes glared down from the portrait, torn across the cheek where a ball from the exploding mine had struck it. Without thinking, I grabbed the golden disk and shoved it inside my coat. "Come on, Kate. We've got to get you out of here."

"What about Radl?" she asked, her voice brittle with pain.

"He's either dead or knocked out cold," I said. "And right now I don't care which one it is."

Kate did not reply. Instead, her eyes rolled back in her head and she began to fall. I lunged to catch her. Gently, I lowered her to the marble floor.

I bent down on one knee, picked Kate up under the arms, and positioned her over my shoulder. Slowly, as I stood, I slid more of her weight toward my back, like I was carrying a rolled carpet. I didn't want to hurt her any worse than she was, but there didn't seem to be any other way to move her. My insides felt squishy. The sensation was like having a bowl of raw chicken in my belly. I'd almost forgotten that I'd been shot too. Blood dripped, making an audible wet splatter as it hit the marble floor. I wasn't sure if it was her blood or mine. *Go. Don't think. Just go.*

They say that in times of extreme stress, people sometimes gain an almost supernatural strength. You read in the paper about the man who lifts a car off a child or the lumberjack who throws the weight of an entire tree off his crushed leg. What happened next was something like that. Somehow I ran up four flights of stairs with Kate on my back. On the last flight of steps I slipped in blood; I was pretty sure this time that it was mine. I reached the apex of the pyramid and staggered out the doorway, then collapsed on the forest floor. Something tore in my side as I twisted to try to keep Kate from falling. My head hit first, driven by the added weight, and I skinned my forehead on a knuckle of root.

I hovered there on my knees, panting, stars dancing in my vision and my side flaming like someone had jabbed in a redhot knife. The trees slanted at an odd angle and began to whirl. That scared me because I knew we would both die if I stopped. All I wanted to do was put Kate down for a minute and stretch out on the dry leaves and pine needles. The beacon was still stuffed inside my coat. I took it out and put it into the empty rucksack I had dropped beside the door, then slung one of the straps over my shoulder. I thought about getting rid of the extra weight, but something made me keep it.

"Come on," I spoke to the silent woods. "Get your ass moving, McCoy."

I surged ahead through the trees. Kate groaned once or twice when I jostled her by stepping into a hole. But at the moment I was less worried about her comfort than I was about simply getting her to help. The thought that she might actually die was like a crushing blow. Choking back a sob, I missed a step and stumbled. I thought of the night back home in Baltimore, of how impossibly tender our lovemaking had been. At the time, I thought two lonely people had come together as they sometimes do and that the night had simply been a kind of oasis. I wanted to visit that place again. I'd be damned if Radl was going to rob us both of a chance at happiness.

"C'mon, Kate, don't die on me," I panted.

I crashed blindly through the trees and underbrush, not really sure where I was going. A sapling whipped across my cheek, stinging fiercely, drawing blood. I forced myself to stop and take my bearings. Getting lost wouldn't do us any good. There wasn't time for that. The trees were all blank and gray. Breathing hard, with the weight of Kate's hurt body bearing down on me, I searched for some sign that I was moving in the right direction. The silence wrapped around us like a cocoon. My breath hung in white clouds in the winter air.

There. Something about one of the trees in the distance looked familiar. It had a knobbed growth on the trunk, like a carbuncle. I shifted Kate on my back and moved again. The only sound was my heavy breathing and the crunch of dry leaves underfoot. After a few uncertain minutes, the gravel road came into view. I could see the car up ahead through the trees.

"Lieutenant Dean!" I shouted. "We need help!"

No answer. Had he fallen asleep? I didn't bother to shout again because I couldn't spare the breath. I struggled on. Not much farther now.

Then I was on the road. I could see Lieutenant Dean in the driver's seat, but he didn't react to the sight of me carrying Kate up the road. What was wrong with him? "Hold on Kate," I panted. "Here's the car."

Still, Lieutenant Dean didn't move. "Wake up, you dumb bastard!"

As I came up to the driver's side window, Dean's eyes simply stared straight ahead. There was a neat round hole in his forehead. Blood covered the seats, already turning thick and gummy in the cold. I put Kate down as gently as I could, then opened the car door and pulled out Lieutenant Dean's body. He was heavy, maybe two hundred pounds of dead weight. Part of me registered the blood and gore in the car, but I turned off that part of my mind. All I wanted to do was get Kate to a hospital.

But there were no keys. Not in the ignition. Not in Lieutenant Dean's pockets. Not clutched in his dead hands. No phone, either. Radl must have taken them.

The thought occurred to me that Radl must have driven there, following us. Maybe his car was up the road, just out of sight.

No time for that. Kate's breathing was shallow, her face pale as the cold of the German soil seeped up into her bones. I wished we had never come to this place. I took off my coat and covered her to keep the warmth in, made a pillow out of the rucksack that held the beacon I had taken from the Wolf's Lair. I took her hand, almost sobbing at the waxy texture of the skin. It was as cold as a mannequin's. "I'll come back for you Kate," I said. "I'm just going down the road for help."

I stood, hoping that Radl had left a vehicle somewhere in these woods. It wouldn't do us much good if I didn't have the keys.

Starting up the road, I thought I heard a sound in the distance. *Whup.* The sound was so low I wasn't sure I had heard it, like distant thunder on a summer evening. *Whup, whup.*

I knew that noise. *Helicopters.*

And then they were on top of us. Two sleek military choppers, skimming the treetops so closely that the topmost branches quivered in the wash from the rotors.

I waved my arms and shouted.

At first, I wasn't sure anyone in the sky had seen me. Then the helicopters pivoted neatly and came around. One hovered overhead while the second machine settled down through the canyon of the trees to land on the road. A hurricane of dry leaves and dust swirled around the car. I ran back and huddled over Kate, trying to shelter her.

A pair of soldiers in flight suits and helmets jumped out, followed by a tall man in a leather jacket. Unlike the young men swarming out the chopper, he moved with deliberate care, his hank of hair shimmering like a whitecap on a stormy bay.

Silas Crockett. He motioned the two soldiers toward us and then followed, leaning into the wash from the rotors.

"She's hurt," I stammered. "Shot."

The medics went right to work, moving me efficiently out of the way. They smelled like diesel fumes. Silas put a hand on my shoulder. "She'll be all right," he said. "This one is as tough as they come."

I hoped he was right. Within minutes, the medics had her strapped into a stretcher and loaded her onto the chopper. Waves of frozen German air thudded against my chest, making it hard to breathe. Silas waved at me to follow. I grabbed the rucksack and ran for the helicopter. Halfway there, I stumbled and fell. I couldn't get up this time. My side felt warm and sticky. Two of the crew grabbed me under the arms, shouting for the medic. They half-dragged, half-carried me onto the helicopter. Lifting off, I thought I could just see the stonework of the Nazi pyramid my father had built, and then it disappeared into the winter woods.

EPILOGUE

Rock Bottom

S ilas Crockett loved low tide. Every morning he walked on the beach beyond the house, bucket in one hand, clam rake in the other. The soft muck of the bay bottom sucked at his Wellington boots. The sea breeze ruffled his white hair, cut short as a Roman centurion's and still thick. He looked the very image of a weathered New England retiree, like a photograph in *Yankee* magazine.

From the kitchen windows, I looked beyond Silas to Branford Bay, which was calm with just a few wispy clouds scudding across the horizon, still tinged pink with dawn. A good sign, considering Kate and I were supposed to go sailing.

A handful of gulls hovered in the old man's wake, swooping down to pluck at the long bands of seaweed left by the tide. The air was thick with the smell of salt, seaweed and wet sand. And something else too, a fresh tang in the morning breeze that was a promise of spring. The morning sun held warmth in it, something that hadn't happened in months. It seemed like since getting back from Germany, I could never get warm enough.

There were a few loose ends in the wake of Time Reich. For one, Radl's body was never found. Apparently, I had not delivered a killing blow. But the Wolf's Lair had been destroyed. Entombed in concrete, beacons and all. This was the decision of the German government, which did not want such a symbolic location to become a shrine to the growing right-wing movement in Germany and the rest of Europe.

An attempt had been made to keep Time Reich quiet, but somehow the story had leaked and made its way onto front pages and news broadcasts across the world. The discovery had encouraged neo-Nazis in Europe. In Austria, they were arresting college professors for giving speeches claiming that the Holocaust had never happened. My agent landed me a contract to write a book about Project Time Reich. My goal would be to tell the truth about that Nazi madness. *Journey of Hope* was to be updated with a new introduction and epilogue for a reprinting. But I wasn't ready to start work on any of that yet.

After getting out of the hospital, Kate spent several weeks recovering at her uncle's house here at Rock Bottom. I was a frequent visitor. Frequent enough that I had learned Silas Crockett's morning routine.

As I watched Silas, it occurred to me that he and my father would have been of the same age if my father had still been alive. In their own ways, both had survived the great test of their time, the bloodiest war in human history.

I took out my wallet, flipped it open. I now carried a photograph of my father taken around the time I was in high school, when I had started sitting across from him at the kitchen table, asking questions while he cleaned the grease from beneath his fingernails. I began carrying the photo not long after I got out of the hospital, when I realized that I was having trouble remembering my father's face. They say that happens with the ones you love the most.

I studied the photograph now. The dark, intelligent eyes that could shift from kind to angry in a single blink. Raven hair shot through with gray. His lined face. Who was he? A Jew. An engineer. Perhaps even a Nazi collaborator, seduced by the desire to build something lasting in the German forest. But he was not a monster. Just a man. A survivor. *My father.* I missed him. And finally, I believed that I had come to know him.

From the window, I watched Silas climb the long rise toward the house, taking the slope easily for such an old man. In the mudroom, he shucked off his boots, put the rake behind the door, and set the bucket of clams in the laundry tub. When he finally padded into the kitchen in his heavy socks, I poured him a cup of coffee and we sat together at the table. Neither of us was much for conversation so early in the morning, so we sat in comfortable silence, drinking our coffee. Silas had brought the salt smell into the kitchen with him and it reminded me of home, of early mornings on my balcony near Baltimore harbor.

"Good day for sailing," he said gruffly, then took a long, noisy slurp of coffee. "Kate still asleep?"

"Yeah."

He snorted. "Just like a teen-ager all over again."

"She's been through a lot."

"That girl needs a man to look after her. I know it's a terribly old-fashioned thing to say, but it's true." Silas seemed intent on his coffee cup as he said it, so it was hard to tell whether or not he was serious. I had learned that Silas found it amusing to agitate.

"Don't let her hear you say that."

"Too late."

We both looked up to find Kate in the doorway, dressed in shorts and a faded sweatshirt. Sailing clothes. On impulse I stood up and hugged her good morning, pressing my face into her hair, not wanting to let go. She smelled like clean sheets and strawberries. I felt Kate melt into me and I soaked her up.

"You okay?" she finally asked. We did that a lot nowadays, asking each other if we were okay. Radl's bullet had almost killed Kate. The one that struck me had done less damage but from time to time I could feel the furrow it cut through me. The flesh had healed into a puckered scar that felt too tight. When the skin and muscles stretched it was like a rubber shock cord snapping painfully inside me.

At the table, Silas cleared his throat. "I'm feeling left out over here."

Laughing, Kate broke our embrace and walked over to kiss her uncle on the cheek. We drank our coffee, ate our blueberry muffins. Along with the muffins, the housekeeper had left the morning paper and Silas flipped the pages noisily like an old-school newshound.

"Let me guess, the new president has been fooling around with the interns," Kate said.

Silas chuckled. "Not this one, although he might be more interesting if he did." He got up and began bumping around the kitchen, pulling out a pot to make clam chowder, checking the refrigerator for a pint of cream. "They don't make 'em like they used to, that's for damn sure. We haven't had a decent president since Kennedy, Republican or Democrat."

Across the table from me, Kate rolled her eyes. She had not been back to OSI since Germany and still had a few weeks of disability leave. Dustin Granger was also healing well and would return to work soon. Kate had sent him a signed copy of *Leaders of the Third Reich*. Meanwhile, Eleanor kept her up to date about what was happening at OSI. Word was that George Foster was being transferred out of OSI to another office at the Department of Justice. Things were still up in the air regarding her old boss's replacement, but Kate seemed like a good candidate for the job.

Kate ate a quick breakfast as Silas assembled his famous clam chowder and put it on to simmer. Then Kate and I packed a picnic lunch: ham sandwiches on thick home-baked bread, some apples picked off Silas's trees last fall, a thermos of hot tea, a bottle of wine. Kate gave Silas another peck on the cheek and the two of us walked down to the beach, where we loaded our picnic items and a rucksack I'd brought along into a skiff. We rowed out to the sailboat moored offshore. Kate climbed on board while I handed up our picnic supplies, wine and the rucksack. This last item was heavy and I felt a twinge of pain as my newly healed muscles strained.

"Okay?" Kate asked.

"Yeah, I'm just stretching something that doesn't want to be stretched."

"What have you got in here, bricks?"

"Something like that."

Leaving the skiff tied to the mooring, I got on board and Kate fired up the engine. She was the sailor, not me, so there wasn't much for me to do as we motored out of the cove toward the deeper water of the bay and Long Island Sound beyond. The sun was out and there was a fresh breeze, the most beautiful day of spring so far.

I had time to admire the graceful lines of the sailboat, a 35-foot Mason called *Liberty*. The boat had a narrow set of steps that descended to the cabin below, which held a dining table, a kitchenette, head and sleeping area tucked up under the bow.

Once we were in the open water of the bay, Kate shut off the engine and we set about hoisting the sail. There was just enough wind to carry us gently and silently through the cobalt water. Kate turned the wheel over to me and we lazed in the stern, drinking hot tea, no sound but the occasional flap of the sail and the water lapping against the sides of *Liberty*. Neither of us said much. We didn't need to.

The wind carried us far beyond the sight of land so that we

were utterly alone, the bowl of blue sky above us and the water stretching on to the horizon. By then it was close to lunchtime so we set a course and let the boat lumber along while we made a feast of sandwiches and last fall's apples with their sweet, shriveled skins.

Afterwards, we took the wine bottle with us and moved up the narrow walkway to the bow. There was not much room amid the coiled lines and gear but we found enough space to spread a blanket. We made love gently to the rocking swells, the sun kissing our exposed flesh pale from the long winter, the salt air raising goose bumps. Afterward we were in no hurry to get dressed and lay for a long time on the deck, soaking up the sun, utterly alone on the water. After a while I got up and came back with the rucksack. Kate propped herself on one elbow, her hair brushing the tops of her breasts as she watched me unzip it.

"What's in there?"

"A little souvenir from our trip to Germany."

I opened the bag and took out a beacon. The polished gold gleamed brilliantly in the spring sun. An eagle was cast across the surface, wings outspread as if it might break free of the metal, a swastika grasped in its talons.

Kate shuddered. "My God, Bram. That's Hitler's beacon. How come you have it?"

"I took it with me when I carried you out of the Wolf's Lair. I didn't want to leave it behind."

She studied the metal disk, then looked at me uncertainly. "Why did you bring it out here today?"

"What if the lair wasn't entirely destroyed, Kate? What if someone else had found this?" I paused. Already, the disk was absorbing the heat from the sun, becoming warm to the touch. "What if it could actually work?"

"I hate that thing. Even as a relic of the Third Reich, it's an awfully powerful symbol."

"That's why I brought it today. I wanted to be sure."

"What are you going to do?"

I stood up, both of us still naked as Adam and Eve, and made my way to the bow. The water was deep here, and cold, far from the sight of land. I held the disk out over the rail.

"Ready?"

Kate nodded. I dropped the beacon into the water. Its smooth metal slipped beneath the bow wake without so much as a splash. For a long way down we could see the beacon's distorted shimmer reaching toward the surface, flashing like a coin tossed down a wishing well. Then the Time Reich beacon vanished into blackness as the sea's depths swallowed Hitler's mad dream.

~The End~

ABOUT THE AUTHOR

David Healey lives in Maryland where he worked as a journalist for more than 20 years. He is a member of the
International Thriller Writers and a frequent contributor to
The Big Thrill magazine. Visit him online at www.
davidhealeyauthor.com
   or www.facebook.com/david.healey.books

Thank you for reading! If you enjoyed the story, please consider
leaving a review on Amazon.com.

Printed in Great Britain
by Amazon